PLAYLIST

DAYWALKER! (feat. CORPSE) - mgk, CORPSE
TROJAN HORSE - SEBASTIAN PAUL
BACK AND FORTH - SEBASTIAN PAUL
Everybody Wants To Rule The World - 3TEETH
With Me - Sum 41
Closer - Nine Inch Nails
under the weather - CORPSE
Mine - Sleep Token
I Don't Even Care About You - MISSIO
Desire - MEG MYERS
fuK u lol - CORPSE
INDULGE - SEBASTIAN PAUL

WHO WRITES WHO?

Cole Carter - Leigh Rivers
Blaise Rowle & Jackson - Harleigh Beck

To all the readers who dream of being chased through the woods and face-fucked by their masked stepbrother.

CHAPTER 1
COLE

The house is crowded. Music blasts through the speakers from every corner of the room, people already drunk and dancing to the heavy bass.

Allie laces her fingers in mine as I lead us through the sweaty bodies until I reach Samson and Keith, my friends from college. They greet me, then nod to my girl.

It's more than what they've done over the last twelve months. They aren't fans of her since she cheated on me last year, always telling me to ditch her.

I didn't care enough to break up with her.

Their eyes lift to the person behind me, and I sigh. "Allie asked Mia to come. Fuckface decided he had to join because he can't go one hour without being stuck to her side."

Blaise ignores me and goes straight to my friends.

Samson leans forward and shakes Blaise's hand. "Been a while, man. How's life treating you?"

Blaise sits down and brings Mia onto his knee. They get into a discussion about football and how my stepbrother wants to do tryouts, and I take Allie to get drinks to try to forget the asshole is here.

For a few hours, I steer clear of him. I've probably done too many shots and smoked far too much weed. I navigate my way from the kitchen to the sitting room, dropping onto the couch in front of Blaise.

"Why are you still here?" I ask him, noticing Mia is dancing with Allie by the stairs. I inwardly huff when they notice us and head over.

"Get fucked," Blaise spits, taking another drink of his beer.

My eyes absently zone into the way his throat moves with each gulp. I wish I could cut it wide open and watch the way his blood flows out. I'd make sure I drained every drop, bleed him dry, then sit by while he turns blue and lifeless.

There's a tick in my jaw, and I drag my gaze to his face instead.

"Stop talking to me," he adds when I don't snap back.

I laugh and kick my legs up on the table between us. "Daddy won't like it if he knows his little princess is drunk the night before practice."

Even though he's done with high school, he still plays on their team for the next two weeks. He grits his teeth and goes to retort, but we're interrupted by my friends.

I'm handed another joint, and I keep my eyes on Blaise as I fill my lungs with the toxic smoke and blow it in his direction. With a grimace, he waves his hand in front of him, giving me the death stare that doesn't even slightly scare me.

"I'm bored," Samson says, sitting next to Blaise. "Let's play a game."

Allie sighs as she approaches with Mia. "Please don't say Never Have I Ever."

Getting comfortable pressed up to my side, she drops her head to my shoulder, lacing our fingers while I inhale on the joint and pass it back to Keith. Blaise only stares at me, his eyes narrowing. I bet the fucking prick will tell his dad that I was smoking weed tonight.

My brow quirks, and he averts his eyes to his girlfriend. Such a fake asshole. Always pretending he actually fucking likes her.

"What game, then?"

Samson hums, thinking to himself before clicking his fingers. "We'll have two teams. One chases the other, and if you catch

2

them, you can beat them the fuck up or just take your point as winning."

Blaise snorts. "What's the point? What do we get if we win?"

"We'll decide later."

"Sounds dumb."

His voice irritates me. I can imagine my fist laying into his smug face, but the idea of letting my mom down again makes me rein it in.

"I'm not on his team," Blaise says as he gestures to me, and my right eye twitches. "He'll cheat."

I scoff. "Fuck off. No one even wants you here."

Mia scowls. "Hey! Allie asked us to come!"

Fuck Allie too. Relationship or not, she fucked me over by asking her friend to come tonight. I never hang out with Blaise. I'd rather rip my own balls off.

The only reason Mia knows Blaise is because I told Allie she could bring a friend to the stupid wedding of our parents. Biggest mistake ever.

He doesn't deserve to be happy. I hope she cheats on him and breaks his fucking heart.

"How many people are here?" Samson asks.

"Twenty-five."

"Great!" He's grinning as he stands. "One can be the referee. Do you still have the masks from Halloween? The black and the white ones with the blank faces?"

"Yeah," Keith replies. "And the black hoodies."

"Let's do it. Twelve on each side. We wear masks and hoodies to hide who we are. Bring a little fun into it."

Keith vanishes, and the party continues. The music gets louder, and Blaise is on his seventh beer. If he drinks any more, I won't need to tell his dad. He'll get caught. But of course, he'll get a free pass regardless of how strict our parents are.

If it was me who had something on the day after partying, I'd get my ass handed to me and kicked out. I'm too broke to survive outside of the house.

Allie pulls my arm. "Let's go back to my place. We don't need to play the chasing game."

I ignore her, downing my drink and looking around, losing sight of Blaise. I can't see his girlfriend either, so maybe they've had the same idea.

My girlfriend looks up at me with puppy dog eyes. "Cole, please. I want to have sex."

Saving the day – because I really can't be fucked with going home and having Allie slopping up my cock or riding me until I force myself to come – Samson returns with a box filled with the masks we all wore at the Halloween-themed football party last year before we all split up and headed for college.

All of them are the same style. Blank face masks with no design. The chasers will wear white, and the runners will wear black.

No weapons allowed. No inflicting fatal injuries. No siding with the other team to beat down the other. No phones.

With my lack of a response, Allie's moved on to kissing my throat. "Let's go upstairs instead. I want to walk around this party with your cum leaking out of my pussy, baby. Come on. Before they pull us into our teams."

My cock shows no reaction to her words, even as she's tugging at me to go upstairs with her and grabbing at me through my pants. She pouts when she finds me soft – the same way I was last night while she was on her knees for me.

It's been happening a lot. I have next to no interest in sexual pleasure. We haven't had sex in a while. Maybe that's one of many signs to break up with her.

Her lips part to say something else, but Samson grabs everyone's attention.

"Okay. Let's choose teams!"

I try to peel Allie off me while she hangs on to my arm like I'm about to disappear. She's so damn horny when she's drunk.

I still can't see Blaise. Hopefully, he left, because the urge to kick his face in during this game is too much. I'll probably kill

4

him if I end up on the opposite team. It would be a damn miracle if I found him first.

When Blaise staggers into the room, I roll my eyes and gulp the rest of my drink, barely registering the burn down in my throat. He drunkenly crosses his arms and leans against the wall opposite me, his hair disheveled.

I look at Mia and roll my eyes at her fixing her skirt, the smudged lipstick, the redness of her throat. I feel sorry for her having to spend so much time with him.

She's best friends with Allie. I might lie and say she tried to fuck me to ruin their friendship. It'll put an end to me and Blaise being at the same parties.

"Why are you staring at Mia?" Allie asks, and I turn to look at her, at the frown between her brows. "Do you want her? Is this because of what happened last week? I'm sorry. I promise I stopped texting him."

She was talking with her professor—flirting, to be exact—and I had to pretend I cared enough and used that as one of the reasons I don't want to fuck her when she cried to me about needing to be screwed.

"Cole and Blaise should choose teams."

My brows raise as I bring my attention back to my friends. They know I hate my stepbrother. They've seen me pin the bastard to his locker by the throat and demand he make his father leave my mom.

I hated him when he came into my life years ago, and I still hate him now.

It takes ten minutes to form teams. Blaise chooses Allie, so I choose Mia. I smirk at his evil glare when she comes to stand beside me and smiles up at me.

She's pretty. I'm tempted to actually fuck her and record it, just to piss him off.

We get our masks and black hoodies, pulling the hoods up to hide our hair, and everyone makes their way to the back of the house. Samson lives in the middle of nowhere with woodland surrounding us – easy to get lost, but also easy to hide a body if needed.

I might kill my stepbrother tonight.

No one speaks a word as the only person who isn't playing stands in front of us. "The runners get a two-minute head start. Remember the rules. Go!"

They scatter, some already tripping over their feet, others shooting off and out of sight.

Hopefully, I don't catch Allie. She'll probably try to make me fuck her into the dirt like some rape fantasy where she begs me to stop. She loves that.

But I can't be bothered with her over-exaggerated moans and clawing at my back when I'm barely inside her. I'm starting to think I don't love her the way I thought I did. The way my therapist insisted I admit to. My feelings are blank when it comes to my relationship.

I forced myself to think I felt that way about her. Mom wanted me to get a girlfriend, and I was trying to please her and prove I'm not a total waste of space after we ran from my father, so I found the best-looking chick at school and told her she was mine.

"One," Samson yells, jumping on his toes as I adjust my mask. "Two."

"I'm hunting down Anabelle and tearing through her cunt," Keith says, his voice muffled by his mask. "She's been giving me the eyes all night."

"The rules, dipshit." Someone laughs, shaking their head at our friend. "Nothing about fucking them."

He chuckles. "Watch me."

"Three. Go!"

Everyone splits up, and I set off toward the woods, my fists clenched and ready to beat the shit out of someone. Especially Blaise for being a wanker earlier. I'll pound his ass into the ground, and he won't even know it was me.

Mom can't give me shit about it this time.

It's dark, so I can barely see once I get deep within the trees. But when I hear screams, it gives me a push to keep running, to catch some sorry fucker and take my anger out on them.

Anticipation ignites within me when I see someone running up ahead. I quicken my steps and begin the chase, enjoying the way my heart races and the adrenaline injects into my veins. They glance over their shoulder, noticing me, the moon shining through the canopy leading me toward them.

They're running so damn fast; I nearly lose them a few times while dodging branches and jumping over fallen trees.

The person stumbles, and I take the opportunity to tackle them to the ground, pinning them face down into the dirt. My body is alive as they thrash beneath me. More alive than it ever has been.

Trying to free themselves by pushing against the dirt, I grab the back of their head over the hood and shove them down. My weight on their back keeps them in place, and I close my eyes, trying to relax the urges.

My heart beats so fucking hard. But that's not the only thing.

The need to hurt this person is there, but it tamps down as I realize my cock is straining in my pants.

Confused, I stare down at where my bulge glows under the moonlight as it presses into the person's ass.

I'm rock solid, stabbing into the person beneath me, who isn't even fighting back anymore or attempting to get away. They're trying to control their erratic lungs and digging their fingers into the dirt.

It's definitely not Allie. She'd be screaming and slapping and demanding I get the fuck off her until she realizes it's me and rips off her own clothes.

Who am I kidding? She'd do that with anyone. I've lost count of how many times she's gone elsewhere for a fuck. I've beaten guys for simply thinking of disrespecting me, but that's the only reason. I don't feel hurt or anger when she fucks around behind my back.

This person is tall like me, has a big build, and I think I might be digging my cock into a guy's ass. Regardless of this knowledge, I hold their nape, keeping them in place as my urge to win takes over, and I rock my hips forward.

Depravity courses through my bloodstream as I feel myself getting even harder.

"Get the fuck off me," the strained, muffled voice warns.

Despite everything within me, telling me to get off this guy and beat him up so he never finds out who just dry thrusted against his ass, my balls tighten, and I force him farther into the dirt by the neck.

"St-op," they whisper, but there's no fucking fight left in them.

I straighten my arms, shoving down the person's hood at the back, pausing when I see short dark hair. Reality hits me that I might actually be hard for a guy right now, but I still don't get off them.

Fuck. My pulse thunders in my ears at the softness of their hair as I slide my hand up their nape and brush my fingers through the wavy strands.

And my cock twitches even more, my lungs burn with the need for pleasure – I haven't felt this way in months. Something inside me snaps. I stand up, roughly yanking the person to their knees by their hair. They don't move as I stare down at the black mask.

Whoever this is, they're submitting. How far will they let me go?

Reaching for the chin of the mask, they don't stop me as I slide it up, and I hesitate, my heart fucking thundering and cock pulsing as I stare down at my stepbrother.

I swallow past a sudden lump in my throat, my eyes zoned into his lips, his fucking mouth.

His heavy breaths – how audible they are.

Why am I getting harder?

The green eyes I need to stare at every day are locked onto

my mask, reminding me that I'll never be as good as him. I'll never be the family good boy or excel in college. I'm the reject, the black sheep who is nothing but a disappointment like my father, and it's all because of this prick.

I grit my teeth as I snatch his jaw, reaching for my belt and unbuckling it quickly, unable to think straight. "Open," I say, doing everything I can to hide my voice. "Open your fucking mouth."

Blaise's eyes widen, but he doesn't refuse or tell me to fuck off. He doesn't tell me he has a girlfriend or that he's not interested. He doesn't realize his eyes are dropping to his stepbrother's cock.

I fist my thick length, precum already leaking from the tip as I rim his soft lips that are begging to wrap around me. I can tell by the look in his eyes. Terrified yet needy.

Blaise is nervous – the breaths falling from his lips aren't from running.

He doesn't even know whose dick is in his face. I wonder how his dad would react if he saw his angelic son sucking his stepson's dick? I don't even have my phone on me to record this moment.

Grabbing a handful of his hair, I tug his head back, rubbing the underside of my cock against his mouth and letting a deep groan leave my strained throat. I should be ashamed of this – I have a girlfriend. And this is Blaise's mouth I'm rubbing my cock against.

"Tongue out," I say, low and demanding.

I tighten my grip on his hair as the heat of his tongue slides against the underside of my cock. As much as this is a way to punish him, I'm dying to slide my cock into his mouth, to feel how good he is at sucking.

I've never had a guy suck my cock before. Fuck, I've never done anything with a guy before. Why is this even happening? Why is my body reacting this way? Why do I want to pin him down and force him to take every inch into his throat?

His hands fly up to push at my thighs as I thrust into his mouth, finally giving me some resistance. And damn, it feels so good. He's trying to shove me away, even as he's wrapping his lips around my cock, making my balls tighten and tingle.

I hold the back of his head, keeping my balance as I pull him toward me, forcing him to take another inch.

There are voices around us. Someone's screaming for someone to stop. I think it might be Blaise's girlfriend. Maybe she's being choked the fuck out, the same way I'm choking her boyfriend out with my dick.

I force my way deeper, feeling his throat contracting around me. His eyes are watering, and I want to take a picture so I can show him. I could use it as blackmail the next time he tries to use my mom against me, the conniving little bastard.

Rage consumes me, thinking of all the times he's made me look like the bad guy to our parents, and I grab both sides of his head and roughly fuck his mouth, reveling in the sound of him gagging and gasping around my thickness.

Is it bad that Allie doesn't make me feel this way? This fucking feral while getting a blowjob? I'm like an animal as I completely ruin him until his hands slide from my thighs, giving up as I control his head.

I don't think he's breathing, but his eyes stay glued to my mask. I guess he's still somehow alive as I repeatedly slam into his mouth.

Another scream from behind, too far away to see what I'm doing to Blaise, so I go faster, harder, feeling the swollen crown bruising the back of his throat until I'm seeing stars.

My head falls back, elongating my neck as I grit out a moan.

The muscles in my thighs bunch as I try to stay at this fast pace, faltering as he whimpers and chokes around my cock. I clench my jaw, groaning as the tightness around my balls gets too much.

Fuck.

Fucking fuck.

I swear through my mask as I still, robbing him of air as I keep my cock buried deep. My cum leaks down his throat in spurts until my vision blurs, and I nearly lose my balance.

He drinks every drop, his wet eyes on my mask as I stay in position, my fingers digging into his skull until I pull out of his mouth and shove him back.

Blaise doesn't get a second to catch up on reality before I drive my fist into his face, knocking him out.

Stepping away, I stuff my cock back into my pants, breathless, my chest heaving as I try to figure out what the fuck I've just done. Blaise is unconscious in the dirt with my cum coating his throat, and I don't regret it.

I've never been interested in a guy. Not that I'm interested in this asshole – I just wanted to ruin him and my cock got in the way.

Blaise's pants are completely tented. It seems my stepbrother liked sucking dick. I can see the wet patch through the material from the moon's glow cracking through the tree canopy.

I chuckle deeply to myself, shaking my head as I turn and leave him in the middle of the woods, officially done with this fucking game.

CHAPTER 2
BLAISE

Scalding water pours down my back as I stare down at my engorged dick that's bobbing against my wet stomach. It's been rock hard since *that* night, when I was chased down by some masked stranger as part of a game and forced to choke on his dick while mayhem ensued all around us, like a twisted symphony of terror. I can still feel my knees sinking into the soft grass, its earthy scent clogging my nostrils. Power thrummed through him as he ripped off my mask.

While I kneeled before him, my heart thrashed madly behind my ribs. He hesitated, and that moment of hesitation, the slight hitch in his breath, made my dick weep behind my zipper.

"Fuck," I mutter, grasping my veiny length and giving it a firm stroke.

I've lost count of how long I've been in this fucking shower, tormented by memories of that night.

I'm not gay.

So, I might have a secret obsession with my stepbrother, but that doesn't make me gay…right?

Besides, I don't know where the hell he was while I was choking on a stranger's dick and loving every twisted minute.

Note to self: New kink unlocked.

Well, until he knocked me out with a single punch.

My obsession with my stepbrother has been a thing of mysteries, never this…tangible as it is now while I drag my thumb over the crown of my cock.

A groan reverberates through me, and I drop my chin to my chest. Fuck, I want a repeat. Only this time, I want my stepbrother in the stranger's place – *his* fingers digging into the side of my skull.

I'd do anything to see him unleash his inner demons and allow them out to cause a little havoc with mine.

Despite what he likes to think, we're not that dissimilar. His violent tendencies and my darker desires circle each other every time we're in a room together.

Pleasure ripples down my spine, and my abs contract as I visualize my stepbrother's cruel smirk.

While I've always been dominant with my girlfriend, never one to offer up my control freely, it's different with Cole. His overpowering presence leaves no room for anything but complete submission.

With a predator like him, my power is found in my submission. If I push back, I lose. However, if I willingly sacrifice myself to his hunger for anarchy and complete destruction, *he* loses.

Though he may think he's the one in complete control, the mask slips when he gives in to those carnal urges.

I haven't succeeded yet, but I will.

My balls draw up tight, and I bite down hard on my lip. The water is slowly turning cold, raising goosebumps on my reddened skin while I jerk my cock as though I have a vendetta against it.

I'm so damn horny, and nothing can satisfy this growing need that's festering inside me—

A slender arm slides around my waist, and I stiffen as Mia trails her lips over my back. "You should have woken me up. I could take care of you."

Gnashing my teeth, I bite back a curse and slowly turn to face her. As she smiles up at me, the cold water hardens her rosy nipples.

She reaches for my dick. "What were you fantasizing about that's made you so hard, baby?"

Her voice is all wrong.

Where Cole has hard muscles and rippling abs, she has soft curves.

Where Cole is sharp angles and vicious glares, she's sweet smiles and peals of laughter.

My cock threatens to deflate as she drops to her knees.

I try so fucking hard to get into it, but this position fails to scratch the itch even as I bury my fingers in her damp locks.

The only person who could satisfy it is blasting music across the hallway like a fucking asshole.

My eyes fall shut, and I force myself to focus on her mouth around my cock. Her head bobs in my hands, and she moans, but no matter how much I try, I can't come.

I just fucking can't.

Not like this, and certainly not with her.

"What's wrong?" she asks in a broken voice as I exit the shower.

Icy panic crawls up my legs and clenches my abdominals while I scrub my hair with a towel, blocking her out behind me.

Why does she have to be so good and pure?

I crave mayhem and darkness.

"Talk to me, baby."

I tie the towel around my waist and then drag my hand through my ruffled hair, smoothing it down. "Nothing is wrong. I'm just not in the mood."

Lies. My cock aches; it's that damn hard.

Mia continues watching me with her doe eyes, but I don't look at her again as I exit the bathroom.

Her steps follow me into the bedroom, and she stays silent while I pull a T-shirt over my head.

After locating my jeans on the floor, I drop the towel and shove my foot through the pant leg.

"You're still hard."

Don't I know it?

"Your point?"

"Why won't you let me make you feel good?"

Sighing, I zip up my pants and then meet her worried eyes.

A part of me wants to reassure her and tell her everything is fine, like I always do when she gets in one of these moods. But I just don't have it in me right now, confused by my stormy emotions. Nothing is clear-cut.

Pausing, I let my eyes drift down her naked, wet body.

Her perfect curves would drive any man crazy, so why could I take it or leave it? Why am I not on my knees, worshiping her pink cunt and making her moan my name?

Why do I feel this inexplicable pull toward my stepbrother's room?

It's all fucked up.

My secret fixation on him shouldn't bleed into my reality.

She turns away from me, and the relief I feel is immense.

Blowing out a breath, I drag a hand down my face, then snatch my phone off the dresser.

My brows furrow as I read over a text from an unknown number.

> Unknown: My dick begs for more when I think of you on your knees, and your mouth stuffed with my cum.

Heart in my throat, I type out a reply.

> Me: Who's this?

His response is immediate.

> Unknown: Your worst nightmare.

Mia walks past me in a cloud of perfume and hurt feelings, her shoulder brushing my chest. "Are you coming or not?"

I look up from the screen, only to be met by her arched brow. My cock twitches inside its denim confines as the phone burns my hand. I pocket it, then hold the door open for her. "After you."

MIA TALKS to Allie and my stepmom, Rachel, while I spend the entire breakfast staring at my phone. Despite how much I hope another message will pop up on the screen, nothing else comes through.

I want to—no, I *need* to find out who hid behind that mask.

A small hand lands on my bulge beneath the table, and I frown at Mia, who ignores me while smiling at my stepmom. She swiftly frees my dick and pumps the hard length.

What the hell has gotten into her today? This is Mia, the good girl, the girl who never steps out of line or takes risks, like jerking her boyfriend in front of his parents.

I'm two seconds away from removing her hand, when my eyes clash with Cole's across the table.

He glances down as though he knows exactly what's going on, and I struggle to decipher the flash of emotion that darkens his eyes. It's stormy, toxic, and unlike anything I've seen on his face before.

Precum leaks from my dick as he holds me captive with his blue eyes that burn with enough intensity to curl my toes.

Beside me, Mia throws her head back and laughs at something my stepmom says.

Her small hand works my cock until I can barely fucking breathe, fighting the inevitable. One more push, and I'll topple.

The way Cole watches me makes my mouth go dry.

My breath picks up, and my knuckles turn white against the edge of the table.

Fuck, fuck, fuck.

Cole leans over and whispers in Allie's ear before straightening back up and smirking like a damn villain.

"I need to talk to you," Allie says to Mia, who pauses with her hand on my dick.

What the hell? I could cry.

"Now?" Mia asks as Allie stands up.

"It's important."

I almost snatch her hand back. Almost tell her to finish me off before she leaves.

My balls throb, and it's all thanks to the asshole across the table, whose smirk remains in place as he picks up his phone. He types out a quick text, and then his eyes are back on me, a dark, deadly abyss I could drown in.

His mom asks him questions while I tuck my aching dick away. Blue balls are the last thing I need.

He leaves, taking his hard glares and heady scent with him, and I pick up my phone and swipe the screen.

No new messages.

My heart sinks, and I tap my thumb against the side as thoughts of my masked mystery man crowd my head.

I need a repeat of that night.

I need it like my next breath.

My phone pings, and I pick it up so fast that my stepmom throws me a startled gaze as she pours orange juice into her glass. My dad, who's spent the last half an hour reading the newspaper, folds it up.

> Unknown: Jerk that fat cock for me and send me a video.

"Are you okay, Blaise? You look flushed."

Torn from my thoughts, I open my mouth to respond, when another message pops up on the screen.

My eyes home in on it like a missile.

> Unknown: Now.

My fingers fly across the screen, and then, after hitting send, I scoot my chair back, offering Dad and my stepmom a smile.

> Me: Not until you reveal your identity.

I've never fled a room so fast before without making it look like I'm running.

> Unknown: You want to see me?

Locking myself in the downstairs bathroom, I plop down on the toilet seat as an attachment pops up on the screen. I click on it at record speed, then gulp at the photo of a veiny dick.

I honestly never thought I'd be into other guys' dicks, but mine jerks a little as I lick my lips.

> Unknown: Like what you see? Stroke your cock for me. Make it leak with precum.

"Fuck," I whisper, unzipping my jeans with trembling hands and squeezing my hard length.

I'm so aroused it won't take much at all.

I record a short video, then hit send before I can change my mind.

His response tingles my balls.

> Unknown: Do you want to know what went through my mind while I pounded your tight throat?

Chest heaving, I reply to his text while a bead of sweat trails down my temple.

> Me: Tell me.

The sound of slapping skin and my labored breaths fill the tense silence as I wait for his reply.

> Unknown: Beg me.

"Fucking cock tease," I mutter.

> Me: Please tell me what you were thinking as you fucked my throat.

More precum seeps from my dick, so I swipe it up with my thumb, then lick it off while imagining *his* taste on my lips.

> Unknown: I was thinking how fucking pathetic you were, gagging on my dick and clawing at my thighs as though I'd let you breathe if you hurt me. Spoiler: I wouldn't. You'd die suffocating on my fat cock first.

Pleasure bursts behind my eyelids, but I manage to hold off from climaxing too soon, like a pubescent boy, greedily awaiting his next message.

> Unknown: Is that what you want, Blaise? To be fucked to within an inch of your life and left ruined and covered in cum?

When I fail to respond, another message pops up.

> Unknown: Answer me.

"Insufferable prick," I mutter.

> Me: Yes, I want you to ruin me with your dick.

His immediate response has my throbbing dick twitching in my grip.

Unknown: Careful of what you wish for.

Unknown: Now film yourself coming all over your hand, then send it to me.

Hands trembling, I press record, stifling a moan while jacking my dick with renewed effort. I'm a savage beast, tapping into desires I never knew existed.

Well, I had an inkling, but I never realized the ferocity behind the desire currently flooding my veins like a powerful, intoxicating drug.

Sex with my girlfriend pales in comparison to this.

Sex never had meaning until now.

Cum erupts from my dick, raining over my hand, and I choke on my saliva as I shudder through the strongest orgasm I've ever experienced.

It never fucking ends.

As seconds turn into minutes on the screen, I milk my dick dry, relishing the image he'll soon see of my hand, coated in cum, as it beats my cock in time with my heaving breaths.

When my pulse returns to a semblance of normal, I hit send—

A loud bang on the door startles me, and I jump ten miles into the air.

"You in there, fuckface? If you're not in the car in five, we're leaving without you." Cole's voice drips with humor.

Oh, right, I need my car fixed so I don't have to catch rides from my insufferable stepbrother.

CHAPTER 3
COLE

Allie's hand feels strange in mine as I walk us down the drive. It's warm, the sun already beating down on my face. I screw my eyes as she stops in front of me, blinded by the sun.

"What?"

"Do you still love me?" she questions, pouting like a child.

I frown. "Why are you asking me that?"

With a sigh, she pops out her hip as if she's bored. "Just say yes or no."

"You're the one opening your legs for other people, handing out blowjobs left and right, sending pictures of your tits to your professor, and you have the audacity to ask me that?"

"I guess I just need reassurance. You said you forgave me."

I hum and cross my arms.

She leans up on her tiptoes and kisses my cheek. "I know you're in love with me, Cole. You don't need to say it and feel bad. I'm sorry I keep messing up. Please have sex with me tonight. I'll make everything better, I promise."

Same speech, different day. I'm starting to think I should break up with her to save myself from looking like an idiot to others. I'm kind of fed up with beating up people she's snuck around with.

Allie hurries around the front of the car to get to the passenger side. I stare at her ass, which is barely covered by the short skirt she intentionally wore to tease me since I'm not fucking her, and it...does nothing for me.

Seeing my girl's ass should drive me insane. I should feel lucky enough to call her mine, if I ignore all the cheating and the shitty personality. As much as she's fucked around on me multiple times, I've never gone elsewhere.

People on the outside of our relationship might think differently, but I have no interest. No attraction. My emotions are apparently nonexistent past anger. I don't look at someone and think "I would fuck them." Nothing that would drive me to stick my dick elsewhere.

Well...unless it was in a brutal act of forced face-fucking and unknown messages to use as blackmail.

I sigh and pull my cigarettes out, lighting one while I open my door.

The phone I bought yesterday dings in my pocket as I settle behind the wheel. Allie's already touching up on her bright red lips in the pull-down mirror like she didn't just spend an hour doing her makeup. I probably have a stain on my cheek.

"How do I look?" she asks me, tipping her head to the side, trying to be enticing.

I move a blonde curl behind her ear. Forcing the softest voice I can muster, I say, "Beautiful."

The blush running up her chest and neck hits her face, and she lets out a giggle and looks away, pulling her phone out to most likely tell the world what I just said with a fake caption. It'll have too many hashtags about having the best boyfriend ever and relationship goals.

I didn't lie. Being with Allie makes sense. I get to be as laid back as I want, and she gets to do whatever the fuck she wants. If I need a date, she's there. If she needs a date, I'm there. It works. It's comfortable. It's—

"Your mom told you to stop smoking in your car."

Blaise appears at my door, reaching through my window to

pull the smoke from between my lips, but I capture his wrist and squeeze harshly. "Don't fucking touch me."

He snatches my throat with his other hand, pinning me to the back of my seat, and squeezes until I struggle for breath. It's a battle of who can squeeze the hardest, and fuck, my eyes feel pressure building behind them, and my lungs burn.

As I nearly crush his fucking wrist, he glares, but doesn't falter.

Allie yanks at my shoulder. "Come on, you two! Don't start fighting again!"

I can't contain the grin, releasing him and waiting for him to do the same. The rage in his eyes tells me he would love to keep going, that refusing my lungs of another full, clear breath would bring him joy. He's got a depraved little mind, even though he's fooled everyone into thinking he's normal and I'm the defective one.

Mia and Blaise get in the back, and I try to keep a straight face when I see how flushed he is under all that pent-up anger, knowing why and what evidence awaits me.

I didn't think he would cave so easily. I expected him to tell me to fuck off and block my number, not do as I told him. For the first time ever, I was intentionally looking at his dick. I didn't accidentally walk in on him and Mia, or him in the shower.

I wanted to fuck with him, make him sweat and panic and wonder whose dick was in his mouth, but the taunting did a one-eighty on me, and I had to slip into the nearest spare room and lock the door. Even when Mia was giving him a handy under the table, I saw the way his eyes glued to mine and his cheeks went red.

He was embarrassed I caught him, but he didn't try to stop her hand or at least look at the fucking wall behind my head. His eyes were on mine.

It annoyed me. How could she do that in front of our parents and he just allowed it? Why the fuck would he stare at me while his girlfriend stroked his cock?

I told Allie that Mia was talking shit about her at the party, which is probably not a lie. I knew she wouldn't wait to question her best friend.

Honestly, I was waiting for them to fight and put an end to their friendship. I already spend too much time with my asshole little stepbrother, and he's now a freshman in my college. Why would I want to see him more?

But as usual, Mia and Allie continue to be joined at the hip. I suppose they do share a dorm room – another shitty point for me to go with the rest of my bad luck.

"How are you feeling now, Blaise?" my girlfriend asks him. "Mia said you weren't doing too good after the party last weekend."

"Yeah," he replies, coughing to clear his throat. "I'm fine."

I turn up the radio to drown out their voices, holding in my scoff. The day after the party, he could barely talk, sounding all hoarse as if he'd been throat-fucked too roughly.

His eye was swollen too from me punching him, and when Mom asked him what happened and he said he couldn't remember, I was to blame for getting him drunk and not looking after him.

He was nearly late for practice because he was in the shower for fucking hours. I had to drive him. He stayed silent the entire time – not that we talk anyway.

It's the same every day. Not even a fucking thank you for letting him ride with me to school. Mom wants me to bond with Blaise more since she knows we can't stand each other. We fight. We argue. We find every opportunity to go against the other.

We live nearby, so we don't stay on campus. It's easier that way. I don't need to worry about surviving on no money or suffering by having an idiotic roommate.

Once I stop outside Mia and Allie's dorm, they both climb out. She leans into my window. "Are you still coming over tonight? Mia won't be home."

I nod and grab her jaw, pulling her mouth to mine and slipping my tongue against hers. I can feel Blaise staring while I kiss her, like he always does when I'm with my girlfriend. It brings me joy when I open my eyes and see through the mirror that he's glaring to the side and ignoring Mia whispering in his ear.

Wiping the lipstick from my mouth with the back of my hand, I drive off with Blaise still in the backseat.

"You shouldn't lead her on," he says, shaking his head. "It's disrespectful and makes you look like even more of an asshole."

I roll my eyes and grab my packet of cigarettes, lighting one up and waiting for him to scold me on that too. But when he doesn't, I turn the radio up even louder and speed off toward the garage while 3TEETH fills the car.

The sooner I get him to this garage, the sooner I can get peace. My head aches, and I need to either smoke a joint or lay my fists into something or someone. Maybe I'll pull the car into an alleyway and knock him black and blue. I'll certainly feel better.

He's forever telling me I'm not good enough for Allie. Even though he cheated on his girlfriend with an unidentified guy, and then sent videos of his cock to them without even putting up a fight. And he has the fucking audacity to say this shit to me?

I stop outside the garage and wait for him to vanish. His presence is irritating me. My neck hurts from when he gripped it, and the smoke I'm inhaling is harsh against my throat.

"Asshole," he mutters under his breath as he slams the door behind him, and I grit my teeth, desperate to throw open my door and punch him again.

Driving to Samson's place, I pull out the second phone and nearly crash as I see the recording. He actually sent it. Multiple minutes long. And instead of laughing to myself and deciding how to use this against him, I pull off to the side and open the file without hesitation.

I click play and watch the way his hand strokes his thick, veiny cock. Not as big as me, but close. It's long, even longer with the way he's working it from base to tip and adjusting his seating position to widen his legs.

I'm with Allie. I don't want Blaise. I'll keep telling myself that too, because this is all to mess with my stepbrother. I don't want him, and I definitely don't check my surroundings and adjust my pants while I watch the full recording.

With sound. Fuck, there's sound. His breathing is heavy, releasing soft groans that have me turning the volume up to its highest.

Who does he think this is for? Everyone who took part in that chasing game was a friend of mine. *My* fucking friends. Does he think I'm Samson? Keith? Someone else?

Who is he imagining while pulling his cock like this?

My body fights against the reaction I shouldn't have, making me shift in place and shake my head. Eyes still on the screen, my breaths quicken. There's heat crawling up my spine, a light sweat on my forehead.

A normal human reaction to sexual interaction, I'm sure. My therapist would be proud of me for trying to get in touch with this emotion. Well, they would be if I still went to see them.

When he comes, he moans deeply, and his cum spurts from the tip of his cock. I need to pause the clip – if I keep watching, I'll grow more confused, and I hate being confused. It aggravates me.

Instead of watching the last few seconds, I type out a message.

> Me: Poor Mia, thinking her boyfriend is innocent and straight. Does she know how much you love sucking cock? That you got so fucking hard having your control taken from you? I can still feel the way you were struggling for breath.

My annoyance hasn't lessened, so I keep going.

> Me: I think Cole would love to know what happened last weekend. I might even send him this video.

I sigh a relieved breath when I feel the tension wrapping around my ribs vanishing. That's it. That's the reason why I'm doing this. Not to get myself a reaction or randomly aroused. I need to stay on track.

The response is immediate, and I can feel his panic and rage through the screen.

> Blaise: Why the fuck would you do that?

Smirking, I lean back into my seat, putting my cigarette between my lips as I type a reply.

> Me: Because I own you now.

CHAPTER 4
BLAISE

Unknown number: Because I own you now.

I stare at the text until my eyes burn while tapping my finger against the side of my phone. I'm restless, and I haven't been able to let this go all day.

I need to figure out who was behind the mask. Whose cock I swallowed.

More importantly, I need to sort my fucking head. What the hell was I thinking, getting caught up and sending a damn video of myself jacking off to a stranger.

A fucking *stranger*—one of Cole's insufferable friends, nonetheless.

A recipe for disaster.

But which one? Samson, Keith, or someone else? There were twelve on his team, and I don't know the names of the other two, but one of them—a ripped guy with more muscle than brains—is known to swing both ways.

Fuck, what's his name again?

Jack? Jackson? Whatever. He's probably the asshole behind those texts who thinks I'll just lie back and take his threats.

"Are you listening at all?" Mia asks.

I blink at her, then snap out of it and pocket my phone while she frowns.

"Are you sure you're okay? You've acted weird for days." She hesitates. "First, you didn't want to have sex this morning, and then you attacked your brother."

I stiffen. "I didn't attack him."

"Blaise...you choked him."

I snort, leaning back against the brick wall while watching students mill about. Of course, she takes his side. Poor Cole. He plays the part of the tormented soul so well that even my own damn girlfriend buys the act. It's fucking stupid.

"You know he acts out. His father—"

"What is he? Five? Stop defending him."

"I'm sorry." Worrying her lip, she slides her palms up my chest, but I refuse to look at her, or I might say something I regret. "I'm on your side. You know that, right?"

Scoffing, I cross my arms, and her hands fall away.

"Why are you pushing me away, Blaise?"

"I'm not having this discussion." I grit my teeth, restless.

"You can be so cold sometimes." Her voice drips with hurt, but I can't find it in me to care as Cole and his friends turn the corner.

He walks with his head down, his broad shoulders swaying with every step. His dark hair falls in his eyes as he adjusts his AirPod in his ear.

My throat goes dry, and I swallow, hating the physical reaction he evokes in me by merely existing.

"I'm here for you, Blaise." Mia slides her fingers into the hair at my nape, and I meet her gaze, but my attention soon skates back to Cole, who lifts his head.

Those blue eyes clash with mine. I'm fucking lost, unable to look away as the crowd parts for him and his friends. His gaze soon slides past me to Mia, and his jaw clenches.

Warm lips press against mine, and Mia's sharp nails scratch my neck. She smells of coconut and vanilla, a warm and exotic scent I used to love. But that was before I took a fucking piss after Cole had a shower, and his citrus and leather scent assaulted me in the steam-filled bathroom.

Fuck. He was everywhere—his handprint on the mirror after he swiped it clean of condensation to look at his reflection, his wet toothbrush in the cup, and his crumpled jeans beside the laundry basket.

I let Mia kiss me, even as my eyes stay locked on Cole. My heart threatens to escape from my damn chest. What is this electric current running through my body when he looks at me like that? Why does it feel like he's undressing me while also plotting ways to kill me? And why do I want him to unleash the fury behind those dark eyes?

Just like that, I'm hard.

Mia notices, nipping at my bottom lip and whispering in my ear, "Want me to suck you before class?"

I might have to take her up on that offer. Shove her to her knees on the dirty, piss-covered bathroom floor and pretend it's my infuriating brother. I wasn't interested in her offer earlier, and I'm still not, but I need release. I'm so damn pent-up.

Cole turns the corner, and I frown as I spot the guy trailing behind with a group of football players. Jack? Jackson?

"Who's that?" I ask Mia while she trails kisses on my neck.

She peers over her shoulder. "That's Jackson, one of Cole's friends."

So, I was right—Jackson.

"Why do you ask?"

"No reason."

Mia opens her mouth to reply, when her friends shout her name from across the hall. Distracted, she meets them halfway and they embrace as though they haven't seen each other in years.

I study Jackson's curly blonde hair and thick arms. For a guy, he's attractive. I'm not gay, but I can appreciate a good-looking dude when I see one, and Jackson is definitely one of those preppy popular guys with cheek dimples and a rich dad who bails him out of trouble.

Could he be my tormentor?

I suppose there's only one way to find out.

When he pauses to talk to a junior in a denim skirt and fishnets, I reach for my phone and type out a quick reply.

I study him closely as I press send.

> Me: What do you want?

Nothing happens, not even a flicker of a reaction on his face, except for the megawatt smile he directs at the girl. If his phone vibrates, he's unaware or ignoring it.

My heart stalls when my phone pings, and I snap my gaze to the screen.

> Unknown: Wrong question.

I scan the hallway, wondering if he's watching me.

> Me: Why?

Mia throws her head back and laughs loudly, but the sound fades into the background as another message appears on the screen.

> Unknown: It's not about what I want from you. The question you need to ask is what I want to do to you.

I play along.

> Me: Let me guess. Chase me? Make me suck your cock again so that you can blackmail me?

Mia returns, smiling brightly and swaying her hips, but I'm too distracted to appreciate the view. Jackson and his friends continue down the hallway, his gaze straying over his shoulder to watch the girl. His phone is nowhere in sight.

Mine pings and I know even before I lift the screen that my

masked tormentor's response will rattle me to the bone, but like an addict in need of a fix, I look down.

> Unknown: Such simple-minded desires, Blaise. I'm disappointed.

The dots appear and disappear.

> Unknown: I'm going to fuck up your world and everyone and everything in it. I'll leave you so broken that you'll crawl on your hands and bleeding knees, begging for scraps, begging for my cum. Begging for me to hurt you.

> Unknown: By the time I'm done with you, nothing will be left for anyone else to salvage.

I nearly drop the phone when Mia pops up like a jack-in-the-box and fawns over me in front of her friends. We're late for class, judging by the almost empty hallway.

Waving her friends goodbye, she steers me toward the bathrooms. I don't stop her. I don't object.

No, when she's on her knees in the claustrophobia-inducing stall, I record a short video of my veiny hand in her blonde hair, twisting the strands, as her head bobs.

> Me: Don't tease me like that. Just look how worked up your cat-and-mouse game makes me. Maybe you want me to chase you instead?

Before he can respond, I send another message.

> Me: You're playing with fire.

"OKAY, let's see what we've got." Ronnie rubs his hands together, eyes alight with excitement as Tiago puts the pizzas down on the table.

Seated beside Ronnie on the couch, Allie looks up from her phone and says, "I ordered a Margarita, a Neptune, and enough fries to feed an army."

"How did you manage to escape your ball and chain anyway?" Luke asks her as he drags the footrest over and plops down.

Seated in the only armchair in the room, I chuckle when Allie preens.

It's not like my stepbrother gives a shit about her. Not really. But she sure loves it when my friends pretend he does.

Why is he even with her when she cheats on him on the regular?

On the other hand, it's easy to figure out why Allie set her eyes on him; he's popular and has that bad-boy vibe that makes girls drop their panties.

Let's just say, she's not the first girl in our town to think she can change him, and she won't be the last.

Why am I even thinking about this?

When Ronnie reaches for the pizza, Tiago slaps his hand and says, "¡Quita de ahí!"

Ronnie pretends to be hurt. "Dude, not fair. I wasn't born in Spain like you."

They banter back and forth, and Allie joins in, too, while Mia grabs us each a slice of pizza.

She sits back down on my lap, tucks her legs up beneath her, and watches me inhale my food. I'm never one to say no to something to eat.

"I don't know where you put it all," she points out, taking such a small bite that I'm sure even a mouse would be unimpressed.

Tiago looks over. Somehow, he got Ronnie in a chokehold,

their food forgotten. "It's all the football he did in high school. When are the tryouts?"

Oh, that.

As if I don't have enough on my plate, I have to try out for a spot on the football team. Guess who's their QB?

Cole.

Of-fucking-course.

Before I can muster a response, the door flies open, and Cole and Samson enter the living room.

When you speak of the devil.

My mood instantly sours.

The look I give Mia says, "You told me he wouldn't be here."

"I didn't know, I promise," she whispers as I grip the armrest with whitening knuckles.

He's everywhere. I can't even have an evening with my friends without him crashing.

Dressed in black combat pants and a hoodie, he saunters across the room as though he owns the place.

"Pizza," Samson exclaims. "Hell yes!"

Elbow on the armrest, I rub my lips. Why the fuck is he here? Allie usually resorts to bribery to get him to show up to spend time with her friends.

As Mia plays with the wayward strands of hair at my nape, I try my hardest not to look in their direction, but it's proving harder than breathing underwater or surviving a fall from the Empire State Building.

Cole drops onto the couch and pulls Allie onto his lap, his smile dark and devilish.

"Fries, anyone?" Samson asks around a mouthful, holding out the container.

"Just…help yourself," Tiago says, and Samson dives in, oblivious to the sarcasm in Tiago's voice.

"I promise, I didn't know," Mia whispers again when I show no sign of relaxing my tense shoulders.

I'll wake up with a sore neck at this rate.

"Why are you here?" I bite out, directing the question at the asshole across the room who stops sucking his girlfriend's face.

It takes him forever to slide his eyes in my direction, and when he finally does, I swear there's a glint of something wicked in those dark depths. His nostrils flare, and then he smirks, but it lacks humor. It's cold, just like his fucking heart. "Dad wants us to bond, remember? Thought I'd make an effort."

"He's not your dad." I'm so fucking triggered that it's difficult to breathe with him in the room. His presence sucks out the oxygen as his eyes burn brighter.

"Blaise..." There's a warning in Mia's voice, but I'm done with her. Done with this. She has defended him for the last fucking time.

Shoving her off my lap, I shoot to my feet and walk out, slamming the door behind me. As I stalk down the hallway toward the bathroom, my hands drag down my face.

Why the hell am I so wound up? I don't even know.

After splashing ice-cold water on my face and spending an eternity bracing my hands against the sink while staring into the mirror, I push off and walk out.

I'll grab my coat and leave. There's no point staying if I have to watch Allie dry-hump Cole all night. Just the thought makes my stomach churn.

I've barely opened the door before a hand grabs me by the throat and shoves me back into the bathroom.

Surprised, I stumble against the bathtub, barely catching my fall.

What the hell?

Cole locks the bathroom door, then looks at me over his shoulders. His mussed-up hair bears the proof of Allie's wandering fingers.

Fingers I want to break.

The raging storm inside me makes me see red, clouding my vision. Striding toward him, I shove him up against the wall and fist his hoodie.

Not one to back down from a fight, he fists my T-shirt fiercely.

We size each other up.

Staring.

Breathing.

"What are you gonna do?" he taunts, flashing a hint of fang.

My eyes fall to his mouth, and my heart rate speeds up.

I swear he can feel it hammering through my T-shirt. Swear he can feel the whisper of breath that escapes me when he drags his tongue across his bottom lip—teasing, taunting, driving me fucking mad with forbidden desire.

Why the hell am I burning up?

I flick my gaze to his, getting lost in those heavy eyes, and hold my hips out of reach so that he doesn't feel how hard I am for him.

"Why are you here?" I snarl, my fingers twitching on his hoodie.

The urge to flatten my palm and soak up the heat emanating from his clothes makes it hard to think. I can smell him.

Smell the citrus and leather on his clothes.

His minty breath.

Those tempting lips spread into a blinding smile that nearly buckles my knees.

How I stay upright is a miracle.

I stare, unable to breathe, while he uses his free hand to retrieve something from his pocket.

A phone.

Confused, I look down.

"Funny you ask." His voice rumbles around me like a summer storm. "Someone sent me an interesting video." Holding up the screen for me to see, I watch the clip I recorded of Mia on her knees. "Care to explain?"

"Who sent it to you?"

"Anonymous number," he explains, then looks pointedly at

my hand on his chest. "Are you going to stop touching me any time soon?"

"Not until you let me go."

Chuckling, he drops his hand, and I reluctantly let mine fall from his warm body. Though my hand tingles. I'm still rattled.

"Why did you send this?"

I frown, confused by his harsh tone. It almost sounds like... jealousy. Rubbing my face to clear the damn haze, I dismiss that silly notion. "It's none of your business."

"No?" Tsking, he takes a step closer. "I can always make it my business."

My heart stutters. "Excuse me?"

"You said it yourself. Your dad isn't my dad, right? From what I've seen, you're the golden boy—always have been."

Gritting my teeth, I watch him smirk.

"Don't you think it's time we shatter that illusion?"

I surge forward, slapping my hand on the wall behind him. Fury heats my veins, and it's a miracle I don't choke him to death. I'm in his face, baring my teeth like a feral animal. "What the fuck do you want?"

"There you are." His smile is manic. "I knew you were in there somewhere, just waiting for someone to come along with a stick and poke you."

Our chests brush with my harsh exhales. He keeps smiling, waiting for me to do what? I don't fucking know.

Reaching out, he pats my cheek, and I whack his arm away with such force that it smacks against the wall behind him.

"Do you know what's interesting?" he asks, flexing his knuckles.

When I remain silent, he levels those intoxicating eyes on me and then trails them down my body until they pause on my straining bulge.

"You claim to hate me so much, yet you're hard as a fucking rock." He reaches out to touch me, but I snatch his wrist, twisting it at an unnatural angle.

"Don't you fucking dare touch me!"

"Why so rattled, little brother? Scared your secret will get back to Mom and Dad?"

I snap.

Moving forward, I press my forehead to his, realizing too late that his body is now aligned with mine, and all I can feel is him. I dig my fingers into the tiled wall as our breaths dance in the small space between our lips.

The need to grind my cock against his crotch makes my mouth go dry, but I force down the urge, whispering, "Stay the hell away from me."

"Scared your dad will find out that you're not so perfect, after all?"

My eyes fall shut and my chest heaves on a ragged inhale. The pull—*his* pull—is too strong. I don't stand a damn chance against his current.

"Scared they'll find out you're dying to touch me?"

My eyes fly open.

Stumbling back, my hand shoots out, and I punch his face.

It all happens so fast.

One minute, he's taunting me, bringing me to the brink of madness, and the next, my knuckles connect with his cheekbone.

His face whips to the side, and he bursts out laughing.

Disheveled hair shifts forward over his eyes, hiding his own descent down the rabbit hole.

I don't think I'm ready to see the look in his eyes.

Instead, I stare at my bleeding knuckles.

Straightening up, he leans back against the wall, his hoodie creased from my grip. "Break up with her, or Mom and Dad will see the video."

When I finally let my eyes lift from my cracked knuckles to his bruised cheek, he shrugs. "Let's see how proud they are of you then."

He walks out without another word.

CHAPTER 5
BLAISE

I love it when a plan comes together without much effort on my part.

It all started when a gravelly voice called my name as I passed by the business building. I looked back to see Freddy, the local dealer, leaning against a tree.

Intrigued, I backpedaled.

We didn't run in the same circles, and we'd never exchanged a single word before now, which made me more curious.

He took a drag on his cigarette, watching me through his lashes. "You party?"

When I failed to respond, he shrugged, blowing the smoke to the side. "Preppy boys like you party, too. What are you into?"

"What have you got?"

His husky chuckle rang out in the afternoon sun. "You name it, I've got it."

An idea sparked—a wicked, evil little idea.

Walking closer, I considered him. Dressed in a Hawaiian shirt and board shorts, he looked so cliché that it gave me a toothache.

"What's the strongest you have?"

"I see..." His amused eyes fell down my body, the cigarette dangling from his bottom lip. He took one final drag before tossing the cancer stick to the grass and crushing it beneath the heel of his Vans. "The preppy boys always party the hardest." Chuckling, he pulled a small bag of pills from his pocket. "This will make you think you're fucking Santa on the moon."

That was three days ago, and since then, my mind has concocted the perfect plan. Now, I'm antsy as hell to trap Cole with his own noose.

A week has passed since my run-in with him in the bathroom.

A full week of him smirking in my direction, taunting me every chance he gets.

I have no doubts about his threat.

Unless I act, he will show that video to our parents. I can't let that happen. Dad would understand—he was young once—but I don't want Cole to have this kind of power over me. It's not about my golden reputation anymore. No, it's about him thinking he can control me, thinking I'll dance to his tune.

Thinking I'm a doormat.

I'm not, and he will soon find out the hard way.

Tonight is Samson's birthday party—an extravagant affair held at a local castle-like mansion that's popular for wedding events. Located in the countryside, it sits nestled amongst acres of woodlands. It is a picturesque place in the daytime and a ghostly setting at night when the shadows thicken and the moon casts an ethereal glow over the turrets.

My veins thrum with anticipation, and I adjust my mask, two seconds away from bouncing on my heels. Samson insisted on a Venetian jester-themed event, and I must admit, the effect isn't lost on me. My mask is gold with bells, while Mia went for red and white, matched with a tulle dress and heels.

"When will they let us in?" she asks, craning her neck to see above the crowd.

Behind us, Tiago shakes his head to make the bells jingle, and Ronnie punches his arm.

Allie is already inside with Cole and the others, and I try not to let that thought bother me as the gates finally open with an ominous creak. Silence falls over the crowd while we wait outside the tall iron gates. Mia interlaces her fingers with mine. I wonder, not for the first time, if I can go through with my plan.

I don't have time to fret, though, because the crowd surges forward, steering us toward the gothic monstrosity that stretches fanged towers toward the sky.

Mia's hand feels so small in mine. Small and fragile.

We enter the building, greeted by rock music and a large chandelier overhead that, if it fell, would kill countless students in one swoop.

The crowd finally thins out as the masked students make their way to the main hall. I barely have time to take in the artwork on the domed ceiling as Mia pulls me along, swaying her hips to the heavy beat. She's in her element now, but I remain stiff. Ronnie's rowdy laughter behind me sounds far away. Distant.

"Allie said to meet them by the fireplace," Mia shouts over the music.

We weave through masked men and women until we reach a seating area. Tiago and Ronnie are nowhere in sight, lost in the faceless crowd.

I know the moment I spot *him*, sprawled on the luxurious couches closest to the lit fireplace, dressed in all black, with one booted foot on the coffee table and his muscled arms spread out behind him.

Goosebumps erupt over my skin, and a chill winds its way down my spine. As the music hits the bridge, his dark eyes lock onto mine, searing me through his striking half-white, half-black mask.

Clashing colors. How ironic.

We stare at each other while I fight against my visceral reaction to the energy emanating from him.

Someone throws themselves at me, and I break eye contact to smile at Allie.

"You came. Thanks for bringing my girl."

"Get off my man," my girlfriend scolds, pulling Allie away while laughing. She plasters herself to my side and flips her off.

Arm flung around her shoulder, I accept the beer Allie hands me, then glance around the room.

Now, on to the next part of my plan.

A smirk plays on my lips as I shift my mask to sip my beer.

Tonight is the night for mayhem.

Chaos.

Destruction.

"C'mon," Mia says, interlinking her fingers with mine and guiding me to the plush couches. I drop beside Samson and pull her down onto my lap.

Music blares around us while I drink my beer, feeling Cole's eyes on me. The urge to get lost in the darkness that swirls around him like shadows has me white-knuckling the bottle in my hand.

I hold the cards tonight. Not him.

Allie appears before us, pulling Mia to her feet.

Samson leans in. "Plenty of fine pussy here tonight."

I take in his green and black Venetian mask with its creepy jester smile. "Got your eyes on anyone?"

He scans the vast room, stretching his arms out behind him on the couch, then leans back in, shouting over the loud riff of music. "Freshman, two o'clock."

Craning my neck, I look behind me, spotting a girl by the tall windows. She's pretty in her white mask and angel wings. Even more so with the starry night sky as a backdrop.

Samson is so close that his mask brushes up against the side of my face. "I'm gonna be balls deep in her pussy before the night's end."

I turn around, and Samson jostles my shoulder, laughing, but I'm caught by the storm on the couch across from us.

If you could define turmoil, Cole is it.

His knee jiggles, and he clenches his hands.

He's pent-up and I like seeing him unravel while the flames in the fireplace cast dancing shadows over his mask.

I almost want to kick the table out of the way, cage him in

with my arms, and ask him why he's so wound up. But that thought soon leads down a dangerous path of grabbing him through his jeans and squeezing his hard dick.

Jesus, fuck.

I help myself to another beer, needing something to cool me off before I do something stupid, like offer him up my power on a silver plate.

Clenching my jaw, I glare at him as I press the bottleneck to my lips.

Tonight, your power is mine, fucker. When I'm done with you, you'll sing to my tune.

Fancy trying to fuck with me.

I think not.

No one threatens me.

The cool liquid slides down my throat, and I see my opening to put my plan into place when Cole rises to his feet.

Rounding the couch, he heads in the direction of the toilets.

Samson kneels beside me, almost falling over the back of the couch as he talks to Keith behind us.

With a final glance around the crowded room to ensure no one is paying attention, I drag the crate of beers closer, then kick my leg out and pull the packet of pills from my pocket. I quickly crush them with a beer can and pop the lid on three bottles, pouring equal amounts into each.

My plan tonight requires more than one sacrifice. I've thought about it, asking myself if it's worth it.

Yes, it is.

I'll happily burn down the world and everyone in it to watch Cole squirm like a worm on my hook.

A smirk spreads across my lips as Cole returns. He flops onto the couch, picks up a beer, and kicks his boot up on the table.

I glance around the room while he drinks his alcohol. For this to work, I need Mia and Allie to return.

Once I spot her dancing in the crowd, I quirk a finger in her direction, pleased when she drags Allie back.

When she falls onto my lap, her mask halfway up her face, I'm ready for her.

Kissing her soft lips, I hand her the beer. "You must be thirsty, babe."

"You have no idea." She smiles, pecking me on the mouth again before she inhales the cold alcohol.

Satisfaction warms my veins as her throat jumps and beer trickles down her chin. I steady her hand, not wanting her to waste it.

Across from us, Allie drinks her beer too. I cock my head to the side, watching her creamy thighs part slightly as she shifts on Cole's lap.

I've never considered fucking her before, but she looks so damn tempting tonight, even more so because she belongs to Cole. I'm developing a taste for his...toys.

The night wears on. More crates of beer appear. Thirty minutes later, I pull Mia to her feet, hauling her against me. Vanilla and coconut swirl around me, warm and spicy. I devour her lips, tasting the alcohol on her tongue.

She's wasted.

Fucking perfect.

Samson and Keith are nowhere in sight.

Whispering in Mia's ear, I quirk a brow at Cole as she runs over to Allie and pulls her to her feet.

"We should explore the mansion."

Giggling, they sway, barely staying upright. Allie drags Cole to his feet, and he comes willingly, shaking his head to clear the haze.

His eyes are glassy, and he is unable to focus. In other words, he's fucked.

How poetic.

I grab the back of his damp neck, shoving him forward. "You want to play, brother. Let's go."

X

IT'S LIKE HERDING SHEEP, I realize, as we stumble upstairs. It's a damn miracle I don't let them all fall down the marble steps.

If I did, they'd lie in a laughing heap of blood and broken bones.

Everything is fun as hell now, apparently.

"Woah, look." Mia points at a deer head on the wall, then breaks down in hysterical giggles.

Rolling my eyes, I open the bedroom door. "Get in."

"So bossy, Daddy." She blows me a kiss on her way inside and winks behind the mask as she pulls a laughing Allie behind.

Grinding my teeth to dust, it takes everything in me not to throttle her. But then citrus and leather invade my senses, and all thoughts of my annoying girlfriend evaporate.

Cole's broad shoulders crowd me against the doorframe. "You put something in my drink."

"I would never do such a thing. I'm a golden boy, remember?" Reaching out, I pull off his mask and swap it with mine. "There, that's better." The smile I offer him as I slide mine back down to cover my face is nothing short of evil. "Have fun."

He sways into me before stumbling into the room when Mia yanks his arm, thinking he's me, too fucked up to realize otherwise.

Yes, I'll happily sacrifice her tonight for the greater good.

They fall onto the four-poster bed together, ripping their masks off, laughing and kissing.

Always one to be in control, Cole has lost all sense of the word now.

While Allie dances in front of a tall window, with her eyes closed and her arms raised in the air, I set up my phone on the dresser and press record, then double-check to ensure it's getting a perfect shot of my dearest brother fucking up his life. Mom and Dad would be so proud.

I watch the screen with my back to the room, ignoring my twisting insides.

The urge to pull Mia away.

And not because I don't like another man touching her, but because she's touching *him*.

Cole motherfucking Carter.

Arms encircle my waist, and I turn around to find Allie smiling up at me.

Her mask lies abandoned on the carpeted floor.

"Why so serious, Cole?"

I tuck her hair behind her ear. One taste won't hurt, right?

She drops to her knees and unbuckles my jeans. I should stop this, but despite what everyone likes to think, I'm not a good guy.

I'm selfish to the core.

Evil beyond measure.

While my brother fights with his fists, I cause anarchy through other less obvious measures.

Her devilish mouth envelopes me, and I fist her hair as I glance over at the bed. Cole has my girlfriend spread like a feast on the plush sheets, tongue buried deep in her cunt.

A cunt I've licked countless times.

I know her taste like the back of my hand. Know the feel of her clenching walls.

Mesmerized, I watch his fingers dig into Mia's thighs while his tongue swirls circles over her swollen clit.

I'm jealous, my grip tightening on Allie's hair, but the sickening feeling twisting my insides is not only intoxicating but addictive, too.

Allie swallows me down, and I grunt, forcing her to take more of my dick. She gags, so I ram my dick as far down the back of her throat as I can.

Something deliciously dark curls around my heart.

My balls throb and my teeth gnash. I pull out, palming my wet dick.

Lifting my gaze, I catch my girlfriend coming all over Cole's face. She's squealing like a little piggy—all inhibitions gone out the window.

I chuckle, pulling on my cock.

Fell right into that trap, brother.

But he's not done.

Crawling up her body, fucked out of his damn mind, he frees his dick.

I push Allie away when she tries to suck me again. A sweet, toxic symphony of slapping skin rings out.

Naughty, Cole.

Allie likes to cheat, but I doubt she takes well to the tables turning.

And with her best friend.

I've got you by the balls now, Cole.

I watch his ass pump, his face buried in her neck.

Allie reaches for me again, clawing at my thighs with her sharp nails. Freddy was right; these pills fuck you up. It's a damn circus in here.

Cupping her chin, I drag my thumb across her plump bottom lip. "You want to suck Cole's dick?"

As my finger swipes the mascara streak on her cheek, she nods eagerly.

"Call me Cole," I order.

Before I've had a chance to drop my hand, she's slurping my cock, teasing me with sweet words like, "Choke me, Cole. Fuck my throat, Cole. I'm your whore, Cole."

I quite like this game of pretending to be my brother while playing with his girlfriend.

My depraved thoughts shatter when Cole's guttural groan fills the room. He shudders, fisting the pillows and sheets. I wouldn't be surprised if my girlfriend suffocates to death beneath his dead weight. I don't think I'd care.

The sight of him with his ass in the air, his damp, mussed-up hair, and jeans halfway down his thighs pushes me over the edge. I grip hold of the dresser behind me as I spill my cum down Allie's throat.

When she's swallowed every drop, I zip my dick away and

grab my phone before walking over to my brother and pulling him off my girlfriend. He's so gone; he just lies there, sprawled on his back with his softening, wet dick dampening the hem of his T-shirt. Chuckles vibrate his chest, shaking his diaphragm as I let the camera roll.

I fucking love it when a plan comes together.

"Lick her clean, Cole," I order. "Don't leave my girlfriend such a mess."

Fisting his hair, I pull him up, and he flays, not yet in control of his own movements. He falls on top of Mia, and his mouth seeks out her cunt.

A ball-tingling groan echoes in the room as his tongue glides through their combined cum.

Mia moans my name, and I stifle a laugh.

This shit is too funny.

None of them will remember what happened here tomorrow, and that thought alone is what makes me end the video and haul my brother to his knees.

My lips are on his in the next second, kissing, biting, and nibbling. A groan claws its way up my throat as I taste their cum on his tongue.

Beneath the tangy flavor is something far more addictive— something salty.

Something entirely forbidden.

Something that feeds this insatiable beast.

It's at this moment, as I devour his swollen lips and tongue, that I realize I'll turn evil for him.

There are no lengths, no stretch of the imagination that I won't go to own every part of him.

Maybe I spent the week planning my revenge, but now, as he moans and pulls on my belt, it dawns on me how meaningless revenge is when I can ruin this broken man and keep the shards for myself.

Pushing him off me, I grip his jaw and snap a picture.

I've never seen Cole so helpless.

So utterly delicious.

So mine.

"Sleep well, big brother."

He collapses back onto the bed, and I pick up Mia, cradling her against my chest. She snores softly, limp in my arms.

I take one final look at the destruction I caused, seeing Cole asleep, and Allie curled up on the floor.

With a final grin and a shake of my head, I walk out.

If he wants to ruin my squeaky-clean reputation with a video, I'll happily implode his world too. If I'm going down, he's sure as hell going down with me.

CHAPTER 8
COLE

There's a crashing sound coming from outside my room that pulls me from my sleep, the door thrown open, making me tense everywhere.

"Did you spill my fucking coffee?" Dad asks in a firm, angry tone.

I kick off my duvet and hurry to get under my bed like I always do when he's mad. He's scary when he's drunk – and he's always drunk.

Mom pulls his shoulder, trying to drag my dad away from coming for me. "I told you it wasn't him! It's only damn coffee, Malcolm! It's three in the morning, go to bed!"

"Stop fucking lying for him!"

"I'm not! Please don't hurt him. He's only ten years old. Please, please don't hurt him. It's only coffee. You need to stop—"

I cover my ears and press my face into the dust-infested carpet the second I hear the slap and my mom crying out. She falls to the floor, facing me with a trickle of blood coming from her nose. Her eyes are telling me to run, to remember what we talked about when he was like this a few days ago.

I'm scared. I love my dad, but sometimes, when he drinks too much beer, he changes. He shouts, breaks things, and when Mom tries to stop him, he hits her.

If I don't hide on time, sometimes he hits me.

Dad grabs her by the hair and yanks her to her feet, and I take the opportunity to crawl from under the bed and run, just like my mom told me to do.

I want to help her, but she'd made me promise to get out of the *house and go straight to the neighbor's place before he gets more violent. If I try to help, I'll only get hurt again. My arm is still sore from when he broke it nearly a year ago.*

He told Mom I fell off the trampoline, but I didn't. He lied. He always lies, and then blames everything on me.

My bare feet smack the ground as I run as fast as I can, reaching Mom's phone, then rushing down the stairs, pausing when I hear a loud scream. I step forward and freeze, a tear slipping down my cheek before I turn and leave the house.

I bang my small fist on the neighbor's front door, full-blown crying now, still hearing my mom's cries for him to stop. The door flies open, and I gasp as my dad grabs my face and drags me into the darkness.

My entire body flinches as I jolt awake in a confused state.

I'm struggling to fill my lungs, a thick layer of sweat all over me.

Hair tickles my nose, and there's a weight on my chest that stops me from sitting up. I'm weak, breathless, and everything hurts like I've been struck by a fucking car. My vision is still completely nonexistent, and I can smell sex everywhere.

There's a bitter taste in my mouth, a mix of alcohol and something else.

I blink a few times, groaning when my head aches, and slip in and out of consciousness while battling with reality. I can't fall back into that dream. I can't. I'll fucking lose my mind if I need to re-live that memory ever again.

Not that my dad was ever arrested for being an abusive asshole. He talked his way out of everything, since the only evidence was the word of a kid and a few bruises on my mom's face that could have been self-inflicted. She was a nurse, after all, so she healed our wounds.

And my dad was a cop. Still is. I haven't seen or spoken to him since I was a teenager.

There's faint music. From behind my eyelids, I know the sun is beaming through the window. Is it the next day already? What the fuck happened last night? The brain fog is fucking me.

I try to tuck my cock into my pants, but my girlfriend hikes her leg over me, and I flinch as her knee skims across my dick. She hums, splays her hand on my chest, and falls back to sleep.

I know it's Allie lying on me, going by the smell of her perfume and her perfect frame pressed against and over me, and the soft way she snores.

From the feel of her tits against my ribs and bare pussy on my leg, she's naked. My jaw hurts, and my head feels like it's about to explode when I try to sit up and fail again.

"Fucking hell," I mutter, and my throat cracks like I've been screaming for hours. "Fuck."

My phone dings from somewhere. The floor? I lift my head, screwing my eyes to faintly see it on the other side of the room.

Allie doesn't stir as I slowly roll her off me, my eyes starting to adjust to my surroundings to see we're in some sort of ancient, fancy room. And when I sit on the edge of the mattress, I look down and see a white-ish stain at the bottom of my shirt. I rub it between my fingers, whatever it is being half-dried.

Is it cum? Mine? Allie's? I glance at the passed-out blonde beside me. How did she successfully get me to fuck her? And why don't I remember it when I only had five beers?

The last I remember, I was sitting with my friends, trying not to jump on Samson and snap his neck for touching Blaise's shoulder. And then I was watching them talk, laughing at something, and the way my friend kept looking at him when Blaise wasn't aware of it.

The annoyance that ran through me could have been the fact my friends were mingling with him, and I hate him. Maybe it's just the fact I hate hanging out with him. Or, it could be that I'm possessive of my friends and don't want them anywhere near the piece of shit.

Blaise might think the masked man and unidentified messenger is Samson, though. Was that why he was so friendly with my guys last night? Was he trying to find out whose dick he sucked?

Surely, he'll know Samson doesn't have an evil bone in his body and does everything for a joke? He's not serious enough to hide his identity and fuck a guy's mouth before stalking the shit out of him.

Then there's Jackson. He's definitely the type. I already know from multiple drunken occasions that he thinks Blaise is a preppy guy he'd fuck. And since Blaise evidently likes cock, going by the way he hardened sucking mine, he might find him attractive.

I groan and rub my hands through my sweaty hair, grabbing my phone from the ground and going into the bathroom to wash my face with cold water and scrub the smell of sex from me. I feel dirty, not because of Allie, but it feels wrong. It had felt wrong being with her sexually before I cut off sex. And I'm still trying to figure out why it feels that way.

The cheating, maybe. The attitude transplant she's in need of, possibly. The six-foot tank who sleeps in the room across from mine, fuck no.

Am I the problem? Is this all my issues getting in the way of me being happy with Allie? Are we a good match, and I'm just fucking it up?

I dip my head, needing the dizziness to ease off before I move from the front of the mirror. I gulp down water from the tap with cupped hands, then I check my phone.

Mom: Did you ask Allie if she wanted to come on the trip with us? I think Blaise asked Mia and she said yes! It'll be wonderful if everyone came. Let me know and I can book a larger lodge so you don't need to share with your brother and his girlfriend.

Blaise: Where did you fuck off to? Allie is looking for you and I'm not babysitting her drunk ass.

Mom: Can you call Blaise? Or are you with him? Gavin can't get a hold of him and he's worried. Please don't get him drunk again, Cole.

Great. His dad can't find him, so they assume I got him drunk.

A few hours ago in the group chat, Keith sent in a picture of them all, asking where the fuck I am in the caption. Samson has his arm over Blaise's shoulder, the latter grinning like he's having the time of his life, a beer to hand. Mia is on his other side and looking completely out of it. Allie is in the background, and she looks even worse than Mia.

I lean out of the bathroom and look over at her. "Allie? Are you feeling alright?"

She lightly snores, so I guess she's not dead. At least she made it to bed with me and not someone else to take advantage of her.

Music plays downstairs in the main hall, and by the sound of it, there are a lot of fucking people drunk still. I can hear screams, cheers, chants, and it only gets louder as I open the room door and lean my body out to look down the corridor.

Strobe lights and colors flash in the distance.

I'm still really drunk somehow. My steps are uncoordinated and I'm swaying, and I keep shaking my head to realign my thoughts when I hear voices I know don't exist.

But I'm not missing out on this. Samson will kill me if he thinks I bailed on his birthday party, regardless of the time.

Taking advantage of the fancy shower, much fancier than the one me and Blaise share, I wash the smell of sex and sweat from my body, grimacing as I pull the dirty clothes back on.

"Allie?" I call her name as I walk into the bedroom.

She groans when I tap her cheek and kiss her lips, her eyes opening slightly. "What?" she croaks.

"The party's still going. Come on."

"But I feel dead."

"Be dead downstairs."

She huffs and sits up, way easier than my attempt. "My head hurts."

I grab her a glass of water from the bathroom, and she sips it slowly while I lean against the dresser and reply to some messages. I intentionally ignore my mom because the idea of spending a full week with Allie complaining about the snow during a ski trip makes my right eye twitch.

It takes her fifteen minutes to wash her face in the bathroom, removing her makeup altogether. I stay where I am, trying to remember what the fuck happened and why I'm still feeling so messed up. The longer she takes, the more ill and hungover I feel.

Which makes no fucking sense.

Did someone slip something into my drink?

"I don't feel good at all," Allie tells me as she leaves the bathroom looking like death warmed up. "I'm really dizzy."

"Me neither." I straighten and stagger, her body distorting through my vision. "We'll go and see Samson and head to your dorm. I have classes tomorrow so there's no point in me going home."

She wraps her arms around my waist and smiles up at me. It's like I'm looking through a kaleidoscope and all I can see is her face in the dozens. "I'm glad we finally did normal couple things. I've missed you."

I huff a laugh. "You tricked me." Sucking on my bottom lip, I feel the tender swelling from being nipped. "You bit me hard."

Her head tilts, and then she pulls me down to kiss her.

Maybe she was the one who roofied me? Would she?

When she reaches down to my soft cock, I pull back. "I think you've had enough. Come on."

She rolls her eyes and takes my hand, both of us looking like death. "We slept for, like, five hours. I have no idea how people are still going crazy down there."

Uncoordinated, we manage to reach the stairs, and she holds on to me tightly as I get us down each step, bumping into the banister as we go. She huffs and stops, placing her hand on her hip. "I didn't drink enough to be feeling this way."

I run my sweaty hand down my face. "Me neither."

"Do you think someone roofied us?"

I think she roofied me, in all honesty. It would make sense, and she could be putting on a show right now to make herself look innocent. She isn't exactly the good girl, and she definitely has the fucked-up nonexistent morals to drug her own boyfriend so he'd fuck her.

If that is the case, then I hope I came and she didn't get a chance to finish. Serves her fucking right.

Did I at least wear a condom? Fuck, I don't know. She's on the pill, but that doesn't protect me from her fucking around with others and transmitting some shit to me.

I take her hand and pull her the rest of the way, stopping in the entrance of the doorway. My eyes instantly find Blaise passed out on the sofa, and Samson laughing and taking a picture of Blaise while trying to balance cups on his head.

Something inside me snaps. "What the fuck are you doing to him?"

My friends stand tall. "Cole's alive! Where did you go, man?"

I ignore them and go to Blaise, crouching down through my dizzy haze and knocking all the shit off him. Grabbing his jaw, I pry one of his eyelids open. His pupils are fully blown, bloodshot, and when I shake him, he doesn't show any response.

"He parties hard," Keith tells me. "Mia left him here and went back to her dorm about an hour ago."

Mom is going to fucking kill me if she finds out he's in this state. Yeah, we're not kids, but we aren't exactly legally allowed to drink either. And if she found out? I'll be shamed in front of everyone yet again and my stepdad will probably cut off all my funding for college.

I stuff my phone in my back pocket and turn to Allie. "We'll take him back to your dorm. His dad will lose his shit if he sees him like this."

My eyes lift to Jackson, who looks like he's trying not to laugh at Blaise as I attempt to wake him again, but there's something else there. Like he's proud of how fucked he is. Why is he looking at him like that? I'll carve his damn eyes out of their sockets and make him eat them.

Keith and Samson help me get Blaise to his feet while I pull his arm over my shoulder. I shake my head, because I'm still fucked up and it's a struggle to focus. Allie calls for a ride, and Blaise groans as I drag his ass to the car when it sounds its horn outside.

Once we reach the dorm, Allie seems more alive while I feel like I'm about to smash right into death, at the same time as carrying my unconscious stepbrother to his bed.

Mia is sleeping on the sofa, so we leave her there. Allie vanishes into her room, and I hurry to get Blaise to Mia's room before I drop him. He groans again, his hand flexing to a fist, and when I lower him to the side of the bed, he blinks his eyes open a little.

"C-Cole?"

Leaning down, I pull off his shoes and socks, and when I go to unbuckle his belt, my hands freeze over the leather, the metal clip pressing to my fingertips.

"This isn't," he starts, hiccupping, "how I saw my night ending."

I roll my eyes and try to ignore the way my cock is reacting as I pull his belt off and drop it on the floor beside me. His body towers over mine as I stay on my knees, looking up at him. Will he let me undress him so he can sleep comfortably?

My cock pulses, and I want to punch it, because what the fuck?

"If you remember me helping you tomorrow, don't you fucking dare let my mom and your dad give me shit for your condition if they find out."

I flinch as his hand reaches to my hair, fisting it and making me pause. "I'm not Mia," I tell him. "Get your fucking hand off me."

Neither of us pulls away, even though I know I should.

"I'm not sorry," he says, slurring each word and syllable.

He falls back on the bed, passed out before I can ask what the fuck he wouldn't be sorry about. I sigh and drop back to my haunches, taking a minute to watch him before I roll him onto his side.

If he's sick in his sleep, I'll get the blame for him dying.

I leave a glass of water beside the bed and exit the room, my head doing overtime, trying to fight my own exhaustion.

Allie is half asleep when I get to the room. I climb in beside her, resisting the pull to go into the room across the hall.

She turns inside the duvet to face me. "Is your brother okay?"

I roll my eyes. "He's not my brother."

"I don't understand why you hate him so much. What did he ever do to you?"

Gritting my teeth, I turn away from her, my fingers gripping the duvet so tight, I think I might rip the fabric.

Hands slide up my back. "Just try with him. You make no effort, and your mom is desperate for you both to get along."

I shrug her off, rubbing my face, feeling the swollen side of my bottom lip from her obvious hard kisses earlier. It's not even something I should be mad at – my girl wanting to be romantic with me. I was before, when we first started dating. I wanted to see her, speak to her, but the feelings were always…confusing for me. Now, everything feels forced to make others happy.

Then again, the look on Mom's face when I brought Allie home pushes me to turn around and face her in the bed. I feel like I need to give her something more. I'm leading her on, and my mom will never forgive me if I fuck this up.

Giving my stepdad and Blaise ammunition against me isn't something I'm seeking out. I'm trying to fucking prove that I'm not the asshole everyone thinks I am.

Well, I am, but not fully. I'm not my father.

Allie smiles when I drag her body closer. Her small frame fits perfectly against mine, but it isn't right. It isn't... I... Something isn't right.

I kiss her, and she kisses me back with her fingers brushing through my hair, and I fight not to pull away. I press my mouth to hers harder, and when her hand drops between us, I snatch her wrist. "No."

I'm giving myself whiplash at this point.

"But..." Her lips move, but no sound escapes. "Why?"

"I'm not in the mood."

She averts her eyes, and I see a tear slipping free. "I promise, I'm not cheating anymore. I blocked my professor's number, and I haven't seen the others in weeks."

My eye twitches. Is it bad that I don't care? It's a huge fucking sign I should end this. "Go to sleep," I tell her. "We're fine, I'm just tired."

"Do you promise we'll be okay? We'll get back what we had?"

I nod. "Yeah."

We both know that's a lie, especially when she falls asleep and I check on Blaise four times before I manage to pass out.

CHAPTER 7
BLAISE

"Cole..." His name dances on my cracked lips in the early morning hours. The sun hasn't risen yet as I blink my eyes open, suppressing a groan. Fuck, my head hurts.

I lift my head, confused for a moment. Where the fuck am I? I rub my eyes. The moon's silvery light filters through Mia's pink lace curtains, casting an almost magical light over the room.

"Were you dreaming of me, brother?"

I stiffen.

What the fuck?

My head snaps in the direction of the corner near the door.

Cloaked in shadows and mystique, Cole smirks. His long legs stretch out in front of him as he leans back against the wall. Fuck, he's a vision, shrouded by the dark as though it's his ally and protector. Or maybe his greatest weapon.

Sitting up straighter, I devour the sight of him. My heart thuds hard in the ensuing silence while we observe each other. I don't want to talk first. I wouldn't even know what to say. Why is he here?

Drawing his leg up, he rests his forearm on his knee. Even in the darkness, I can make out his long fingers, the leather bands around his wrist, and the veins that paint a roadmap on the top of his hand. He's effortlessly attractive in a devastating way. We'll ruin each other. It's not a matter of if but when. We circle like magnets.

"Don't flatter yourself." I glance around the room.

"Mia isn't here."

My attention skates back to Cole, who rises to his feet, the shadows thickening around him like the night.

"We're alone."

He emerges from the shadows, his large boots sinking into Mia's white, fluffy rug. He's even more breathtaking in the moonlight.

I struggle to focus when he runs a hand through his mussed hair before setting his eyes on me. Something pulses between us. Something elusive.

"I know what you did," he says in a tone that caresses my senses like a whispered kiss against my collarbone. I shiver, watching his approach. This side of Cole is uncharted territory.

When he levels those intense eyes on me, I'm lost in an enchanted forest, called forward by a bewitching voice in the distance. My heart thuds harder, throbbing in my throat, and I wet my dry lips.

The floorboards creak beneath his weight as he comes to stand beside me. Anticipation thrums through my bloodstream, and I hold my breath while he slowly fingers the quilt, watching me the entire time. I drown in that drugging look. What will he do next?

He rips the quilt away, making me jerk.

"Cole?"

"Shut up for once." Walking around me, he comes to a halt at the foot of the bed, and my lungs burn. I need to inhale a breath—just one. I'm caught in him and the curve of his sensuous lips.

He climbs onto the bed, cloaked in the night's mysterious pink and silvery hue filtering through the lace curtains.

"Cole?" I question as his hulking frame stalks me, the mattress shifting beneath his heavy weight. "What are you doing?"

"I changed my mind."

"What do you mean?" I ask breathily, my cock straining inside my unbuckled jeans.

"I told you to get your hands off me, that I'm not Mia."

What is he talking about? When he curls his fingers inside my waistband, confusion mixes with the primal arousal coursing through me.

"I'll make you feel so much better than she ever can." Yanking down my jeans, he grips my weeping dick before I can choke out a response. My hips buck and I grunt, caught in his wicked eyes. Fuck me... A ragged exhale claws its way up my throat.

He strokes my length and swipes his thumb through the precum seeping from the crown. I'm caught defenseless against him with nothing but my waning dignity to keep me together. I'm a lost cause. Alone on this battlefield.

Choppy breaths hover on my lips as he leans down to drag his flattened tongue from root to tip.

"Fuck..."

Cole's eyes flick up, a hint of fang gleaming in the moonlight. He slides his hand down the length of my cock, over the angry veins, then palms my balls and chuckles low, squeezing with enough threat to make my breath hitch. "You folded so easily. Look at you..."

Another squeeze.

Shudders ripple down my spine, and I tip my head back. He'll be the death of me before the night's end if he keeps touching me like this. I'm fucking dying, my cock throbbing and leaking. It won't take much at all to make me blow.

"So powerless with your balls in my hand." He massages them between his fingers, tracking my every quivering exhale. Leaning down, he grips my dick and sucks my balls into his mouth, slurping and groaning low in his throat.

My heart beats through my chest, and I clutch the crumpled bedsheet like my life depends on it. I can't control my breathing anymore, not when he scrapes his teeth over the sensitive skin and squeezes my crown. More precum weeps from my dick, and I swallow down the saliva in my mouth as my hips shoot off the bed.

I've never been this aroused before. Mia gives good blowjobs, but this is on another level. Or maybe it's not about the technique. Perhaps it's him.

Dragging his tongue over my balls and shaft, he trails the angry vein that runs up the underside of my throbbing dick and swallows me down. He sucks me hard, his head bobbing before me.

White knuckling the bedsheet, I watch him bleed me dry of my sanity and self-control. He drives his sword deep, and I fall to my knees on our battlefield, staring up at his blood-streaked face. I should have known all along that I stood no chance against him. Not in a world where emotions are foreign concepts and nothing more than learned behavior for me. Yet this guy, this broken, ruined guy, makes me want to lose this war between us. Even if only for this moment.

As soon as dawn chases away the night, he better run. I'll fuck him up for thinking he can catch me defenseless and exploit my weakness—my dick in his mouth.

Because fuck, I can't fight back against this growing obsession.

I release the creased bedsheet and slide my fingers through his soft hair, gripping the strands tight. Fuck everything good and holy. I've never seen a more erotic sight. He slurps and sucks, humping the mattress while I bite my lip hard enough to taste blood on my tongue.

Someone could walk in any moment now, but I don't care. I'll murder anyone who sees him like this. Snap their fucking neck like a fragile twig. Bathe in their damn blood and use it to lube up Cole's pretty ass.

And it's that thought of bending Cole over and smashing his face into the mattress that finally tips me over the edge.

A strangled grunt chokes me as my cock pulses in his mouth.

My eyes roll, head thrown back, as I reach a hand up to fist my sweaty strands until my scalp prickles with pain—

I wake with a start, choking back a groan. My body shudders. Mia pops up from beneath the quilt, her hair disheveled and a wide grin spreading across her lips.

"Good morning, baby." Her smile widens even more, and she crawls up my body and kisses me, slipping her tongue against mine.

I can't think straight, reeling from the strongest orgasm I've ever had. What the hell just happened? Did I dream about Cole while my girlfriend blew me off in my sleep?

Mia's chin is smeared with cum, and her breath is laced with last night's alcohol and sex. She whispers against my lips, "Did you like your wake-up call?"

Dragging a hand over my face, I push up on my elbows and blink at her. What the hell happened last night? I executed my plan to perfection, but then what? I don't remember a damn thing after carrying Mia out of the bedroom and tucking her into bed in a spare room so that she could sleep it off while I returned to the party downstairs. Samson and Jackson supplied me with alcohol, and I played along. I've perfected the social game, or so I thought...

Mia's tangled hair is a rat's nest on her head, and her lashes are clumped. She's a fucking mess, but I'll admit that she has never looked more enticing to me than she did last night while Cole fucked her senseless—a warm hole to empty his load inside.

I'm strangely stirred by the memory as I finger a strand of Mia's matted hair. I rarely feel emotions past this 'desire' to control my environment and the people in it, but something about seeing Cole pump her full of cum piqued a deep-rooted curiosity in me. That need to control my environment has now homed in on him. Everything else fades in comparison to the overwhelming urge to possess him. I don't even know what it is, but it quirks a finger at me from the shadows.

Mia's cheeks redden when I tuck a strand of hair behind her ear.

"You surprised me." I smack her ass, the sound echoing in the small room. "Sit on my face. Let me return the favor."

What I don't say out loud as she settles over me with her knees on the mattress on either side of my head is that I want to see if I can still taste Cole on her pussy and the inside of her thighs.

Gripping her ass cheeks, I pull her down, sucking on her dripping pussy lips. I can, in fact, taste his dried cum as I feast on her puffy cunt. She writhes and moans. I'm usually bored, going through the motions of sucking and licking while she rides my face, but today is different.

My fingers bruise her pale ass. I lick her clean of Cole, stirring the darkness further, enticing and playing with the mysterious sensations he lures to the surface. Color me intrigued. I want more.

My STOMACH OBJECTS to the scent of scrambled eggs and bacon, which greets us as we emerge from the bedroom.

Allie beams at us as she plates the food. "Just in time for breakfast."

Unlike my girlfriend, Allie is dolled up to the nines.

With a wince, I collapse onto the chair, pulling Mia with me, if for no other reason than to provoke a reaction from Cole. He looks extra tormented today, dressed in last night's clothes. I'm surprised he's still here, tolerating Allie's sunshine mood.

Shutting the fridge door more forcefully than needed, he stalks to the table and gives me a glare. Nipping Mia's earlobe, I pretend I don't notice his animosity while she giggles like a schoolgirl.

"Though judging by the sounds that came from your

bedroom not five minutes ago, you've already had breakfast," Allie teases.

I glance at Cole as I tug on Mia's earlobe with my teeth. "I'm ravenous."

"Gross," Allie laughs, plopping down onto her seat and picking up her fork. Then she looks up at Cole with a frown. "Aren't you going to sit?"

He pulls out a seat and lowers himself down. Tension radiates off him in waves, but Allie and Mia are oblivious as they discuss last night. Who fucked who, and who passed out where. All boring, mindless chatter I care little for.

I do, however, care a lot about the daggers Cole glares in my direction. I wonder what has gotten him so worked up this morning. It's amusing as hell.

"Eat your food," I say, smirking in his direction as I tip my chin.

Those long fingers curl around the fork, and he stabs the bacon on his plate, a muscle working in his jaw. The fork connects with the porcelain violently as he holds my gaze.

My dick jerks in response, and I lean in to sink my teeth into Mia's neck. If he only knew we have both filled her hole, though not at once. However, that's another stimulating thought. I wonder if she could take both our dicks if we had her trapped between us, using that pussy until she milks the cum from our balls.

Shifting Mia on my lap, I squeeze my now throbbing dick to ease the ache while I imagine what it would be like to feel his thick cock move against mine inside my girlfriend's cunt, stretching that tight hole to its limit. Maybe even breaking her.

He finally looks away to inhale his food, and I watch his jaw work, his hair falling over his stormy eyes. Allie leans into him, and my interest piques further when he flinches. It's sudden. Gone just as fast.

His eyes clash with mine again, and I raise a brow. What are you hiding? What are you not telling the world? Is that pretty girlfriend of yours not satisfying your needs?

After we've finished eating, I wash the dishes while Mia escapes to have a shower, and Allie locks herself in her bedroom to answer her mom's phone call.

Cole hovers, leaning against the fridge like a storm cloud, watching me the entire time with his head tipped back and his booted feet planted wide, hands buried deep in his pockets.

I wait him out, soaping up the plate in my hands. The water is too hot, but I welcome the burn. I like the heady sensation of his eyes drilling holes into the back of my head.

What's going on inside his skull? What is he doing here?

"Why did you drink so much last night?" he asks, his husky voice drifting over my nape like a caress.

I shrug, squeezing soapy bubbles from the sponge, imagining it's his cock in my hand and I'm milking the cum from his balls. "Jackson challenged me to drink."

"Jackson?" There's an edge in his voice.

He's on the move, prowling closer while I slide the sponge in a wide circle over the plate. I squeeze again, coaxing more creamy foam to the surface, and it slowly slides down my fingers. *"You like that, don't you, Cole? Give it to me."*

I smirk. "You sound tense."

His heat lines up with my back, warming more than just my skin beneath the T-shirt. I feel him everywhere, his breath wafting over my neck to tease the short strands curling around my ears. I focus on the sponge in my hand and trail my thumb through the creamy foam. *"Such a good boy for your little brother. Look at all that cum."*

"I told you to break up with your girlfriend. I'll show the video—"

I spin around and curl my fingers around the counter's edge. "You'll do no such thing, Cole."

His jaw twitches, and then he scoffs, shaking his head. He looks away, but I grab his stubbly chin with my wet hand,

67

momentarily transfixed by the foam seeping from between my fingers.

I pull him to me until his lips are a hair's breadth away from mine, and he comes willingly, crashing into me like a furious wave. "Don't play with me, Cole. You don't know me. Trust me, you have no idea what I'm capable of if you corner me. I will bite, and it will hurt." Turning his head, I brush my lips against his ear, feeling his dick twitch inside its denim confines. "Maybe that's what you want?" I shove him away, and he stumbles back.

His eyes flicker briefly with an emotion that's as unfamiliar and elusive to me as the organ that thuds harder behind my ribcage. He surges forward to trap me against the sink. "You want to test me, Blaise? Go ahead. Provoke me. See what happens."

When he looks at me this way, it's too much, so I focus on his clenching jaw and the slight hitch in his breath. Every part of me, from my throbbing heart to my straining dick, aches for him. We're a toxic mess of pushing and pulling until one of us breaks. I'm not used to emotions or the onslaught of them as his intoxicating scent and venom assault me, seeking weaknesses in my shield.

"You want me to provoke you?" I ask, wetting my lips.

"If you dare," he challenges.

Laughter climbs up my throat. Is he serious? Of course, I do. I flash him a wide smile, appreciating this side of him that takes no prisoners, that wants to see me fold.

"Oh, I dare." Straightening up, I grab his dick through his jeans and palm the rock-hard length, making his breath catch in his throat.

"Interesting," I muse, caressing the wet patch. "I saw how you flinched when Allie leaned into you earlier."

His choppy exhales crash against my lips, but he doesn't move away from my touch or tell me to stop.

Very fucking interesting, indeed.

I squeeze his dick, breathing a laugh as mine grows impossibly hard. "You're not flinching now. Interesting, don't you think? Remember the other day when the roles were reversed in the bathroom. You threatened to expose me to my parents and accused me of being aroused. Funny how the tables have turned."

His throat jumps and he lifts his chin defiantly as though it takes everything in him not to beat me to a pulp. He wants to lay into me with his fists. Make me bleed.

This is a battle of wills. Who will fold first? Who will back down?

"Let me guess. She doesn't satisfy you. Maybe you pretend to like pussy, when all you really want is to choke on a big, fat cock?"

This time, he slaps my hand away and steps back. I revel in the victory, watching him from beneath wavy strands of my dark hair. Ragged exhales split the silence as he fists his hands rhythmically, trying so damn hard to regain his composure. There's a softness beneath the anger, a fragility I find more enticing than his next trembling breath or the lick of his lips.

If I had my way, I'd peel him open, layer by layer, until I get my hands on what's hiding at the core of him. What's behind that vulnerable look he throws at me.

Allie stumbles out of the bedroom, disturbing this tense moment of his walls crumbling to dust. "Phew, she never stops talking." Her voice reminds me of nails on a chalkboard, and the urge to throttle her with my bare hands tingles at my fingertips.

Cole turns around and slams his lips to hers in a display meant entirely for me. I'm intrigued nonetheless as I watch the muscles shift in his stiff back. His fingers drift to her hip, teasing a soft moan from her lips, trailing over her skin where her tank top meets her shorts.

Amused, I push off the sink and saunter past them. He won't fuck her. No matter how much he tries to convince me otherwise.

Before I turn the corner, I peer over my shoulder. Cole is

already watching me from beneath his lashes while cradling his girlfriend's face in his big hands and feasting on her mouth.

I lean against the doorframe and cross my arms, the muscles bulging.

Show me what you've got, Cole.

He kisses her like she's the air he breathes, and I must admit that he does a convincing job, but he can't fool me. We're both chameleons in our unique ways, hiding behind impenetrable walls and cracked masks.

Chuckling, I step away, exiting the room.

CHAPTER 8
COLE

Coach is giving me a fucking headache, probably worse than Blaise did yesterday. The audacity of that motherfucker to even think about laying a damn finger on me. Who the fuck does he think he is?

He openly grabbed me, as if he did it every day, and the more I think of it, remembering the way he swallowed my cock with very little fight, he might enjoy it.

Fuck.

I've never indicated to him that I wanted his hands anywhere near me. Yeah, a few times I've teased him, called him out on his bullshit and demanded he break up with Mia, but I've never given him any ideas that I'd want to, and I quote, "choke on a big, fat cock."

Fucking asshole.

A shoulder hits into me, and I nearly deck it.

"Pay attention, Carter."

I grit my teeth and glare at Samson, not giving a fuck that he's my friend. I'm in no mood for bullshit today. And to make this glorious fucking afternoon better, Blaise stands at the side, impatiently bouncing on his heels while he waits for the second day of tryouts to begin.

For *my* team.

My stepdad is kind of best friends with the coach, so it's inevitable he's going to get onto the team. He probably doesn't even know how to play with college guys. The privileges of being a good boy, I guess.

"You think he'll replace Samson?" Jackson asks beside me, tightening the clips of his helmet. "From what I heard of the tryouts yesterday, he's a good linebacker."

"Coach won't replace Samson, he's too good."

"Hopefully Keith. He's been slacking."

I snort. "Says the one who comes to practice late and still drunk."

He shrugs and runs off to his position, and I try not to look at Blaise while I finish my game, my throat sore from yelling every two seconds.

Sweating, I wipe my face with my shirt, my eyes clashing with Blaise, whose gaze lowers to my abs. He averts his stare as soon as he sees he's been caught, and follows the coach's assistant to start his tryouts.

I keep looking over at him, though. He moves with fluidity, and seems to know what he's doing, which irritates me. Twice, he gets tackled, and I fight the urge to get involved when another student gets in his face.

Not my fucking problem.

"Fuck, Carter!"

I stare down at Samson, his eyes wide. Did I tackle him?

"I think you broke my ribs."

"Stop being dramatic," I retort, helping him up. "I wasn't paying attention."

"Because the walking thumb is giving Blaise shit? I thought you hated him."

"I do," I reply, shaking myself off as we fall back into position. "His dad thinks he's a kid still and everything bad that happens to him is my fault."

"That explains the glare you're sending the thumb's way."

Sure. Let's say that's why. I just don't like the way he's scowling at Blaise as if he wants to devour him then snap his bones. He's a big fucker; I'd get five minutes of fight time before I was a goner, but if I need to, I'll fight him.

Blaise is soaked in sweat half an hour in, and he keeps brushing his hand through his unruly dark hair, the white shorts covered in dirt from tackles, and his muscles are bulging in his legs.

He has huge thighs to match the powerful back.

Shit. I think if we had a one-on-one fight, the fucker might be able to scrub the floor with me.

Our eyes clash again, and neither of us looks away, both trying to catch our breaths. Someone grabs my shoulder, a voice in my ear, but it doesn't matter. The plan is already concocting in my head.

He threatened me.

No one threatens Cole Carter without getting fucked up.

Once I'm done, I head to the showers, checking my phone and seeing a text from Allie, asking me to come over tonight.

I decline. I'm not in the mood for her company. As soon as Blaise vanished from the kitchen the other morning, she tried to fucking mount me, but I shrugged her off and pretended I was late for class.

I wasn't.

Blaise and the others from the tryouts are sent to the other locker room. Thank fuck. I think him getting naked in front of everyone would have pushed me to my limit. They would all comment on his size, then compare him to me, and then I'd need to kill them all.

Everyone's washed and getting dressed.

By the time I finish sorting my bag, I'm alone in the locker room, and when the door opens, I glance up to see...

"Mia?"

She hugs herself, sniffs, her eyes red like she's been crying. The door closes behind her, and she edges in. "We really need to talk."

I frown. "Blaise is in the other locker room."

"I know. I'm supposed to meet him, but I had to see you first."

Slinging my bag over my shoulder, I tilt my head. "What's wrong?"

"It was a mistake. Please, please don't try to make him break up with me."

My brows hike up to my hairline. "What are you talking about?"

"I was drunk, but I remember some of what happened the other night. Blaise can't know, but it won't ever happen again. I love him."

"I haven't the slightest clue what you're insinuating." How fucked up was she the other night? I was with Allie.

Mia obviously thinks Blaise was me.

"You need to lay off the booze, Mia."

She worries her lip and averts her eyes. "I heard you telling Blaise to break up with me the other morning."

It takes me a long second to figure out what she means, and I let out a snort. "I was fucking with him, but you can do better."

"I don't have feelings for you, Cole. I love Blaise."

Confusion hits me again. "You're Allie's best friend. Why would you have feelings for me?"

"Good." She nods. "If we're going to pretend it didn't happen. Okay. But please don't tell him to break up with me. It was a mistake and it'll never happen again."

The door opens, and she flinches as if she was right in front of me and tries to get distance as Blaise walks in, fresh from his shower, his face red. "Did you—" He stops when he sees his girl-friend. "Ah, there you are. Ready?"

He doesn't even ask her why she's been crying, which is fucking evident. She nods, glances at me briefly, then walks out. Blaise follows her, pausing in the doorway. "You can barely control your own girlfriend. Stay the fuck away from mine."

The door slams, and my right eye twitches, both confused as fuck and filling with fury. I drop my bag and fish my phone from my pocket, finding my friend's contact. He answers on the third ring.

"Do you still have those masks and hoodies?"

"Yeah, man," Samson replies. "You need them?"

I smirk to myself, already imagining the scene. "Yeah."

I STARE AT MY PHONE, my knee bouncing, needing to get rid of this anger, but punching a bag or hitting the gym did nothing to lessen my rage.

Mom texted me earlier, asking me to leave Blaise and his girlfriend alone, and that, with the combination of his words earlier and the way he spoke to me the other morning, I'm about to snap.

Maybe I already snapped?

I type the message out four times, deleting it each time, lying back on my bed and listening to how loud Blaise's TV is. Mia is in there. I can hear her giggling, and I want to break through his door, tell her to fuck off, and punch Blaise so damn hard, he passes out.

The white mask and black hoodie I got from Samson sit on my bedside cabinet. I had a plan. But now I think I might kill him instead.

Fuck it.

I type out the message I've been desperate to send.

> Me: Wanna know who I am? Meet me at the college's swimming pool at 7 tonight or everyone will see our text messages. I'm sure your girlfriend would be thrilled to know how much you love sucking dick.

Sighing, I toss my phone down and get dressed. He won't refuse. He'll shit himself and demand answers. He'll probably try to find out who I am, but I won't let him figure it out.

My phone buzzes, a ding following right after, and my heart ricochets when I see it's a response from Blaise.

Of course it's from him. He's the only number I have in this piece of shit burner.

Blaise: Fine.

I snort at his blunt reply, a ball of excitement growing within me as I finish getting ready, hearing him and Mia arguing as they bypass my bedroom door. He's trying to get her out so he can play a game of tag with his unidentified stranger, readying to choke on his cock again.

I harden at the thought and stare at my bulge, frowning. Why do I keep getting rock solid at the thought of my stepbrother? I want to fuck with him, not fuck him.

Regardless, I pulse at the memory of his throat tightening around my engorged head and the sounds he made as he gagged, and I have to adjust myself into my waistband.

I hear Blaise walking back upstairs and down the corridor, slamming his room door loudly. I smirk, knowing he's angry, but he'll love the way I make him feel when I make him run for his fucking life.

When it hits six, I pack my bag and tell Mom I'm heading to Samson's. She kisses my cheek, and I ignore my stepdad as I leave.

The drive there is short. I go over the speed limit, adrenaline coursing through my veins and making my heart race.

I pull on my hoodie and slip the mask over my face, parking my car between two buses so he doesn't recognize it.

The school is closed, and I don't bother turning on the lights while I find my way to the room filled with all the sporting equipment. Using the light on my phone, I hunt for a weapon, settling on a hockey stick.

My phone buzzes.

Blaise: I'm here. Did you pussy out?

Rolling my eyes, I leave my bag in the room and grip the hockey stick tightly, cracking my neck side-to-side. I make my way to the offices, scouring the screens and communication devices until I find the Bluetooth settings that's connected to all the speakers in the school.

My teeth capture my bottom lip, and I grin as I pull up my playlist, click on a rock song, and wait for it to filter through the entire building. I turn the volume all the way up, grab the hockey stick, and make my way to the pool.

When I get there, he's got his back to the door, head lowered, staring at his phone in his hand. Since the blaring music muffles the sound of me approaching, he doesn't get a chance to look up before I swing the hockey stick, smacking into the side of his head and knocking him into the water.

He splashes, sputtering out breaths as he breaches the surface, glaring at me, my face hidden beneath the mask.

There's a trickle of blood-stained water down the side of his face, and fuck, my balls ache to empty at the sight.

He climbs out, tensing his jaw, holding the side of his head.

"Run," I say, loud enough for him to hear over the music, but muffled enough he doesn't realize I'm Cole Carter.

My chest tightens some more as he steps back, then again, and again. He could easily fight me. He could rip the mask off and see who I am, but instead, Blaise, soaked to the bone with blood down his face, turns on his heels and runs.

I wait ten seconds before I give chase.

Out in the corridor, within the darkness, I can see his shadow in the distance. I forget sometimes he can run like fuck, but unlucky for him, I'm faster.

I catch up to him just as he pushes open a door to a closet in an attempt to hide, throwing the hockey stick at his feet, causing him to hit the ground.

I'm getting flashbacks from when I chased him in the woods.

I lower to my knees beside him, snatching his nape to restrain him enough he can't get up. I'm throbbing in my pants, my precum already leaking as I see the blood soaking his hair.

"Who the fuck are you?" The heavy metal music blasting through the school drowns out his words, but I can just make them out.

I lean down to lower my body on top of him, my urge winning against my confused hard-on as I press my cock against his ass, letting go of his nape and grabbing his hair.

Fuck.

Fuck me, why does this feel so right?

I push my cock against him harder, ignoring the way he's kicking his legs and telling me to get the fuck off him. He's strong, and I struggle a little to stay in position as I reach between him and the floor, grinning when my hand grabs his raging hard cock.

Blaise Rowle gets off on the chase.

Squeezing his cock, I thrust against him, fighting a moan. He's still trying to get free from me, even though his movements push him against my cock and his cock into my hand.

"Such a good fucking boy," I whisper in his ear, keeping my voice low and undetected.

His elbow flies back and connects with my mask, nearly knocking it off me. I quickly stand to fix it, feeling some of the plastic snapped around my eye and cheek.

Blaise hurries to his feet, his cock tenting his pants as his chest rises and falls, before he turns and takes off running again.

CHAPTER 9
BLAISE

"*Such a good fucking boy.*"

Fuck me dead. Those whispered words and the anger they evoked when he used them as a weapon to taunt me drove me mad, but not only that—desire licked over my heated skin beneath my soaked clothes.

Trapped in my pants, my cock pulses as I sprint down the hallway like my life depends on it, pushing myself more than I ever have on the football field.

My boots thunder on the floor, and my legs pump harder and faster. Beneath the consuming fear and anticipation burns a fire that sets me alight. I'm alive.

I go flying around the corner, colliding with the wall opposite, my shoulder taking the brunt of the impact. The pain barely registers. My head already throbs from the blow that sent me flying into the swimming pool. I didn't see it coming, and that's what's so fucking thrilling. I felt his hard dick grind against my ass back there, his fingers twitching in my hair, the barely restrained control behind every breath.

Expecting him close on my heel, I throw a quick glance behind me, and my heart rate spikes to dangerous levels when I find the hallway empty. I skid to a halt, spinning around. Where the fuck is he? I swear he was behind me seconds ago. Music blares, throbbing in my veins. I slowly back up against the wall, scanning the dark hallway while trying to catch my breath.

My attacker is aroused by the chase, and the small flicker of doubt of not knowing what his true intentions are sets me on fire. What does he want with me? How far will he take this? Who the fuck is he?

I swipe my damp sleeve across my eyes to wipe the blood away as my heart thrashes. I might need stitches.

"Jesus," I whisper, closing my eyes and wincing when another sharp stab of pain sears my skull. He didn't hold back when he knocked me down.

No, focus, dammit.

Shaking my head, blood pouring in a steady stream from a cut on my eyebrow, I push off the wall and continue down the hallway, glancing behind me every few seconds.

He's nowhere in sight, and I soon find out why when I turn the next corner.

Moonlight streaks through the window beside him, bathing his imposing form in an ethereal glow as he watches me from behind his mask.

I'm unsteady on my feet, dizzy from the blow, and he cocks his head, intrigued.

I sway, trying to focus, but it's difficult when I see two of him.

Tightening his grip on the hockey stick in his hand, he steps toward me, and I inch back, cursing my fucking dick for twitching at the sight of the weapon in his hand—the damage it can do if he catches me.

Focus, Blaise.

I need to remove his mask somehow. Expose his identity so that I can destroy him for thinking he could threaten me without consequences.

His blurring shape morphs again, splitting from two into three before merging back into one. I chuckle as I stumble back, blood stinging my eyes. I'm so fucking screwed. But hey, that's what makes it so damn exciting, right? Very few things in life thrill me, and this masked man might be as unhinged as I am.

I extend my arm, pointing at him, and flash a feral smile.

"Catch me if you can, fucker." Spinning around, I run in the opposite direction, flying down the next corridor, ignoring the stabbing pain in my skull and the burning muscles in my thighs.

The faster I run, the more excited I get, and the more I wish—no, *hope*—that he'll beat me bloodied with the stick before fucking me hard and making me feel something real for once.

Wait?

Fuck me?

Yeah, I've lost it.

The thought has more laughter spilling from my lips. I must have a concussion. Why else would I be this enthralled by a masked psychopath with an erection chasing me like a blood-thirsty lunatic? This is the stuff of horror movies, and I'm here for it.

I throw a glance behind me, seeing him getting closer.

Shit…

Darting inside the nearest lecture hall, I slam the door shut, ramming my shoulder against it, but I'm not fast enough, and the wood crashes against his hockey stick.

Jesus fuck… I grunt, shoving harder against the stick, then spin around, my eyes darting across the empty hall. The only other exit is across the room.

When the door pushes against my back, I make a rash decision to dash for the rows of raised seats.

I fly up the steps, throwing myself into one of the rows, jumping over the back of seats, ascending higher and higher. I'm weak, and my attacker laughs, knocking the hockey stick against the furniture.

"Where are you going?" he shouts as I scale a bench, and the sound of his voice sends me crashing to the dirty floor between two rows.

I wince in pain, clutching my elbow. Fuck me, that hurt! My chest shakes with silent laughter. How the hell did I find myself trapped in a lecture hall by a fucking madman whose cock I've sucked?

Grabbing hold of the nearest seat, I pull myself up, grimacing as pain jabs at my skull. I'll feel fantastic tomorrow.

I breathe through gritted teeth, my eyes tracking his every move while I try to gain control of my body. There are two more rows behind me. If I'm quick, I might reach the doors at the top.

When he's at the end of my row, I swallow down a spike of exhilaration, watching him approach. Dark eyes peer at me through his mask. He takes his sweet time, one booted step in front of the other, his black jeans straining against his muscular legs.

Kneeling on the floor with my injured elbow clasped tightly against my heaving chest, I bare my bloodied teeth while trying my damn hardest not to stare at his thick bulge. But fuck me; I can see the outline of his hard dick. I'm an injured animal, playing dead at the feet of his attacker. Something about that turns me the hell on.

Not only that... Something about my attacker reminds me of Cole. I can't put my finger on what it is, but it's there in the tense sway of his broad shoulders and that searing gaze.

My heart thuds harder in response, and I allow myself to indulge in the fantasy of my tormented stepbrother being my late-night stalker. How far would I let him descend into the dark night with me before steering him back into the light where he belongs? Or would I take him hostage, dragging him farther into the shadows? He's too good for a soul like me and too fucking pure, but that's what makes him so irresistible. I want a taste.

As the hockey stick slides beneath my chin and tilts it up, I stare into the gleaming eyes behind the mask, and for one moment, it's Cole who stares back at me—conflicted, aroused, fucked up.

A smile plays at the corner of my lips, my heart finding a steady rhythm as I dig my fingers into my palms. The thing about injured animals who play dead is that they don't stay down for long. It's a ruse—a game of 'pretend' to buy time.

I launch myself at his ankles, taking him by surprise and

sending him crashing to the floor. He throws his arms out, but it's too late—his breath gets knocked from his lungs.

Hurling myself on top of him, I try to grab his mask, fighting with his flailing arms and wriggling body. We roll in the small row like tumbleweeds, knocking against the seats, grunting and cursing, flinging punches until we're both sweaty and out of breath.

When I start to succumb to my injuries, the weaker of us, I jump up and try to launch myself over the back of the row, but my attacker grabs hold of my ankle and hauls me down.

Fuck, fuck, fuck.

I'm on my back, and he's hovering over me with the hockey stick pressed against my esophagus. This is it. I can't fight anymore. I'm too weak and dizzy, coughing and spluttering beneath the unyielding pressure on my throat. I attempt to shove the stick away, grunting from the effort. My attempts are pathetic. Kicking my legs out on the floor, my hips buck.

"I can feel how hard you are," he taunts, his voice getting lost in the music, but I hear the hunger behind those cruel words. He rolls his hips, grinding his thick dick against mine, and I whimper, unsure if I want to fight him as he thrusts into me again.

"Say it," he urges, obliterating my defenses with his next crash wave against my throbbing length.

Our cocks rub together through our pants. I part my legs, inviting him closer, and we stare into each other's eyes.

Who are you?

My trembling breath twirls past my parted lips, and I clutch his hoodie at his sides, wringing and creasing the fabric.

He rocks harder against me, then tosses the stick aside and wraps his hand around my throat. "Say it."

"I'm a good boy."

Shifting, he keeps me pinned to the floor while ripping my pants open and fisting my weeping dick. This is it. I could tear off his mask and find out who he is once and for all, but my eyes roll back when his calloused hand slides over my length, from root to tip and back down. I crane my neck, raking my teeth over my bloodied lip, losing myself in a dangerous fantasy.

"Such a good fucking boy, huh?" His words are cruel and cold, yet heated, dripping with something...all too familiar.

Cole...

Images of him laughing on the football field with his helmet balanced under his tanned arm, covered in sweat as Samson ruffles his already mussed-up hair, flash through my mind—the feel of his warm chest against my arm when he brushes past me in the kitchen doorway, his eyes burning into mine for a split second before he's gone again.

I bite my lip hard enough to hurt, needing the pain to settle my throbbing heart, thrusting into my tormentor's next stroke.

A ragged breath cuts me open as it expands my aching chest. This is more than bodily pleasure. This is rapture...surrender.

I'm coming apart to thoughts of my stepbrother while a stranger jerks my dick.

"Look at me," he orders, releasing my throat to clasp my chin, and our eyes clash, sending sparks to my pulsing dick. "I need those eyes on me when you come all over my hand."

Who are you?

He digs his ruthless fingers into the stubble on my chin, his eyes burning into me. My hips meet his touch, rocking and thrusting. I'm trembling.

As he increases his pace, I struggle to keep my eyes open. Fuck, I'm so close. His grip tightens when my lashes threaten to flutter closed, and I break out into a cold sweat, my balls drawing up.

Moaning, I fist his hair, needing to feel the soft strands between my fingers, but he bats me off before trapping my wrists above my head in one of his hands.

His eyes fly over my face as I shudder beneath his weight. Where do I know those eyes from? I imagine it's Cole's eyes staring down at me with his hand on my cock, stroking and smearing the precum over my veiny length.

My damp clothes stick to my skin, cool against my heated flesh. I'm burning up, caught in those eyes.

I'm helpless.

Defenseless.

"Good boy," he praises, grinding against my thigh.

We move like frothy waves on an ocean, rocking on the grimy floor while gazing at each other. I can't hold back the climax, not when I scan the crack in his mask, seeing the tanned skin beneath. What if I remove it and find Cole staring back at me with his ruffled dark hair and tormented eyes?

Fuck...

I come all over his hand, quivering, as moans rip from my throat. I bite down hard on my lip to suppress them, but I don't look away from his eyes. No, I lose myself in him completely as pleasure stiffens every muscle in my tender, bruised body.

I'm ruined.

He slows his slick hand on my dick and stares at me for a fragile, throbbing minute. We don't speak.

A line has been drawn in the sand on this battlefield.

Then he's gone, fleeing the room before I recover from his onslaught.

Wise choice.

"Fuck it all to hell," I curse, dragging my hand down my face.

It comes away slick with blood, a crimson rivulet trailing from my palm down my wrist before soaking my sleeve.

My teeth grind together, and I fist my trembling hand, lowering it by my side.

I feel dirty, but not because I let some stranger with a hockey stick ravage me like an animal. No, I loved the chase and adrenaline, but it wasn't Cole. It wasn't my infuriating stepbrother— the one guy who could cut through this numbness with a single look. What the hell is wrong with me? Why am I pining after him? And why do I feel this foreign sense of loyalty?

CHAPTER 10.
COLE

The ringing of my phone wakes me from my deep sleep, and I wince when I try to move, my body battered and bruised from last night's antics.

Everything is tight and tense, and so is my rigid cock standing to attention beneath my duvet, straining in my pants.

I shove my hand south and fix it to a comfortable position, groaning from the tingling sensation. I didn't get off last night. My full attention was on Blaise and making sure I owned full dominance.

I think, deep down, I didn't want to dominate him – wearing the mask and hiding who I was just made it that bit easier to breathe.

What exactly was it I wanted? To beat Blaise? To touch him?

No.

I'm just confused with the way I'm feeling. Allie claims to love me, yet spreads her legs for anyone and everyone, and then Blaise is just...everywhere.

Another buzz from my bedside, and I sigh and rub my hand down my face. I need to go back to sleep, I'm exhausted.

With one eye open, I reach for my phone, rejecting the call from Allie. It's three in the morning, and going by the bazillion messages apologizing, she's cheated on me again. I should call her back and demand to know who she's fucked – and I will, just so I can save myself any embarrassment and go beat up the asshole, but she can panic for a little while longer.

She calls again and again and again. Exasperated, I give in and answer the phone. "What?"

"Baby," she cries, and I want so badly to hang up. "I didn't mean it. I wasn't planning on doing anything, I just needed to talk to him about my course work!"

"You fucked your professor again." Not a question, and by the way she starts sobbing, I'm correct. "Why exactly are you with me if you keep fucking around?"

Sniffing, she coughs, and then I hear a door opening and closing. Her voice lowers. "We haven't had sex in months, Cole." Her throat cracks. "You don't come near me, and if you do, you pull away. We barely talk. We barely message each other. When we do, you're dry or emotionless or you just seem bored with me."

"So instead of breaking up with me, you cheat?"

"I think you're cheating on me too."

I snort out a laugh. "That's the most ridiculous thing you've ever said." Technically, I have cheated. I fucked Blaise's throat and stroked him to an orgasm, but that doesn't count. "I've never given you any reason to think I've cheated."

She sniffles, and I pinch the bridge of my nose.

"We had sex at Samson's party," I say, sitting up, leaning my back to the headboard.

When she stays silent, I shake my head. "We should probably just call it quits, Allie. You obviously want the single life, and I'm not going to embarrass myself any further."

"No!" she shrieks. "Please. Please, don't end this. I'll do better."

I sense movement in my dark room, and I glance to the side to see the shadow of someone sitting on the floor with their back to the wall.

She's still crying and begging me, but I hang up on her.

Blaise.

Leaning over, I turn on my lamp, lighting the room with a soft glow. My eyes land on all the bruises littering his face, the gash on the side of his head covered in dried blood, the swollen eye from my fists.

"Blaise?"

He doesn't look at me when I say his name. His hair is a mess, as if he's been running his hands through it. And he's in the same clothes. They're still damp, surely?

I gulp and sit up more. The silence is deafening, and I'm getting a little nervous at the tension here. There's a tightrope between us, and I don't know if it's wrapping around my throat or pulling me toward Blaise.

"What happened to you?" I ask, knowing fine well it was my fists that did all that damage. "You look like shit."

He doesn't give me any response, or even acknowledge that I'm asking him anything. He's vacant, unblinkingly staring at the wall opposite him.

The urge to go to him annoys me. Why the fuck would I do that?

I grab my ringing phone, silence Allie and, for fuck's sake, a message from Mia pops up asking if Blaise is home.

Why is everyone awake at this fucking time in the morning?

I frown at my screen, then look at him again. "Mia is looking for you."

Nothing. He's not even asking why his girlfriend has my number. I don't have hers saved, but from the millions of times Blaise has called me from it to either give me shit, ask me to pick him up, or to get ahold of one of our parents, I recognize the number.

Why is he not speaking? Did I fuck him up that good?

"Rough night?" I ask him, and I feel like slapping myself.

Of course it was a rough night. I beat the shit out of him, then forced myself on him. Rough night is an understatement. Saying that, my body hurts too. If he really wanted to, he could have stopped me. There was an opening he could've whipped off my mask, but he chose pleasure from an unknown.

And I was hard from it – the thrill of chasing him, watching him, hitting and touching him. I was so hard that I was losing my vision. I nearly took it too far, wanting more, to go further, to fuck him up really good and to feel from it, but the look in his eyes when I wrapped my hand around his cock? It floored me.

What the fuck is wrong with me?

Chewing my lip, I glance around my room to make sure I definitely packed away the mask and black hoodie – they're in my bag in the closet.

I don't have any bruises or cuts to my face to show that it was me, but what if he recognized my voice? My left eye was visible through the crack. Did he realize?

Maybe it was my cologne. Fuck. Does Blaise know I'm the unidentified masked man who's been fucking with him? Does he know his stepbrother forced him to suck his dick, then stroked his cock until he came?

I swallow and sit on the edge of the bed, my knees bouncing, stopping when I lean my elbows on them. "Are you going to stay silent and stare at nothing, or are you going to tell me why you're in my room?"

He's only been in here twice since me and Mom moved in years ago. Once when he was drunk, and I had to lead him to his own room and hide the fact he was fucked up. The second time, he stormed in after an argument and tried to choke me out. We fought for what felt like hours before his dad broke us apart and blamed it all on me. I was the bully, and he was the victim.

Every. Fucking. Time.

"Did you take something?" I ask, nerves catching in my throat.

"Just..." He sighs, closing his eyes. "Let me sit here."

Why does the way he says those words stab me in the chest?

For the next ten minutes, we stay silent, my phone buzzing repeatedly from Allie – but this is more important. I hate Blaise. I really fucking hate him, but there's something within me that also wants to protect him. Plus, I think he knows and he's trying to process it. Maybe he's readying himself to walk down for breakfast in a few hours and tell our parents I basically forced sexual acts on him. He knows I'll get disowned and my schooling will be done. I'll lose my spot on the team, and if I get kicked out, there's a high chance my dad will try to swoop in to save the day.

Not that he will. We ran when Mom finally had enough, and he never tried finding me.

I was the son nobody wanted.

MOM HAS SET a spread for breakfast like she does every weekend morning. If she's not at work on the ward at our local hospital, she's in the kitchen with her cookbooks and enjoying every second of it.

My stepdad stares at me from across the table. "Where were you last night?"

I raise a brow. "Samson's, why?"

"We heard the front gates opening in the middle of the night."

Dropping my gaze to my plate, I shrug. "Wasn't me."

The table shakes as his hand slams down on the surface. "Don't lie, boy."

"Gavin," Mom scolds. "He said it wasn't him."

"Well, it wasn't my son."

He likes to point out on the regular that Blaise is his son, that I am not anything of biology to him, and that he has a strong bad taste toward me. He thinks I'm my dad. I look like him, and apparently, I'm going to grow up to act like him too.

If I ever become a family man, the last thing in the entire world I'd do is abuse them. I wouldn't force my son to drink gasoline and make him puke it back up, and I wouldn't make my wife terrified of me.

Never.

I fill my mouth with food and ignore him, despite wanting to slam his face into his bowl of oatmeal.

Blaise walks in, and I freeze my chewing as my eyes follow him. In the daylight, he looks worse. The bruising is more noticeable than earlier. He hasn't even tried to cover them up or wear a hoodie or sweater to make sure our parents don't see.

Gavin stands. "Christ, Blaise. What happened?"

He ignores him and takes his seat opposite me, the purple ring around his eye nearly swelling the lid shut. Filling his plate with food, he pours himself a cup of orange juice.

"Did someone hurt you?"

He nods once.

I don't know why, but I get pissed off, the confused, possessive side of me forgetting that I was the one who hurt him.

My stepdad sits down and grips his cutlery, scowling at me.

"What's the point in pretending to be a big brother if you can't protect him?"

I glare at him and my mom. "So I'm to blame when Blaise is a dick and gets beat up?"

"Yes," Gavin replies. "I'm going to have a word with your school. You get far too much special treatment because of me, and you repay me by allowing this to happen to my son?" He tsks, shaking his head. "You should have stayed with your father."

I push back in my seat and knock his plate from the table, smashing the ceramic on the wall. "Say that again, asshole."

"That's enough!" Mom yells. "Blaise, Cole, go to your rooms. Now."

Blaise gets up and leaves with no words, but I stay in my chair.

"I'm twenty, not thirteen. Stop talking to me like I'm a child." I turn back to Gavin. "If you ever bring up my father again, I'll make you fucking regret it."

"You live under our roof, boy, so you'll start respecting us, or you'll be out with no money and no college funding."

"Gavin," Mom snaps.

He raises his hand to stop her from saying anything else. "I own your entire future. If I want my son to replace you instead of Jackson on your football team, I will. If I want you on the streets, you will be. If I want you to jump, you will ask me how high."

"Blaise can stick up for himself," I grit out. "You need to get your head out of your ass and see he isn't the little fucking angel you paint him as. He got beat up because he's a prick, just like his father."

"Cole." Mom pulls my sleeve. "Stop."

Begrudgingly, I listen and leave, wishing I could punch this motherfucker. But he's right. My entire future is in his hands.

I hate him just as much as I hate his son.

THE BACK of my skull hits the tiles, my eyes closing as the hot water soaks my hair and skin. Each long stroke has my balls pulling tighter to my body, my lungs forcing out air as I breathe.

I've been hanging on the edge since last night. I wanted to find pleasure instantly. I couldn't fuck my own hand while in bed, with Blaise sulking in the corner of my room, and I couldn't do it when he got up and left before we went down for breakfast, and now, hours later, my swollen crown leaks with precum as I slide my hand up and down my rock-hard shaft.

I let out a groan, my hand slamming into the glass door, and when my palm slips, wiping away some of the condensation from the steam, my eyes collide with green ones.

I freeze all over, staring at Blaise, my dick pulsing in my palm. From what I can see through the steamed glass, he's leaning against the sink, his arms folded. He's wearing a sweater now, probably already packed for our ski trip with our parents and Mia.

"Don't stop," he says, his voice strained.

For a long moment, our eyes stay glued, my heart accelerating to a dangerous pace, feeling like it's about to bound out of my fucking chest.

His gaze dips to my hand around my cock. He'll be able to see it faintly through the glass. "Keep going."

My hand stays around my length. "You just have to ruin everything, don't you?"

He nods. "I said...*keep going.*"

My grip tightens, and I grit my teeth to hide the way it's making me fucking feral – him looking at me like I'm next for breakfast, his face, his deep voice, the corded muscles I can see through his clothes. His hands have veins, and I picture the touch being his hand wrapped around me as I absently thrust into my own palm.

From outside the bathroom, my bedroom door opens. "Cole?" Allie calls out, and I pause. What the fuck is she doing here?

Blaise reaches over and locks the door. "Keep going," he demands again quietly, crossing his arms and leaning against the sink once more.

His chest rises and falls with heavy breaths, matching my own, and I clench my jaw, needing so badly to move my hand, my fingers flexing around the throbbing girth.

Blaise's body is so relaxed, watching, waiting, and I'm as tense and rigid everywhere.

"Cole?" Allie calls my name again, and the bathroom door handle jiggles. Neither of us look in that direction. I'm trapped under his spell, eyes locked through each slow, tight stroke. I hate myself for doing it, for listening, but for some reason or another, the pleasure wrapping around my spine intensifies with him watching me.

"Can you let me in? Please, talk to me, baby. You can't break

up with me!" Her little fist smashes into the wood, a sob following. "Please, Cole. Your mom asked me to go on this trip since
you didn't ask me. We'll make it work. I'll be a good girl."

She lowers her voice. "I'm always a good girl for you,
aren't I?"

Blaise tilts his head to the side, both of us ignoring her. "Is
she always a good girl for you, big brother?"

"No," I breathe, biting my lip. "I'm not your fucking
brother."

He chuckles, and fuck, my balls nearly explode. "What do
you think she'd say if she knew you were in here, touching yourself, fucking loving it too, as I watched?"

Depraved. I'm depraved and sick and I love it.

"I knew she didn't satisfy you," he says, smirking as he
comes closer to the glass. "You want a cock. And not just any
cock. I think you want mine."

He slides open the glass door, the bathroom far too steamed
up for him to see the faint bruises from last night. His proximity
has my body feeling alive and I hate myself for it.

My eyes roll as the back of my head hits the tiles again, the
muscles in my thighs tightening while I fuck my hand. I'm
unable to stop the deep moan from rumbling in my chest.

Listening to Blaise's voice, I feel him press his hand to my
pec, siding it up to grab my throat, strangling me, robbing me of
air, but not enough to cut off my words.

"Don't...fucking touch me," I say through gritted teeth,
slowing my strokes despite wanting him to drop to his knees
and suck my cock again, to feel what it's like to slide into him.

Blaise's eyes brighten, soaking himself under the shower. His
fingers wrap around my wrist, forcing me to keep going.

With a groan, I release so damn hard I see stars under my
eyelids. I come all over his wrist as he makes me keep jerking
myself through my orgasm while he sucks his bottom lip into his
mouth. "Hmm," he hums. "I knew it. You need to get out of the
closet, *big brother*."

The grip on my wrist and the hold on my throat vanish as he slaps my cheek. I stand there, unmoving, eyes closed, listening as Blaise leaves through the door to his bedroom, before my back slides down the wall.

What the fuck just happened?

I blink away the dizziness, looking down at the cum painted on the tiles just as Allie knocks on the door again.

CHAPTER 11,
BLAISE

"**K**iss me, Cole," Allie's voice drifts through the door, and I fist my hands, ear pressed to the wood. "I've missed you. Did you miss me?"

I can't hear Cole's response, my brows knitting together as I strain to listen. Are they kissing? Does he want her?

I grind my teeth, cursing myself for hovering outside my brother's bedroom door like a peeping Tom, but my skin crawls at the thought of his girlfriend anywhere near him after the way he looked at me from beneath his heavy lids in the shower. I can't stop thinking about his soaked hair plastered to his forehead or how the water beaded on his lips, a droplet clinging to the end of his nose while he stroked his hard dick. *Fuck me...* I'm ruined after seeing him wet and horny, surrounded by steam. The way he stared at me as he pleasured himself, trying to reach a high that seemed far away until I curled my fingers around his wrist.

He didn't stop me.

I should have stayed away, but I didn't.

Despite my better judgment, I reach for the door handle, hesitating. What am I doing? Why am I here?

I let my hand fall away, then form a fist. Allie giggles on the other side of the door, and something ugly stirs from deep within. My knuckles turn white as I inhale a steadying breath, feeling my chest expand.

Get yourself together, Blaise.

I slowly uncurl my fingers on an exhale, my heart aching and throbbing.

Fuck this…

Turning on my heel, I drag a trembling hand through my hair. I'm a fucking mess, and my emotions are all over the place after I let a stranger touch me last night. What started as a fun game, a thrill to add a little color to my boring life, soon left me empty and restless.

I'm no closer to figuring out who hides behind that damn mask. Why's that? Because I got too caught up in the moment.

Fucking weak.

I enter the kitchen and open the fridge, allowing the cool air to clear my head.

Cole didn't pull away or tell me to fuck off. No, he came almost as soon as I touched him, his wet lips parting with a shuddering breath as cum rained over my wrist.

"Fuck…" I slam the fridge door shut but pause when the landline rings, the shrill tone tensing my shoulders. Who the hell could that be now? Dragging my hand down my face, I blow out a long breath, exhausted and fed up with my internal turmoil.

It rings again, so I cross the room and pick up the phone without checking the caller ID.

Leaning back against the counter, I balance it between my shoulder and ear as I fish my mobile out of my pocket.

"Hello." I swipe the screen, noting a new message from Tiago.

"Cole? Is that you?" a slurred voice rasps.

I stiffen, looking up as the man in question and his annoying girlfriend enter the room. They stop in the doorway as though they didn't expect to see me there.

For once, I'm swallowing thickly for a different reason.

A pang of…*something* throbs behind my ribcage.

"It's me…your dad. I've been thinking…" His words fade into the background when Cole's eyes clash with mine.

He walks past, his leather scent lingering for long moments. I clench a muscle in my cheek, staring at the expanse of his broad back. His gray T-shirt is stretching over his shoulders, and his combats sit low on his hips, accentuating his toned legs and fine-as-hell—

"I want to see you," Cole's dad slurs through the line.

I turn my back and stare out the window, watching Mia pull up outside. After exiting her car, she talks briefly to my dad, who shuts the trunk on the suitcases.

"Cole? Talk to—"

"Wrong number," I grit out, lowering the phone from my ear and ending the call.

"Who was that?" Allie asks, seated at the table, peeling a mandarin while Cole roots through the fridge.

Placing the phone back in the holder, I tear my gaze away from the window.

Some people peel off small pieces, but not Allie. No, she makes a game out of creating a long spiral. I watch her, feeling Cole's eyes on me as he shuts the fridge.

Guilt eats me up from the inside despite the overwhelming sense of protectiveness, which has my chest tightening. His father is an asshole who only calls here when he's drunk. Sometimes, he's regretful, begging for forgiveness. Other times, he shouts abuse.

I've managed to intercept every call, but there will come a day when Cole picks up. I told his mom once, and she changed the number, but it didn't stop him. Nothing does.

"Mia is here," I say, pocketing my phone, and Allie cranes her neck to see outside, her face lighting up.

Cole lingers behind when she leaves the room in a cloud of citrus fruit, perfume, and undertones of her boyfriend's cologne.

I fucking hate his smell on her.

Leaning back against the counter again, I finally lift my gaze, my heart thudding as our eyes clash in a hurricane of unspoken words.

Why does he make me feel this way? I want to blur the lines for him.

I mean, fuck, I sought him out last night, hiding in the shadows of his room, listening to his steady breathing. When he woke up, I felt...relief.

I could finally breathe again.

He speaks first, staring at me from across the table. "Why did you do it?"

"Why did I do what?" I ask, letting my eyes fall down his body and back up, lingering on the veins in his arms and his tense jaw.

How can he have such a chokehold on me? I don't get it, yet here I am, feeling my heart pound harder while he grinds his teeth. I wonder if he can sense this pull between us or if it's all in my head. When he looks away, I want those conflicted eyes back on me.

I'm growing addicted to how it hurts when he looks at me with such fury.

"Don't play games with me."

"Isn't that what we do?" I question, and he reluctantly trains his attention back on me. "Play games."

"You..." he starts, breaking eye contact and shaking his head before raking his fingers through his hair, twisting the strands as though he needs the pricking pain to help him focus. "Don't fucking touch me again."

"You didn't stop me."

He drops his hand to his side as a look of disgust or anger—maybe both—twists his features. I try so fucking hard not to let him sink the knife deeper into my chest, but I know it's a lost battle when he looks at me again. I felt numb for so long and lost in a gray world. Then he entered the picture. I'm not numb anymore, not when he cuts me wide open with his tormented gaze.

I never want him to turn away.

He swallows, his voice trembling as he lifts a shoulder in a small shrug. "That doesn't mean anything."

The charged air between us pulsates while we stare at each other.

"Just…" He clears his throat. "Stay the fuck away."

Then he's gone, brushing past me, his scent curling around my aching heart like tendrils of ivy. I stare at the empty doorway with my hands in my pockets until I'm forced to blink because my eyes burn.

Turning to face the window, I watch Allie glue herself to his side the moment he walks outside, batting her wispy lashes and looking so fucking happy.

When he wraps his arm around her shoulder and pulls her into him, I feel sick.

I swing back around before I can do something stupid, like storm outside and haul her off him in front of our parents.

I need her out of the fucking picture.

My eyes catch on the lilies on the kitchen table. Cole's mom's pride and joy. Pushing off the counter, I cross the small space and pick up the vase, then hurl it against the fridge. The glass shatters on impact in a spectacular explosion of broken shards and destruction, but the loud crash does nothing to calm me down. If anything, I want more violence. My chest won't stop aching.

COLE IS DRIVING us to the airport, and our parents are in their own car a few vehicles ahead on the stretching country road as music drifts through the speakers.

Cole drums his thumb on the steering wheel in time with the beat, his other hand surfing the wind outside the open window while the warm breeze teases the dark hairs around his ears and nape. I regret my decision to wear a sweater so soon. We're not even on the plane yet. Sweat beads on my forehead as I reach behind me to pull the extra layer off, messing up my hair in the process. I toss it beside me, my eyes clashing with Cole's in the rearview mirror.

"Stay the fuck away."

His words from earlier turn my stomach, and I look away first. Trees pass by in a blur outside as I listen to the guitar riff, jiggling my knee, restless as hell.

A soft touch to the top of my hand makes me stiffen. Mia smiles at me and trails her nails over my knuckles. The urge is there to pull my hand away, but I keep it on my thigh while she threads her fingers through mine. We're traveling to a ski resort, yet she's wearing a short skirt and heels.

She sneaks a furtive glance toward the front, then guides my hand to her smooth thigh, parting them in invitation. Unease twists my insides when she sucks on her lip. Why am I feeling this...confused? I've never hesitated to touch her before, yet when my fingers graze her damp lace panties, I want to recoil.

But then I feel it.

Cole's eyes on me.

I lift my gaze and trail the edge of Mia's panties. He's no longer tapping his thumb on the steering wheel. Now, he wrings it until his knuckles turn white against the leather.

I dip my fingers beneath the lace, and when Mia realizes we have an audience, she grips my wrist to stop me. Parting her soaked pussy lips, I slide my middle finger knuckle deep into her tight little cunt.

That sensation of wanting to recoil? It's gone.

I shove my finger deeper, feeling her pussy tighten as I smirk at Cole.

You want me to stay the fuck away from you?

One finger becomes two. I fuck her with slow, sensual strokes while the rock music drowns out her panting breaths and pathetic little moans that don't do shit for me. Cole stares the whole time, glancing at the road every few seconds.

This is what he wants. What he asked for. I'm staying away.

Mia's pussy pulsates around my fingers, her grip turning

slack on my wrist. The fight is gone. Now that her climax is within reach, she doesn't care about an audience. She cants her hips and guides me deeper, rocking to meet my touch.

When I look at her, she spreads her legs wider, her heaving tits rising and falling with every ragged breath from her parted lips. I've fucked this pussy enough times to know how to get her off in minutes, but I keep her on the edge, slowing down every time she comes too close.

I meet Cole's stormy gaze and smirk, my hand moving inside Mia's bunched skirt. He tracks the movement, then swallows thickly before glaring at the road ahead, but his eyes soon return to me—haunted.

As he looks away again, I finish Mia off.

I know the minute she comes apart around my fingers, and I hate how she ripples and pulsates, squirming beside me. But I don't pull out or allow my mask to crack. Cole can't have the cake and eat it, too.

I will break him open one way or another.

When he rolls up the window and glances at me again, I slip my fingers from beneath Mia's skirt and suck them clean, pretending to savor the tangy taste.

I used to love the taste of pussy, but now I have a craving for something else.

Someone forbidden.

And that someone is currently staring at me with a frown between his brows.

"I CAN'T FUCKING BELIEVE THIS," Cole mutters, sliding his duffle bag from his shoulder and tossing it onto the bed. He turns around, his eyes sweeping over the small room and the bed.

"Trust me, I don't want to share a room with you either," I grumble, plopping down onto the couch across from him.

He looks at me then, and we watch each other while the girls giggle in the ensuite bathroom. I wish I could read his thoughts. The air is tense, but neither of us says a word. His eyes fall down my body and then back up. He turns away just as quickly, unzipping his bag.

His shoulders tense when I rise to my feet, but he doesn't turn around or ask me to leave. I'm so close I can smell his cologne, and it's all I can do not to lose my sanity.

"You want me to stay away?" I whisper against the nape of his neck, lining my chest up with his broad back. He stops breathing when I reach around to tease the sliver of skin where his hoodie meets his combats. His stomach is smooth and warm, and I almost growl as I dip my fingers below the waistband. Shivers erupt over his skin, his pulse pounding. I press my lips to the curve of his neck, where his hair curls enticingly. Fuck, I've longed to taste him for so long.

"Are you sure that's what you want?" I ask, sliding my hand lower, avoiding touching his dick.

"Yes," he whispers even as he melts into me. "Stay the fuck away—"

The girls giggle in the bathroom, and he stiffens, ready to bolt. I chuckle, wrapping my hand around his dick in a possessive hold before he can make his escape.

I don't stroke him. I hold him, feeling his cock swell in my palm.

"Has your girlfriend ever told you how perfect your dick is, brother?"

"Don't call me that."

"No?" I kiss his neck again, sensing his shiver, then pull his earlobe between my teeth, nibbling and sucking. "Admit that you were jealous earlier."

"I don't know what the fuck you're talking about." His voice breaks when I give his dick a small tug.

"Sure, you don't." I pull my hand out of his pants when the bathroom door opens.

Mia enters first, with Allie close behind, having reapplied her lipstick and combed her shiny hair.

Without a glance in their direction, Cole escapes to the bathroom, brushing past his girlfriend as though she doesn't exist. Call me selfish, but it gives me a sense of satisfaction knowing she fails to rattle him as I do.

Mia asks me something, but my attention snags on Cole's bag, and I do a double take, pulling it closer to me on the bed.

A mask peeks through the creased clothes shoved inside.

Curious, I pick it up.

What the hell?

I stare at the crack, unable to believe my eyes. It was Cole all along? He was the one who chased me with the hockey stick? I broke his mask—*this* mask... Was it him that first time, too?

What about the fucking messages? My eyes widen.

He sent them...

The mask trembles in my hold, my heart slowing to heavy, insisting thuds. I can't think. Fuck... It was Cole.

The girls' annoying giggles fade into muted background noise as my mind spirals out of control.

Glancing at the closed bathroom door, I set my jaw.

I should have guessed that he likes to play games, scared to let the world in on his little secret.

Looking back down at the cracked mask, I trail my thumb over it, then shove it back inside the bag.

He wants to play pretend? Threaten me one second and jerk my dick the next?

Mia comes up behind me and slides her hand over my back. "Are you okay, baby?"

Turning around, I pull her into me. "Never better."

CHAPTER 12
COLE

B y the time we unpack, Mia and Allie are already out shopping with Mom, and wanker-face Gavin is trying to tell his son that there's no chance we can get a larger lodge since Mom asked Allie when she called up in the early hours to join us, and now we have to figure out how the four of us will fit in one bed.

Call it pride, but I refuse to be on the sofa with a girlfriend who sleeps like an octopus.

So we're stuck sharing a room – a bed. Being so close to Blaise for a solid week was going to be bad enough, this is just a fucking nightmare.

My phone buzzes in my pocket. It's the group chat with my friends. They're all planning a party this weekend and asked if I can slip away.

I snort and sit on the edge of the bed, typing back a reply that we're over a thousand miles from California, but to have extra drinks for me.

Samson sends a thumbs up, Keith sends a sad face, and Jackson stays silent.

He's been quiet since the tryouts. I think he already knows Blaise is taking his spot on the team and he's fucking fuming about it. I would be too. He worked his ass off to get to his position until he decided that partying and showing up late were more important, but still. No one wants to be kicked from the team at such an important time in our lives.

I open social media, seeing Allie has tagged me in a post. I don't bother looking at the fake crap. Instead, I click on Mia's page, my right eye twitching at the most recent post from an hour ago of her and Blaise standing in front of the lodge, him kissing her cheek while she beams a high-voltage smile.

My reaction is vicious, like a fist is shoving itself through my chest cavity. Something like jealousy whips around me, and I click off social media and toss my phone on the bed behind me.

Lying back, I rub my hands down my face, exasperated by this entire ordeal. "Fuck this," I mumble. "Fucking fuck this."

"Talking to yourself?"

At the sound of his voice, my hands drop from my face. Blaise walks into the room with a subtle smirk, pulling his shirt off and tossing it on the floor. Gaze locked on his back, I watch him. Or more so, I watch the way his muscles pull taut with his movements as he snatches a towel from his bag and heads to the bathroom.

Clearing my throat quietly, my mouth fills with saliva as he kicks off his sweats. His body is still bruised, and I want to high five myself for hurting him, but I also want to mark him some more.

It's like my claim is all over him, even though he doesn't know it's me he belongs to. I don't think I'll ever reveal myself to him. I like being able to do whatever the fuck I want to him without worrying about the repercussions of fucking with my stepbrother.

With the mask on, I can be whoever I want.

I don't fill my lungs with air until the bathroom door shuts. Before I can second guess my next move, I rush to my bag, fish out my second phone and type out a message.

> Me: Did you know there are cameras in every classroom at the school? With a click of my fingers, I can have it all sent to your brother to use against you.

The response is fast. The fucker must be sitting in there on his phone instead of turning on the damn shower.

Blaise: What do you want this time?

I smirk and type a reply.

Me: Surprise me.

My forefinger taps the side of the phone, and when the shower turns on, I sigh and toss the phone down beside my other one. Allie will be back soon, and I need to sit her down and have a serious talk with her.

When my phone lights up, my heart nearly explodes. Blaise has sent his secret stalker a picture, and instead of feeling like I'm winning, I feel something ugly crawling under my skin.

That bastard was right there in the shower with me – he watched me. He fucking grabbed my wrist and made me fuck my own hand.

Blaise had his fingers around my cock not even an hour ago.

I know this feeling. It's what I should feel whenever my girlfriend cheats on me. When she fucks off and flirts with people right in front of my face, then lies and calls me a psycho.

I feel betrayed.

I THINK my girlfriend just asked me something. She's smiling up at me with her big, beautiful blue eyes, her blonde hair whipping around her face from the cold wind. The corner of my mouth curves ever-so slightly in response to whatever she's said.

I can't pay any attention to her. She shouldn't be here anyway. I broke up with her and she barged her way back into my life in a matter of hours and infiltrated our trip to Aspen.

She called my mom completely hysterical, begging to speak

with me. Instead of coming to me, Mom tells her to pack a bag and join us. Now I'm stuck with her for a week, in a room I need to share with Mia and Blaise, while my cock tries not to stand at attention from the memory of the way he touched me.

I'm the one who dominated him when I had the mask on. Me. Yet without it, when he knows it's me, he's forceful and…I like it. But right now, I'm in even more of a mood with him than usual.

I shake my head and fix my gloves into place, then help Allie do hers, checking her helmet is clipped properly.

I feel eyes on me, but I ignore them while we sort out our protective gear.

Allie wraps her fingers around my wrist to stop me when I clip her in. "I love you," she says, her eyes shining.

"Sure you do," I retort, taking a step back so she releases me.

Mia is giggling, and I glance over to see Blaise smashing snow into her face before they start throwing snowballs at each other and laughing.

They look happy. I want to kill them both.

My nostrils flare, and I look back to Allie. She tilts her head. "What's wrong? Why do you keep staring at them?"

"I'm not," I lie, waiting for the instructor to come and take us to the bunny slope.

Blaise and I haven't been skiing before, so we're not allowed on the big slope, but Mia and Allie have been plenty of times with their families. Our parents think this will be a great bonding experience since they've noticed how tense the atmosphere has been around me and Blaise.

If only they knew.

There isn't tension. I just want to fucking strangle the bastard while he wraps his fingers around my cock again and—

"Hold my hand," Allie says, breaking me from my thoughts. "I'll catch you if you slip. Make sure you're pointing your toes together. The motion will act as a break. Or if you go too fast, you can slow down by doing it too."

"I'm sure the guy over there is about to talk us through it."

I flinch at the voice beside me, too close, yet too far away, enough to make me shiver. Blaise huffs, his shoulder bumping into mine as we make our way to the small group gathering around the instructor.

He draws on about safety and rules and everything else while me and Blaise try not to slide on our asses during practice. Allie and Mia ditch us to go on the big slope, and I shove Blaise when he slips and tries to grab my arm.

"Really?"

I look down at him in the snow. "I told you not to touch me."

He scoffs and shakes his head. The instructor goes on for an hour before we feel semi-confident to go to the top of the bunny slope. It's not big, but it's way more slanted than I expected, and when I go to straighten my skis, I stop.

Blaise glances over at me, with two kids between us, just as they shoot off down the slope with no care in the world, cheering and asking their parents if they saw them.

"Scared?"

"Why would I be scared?" I frown at him. Deep down, I'm nervous. I'm not afraid of heights, but this feels dangerous.

"Such a fucking pussy." Blaise moves slowly down the slope until he's halfway, straightening his skis so he zips down the rest.

I wait for him to topple over, to fall and decapitate himself on a snowball, anything. But he reaches the bottom, glancing over his shoulder up at me with a smirk.

Asshole.

When I straighten my skis, I hold my breath and try not to close my eyes. I'm not scared – there's an image flashing behind my eyes of my dad dangling me from the top floor window by the scruff of my shirt, Mom screaming at the bottom, begging Dad not to let me go. My leg itches at the memory of him – the scars covered by ink to hide the abuse and forget it ever happened.

I collide with someone trying to catch me, dragging them down into the snow and off to the side so we're in a ditch.

"Fucking hell, Cole," Blaise groans. "Watch where you're going! You were going too damn fast!"

His nose is bleeding. He touches it, and the ruby red has me mesmerized and desperate to feel the warm liquid between my fingers. To reach up and wipe the droplets away, but I stay frozen beneath him.

Because he's on top of me, pinning me into the snow, and I can feel all of him pressed against me.

A droplet of blood drips onto my cheek. Blaise follows the trail rolling against my skin, his heavy breaths hitting my face.

Blaise tuts. "Why do you always need to fuck things up? You can't even go skiing without making a mess of shit."

My eyes darken as I glare, and the force of me throwing my forehead into his face knocks him off me. It takes him half a second to catch his bearings before his fist flies into my cheek. Sometimes I forget the asshole has muscles, because I'm certain my jaw just nearly shattered.

Through the burning of pain, I unclip one of my skis and get to my knees, grabbing the ski and swinging it at his side, knocking him off his skis completely.

"What the fuck!"

I drop the ski and unclip the other, traipsing through the deep snow to grab him by the hair, now on his knees in front of me where he fucking belongs.

The blood on his face is making me hard, my pulse elevating. Fuck.

Before I can hit him again, he tackles me once more, back into the same position with his hands around my throat, pressing his forehead against mine. "You're taking this too far." He forces his forehead harder. "Too fucking far."

"Then do something about it," I spit out, my throat closing from his firm grip.

His nose bumps mine, and I freeze all over as he snatches my bottom lip between his teeth, a burning sensation searing as he bites harshly and tugs until it snaps back into place.

Fuck. I'm breathless, and I don't think it's because of his hold on my neck. I don't even register the coldness of the snow surrounding us with the heat growing between my legs, making my cock swell.

I gulp under his grip, and as his head lowers once more, I have an inner war to either headbutt the dickhead or feel his lips on mine.

The fuck?

"Do that again," I manage to say through the tightness in my throat, "and I'll rip your fucking face off."

Blaise glances down between us, and I know I'm tented. He can probably feel it.

I can feel him too.

He straightens his arms and squeezes his fingers around my throat to a point that it hurts, but I don't stop him or try to shove him off. I lie in the snow, his legs straddling my hips, as he cuts off my airflow.

Tighter. Tighter. And even tighter.

I can't breathe, my vision blurring, his image above me distorting as I refuse to beg him to stop, to release my throat. His face is shaking with his rage, his eyes on fire. No one can see the attempted murder with us in a snowy ditch. Icy flakes fall from the sky, coating our thick clothes, and I hear someone yelling in the distance as if their kid just fell and hurt themselves.

"Why?"

I try to blink through the pressure behind my eyes. *Why, what?* I want to ask, but I can't talk, the world vignetting around his form as he keeps strangling me.

I'm painfully aware of how rock solid my dick is. He's full of blood and his large, veiny hands are around my throat, and they're all I can think about. But then I think about the masked stranger he's messing with, and even though it's me, I feel the stab of betrayal in my chest again.

His phone rings, and it's the only reason he lets go of me. I gasp in as much air as I can, filling my desperate lungs. My body automatically curls to the side, and I choke into the snow. He stays straddling me, blood staining his face.

"What?" he grits through the phone. "Fine. We'll meet you at the burger shack."

Hanging up, he shoves his phone back into one of his pockets. "Allie fell and hurt her leg. Go tend to your needy, cheating girlfriend."

CHAPTER 13.
BLAISE

S eated beside Cole on the couch, I watch the flames flicker in the fireplace. Above it, a moose's head with big antlers is mounted on the wall.

My father paces in front of us, pinching the bridge of his nose, thoroughly pissed off.

When we returned to the cottage, he ordered us into the living room, away from the girls. I swear his eye twitches when he levels Cole with a glare.

"I asked for one damn family holiday without you causing a scene. One! But you just had to start a fight on the first day, didn't you?"

Cole is stiff beside me, and tension radiates off him in waves. He remains quiet, staring straight ahead at the fireplace.

"This was supposed to be a chance for us to bond as a family. How do you think it makes your mother feel when you fight with your brother every chance you get?"

I glance down at Cole's clenched hands on his thighs, and when I lift my eyes, a muscle tics in his jaw. There used to be a time when I would get a sense of satisfaction from seeing my dad lay into him, but something feels wrong tonight. *I* feel wrong.

"She's tired of your behavior, too. It doesn't matter what we do or how many chances we give you, Cole. You go out of your way to ruin everything." He points a finger in Cole's direction and narrows his eyes. "It ends now."

The muscle in Cole's jaw tics again, and the ache that's pressing on my ribs intensifies.

"Do you hear me, boy?"

"Dad..." I rip my eyes away from Cole, then rise to my feet. "He gets it, alright?"

Dad looks at me, blinking like he'd forgotten I was here. I've never thought about it until now, but I'm embarrassed. Cole is an asshole, sure, and he's temperamental, argumentative, and... broken. But my dad never gave him a chance. No, in his eyes, Cole is cut from the same cloth as his alcoholic father.

"He gets it..." I emphasize, pleading with him to drop it.

My chest fucking throbs. What's that shit about?

I don't like how my father skates his attention to Cole, and I like it even less when a look of disgust flashes in his eyes.

It dawns on me that I'm protective of Cole. The instinct to defend him tingles my fingertips.

No one hurts him but me. No one gets to crawl beneath his skin.

I swallow down the lump in my throat. "I started it."

Cole looks up at me. I stare at my dad, fighting the urge to check on him to ensure he's okay.

I'm so confused.

Dad tightens his jaw, looking between us. Then he points at Cole again. "I will not tolerate you ruining this family holiday."

Then my father walks out without another word, all but slamming the door shut behind him. I want to run after him and shove him so fucking hard that he crashes into the opposite wall and breaks his fucking nose.

I peer down at Cole, but he's not looking at me. "He shouldn't have treated you like that."

Cole sucks on his teeth, the flames casting flickering shadows over his face. "Why did you do it?"

"Why did I do what?" I ask.

"Stand up for me." His eyes lift, hooking my heart and tugging at something inside me. I take him in, sweeping my gaze over his lips and the stubble on his jaw—lips I want to feel pressed against mine. The emotions he evokes when he looks at me scare the living daylights out of me, yet here I am, unable to break eye contact.

My throat jumps. "I did what I thought was right—"

He flies to his feet, standing so close that his heated breaths fan my mouth. "Next time, don't."

I frown, bouncing my eyes between his. Why is he so angry? What have I done wrong now? My father was a dick to him, and I couldn't just let that slide.

"I don't want you to defend me, Blaise," he seethes. "I didn't fucking ask for it, alright? I can look after myself."

"I know you can," I reply, struck with the need to explain. "I didn't suggest otherwise."

"No? Then why the hell are you getting involved? Do you think your dad is the first asshole I've had to deal with? That I can't stand up for myself? I'm not fucking weak."

"I never said you were—"

"Stay out of my fucking business, *brother*," he sneers before turning on his heel and walking away.

I stare after him.

What is wrong with me? I almost feel like I want to...cry or punch something.

No, fuck that.

"You're scared, Cole," I call out, and he pauses in the doorway with his back to me. "You're so used to being treated like shit by everyone—your dad *and* mine... It's where you feel safe. You would rather push everyone away than allow yourself to be vulnerable."

When he stays silent, I throw my hands out defeatedly. "Not everyone is against you, Cole. Sooner or later, you will need to let someone past those fucking walls you've built so damn high. You want to hate me? Is that what you need to feel good? To feel safe? You want a villain? Fine. I'll be your worst fucking nightmare."

This time, when he walks out, I slump.

What the hell was that? He makes no secret of hating me, but when I try to do the right thing, he throws it back in my face. I can't fucking win. Screw him and his wounded pride. I couldn't just stand by while my dad was being a dick.

Grinding my teeth to dust, I rip my eyes away from the door, then glance up at the moose's head. The huge antlers cast grotesque shadows over the walls, and its eyes are as dead as my soul once used to be before Cole fucking Carter had to go and awaken these foreign emotions. I don't know how to handle them, which pisses me off.

"What the fuck are you looking at?" I sneer at the moose.

IS THERE anything cheesier than board games? I think not.

Cole's mom came prepared on this trip, and now we're seated around the dining table, playing Monopoly while it's snowing outside.

I'm bored out of my mind, slouched in my chair, arm stretched out on the back of Mia's chair. I twist a curl of her hair around my finger while making no secret of watching Cole. He hasn't looked at me once.

Fuck him.

He tries so hard to play the perfect boyfriend, but I see through him. Unlike me, who has perfected my social game to fit in, he can't hide his disinterest in his girlfriend. Every time she leans into him, he shifts away, even if it's only slight. When she plays with the curls at his nape, he stiffens. His smiles are forced and don't reach his ears. But he tries. He tries so fucking hard to keep his eyes off me while giving her flirtatious looks, engaging in a far more intriguing game than the one spread out before us.

The only time Cole feels safe is when he's hiding.

It's what he's good at—hiding behind masks, walls, and harsh words.

With that thought in mind, I discreetly unlock my phone beneath the table and send him a mirror selfie I took earlier of me naked and wet from a recent shower.

Me: I fantasize about you chasing me again.

After placing the phone on my thigh, I reach for my Coke bottle, watching him closely while taking a swig. He must have his burner phone on him. I bet my girlfriend's non-existent virginity on it. He's too fucking curious about me to leave it with his things back in the room.

"It's your turn," Dad says, dragging me from my musings.

I pick up the dice and toss them on the board. Two threes. I move my wheelbarrow.

"Go straight to jail," Mia sniggers, leaning into me and scratching her nails over my thigh beneath the table.

Curling my fingers around her wrist, I'm about to shove her off.

What the hell am I doing? I didn't even think as I gripped her. It was instinct. I didn't want her to touch me because of the asshole across the table.

Fuck him and the effect he has on me.

I loosen my grip, stroking my thumb over her wrist. My lips curve when Cole digs something out of his hoodie's front pocket. His hair falls over his brow as he looks down.

Gotcha.

He stiffens, ignoring Allie's excited squeal beside him when she throws two sixes. I hide my smile behind the rim of my Coke while he works his jaw before typing out a response.

The phone vibrates on my thigh.

Cole looks up at me, straightening in his seat and flicking his hair out of his eyes.

My dick likes that he looks annoyed. Maybe even angry. Whatever the emotion is behind the hardening of his eyes, I like it.

I've crawled beneath his skin, and I have every intention of burrowing deeper.

His hand trembles as he swipes up the dice, rolling them in his closed palm before tossing them back down. Two fives. He moves his piece past mine and picks up a card.

Dad drinks the last of his red wine, then refills it to the top. Cole follows the movement, watching him place it back down. He pays the bank and settles back with his arm stretched out on the back of Allie's chair.

I finally have his eyes on me, and I pretend I don't notice as I unlock my phone beneath the table.

> Cole: You want to choke on cock that badly, huh?

I almost chuckle out loud. Now that I know it's Cole behind the messages, I get one heck of a kick from riling him up.

> Me: Not just any cock. Yours.

I look up through my lashes, smirking.

Allie throws her head back and laughs at one of Mia's stories while Cole stares at his phone beneath the table. Then he types, and I wait.

My dick likes seeing him visibly rattled like he is now. He tries to hide it, but I track every subtle stiff shift of his muscles.

When Allie beams at him, he drags his eyes away from his phone, but his attention is elsewhere. A bead of sweat trails down his temple as his eyes flicker my way, then back down.

My phone vibrates.

"Isn't this nice?" Cole's mom asks, leaning into Dad. "Us here, together as a family."

He makes an affirmative noise, his eyes narrowing on Cole as he picks up his glass of wine. I watch the movement while grinding my teeth. What is his fucking problem now? I never realized what a fucking ass he is to my stepbrother, and it doesn't sit right with me.

I reach for the phone to distract myself, typing in the passcode one-handed. Mia trails her nails over my back, picking up a card. Imaginary spiders crawl down my spine as her nails scratch me through my hoodie. It's a physical struggle not to shake her off.

Fuck...

I don't want her to touch me.

> Cole: I'm blackmailing you, yet you still want to suck my dick. Are you that desperate?

Chuckling, I wet my lips.

He's so damn serious, frowning across the table. It's simple—I want to make him jealous. Now that I know it's Cole behind the mask, I can't stop replaying how he chased me down and showed me a rare glimpse of the true him.

He has urges no one knows about, and I like that knowledge a little too much.

> Me: Your threats have me in a chokehold.

Cole looks down at his phone beneath the table.

Shifting in my seat, I type out another message.

> Me: I like it when you steal my breath.

My fingers fly over the screen, and I glance up at him as I hit send.

> Me: You have me by my balls, so I might as well enjoy it. Besides, I can't stop thinking about how you stroked my dick.

What intrigues me about Cole is that he looks conflicted for reasons other than the mere question of his sexuality. He almost looks...jealous. His jaw is tight, and his eyes are hard.

He shoves his phone into his pocket and swipes his Coke bottle. Allie startles at the sudden movement and asks him if he's okay.

Ignoring her, he swigs his drink, his eyes burning into my face. I whisper in Mia's ear, and she giggles.

This is the difference between me and Cole. I've mastered this game, whereas he's struggling to read the rulebook. I can play the doting, loved-up boyfriend and make it look real.

Mia's eyes glitter with happiness, and I know that I should feel bad for using her as a pawn on this playing board. But everyone plays a part in the grand scheme of things.

The only person I care about, and who stirs the numbness inside me, is the boy across the table.

He looks at me, and I tilt my head.

What are you thinking about, Cole?

"It's your turn to roll the dice, son," Cole's mom says to him, reaching for her wine glass.

Seconds pass while we watch each other, caught in our own world. Flames flicker in the fireplace, and snow flurries sail through the air outside, but he's all I see.

He looks away first, picking up the dice and shaking them in his palm. With a flick of his wrist, they fly across the board, knocking over my wheelbarrow in the process.

Two sixes.

I raise a brow, and he smirks.

Well played, Cole.

SHARING a bed with Cole and our girlfriends isn't how I imagined this trip. Needless to say, I can't sleep.

Not when my cock is hard, and Cole looks so damn irresistible asleep on his front with his bare back on full display.

Mia was pressed up against me earlier with her thigh over mine and her cheek on my chest. I was too hot and restless to sleep.

Instead, I found myself hovering by Cole's bedside. I'm hard. Frustrated. His dark hair obscures his eyes, so I reach out to stroke it away. Why does my heart thud harder when I feel his warmth?

I linger on his skin, tracing my finger on the scar on his hip, glancing at the girls, who're fast asleep, snuggled up together. They'd make a perfect couple if they didn't like cock so much. I can't blame them. Cole's dick is all I can think about these days.

I lift my eyes to the girls one final time, wetting my lips in anticipation of what I'm about to do. When I'm reassured that they won't wake up after I spiked their drinks with Rachel's sleeping pills, I straddle him naked on the bed. He startles awake, and I loop my belt around his neck while he tugs on the restraints that I used to secure his wrists to the bed frame. What can I say? I came prepared. Did he think I would make this easy on him?

His words are muffled behind the duct tape on his mouth, and he tries to look at me over his shoulder. I pull the belt tight, then lean down to whisper in his ear, "You want a fucking villain, Cole?"

He stiffens, throwing a panicked glance at the girls.

"Villains don't ask nicely," I whisper, circling the belt around my hand. "They take. Is that what you want? A bad guy who steals your choice?"

His back breaks out in a cold sweat, and I smile against the shell of his ear before tracing it with my tongue. I bite down, making him grunt from the sharp sting. "Do you know what I think, brother?" Shifting, I settle on top of him. "Beneath your bad attitude, you're a slut."

When I yank down his boxers to expose his firm ass, his struggle renews, and he pulls on the restraints as he tries to wriggle out from beneath me, but soon stops when I pull on the belt.

"Shhhh. You don't want to wake our girlfriends."

My big cock nestles between his ass cheeks, and his harsh breaths rattle his chest. I pull his short hair with my free hand, forcing a groan from his throat, then rock forward, sliding my dick through his ass crack.

"Fuck," I grunt, looking between our bodies. It's dark in the room, and I can only just make out the outline of my weeping dick.

"I guess you're weak, after all." I chuckle, shoving his head into the mattress. "Fight me all you want. You're taking my dick tonight whether you want it or not." Swirling my tongue through the sweat on his nape, I breathe against his ear, "But we both know you do. Your ass feels empty, doesn't it? Want me to fill you up and fuck you until you can't walk tomorrow?" I hum, grinding against his ass. "I like thinking of you waking up next to your girlfriend, with your brother's cum leaking from your ass. Does she rim you, Cole? Do you let that pretty girlfriend of yours lick your ass?"

He yanks on the restraints, breathing harshly through his nose.

If I hadn't tied him up, he'd shove me off and ram his fist into my face. Punch me bloodied. Why does that thought turn me on? I like him naked and defenseless.

I bet his dick throbs as much as mine.

"You love it, don't you?" My breaths tremble against the curve of his neck, and I suck his earlobe between my teeth. "You love that you have no choice but to take it." I shudder, grinding harder against him. "I want to fuck your ass, Cole. I bet you're tight."

Jesus Christ... I'm so screwed.

I chuckle breathily against his ear, but it's not to taunt him. No, he has all the power without even realizing it. I'm powerless against him when he shivers beneath me—tied up, naked, and trembling.

"Why do you drive me so fucking insane?" I'm struggling to keep my wits about me when he feels this good. He throws his head back, and I barely dodge in time.

"Fuck," I laugh and dig my fingers into his sweaty neck. "Nearly broke my nose. Naughty boy." Pistoning against his ass, I pound him into the mattress.

My hair falls over my brow as I watch my dick slide through his ass cheeks. Fuck me. It's the most erotic thing I've seen.

I sink my teeth into my lip, circling my hips. I've never been this aroused. Not even with Mia.

Sliding my fingers through the damp hair at his neck, I press his face into the mattress. "I'm in control, Cole. You can build your walls as high as you want. I'll demolish them every time. Don't you think I can feel you humping the mattress?"

Braced on my elbow, I squeeze his hip, grinding harder against his ass. "One day, I'm going to fuck you. Remember that tomorrow when Allie asks you if you love her."

I glance down in time to see cum squirt from my dick, and I collapse forward, panting against his neck. Cole's out of breath, too, and his sweaty back is slick against my chest. I kiss his neck and shoulder before pushing up and climbing off the bed.

Cole turns his head away from me while I free his wrists, and I hesitate, struck with a pang of regret. What if I hurt him? What if I took it too far? But then again, so what? He asked for a villain, and I'll be whatever he needs. Even if I turn into the bad guy.

When he's free, he turns his body away from me, too.

"Don't ask for a villain, Cole, if you don't want to get hurt." I stroke my fingers through his hair, and he flinches. "Do you feel safe now? Protected behind your walls. You didn't get to come. I bet your dick is throbbing, huh?" Fisting his hair, I pull hard, and he shoots up from the bed and fights me off, causing me to stumble back several steps.

I'm relieved, to be honest, to see the fire back in his eyes. The way his nostrils flare as he rises to his feet, ripping off the duct tape.

"You like this, don't you?" I taunt. "It feels good to hurt, right? This is what you want. To be treated like shit."

Cole comes for me, and we crash into the wall, knocking down a painting.

"What did you do to the girls? Why the fuck are they still asleep?"

"I told you," I whisper, "I'm not a good guy. Do you think I'll let our girlfriends stand in the way of me hurting you? Owning you? I did what I had to do." I fist his dick, stroking the firm length from root to tip and smiling. "So fucking needy, huh?"

He grunts. "I fucking hate you."

"Good." His dick pulses in my hand. "You can hate me while you come all over my fingers."

"Fuck you," he growls, thrusting against my palm, his choppy breaths fanning my mouth. "Fuck you to hell and back."

"You'd like that, wouldn't you? My dick in your ass."

"Shut up."

I grin, nipping his jaw when he pulls away to look down at his cock in my hand. "You're leaking all over my fingers. Such a filthy boy, hmm?"

Grabbing my chin, he shoves my head against the wall, and I laugh harder.

"Just admit that you love this."

"Stop talking." He shudders before crashing against me as cum erupts from his dick.

Seconds pass. Cole stays pressed against my chest, his face buried in my neck. Neither of us moves.

"Your heart is pounding," I whisper against his shoulder, feeling the organ thrash behind his ribs.

He shudders, inhaling a ragged breath.

This is us.

This is our push and pull.

Our battlefield.

"If you ever touch me again," he breathes against my skin, "I'll kill you. I won't hesitate to end you."

Trailing my fingers through the sweat and cum on his back, I hum while his muscles shift and ripple. "That sounds like a promise."

His husky voice drifts over my ear. "Stay away from me, Blaise."

"That's right, I almost forgot," I say, feeling his shoulder blades move beneath my fingers. "I forget that you want me to hurt you. You're not scared of me shoving you away or punching you in the face."

His pulse thunders in his throat as I trail my lips over the curve of his neck, and I dart my tongue out to tease his earlobe, whispering, "You're scared of what would happen if I hugged you now. If I held you close and told you how fucking perfect you are. You'd sooner cut yourself open on your own blade than let someone hold you after they're done fucking you." Though it pains me to do it, I press my palms to his chest and shove him away.

He stumbles back, and I walk past him. "Don't worry, Cole. I could never fall for you. You're safe."

Lies.

Fucking lies.

CHAPTER 14.
COLE

Strobe lights flash, music pounding against every wall in the club, and my headache intensifies every minute I stay in this fucking place.

Blaise and Allie are at the bar, and Mia is walking back from the bathroom, her eyes flickering to her boyfriend, to me, then back to the bar.

In her tight little dress, she doesn't sit where her drinks and bag are, she lowers onto the chair beside me, turning her body so her knees point right at me.

"Can we talk?"

I narrow my eyes. "Talk about what?"

She's glancing at the bar again. "Not here. Can we slip away and talk? Maybe at the cabin? Your parents aren't there."

"Why would I sneak away from my girlfriend to talk to my stepbrother's girlfriend?"

Nibbling her lip, she fidgets her hands in her lap. "I just thought...maybe...I don't know? We could talk."

Her shoulder raises when I blink at her with no words as a response. "Maybe we could try something."

"Try what? You need to be clearer here, because all I can think is that you want me to fuck you and that's not happening."

Her eyes widen to saucers. "That's not— I mean, we could... I'm..."

"I'm not interested. I'm with Allie. If you drop this, I won't tell her you're trying to fuck her boyfriend and you can continue

playing the good little angelic girlfriend with the perfect relationship."

"Allie cheats on you all the time."

"I'm very aware," I reply, taking a gulp of my drink. "And it
seems you cheat on Blaise too if you're so eager to get on your
knees for me." I shake my head. "What's gotten into you? Why
are you all of a sudden all over me like a fucking rash? You're
either staring at me, staring at me holding Allie's hand, or when
you're kissing Blaise, you're seeing if I'm looking. I don't get it at
all."

Her voice lowers. "But you're always looking at me too."

I pause, because that might come across as true. I'm not
looking at her – my eyes are glued to the asshole she's hanging
off of. It's automatic when I'm near him.

Again, I shake my head. "You're mistaken. I'm not interested
in playing any games with you. How many times do I need to
say it before you fuck off back to your own seat and stay on the
dick you're tied to?"

"You're making me look crazy."

"If the shoe fits."

Her face contorts. "Fuck you, Cole."

"No thanks." I flatten my lips and my gaze lifts to the bar.
"And if you're trying to be sneaky about whatever it is you're
doing, your loverboy is on his way over with your best friend."

She darts to her feet and shuffles to her seat, her face going
bright red with embarrassment. What's her deal?

"That took forever," Allie says, placing drinks on the table
while Blaise leans down to whisper something in Mia's ear. She
grins up at him—fake as fuck—and then puts her hands on each
side of his face and drags his mouth to hers.

I'm glaring. I know I'm fucking scowling at them. But when
Mia opens her eyes mid-kiss, they clash with mine, and I want to
snap her neck.

A hand rests on my thigh, and I glance down to see Allie's
manicured nails strumming against my pants. She hums along to

the song, her head bobbing, before she turns to look at me. The corner of her lips curls, then she rests her head on my shoulder.

"I'm sorry," she says over the music. "I know you don't want me here, but I had to come and try to fix this between us. What can I do?"

I readjust myself on the seat, causing Allie to straighten. Draping my arm behind her chair, I avert my eyes from Blaise eating Mia's face off while her hand slips down his chest. They're so open in public. He could finger her right here and neither of them would care about where we are or the audience they'd have.

I don't want to see it.

"Do you want to go back to the cabin?" I ask Allie.

Her eyes light up. "Really?"

I nod. "Yeah. This place sucks."

Blaise pulls away from Mia when Allie and I get to our feet. "We're heading back," my girlfriend tells them.

"Please stick to having sex on your side of the bed," Mia says, smiling, but there's a hint of something vicious in her tone. She glances at me with silent words I have no idea what the fuck mean, then turns back to Blaise.

He's watching me as I wrap my arm around Allie's waist and walk her in the direction of the bar's exit.

As soon as we're through the door, Allie glues herself to my front, wrapping her arm around my neck and latching her mouth to my throat.

My bruised throat from Blaise strangling me.

I close my eyes and try to enjoy it, to like the way her tongue runs across my skin or the rushed way she unbuckles my belt.

I usually stop her and tell her I'm not ready, but after last night, and the way Blaise made me feel, I have to shadow it all with something else.

Weak.

I was weak. Always weak. The weak piece of shit who—

"Come on," Allie whispers, grabbing my hand and leading me to the bedroom, to the bed we share with Blaise and her best friend. "Please don't stop me."

She slides the straps of her dress from her shoulders, the material dropping and pooling at her feet.

I'm looking at her, and my eyes are on the marks on her breasts that I didn't create. Someone else was on her only a matter of days ago, and she hasn't even tried to hide it from me.

My gaze drops to the bruise on her hip, and she follows my line of sight. "Oh..." She hesitates and covers the blue-tinted skin with her hand. "Please don't judge me."

"Did he bend you over his desk again?"

The last time she had those marks, her professor made them. She got drunk and went into detail of how he worshipped her body while bending her over his desk, fucking her from behind while she imagined it was me.

Her bottom lip wobbles. "Yes," she says quietly. "I won't do it—"

"Stop lying," I snap, interrupting her. "You will do it again. I honestly think this is the eighth, maybe ninth time. Why are you with me? Give me a good reason, and I'll forgive you."

"I love you."

"Not good enough. Your actions speak louder than words, Allie. Why, after two years of you fucking around behind my back, should I stay in this relationship? You make me look..."

Weak. Blaise's voice is in my head, and I want to crack my own skull to pull him out.

She remains silent, tears building behind her eyes.

I step forward, anger growing the more I think about the shit she does and how it makes me look.

Weak.

I look weak.

"I don't love you anymore. I don't look at you and see a

future, or think about ripping your clothes off and burying my cock inside you. The first time you cheated, I wanted to kill the guy. I wanted to kill you. But instead, I forgave you and let you do it to me again and again and again."

I walk toward Allie until her back hits the wall, caging her in. "I don't care about you. I don't miss you when you're not around. I don't grab my phone to check if you've called. You broke me the first time you opened your legs for someone else when you belonged to me, and I'm not fixable, Allie."

She tries to grab my face, but I snatch her wrists and pin them above her head, holding her against the wall. The movement lines our bodies up, her bare tits against my chest.

My dick doesn't care.

"I want you to go home. My mom will drive you to the airport tomorrow. Go to my room and pack everything you have there, and I swear to fucking god, Allie, you better not be there when I get home."

"No," she croaks. "Don't. Please, Cole. Don't do this. I'll... I'll do better! I can—" She frees her hands from my grip and lowers to her knees. "Let me make you feel good. Give me a chance to make you fall back in love with me."

Breathing heavily through my nose, I grit my teeth as she hurriedly unbuttons my pants and yanks my soft, disinterested cock out and wraps her fingers around it.

Not a single twitch as I try to pull back, but she digs her nails into my thighs and forces her mouth on me. The snatch I have on her hair makes her cry out around my flaccid dick, and pauses, looking up at me through her lashes. "Please," she mumbles around the soft muscle.

She's sucking, trying to swallow me, but nothing happens. My body doesn't even betray me the way it has in the past.

I sneer, pulling away from her so my cock is free of her mouth. "Give up, Allie. We're done." I toss the short dress at her. "We're just going to drag on the inevitable. If you keep running back to your professor, then why don't you just be with him?"

She sniffles as she slides the dress back on. I sit against the dresser, crossing my ankles while I refasten my pants.

"He's married," she says, hugging herself. "I only went to him because he gave me attention and was helping me with coursework. I never had any intentions of becoming physical with him."

I nod a few times. "Which professor is it?"

The door opens, and she pauses her reply as Blaise walks in, his hand securely around Mia's. "I don't think your girl is supposed to cry after you fuck her," Blaise says to me, tipping his head, drunk as fuck. "Our wonderful parents decided to rent a second cabin so they can have privacy. I'm not sleeping in their bed."

Mia rushes to Allie. "What's wrong?"

She breaks down into a string of forced sobs. Huffing, I run my hand through my hair while Mia comforts her, and Blaise follows me out of the room as I go to the kitchen.

"What did you do?"

I turn around, nearly causing him to crash into me. "Stop talking to me. Stop doing all this fucking shit." Grabbing his jaw, I seethe. "And don't you ever do that to me again."

"Do what?" He smirks. "Make you feel good?"

My fist is flying before I can stop it, my knuckles smashing into his cheek so hard, my wrist aches and Blaise hits the ground.

For once, he doesn't fight me back. He's sitting on the ground at my feet, scowling up at me, his cheek red and slowly swelling.

Chest tight, my heart races, and I want to kick him in the face, to grab his hair and drive my knee into his nose and tell him never to come near me again, to stop ruining my fucking life.

"I'm not weak," I say through gritted teeth. My nostrils flare at his silence, the building rage behind his eyes. "And put a leash on Mia."

He frowns at my change in subject, getting to his feet. "What the fuck are you talking about?"

Just to be a dick, because he's pushed far too many buttons, I say, "She's randomly started approaching me as if we have something. I can assure you that I've never laid a fucking finger on your girl, but if she comes looking for my cock once more, I'll give it to her."

CHAPTER 15
BLAISE

Allie is crying herself to sleep in the other bedroom. Cole went outside to clear his head after he informed me of my girlfriend's sexual advances. I'm not even surprised. I've seen how she looks at him when she thinks I'm not aware, but she fails to realize that I miss nothing. Maybe that's why I keep her around. At least I know where she is when she's riding my dick.

"Allie is upset, Blaise." Mia reaches for my hand. "I can't let her sleep alone tonight."

I look at our interlaced fingers, stroking my thumb over her pale wrist. It's such a gentle move, sweet almost.

How fucking ironic.

I snatch her wrist, making her suck in a surprised breath. The move is sudden and unexpected. That's the thing about Cole. He brings out the darkness in me. Now, that poison is bleeding all over the girl I've pretended to care about for far too fucking long. I won't hesitate to snap her neck if she touches him again. I'm nothing but a cold-hearted, unfeeling, and uncaring monster. The truth is there in her eyes. I scare her.

"Blaise?" she asks, nervous.

As I stroke a strand of hair behind her ear, she holds her breath. Something about the flicker of doubt in her eyes soothes my inner turmoil. Even so, I cup her chin and claim her mouth. Our lips crash, and I frown, kissing her harder.

Why the hell is it that I feel nothing when I touch anyone but

Cole? My girlfriend could be an object. I taste the coppery blood on her tongue, and my heart remains a dull, steady beat. It doesn't matter how hard I kiss her or claw at her clothes, skin, or hair. I don't feel a thing. It never bothered me before to use people for my gain, like pieces in a chess game, but now it seems like I have a queen on my board—the most valuable player—and I can't fucking get to it. Cole smirks at me from behind a wall of pawns, protected by his rooks and bishops. My king can't defeat his army, and I'm yet to decide if he's a coward or if he's smart for building his walls this high.

"Blaise," she breathes when I spin her around. "Allie is upset in the other room—"

"Shut up!" I yank down her pants, palming her bare ass while keeping her cheek pressed to the wall with my fingers around her neck. I smack her pale skin, and she yelps, but I still feel nothing.

Not a fucking thing.

Numb.

Empty.

I attack her neck with biting kisses. Moaning, she juts her ass against me. The bitter taste of her flowery perfume assaults my taste buds. I rip my belt open, determined to feel...something.

"What's gotten into you?" she asks as I free my dick.

I clamp my hand over her mouth to shut her up, and she whimpers, aroused and scared.

I've always played the perfect boyfriend.

Always been what I thought she wanted. I've tried to fit in.

"If she comes looking for my cock once more, I'll give it to her."

Cole's words taunt me, slithering beneath my veins like prickly thorns. Fuck him and his threats. He won't be touching anyone without my permission.

Mia's eyes roll back into her head when I ram my dick into her tight cunt.

I still feel nothing.

She squeals, and I pause when the door creaks. He's here,

watching me fuck my girlfriend. Cole sets me on fire as he drops a metaphorical matchstick to the gasoline trail on the ground.

I feel again.

My heart thuds to life, beating so damn hard that my chest aches. Mia's walls ripple around me as I sneak my hand beneath her wooly sweater to palm her tits. She doesn't arouse me, but the thought of riling up the man behind us sure as hell does.

It's easy to ignore her sickly perfume and squealing whimpers when every snap of my hips knocks another pawn off his board.

I'm hunting his fucking queen.

"Moan for me, Mia," I growl in her ear, pinching her nipple. "Let my brother hear how good my dick feels. How you love it tearing through your cunt."

She stiffens, but soon melts into my touch, and I slip my hand from her top to play with her clit. I've barely grazed her slick pussy lips, when I'm wrenched away and punched in the face. Collapsing to the floor, I laugh like a fucking maniac. "You're so predictable."

Cole glares at me and my still hard, slick dick. I push up onto my elbows and smirk at him while Mia hurries to pull her pants back up. She flees the room, mumbling apologies.

"Why so angry?" I taunt.

My dick pulses against my T-shirt. There's a wet patch on the navy fabric. Cole grinds his teeth as he stares at it. He pulls on his short hair before kicking me hard enough to make me double over and choke out a strangled laugh.

"Fuck!" I cough, cradling my stomach. "That hurt."

I'm finally alive again. Alive in ways I've never been. So what if I have to hurt him to taste freedom from the suffocating darkness? It's worth it.

He is worth it.

"You can't keep your fucking hands to yourself, huh?"

"What's the problem? Don't you like it when I fuck my own

girlfriend? Maybe I should fuck yours instead. Oh...that's right, you broke up with her."

Cole grabs my hair and knees me in the head.

I laugh even harder. My nose is busted. I swipe my hand through the pouring blood before collapsing onto my back, tasting iron at the back of my mouth. "Feel better yet?"

Walking past me, he plops onto the bed, shoulders slumped. He puts his elbows on his thighs and drags his fingers through his hair.

I frown as I sit up and wipe more blood from beneath my nose. It's everywhere, coating my arm and soaking the front of my T-shirt.

"Why are you trying to piss me off?" he asks, tugging on the strands.

I glance at him. "What makes you say that?"

"Why the fuck are you doing this?" As he lowers his hands, he levels me with a look that cracks my heart wide open. "Why are you putting on a show?" He motions to where I fucked Mia not five minutes ago, and I look over as though I'll see what he saw.

"You think me fucking my girlfriend was a show?"

"Wasn't it?" His voice crackles. "Everything you do is a show. The girlfriend. Your grades. Your friends. Football." He glances away, fisting his hand, and then he looks back at me. "What's real, Blaise?"

My heart clenches tight, and I look past him at the snowflakes outside. "I don't know." An inch of snow lines the bottom of the window, but it's warm in here. Warm and safe in a way I only ever feel when Cole is around. I can't place the ache in my chest.

"I broke up with her because I can't pretend with her anymore. My feelings are just...nonexistent."

When I look back at him, the ache in my chest burns brighter. I want to crawl closer, but I stay rooted to the floor. My dick is still out, flaccid, but Cole never looks down. His eyes search my face, offering me a rare glimpse behind the anger that's always close to the surface. Beneath it hides a depth I doubt many have witnessed before. It's both intriguing and scary as fuck. I realize, as he breaks eye contact to look out the window, that I want him to trust me.

"I don't do feelings either," I admit, trying to explain something I struggle to comprehend myself.

A muscle clenches in Cole's jaw. He stays silent, watching the peaceful night.

"Not because I don't want to." I continue, feeling my heart thud harder. Why is it scary to be vulnerable? Especially with someone like him, who has always tried to cut me down. Even if he did it to keep himself safe from further hurt. His father fucked him up, and Cole still carries the scars under his ink. Meanwhile, I'm just faulty.

"I just can't…feel."

Cole is still looking out the window, his knuckles bloodied.

I zip my dick away before climbing to my feet and hobbling over to the bed. "Fuck," I snigger, flopping down beside him. "You got me good. My ribs hurt like a motherfucker."

His lips curve, and he tears his eyes away from the window to look at me. Then he shoulders me, and we chuckle. "You're an asshole. You know that, right?"

"Yeah…" I wet my lip, tasting blood, but I can't stop smiling. Something warm spreads through my chest when he looks at me this way. "You're an asshole, too."

This time, when he laughs, I smile so big my cheeks hurt.

We fall silent, watching each other. The urge to kiss him strikes me like a boomerang. I clear my throat and look anywhere but directly at him.

When he sighs out and looks down at his hands, I swallow thickly. What is he thinking about? I hold my breath when he shrugs.

"You say you can't feel…"

I stay silent, my heart thrashing madly.

I feel now.

"I don't believe you."

Staring at the side of his face, I sweep my gaze over his sharp jaw. Why does he hold this much power over me?

He focuses on his fingers—his nailbeds. "You wouldn't have defended me the other day if you didn't."

"I don't think you're weak," I rush out.

His brows furrow as he nods, looking pained. "I know…"

"What scares you, Cole?"

He pauses and looks up at me, his blue eyes flicking between mine.

I lower my gaze. "You don't have to answer."

His attention burns the side of my face for a moment longer before he sighs and runs his fingers through his hair. "Being alone."

When I don't answer, his chest expands on a shaky breath. "I don't know how to explain it."

"You don't have to."

"I know…"

I lift my gaze to his face, and he smiles weakly. "I fear being alone, so I push people away. Ironic, isn't it? I'm alone because I don't let anyone close. I guess…" With a shrug, he screws up his face. "I guess it's easier to push people away than face rejection. People have a way of hurting you in the end."

I study the side of his face, craving more of his truth. Fuck, I'm falling for him and the pain he exudes with every breath.

"How about you?" he asks as he rubs his neck.

I answer without thinking twice. "I'm scared to kiss you."

He stills.

I stare at the doorway. Why the hell did I tell him that? Some truths should stay guarded. This was one of them, but now my truth is out there, searching for a way past his impenetrable walls.

The ache in my chest burns brighter. "You need a villain." I meet his eyes, letting him see what lurks beneath my own surface. "I fear being the hero."

A myriad of emotions flickers in his eyes—emotions that are as foreign to me as the whisper of his breath on my lips.

Like a tidal wave pulled toward his sandy shore, I press my lips to his. I don't even think as I invade his space. Cole stiffens, but he doesn't pull away. Maybe he's too shocked. A small part of me—one of pure longing—wants to believe his heart beats as frantically as mine.

He's not breathing or moving a muscle. I kiss him harder and tentatively reach up to cup his face. The moment my fingers graze the stubble on his cheeks, he pulls away. It's not a sudden move. He doesn't wrench away like the thought of kissing me repulses him—it's a subtle move, a slight tilt of his jaw, but he could have just as well smacked me. I feel dazed, disoriented.

"Don't," he says, his voice cold and detached.

Outside, the snow sails through the air.

Peaceful.

Soundless.

Cole stands up without another word and walks out, leaving me behind to swallow down the hurt lodged in my throat. The door clicks shut. I fall back onto the bed and dig my fingers into my eyeballs. "You stupid idiot. What the hell is wrong with you? Why the fuck did you do that?"

CHAPTER 16.
COLE

I'm not a vulnerable person. Even when I was a kid and I watched havoc rain down on my life every single hour, I held myself together.

Letting someone else into my headspace when it's like a wrecked fucking battlefield with debris and blood and horror, is not something I can do. Even when I was all for being with Allie, I couldn't let her in. She still doesn't know much about my past. Just the little tidbits I've shared when I was drunk and needed someone to talk to. There's never been a reason to tell the people around me. Mom knows, and she's the only person who needs to know. She witnessed most of it, after all.

She told Blaise's dad, who most definitely told his son, maybe as a heads up on having a fucked-up stepbrother, going on the words he threw at me at the cabin. I need to lower my walls down and let people in.

Why? What good does that do to let others see my different shades of messy bullshit? For them to know everything my own piece-of-shit father did to me?

The thought alone has my leg itchy, making me shift uncomfortably in my seat while I drive us home from the airport in the middle of the night.

Blaise is the passenger for once – he usually sits in the back – and Mia is asleep in the backseat, with a blanket wrapped around her that her ever-loving boyfriend threw over her. He cares about her, that much is obvious, and it fucking annoys me. And it annoys me that it annoys me.

I want to break his hands when he touches her. When he kisses her, I'll know it's the same set of lips that softly brushed mine before I took too long to pull back and got the fuck away from him.

My fingers tighten on the wheel when he glances over his shoulder to check on her, then sighs and slouches in the seat. His eyes go to his phone screen, lighting up the contours of his face, and when he flicks his eyes to me, I quickly look away.

Sebastian Paul plays on the radio, filling the intense, awkward silence – but it isn't drowning out the fucking thoughts in my head. The voices. The taunting. The fucking—

"Did Allie really steal your sweater?"

I glance at him. "Yeah," I reply, rapidly tapping my forefinger on the wheel. "She sprayed her perfume all over my clothes too."

He flattens his lips in an attempt to stop himself from laughing, and I shake my head, rolling my eyes as I give the road my attention.

"Stop talking to me like we're friends," I say. "What goes on between me and Allie has nothing to do with you."

"I asked if she stole your sweater. Calm the fuck down."

Maybe if I crash, he'll die, and I'll be free of him.

I stare at the possibilities, all the trees I pass by, the signposts that'll tear the car in half if I smash into them fast enough.

A few minutes later, he talks again. "She's kinda nuts, ain't she?"

I feel my right eye twitch.

Another minute. "She must be nuts if she put up with you for two years."

He laughs at my lack of a response, my eyes flicking to him, my gaze on his smiling mouth. He has a dimple, and it's a deep one too. Why have I never noticed that before? He stops laughing, leans his head back, closes his eyes with his throat elongated.

My mouth starts to water, and I gulp and watch the road, speeding up a little as I increase the volume of the song.

The atmosphere feels like it's shifting. I hate him, he hates me, but something is different. We had a truce, of sorts, but it was awkward for me to pretend. Sure, it was good to be normal for a day, but we aren't normal.

Stepbrothers aren't supposed to know what their cocks feel like in each other's palms. It's not normal for me to know how tight Blaise's throat strangled my cock when he—

I shift position before Blaise notices me getting hard over a stupid memory of him kneeling before me.

It reminds me of the two times I wore my mask and could be the real me, the version I want to be, and I'm smashed with a bag of jealousy. Because he doesn't know it was me – who else has he been fucking around with?

After what's happened between us on this trip, the obvious shift that's confusing the shit out of me, will he still engage with the unidentified man?

"I need to get gas," I say into the silence, turning off the freeway.

When we reach home and climb out of the car, I try not to look at Blaise wrapping his arms around Mia, trying to heat her up while I open the trunk for our things. She buries her head into his chest, and I narrow my eyes, watching him kiss the top of her head, his eyes dragging to me.

I look away quickly, toss all the luggage on the ground, and light a cigarette. My phone has been going nuts for the past hour. The group chat. And I have a message from Samson and Keith.

Samson: J is pissed. He got kicked off the team!!

Keith: Woah, dude, really? Blaise is replacing
him? You need to fix this.

There are multiple messages from my friends going in on me,
telling me to deal with him and make sure he's not physically
able to play. They want me to beat him up, make him disappear,
or threaten him.

I exhale a cloud of smoke as I glance up at Blaise. He's
already looking at me while Mia holds his hand and sways into
him, half asleep.

I should give him the heads up.

Or at least tell him I'll deal with it.

Shutting off my screen, I pocket my phone, puffing the rest of
my smoke until my mom and stepdad pull up in the driveway.

Mom stops me and places a hand on my cheek. "Are you
okay? You look tired, sweetheart."

I pull away from her touch. "I'm fine."

I hate when people touch me. Mom knows this.

Her lips press together and she turns away, shaking her head
when she reaches Blaise's dad. He glares over at me, like I'm
some sort of problem, and whispers something back to her.

Why do I put up with this shit?

I'm twenty. I'm old enough to move out and live my life.

But then I'd have no money, and I'm nearly done with
college. So fucking close, and I can get the fuck away from here
for good and not feel like I'm a delinquent or a burden.

"You're not fine," Blaise mutters under his breath as Mia
grabs her bags. "Walls, Cole. You need to bring them down."

"And you need to mind your fucking business."

His gaze searches me, his brows furrowing at my snappy
tone, before he too, shakes his head and walks away from me.

Mia grins at him at the entrance to the home I hate, and I turn
away when he leans down to kiss her.

There's a gasp as soon as I walk through the door. Mom is

covering her mouth and Blaise is dropping his bag on the floor and pushing Mia behind him.

Everything is destroyed. As if someone barged in here with bats and wrecked it all. The sofa looks like it's been ripped with a blade, and there're gashes down all the walls.

I frown and walk farther in, dodging Mom trying to grab my arm.

"Call the cops," I hear my stepdad say.

"Who would do this?" Mom cries.

Their voices fade as I make my way through the debris, seeing the kitchen demolished, the hallway splashed with red paint. Mom's nurse bag is emptied on the dining table, her pills crushed.

I take two steps at a time, stopping at the top when I see it's untouched up here. The rooms are fine. My room is fine. Only downstairs.

I hurry back down when I hear my mom sobbing, Blaise's dad on the phone to someone, and his insufferable son is still protecting Mia like someone is going to jump out and shoot at us.

"The house is clear upstairs."

"Do you think it was Malcolm?" Mom asks, mascara down her eyes, then she gasps again and rushes to the back window. "The family portraits are burned in the yard!"

Blaise sighs with a low chuckle. "This is messy."

My head snaps to him. "Do you think this is fucking funny?"

"Don't you two dare start arguing right now," Blaise's dad warns. "I don't think it was Malcolm."

Swallowing, my eyes are on my mom as she worries her bottom lip and looks around the destroyed room. "Can you think of anyone else who would do this?" she asks.

"I broke up with Allie," I tell her, shrugging. "She might've went crazy and—"

"I thought you said she had to go home for college assignments?" she interrupts, her brows knitting together. "You broke up with Allie?"

I stare at her, knowing she's just caught me out on a lie. But then I remember I'm fucking twenty and don't need to be schooled like a goddamn teenager. "We weren't getting along. You can't force me to stay in a relationship with her, Mom."

Blaise's dad tuts and shakes his head. "Typical. Are you even surprised, Rachel?"

I turn away from them and storm out the room, not taking a breath until I reach the top of the steps. My hands fist, and I wish I could punch Blaise's dad hard enough he becomes unrecognizable.

Blaise is following me. I can feel and hear his footsteps behind me. "Cole."

"Fuck off."

He grabs my shoulder, but I shrug him off and try to get to my room. My head is all over the place, a devil on my shoulder whispering shit that isn't true, and I think I might be sick.

I'm dizzy, and my chest feels tight.

"It might not have been your dad. You don't need to be scared."

I spin around, and he crashes into me, only staying on his feet when I snatch his throat and shove him into the wall beside my door. "What part of fuck off do you not understand? What are you doing?"

"He's not going to get you."

Grinding my teeth, my eyes burn as much as the pain in my chest. "You don't know that. And even if he does, it has nothing to do with you." I let go of him and stand back. "Stay in your lane, Blaise. You don't fucking belong in mine. Stop touching me. Stop coming near me. If you do it again, I'll choke you."

I slam the bedroom door behind me, leaving him in the hallway, my vision blurring even more. My eyes zero in on my bed, and the inner child in me screams to hide.

Sliding under the bed, I try to control my breathing as I close my eyes. He's not here; my dad isn't coming for me.

He won't.

I feel a tingling sensation at my toes and fingertips, and I screw my eyes shut tighter and try to stop hyperventilating at the thought of him barging into my room and dragging me from under my bed.

He'll hurt me.

He'll hurt Mom.

I need to stay quiet.

If I stay silent, and not move, or cry, he won't know I'm here. My leg aches, and I hold my side. Memories are ruining me.

My phone buzzes, pulling me from my panic momentarily when I realize it's my burner phone. I pull it out and see the screen.

Blaise: I'm home now.

My eyes glaze over with rage. How fucking dare he fuck around with me on the trip, then hop back into this shit?

He can't fuck around with me, with my head, then expect to go home and move on to this masked man who degrades him, makes him run and submit.

My chest tightens, but in a different way. My anger is there, but it's forming into spiteful jealousy, and I stop hyperventilating like I'm about to pass out.

I crush my teeth together as I type back a location and time, knowing fine fucking well I won't be meeting him there.

CHAPTER 17
BLAISE

W hy do I even bother when all he does is turn me away? More importantly, why do I even care? Why do I want to storm back to his room and hurt him like he hurts me? So many fucking questions without answers.

I drive my fist into the wall, but the pain barely touches the rising anger inside me. Is that what this is? Anger? I don't fucking know.

"Are you okay, Blaise?" Rachel asks as I thunder down the stairs.

I storm past, biting back the clogging sensation rising inside me. My chest feels too small to contain whatever shit this is. Is it supposed to hurt like this? To be this hard to breathe? I emerge into the afternoon air and pause outside the front door, trying to inhale a ragged breath, but it catches in my throat. The backs of my eyes burn. Before I know what the hell is going on, my chin wobbles, so I crouch down and fist my short hair until my scalp prickles. The urge is there to scream, but I squeeze my eyes shut instead. Is life always like this? Polar opposites? First, I felt nothing, and now this...tumultuous roar in my head? The pain becomes almost unbearable, and I punch my skull.

What do I want?

Did I want Cole to let me in? To trust me and stop looking at me like he hates me? Or do I want to stop feeling and return to the emotionless, bored shell I was before he came into the picture?

What's wrong with me? Why the fuck do I let him affect me like this? No one should have this control over me, let alone my own stepbrother.

I punch my head again before shooting to my feet and walking down the street without direction. Well, that's not true. I wipe tears from my eyes and dig my phone out of my pocket. Cole texted me an address and a time.

Gritting my teeth, I crush the phone in my hand and glance at the setting sun in the distance. A myriad of orange, pink, and purple streaks paint the sky. I shouldn't let him chase me again. Why the hell should I play his games? My thoughts drift, and I bury my hands in my pockets.

With my eyes on my scuffed Chucks, I walk with my head down, kicking up rocks. I wonder what he's doing now. Is he hiding under his bed again? I overheard his mom talking to my dad about it, who grumbled under his breath. It was the first time I wanted to bang my dad's head against the wall. But I didn't give it much thought back then. Dad was Dad, and I was used to his eye rolls and dismissive sighs. I never thought it was something…more.

After sliding my phone back out, I bring up Mia's number.

Music drifts through the open window of a red sedan as my steps slow. I press the phone to my head, watching it drive past.

Mia answers on the third ring. "Blaise, where did you go? You ran out of the house and…" Her voice drifts into the distance as I watch a bird dip sideways in the mild breeze. "Blaise?"

I hang up, then lower my phone by my side.

I feel nothing for Mia. In fact, I could break up with her now and not care. What do I make of that? On the one hand, it's safe. She can't hurt me by slamming doors in my face. No, this storm inside me belongs solely to my infuriating stepbrother, as if he has laid a damn claim on my emotions.

I've lost my fucking compass.

Blowing out a tired sigh, I cut my gaze from the sky. Fuck

this. I'll give him one more fucking chance. Maybe it's better to hurt than feel nothing at all? If he wants to cut me wide open with his games of hide and seek, who am I to stop him? It's not like I have a choice.

I kick a rock before running a hand down my face. What am I doing?

My conflicting thoughts war the whole way there. Once I reach the abandoned train bridge, as per his instructions, I lean my elbows on the rusty railing and gaze out over the water. Undercurrents ripple the surface as the sun dips behind the fir trees in the distance.

The longer I wait, the more the burn in my chest intensifies. I clench my jaw and fix my gaze on the horizon.

He will show.

He *has* to show.

But he doesn't.

Soon, darkness settles over the river, and the silvery moon rises in the sky, reflecting off the glassy surface. In the distance, a chorus of bird caws echoes off the water. I dip my chin to my chest and breathe through the throb behind my ribcage.

He shut the door on me again.

I'm done.

So fucking done.

He wants me to back off? Fine. He can have his damn wish. I don't even know why the hell I tried to build a bridge in the first place. He confounds me.

"Blaise?" a voice pulls me from my thoughts, and I look up to see Jackson approach me on the bridge. "What are you doing here?" he asks.

His dark jeans hang low on his hips, and a sliver of skin shows when he scratches the back of his neck.

"I could ask you the same," I reply, straightening up and leaning an elbow against the railing.

He chuckles and shrugs as he steps closer. I'll admit that he's a good-looking guy, and his red backward cap adds to his allure.

The girls flock to him like flies to a pile of shit. But he's not Cole, and that thought pisses me the fuck off.

"I got kicked off the football team," he says, leaning beside me against the railing. "My dad didn't take the news well." He peers at me sideways, and I make no secret of studying his face. Why the fuck am I so hung up on Cole? I feel nothing for Mia and can't even muster a spark of interest in Jackson.

"It's fine," he says, looking out across the water.

"You can punch me if you want," I reply, and he looks back at me. "It might make you feel better."

We stare at each other for a beat, and then he chuckles.

"Why are you here?" he asks.

"I'm here for the birdsong," I joke as he turns back to face the water. He's smiling now, and I don't know what to make of the look he tosses my way.

"Cole hates you, huh?"

My shackles rise at his question, but I keep my face neutral as I shrug and cross my arms. "It's not a secret."

"Secrets," he muses, lifting a brow before he straightens up and inches closer. I can't read him. Alarm bells blare, and I watch him pull his phone from his pocket. The shrill dial tone soon cuts through the birdsong in the distance, and my eyes widen when Cole's voice drifts through the speaker.

"Jackson?"

"Hey, man. What are you doing?"

Cole sounds like he's talking around a mouthful of food. "Watching TV."

"Yeah? I caught a rabbit."

"What the fuck are you talking about?"

Jackson grabs my neck and jostles me. "Say hi to your brother, Blaise."

Chuckling, I shove him away, but I'm not amused. Not even a little.

"Hear that?" Jackson asks Cole. "Let Blaise's dad know he

might be home after curfew." Then he hangs up before Cole can reply and shoves the phone into his pocket.

My mouth falls open, and I blink at him.

"You can thank me later." Leaning back against the railing, he kicks his foot up behind him.

"Thank you for what?"

"Now your parents won't worry about you," he replies with a shrug, but I don't miss the note of amusement in his tone. "What's up with you and Mia?"

With a frown, I bend down to pick up a stray rock. "What do you mean?" I pull my arm back and send the rock flying.

"Are you solid?"

"Solid?"

A warm breeze teases the hairs at my nape. The temperature is dropping rapidly now that the night is drawing in. I haven't even checked the time. Overhead, stars twinkle, and crickets sing in the tall grass.

I freeze when Jackson corners me against the railing and puts his hand on my bulge.

What the—

"I like you, Blaise."

My brain is slow to catch up. What does he think he's doing?

I grab his wrist and remove it from my soft dick. "Don't ever touch me again."

Skin crawling, I suppress a shiver.

Jackson laughs under his breath, unperturbed by my icy stare. "Solid…I get it. Worth a shot, though."

When I get home, it's late—much later than I intended. The house is quiet, and the lights are out.

After Jackson left, I dug my phone out of my pocket. Cole tried to ring me twice, but didn't leave a voice message. I stared at the missed call notifications for a long time, cursing myself for wondering why he tried to contact me after slamming the bedroom door in my face. It couldn't be because of Jackson, right? I squashed that thought. Cole hates me. My dad most likely asked him to check up on me, like he does sometimes, much to Cole's annoyance.

I'm old enough to stay out all night if I want to, but my dad and stepmom still like to know where I am.

I bypass my bedroom and walk on light feet to Cole's room, carefully avoiding the creaky floorboards. It's not as easy now that I'm older and pack a lot more muscle.

My brain screams at me to turn back, but like an addict on crack, I crave one more hit. Just one.

I pause outside his bedroom door and press my ear to the wood. It's quiet on the other side. I should hope so; it's in the dead of night.

Cole's room is dark when the door creaks open. My heart pounds and sweat clings to my nape. Isn't it funny how he sets me alight like this?

I pause at the threshold, seeing his sleeping form on the bed. Seconds pass while I listen to his breathing. Each soft exhale calms the storm.

Before I can change my mind, I walk deeper into the room. Just one more hit. One more taste.

Pausing at his bedside, I sweep my eyes over the muscles in his back. The quilt pools at his narrow waist, low enough to reveal the top of his boxers. I step closer and pause. Something sticks out from under the bed. Frowning, I crouch down to pull it out.

It's Cole's bag, and it's unzipped.

Swallowing, I remove the mask and turn it over in my hands. It looks grotesque in the dark, and a chill slithers down my spine when I recall Cole chasing me—the sheer thrill of his pounding footsteps, every ragged breath that escaped my lungs.

I trail my thumb over the crack, and my lips curve. Cole's a sneaky little fucker. What is it about this mask that allows him to hide from himself?

Intrigue wins out, and I slide it on before rising to my feet. Cole is still on his front, with his arms beneath the pillow. My breaths puff against the plastic as I watch him. It must be nice to enjoy the reprieve dreams allow. Meanwhile, I've spent the night haunted by his cruel words and clinging to some elusive hope that he would seek me out.

I hover with my hand inches from his shoulder blade before trailing my fingers over his warm skin.

Fuck me...

I hold my breath.

His muscles ripple beneath my hand, and he mumbles something unintelligible.

I wait until his breaths deepen, and then I glide my fingers higher and wrap them around the back of his neck. His pulse thrums and my cock takes notice.

I like how vulnerable he feels and how easy it would be to snap his neck. For once, he can't hurt me, not unless I allow him to. My fingers twitch on his skin when I imagine pinning him down and making him regret shutting me out.

I bet he would sing a different tune then.

Cole sleeps like the dead, so shifting him onto his back and removing the quilt is surprisingly easy. Maybe he's so used to sleeping beside someone that he's no stranger to...

No, I squash that thought. The thought of him with Allie or anyone else makes me see red.

His dark hair falls over his brow, so I brush it away and stroke his jaw. My fingers drag over the scratch of his stubble, and I bite back a pained groan. I can't stop touching him or marveling at how perfect he is beneath all that fear and anger, which he wields like sharp weapons to keep others at a safe distance. My heart pounds harder when I wrap my fingers around his throat. The urge is there to steal the last breath from his lips. Maybe then he'd wake up and fight me. I squeeze lightly, careful not to wake him.

His heartbeat kicks up, and I tilt my head, watching him through the holes in the mask. "You like to hide, brother?" I release his throat. "You think I won't find you?"

Fuck...

I study his mussed hair and the expanse of his muscular chest. My eyes have adjusted to the darkness. If anything, the shadows cling to his skin like they're a part of him.

Pressing my hands into the mattress, I bring my face close to his—close enough that my breath would skim his parted lips if it weren't for the mask.

His pulse flutters in his neck, and his eyes move behind his eyelids. What is he dreaming about?

I wet my lips and trail my gaze over the expanse of his chest before pausing on the bulge inside his boxers. Cole is big, but I already knew that.

My mouth waters at the memory of his swollen dick.

No, Blaise.

Don't fucking do it.

I stare at his cock hidden under a thin layer of black. My teeth grind together, and I swallow. He'd kill me if he knew I was here, so why does the thought of touching him without his knowledge stir the shadows?

Fuck it.

My heart hammers harder as I pull his underwear halfway down his thighs to reveal his soft cock.

After one final look at his face to ensure he's still asleep, I palm him and tug the length while holding my breath. It doesn't take long for him to grow hard, his hips chasing my touch.

I love the feel of his dick in my hand. It's bigger than mine, but not by much. His eyes move rapidly beneath his lids as I stroke his length until he hovers right at the edge. I keep him there, suspended, swiping my thumb through a bead of precum.

His chest expands on a ragged inhale, and he fists the sheets as he cranes his neck. Is he dreaming about me?

I rip the mask off, toss it to the floor, and take him in my mouth.

The moment my lips stretch around his dick, his hips shoot off the mattress, and his cum fills my mouth. I swallow every drop, my heart pounding so hard that I'm growing dizzy.

When his breathing evens out, I suck him down one final time.

Even now, as he throws an arm over his eyes, I wish he would look at me. But he's asleep, and I stole a part of him like a thief in the night.

I straighten up and trace my thumb over his mouth.

My heart swells as I whisper, "One day, you'll beg me to kiss these perfect lips, big brother."

CHAPTER 18.
COLE

J ackson doesn't answer on the fifth ring, and Blaise isn't replying to my anonymous text. I arranged to meet up last night—I ghosted him, expecting to hear him throwing open the front door and stomping up the stairs, but it's now the next morning, and he isn't in his room. It was supposed to piss him off, some payback for thinking he "knows" me so well. For thinking I need his help or reassurance over my dad or everything else going on.

He doesn't have a place in my life. He's the fucking poisonous stepbrother I was given, the world's favor for surviving Malcolm Carter.

Who does he think he is to not reply to me now? He's not even gracing my masked self with a reply, and it enrages me.

I'm getting fucking annoyed, with a hint of...something else.

My cheek hurts, and I think Blaise nearly cracked a tooth when he hit me, the fucking asshole. Maybe ghosting him as the masked man was a bad idea?

On the eighth attempt to call Jackson and getting nothing, I shoot him a text asking where he is, and if he's with Blaise.

My lungs halt when he replies with a winking emoji.

A fucking wink emoji.

The fuck?

Does he have Blaise on his knees right now, fucking his face and he's enjoying it? Maybe Jackson lets Blaise kiss him. After all, I pulled away.

Is this his version of payback?

Thump. Thump. Thump.

Jackson has said multiple times that he loves nothing more than to fuck his cock into a tight hole, preferably the back one. Blaise wouldn't let him do that to him, would he?

Thump, thump, thump, thump, thump, thump.

I stare at the ridiculous response while my hands fail to stop shaking, the roaring in my ears drowning out anything around me. What does it mean? I send a few question marks, waiting and waiting and fucking waiting, but as fifteen minutes fly by, he ignores me. Instead of being anonymous in my burner, I pull up Blaise's contact on my normal phone and type, my heart pounding faster than I care to admit as I pace the floor.

> Me: Where the fuck are you?

I'm in two states of unsureness. One side, Blaise obviously likes cock and so does Jackson. I know, from previous conversation, that Jackson thinks Blaise is hot and would fuck him. But Blaise wouldn't go near him, right?

Maybe with me, he's just exploring the basics and seeing if it's something he's actually into before he fucks off to someone he can really...

I grind my teeth to dust and drive my foot into my door, making it slam shut with a bang.

But Jackson just got kicked off the team so Blaise could slide in. What if he hurts him? He's capable of lashing out on him.

He's also capable of setting him up and leading him into a fucking murder house with all my friends waiting with bats. They won't grant him any mercy—they'll probably record it all and post it all over social media with their faces covered and Blaise all busted up and bloodied on the floor.

Fuck.

I quickly shower, pull on clothes, and check my burner phone

one last time before ditching it in my dresser drawer and packing my bag.

Still nothing from Blaise or Jackson. Samson doesn't answer, and there's nothing posted online. The group chat is silent too.

I huff as I bring up a contact I refuse to save in my phone. She left when Blaise told her to leave after seeing the house in ruins.

It rings four times before it stops. "Cole?"

"Mia," I greet, giving her a tone like I didn't just spend a week with her at close proximity. "Is Blaise with you?"

"No," she whispers, a door closing in the background. "I'm with Allie. She's been a mess since—"

"Where's Blaise?"

She's quiet for a few seconds. "That's why you've called?" Mia couldn't sound more defeated if she tried. "I thought..." she trails off into silence.

Closing my eyes, I pinch the bridge of my nose. "Why else would I call you? Do you know where he is or not?"

"No, he hasn't replied to any of my messages or calls. Do you need help finding him? I can drive over and pick you up?"

My jaw clenches as I shake my head. "Let me know if you hear from him."

I cut the call before she can say anything else. I don't really know what her deal is with me all of a sudden, and it's frustrating. She's my ex's friend, surely, there's a rule to stay away from the other's ex? Maybe if I tell Allie, she'll back off and leave me the fuck alone. Then my ex might want to know why she out of the blue wants my cock, and she'd believe Mia's warped memory of that night over me and I'd be labeled as a cheat and she'd make my life hell.

Maybe I should just fuck her. I'll make it hurt and bruise her inner thighs so she never looks in my direction again. Not only will it make her scared of me, but it'll piss Blaise off and hopefully Allie will stop blowing up my phone with drunken voicemails. She'd hate me too, and that's fine.

It's such a great plan that I contemplate calling Mia back to sneak away from my ex. It'll be a fucking nightmare for her, but worth it.

I know for a fact if I told Mia to get on her knees, she would in a heartbeat, and that's concerning considering she has never been like that with me.

I think for a second about all the implications of those actions. One, I don't have any attraction to her. I doubt I'd even get hard. And she might like it rough and want me more. If she told Allie... I shiver at the thought of that bomb dropping and all the evil things Allie would do to me.

Nah, I won't fuck her. She's not my type and she's clingy and annoying.

And Mia belongs to Blaise.

I reject her incoming call and leave the room.

Reaching downstairs, I pause in the entrance of the sitting room, seeing my mom crying into Blaise's dad's chest. My bag slides down my arm, dropping it on the ground. The heavy chains, mask, and hoodie I put in clank on the laminate, where I leave it and walk to my mom.

"Are you okay?" I ask, my voice soft.

Ignoring me, she buries her head into his chest more.

My stepdad glares at me. "Can you not leave your mother alone for five minutes? She's obviously upset, boy. None of this would even be happening if it wasn't for you."

I narrow my eyes. "How the fuck is this my fault?" I gesture to the wrecked surroundings, most of which my mom has cleaned up. "I didn't do this."

"Same blood," he snarls.

I laugh, because it's the same tune from him every damn day. "When I leave, I hope you know I'll be kicking your ass."

Mom snaps her head in my direction. "That's enough! Get out!"

I want to tell her to fuck off too, but I won't.

Mom will be upset and that's why she's shouting at me. She's been through enough without me making things even worse as usual. So I do as I'm told and leave, throwing myself behind the wheel of my car and starting the engine.

I pause when I see a text popping up on my screen.

> Jackson: Does bro code still count if I fuck your brother? If not, then my bad, dude. He wanted it and I'm nothing but a gentleman who has needs.

At the same time as my entire body seizing, I glance up when I sense movement, seeing Blaise with his hood up, hurrying his steps down the driveway, not sparing a look at my car to see if I'm in it before he vanishes down the road.

I slump in the seat and chew my lip. He's not dead, and he's not with Jackson like I thought. He was in the house all this time, so I have no reason to feel like I'm on the verge of being sick, right? Am I just losing my mind?

My phone vibrates again, and I see a text from Allie, asking to meet up to talk. She wants to be friends.

Nope.

I block her and turn my engine off, staying here until the sun goes down and my eyes are heavy. I only leave the car after watching Mia and Blaise get out of her car and rush into the house.

SOAP LATHERS ON MY CHEST, the music from my phone drowning out my surroundings. It vibrates, interrupting the song for a second, but I ignore whoever it is and stay under the water.

My head is spinning. I think the lack of sleep over the past few days, and being pissed off and ignoring all of Blaise's messages to his stalker, and pretending he doesn't exist in the house, is all starting to get to me.

I went to practice, and sure enough, Blaise was there, standing right in the spot Jackson usually is. My friend did show up, and I caught him whispering something to Blaise before laughing and going to the stands.

As if they were friends.

Or more.

The bathroom door opens – I thought I locked it?

Thinking Blaise will pop his head in, I'm mistaken when Mia slips inside and closes it behind her.

I narrow my eyes and tilt my head. "What do you want?"

Thankfully, the frosted, steamed-up glass hides my junk. Not that she's caring since she's pulling off her shirt and unbuttoning her pants.

I hesitate. "The fuck are you doing?"

"Shut up," she retorts. "You're starting to annoy me, Cole."

I raise a brow and back away when she slides the shower screen over, stepping into the steam completely naked. "Are you still going to pretend?"

"If you don't leave, I'll tell Allie and Blaise you keep throwing yourself at me. It's pathetic." I keep my eyes on her face, refusing to look down at her body. "Mia. Whatever it is you think is going on, you need to stop."

"I had to take a Plan B, then get checked for STDs, and you still think this is me throwing myself at you? Why are you pretending nothing happened that night?"

When she comes closer, rage hits me, and I snatch her throat, slamming her into the tiles. She gasps, her cheeks going bright red, but then her eyes widen when they slide to the side.

"Blaise," she breathes.

I turn, keeping her in place still, to see him closing the door behind him and locking it. His eyes are snapping back and forth between me and my hand on Mia's throat.

My grip tightens, feeling her pulse racing faster now that her boyfriend is here, her boyfriend, catching her in the act that isn't an act but definitely looks like it.

Blaise's attention isn't on her at all, but me, his nostrils flaring. "What the fuck is going on in here?"

"It's... It's not what it looks like," Mia cries, gasping and clawing at my wrist. I release her and step back. "We were just talking."

Stepping forward, Blaise glances down at my cock, that thickens from his presence, painting me potentially guilty for trying to fuck his girl. Backing away from her more, I put myself under the sprays of warm water. "Get out," I tell them both, giving them my back and bare ass. "I'm trying to shower."

"Kneel."

I freeze as I hear clothes hit the tiled floor. His shirt and pants are in my peripheral. Briefs next. Fuck, what is he doing?

Mia hesitates. "Right here? You want me to blow you in front of Cole?"

Glancing over my shoulder, I see him shake his head slowly, a glint of something in his eyes. "Kneel. I won't repeat myself, Mia."

Her eyes flicker between us as she lowers to her knees, but I'm trying not to look at Blaise naked. I've obviously seen him before, but I can't help my body's reaction. I'm getting solid, and my heart races in my chest.

"So beautiful," Blaise says, and my jaw tenses at the way he looks at her. He glances over at me. "My girlfriend looks good on her knees, right?"

I turn to face him again, not bothering to cover my junk. "What the fuck are you doing?"

"You want her? Go, have her. Right now."

I roll my eyes.

"Blaise..." Mia goes to stand up, but Blaise holds her in place by the shoulder.

"Stay the fuck down."

"What are you doing, man?" I ask again, both confused and...something else at the way he's trying to dominate the situation.

"You're hard," Blaise says, smirking as he looks down at my

stiff dick. He takes Mia's jaw, squeezing to open it. "Suck him," he orders.

Her eyes widen.

I step away, but he grabs my throat and tugs me back. My cock jumps, hitting Mia's cheek, and I struggle to keep my groan in when Blaise lets go of my throat and wraps his fingers around my cock, dragging the swollen head across his girlfriend's lips.

"Open up," Blaise coos. "Make him feel good like the little whore you are."

I don't fight it. My eyes close as Mia's tongue slips out and strokes the underside of my length, hesitant at first, but when she takes me into her mouth, my balls tighten. Blaise releases me, pushing her head so my tip hits the back of her throat and makes her gag.

"Keep going," Blaise demands, stepping back from us completely, watching Mia sucking me off and sliding her hands up my thighs.

It feels good, but the fact Blaise is watching drives me insane. I'm thickening with every suck and lick, and my hips meet each bob of her head.

I open my eyes, watching him watch us, looking painfully hard.

We keep our eyes locked as Mia gags and slurps and deepthroats me. The sensation rushing in my veins isn't from the blowjob, it's from the way Blaise is both pissed off and turned on.

Blaise groans deeply, coming closer to whisper in my ear while Mia's throat accommodates my cock. "How do my girlfriend's lips feel around your cock?"

I'm silent, because his voice and nearness and the smell on his fucking skin has my balls tingling, the head of my dick hitting the back of Mia's throat.

"We…" I stop, taking heavy breaths. "We shouldn't be doing this."

"Why?" Blaise asks, smacking Mia's ass so she screams

around my cock at the same time as fisting the hair at the back of my head and tugging so I'm gasping up to the ceiling. "Because my girlfriend is here, or because we're stepbrothers?"

Both. Neither.

Because there's an extra person here I don't want.

"Blaise," I whisper as Mia takes me deeper, swallowing around my thickness. "F-Fuck you."

"I think you'd like that," he murmurs back. He brings his mouth to my ear, his voice drowned out by the water so Mia can't hear. "I think you'd love it if I was the one on my knees, taking your cock in my mouth, sucking you dry like I did the other night while you slept."

My brows knit together. I thought that was a dream?

"Mia," Blaise snaps, pulling away from me and yanking his girlfriend off my cock and onto her feet. "Bend over."

She does as she's told, and without direction, or any refusal from me, she takes my cock back into her mouth. Forced breaths leave me with each suck, the way her warm tongue runs up the underside and around the crown, taking me deep.

"Fuck," I mouth breathlessly, needing more. I grab her hair and thrust my hips, fucking her throat while he watches.

"Does this make you mad?" I ask, gritting my teeth as I thrust harder. "Watching me do this to your girl? Hearing her choke and gag and cry while she pleases me?"

Blaise's jaw tics, and he licks his lip. "Hmm," is his only reply.

He fists his dick and strokes it, coming up behind her. "Have you ever fucked an ass before, Cole?" he asks as he pushes his thumb against Mia's back hole, making her moan. "It's so fucking tight, it sometimes feels like your dick will get stuck."

Spitting on her ass, he fingers her there, forcing two, three fingers in, causing Mia to grab my thighs and sink her nails into my skin. The bite of pain makes me harder, especially when Blaise grins at me like a psychopath.

"I'll make it hurt," he says, pulling his fingers out and replacing them with his dick.

He doesn't give her a chance to get used to it—maybe because he does this all the time—fucking her ass like he's on a mission and forcing her on my dick.

She moans my name around my cock, and I see the way everything snaps behind Blaise's eyes. He grits his teeth and pounds into her tight ass faster, the slapping of skin filling the bathroom, louder than the music still playing from my phone.

My stepbrother is mad, really fucking mad.

Good.

I hope he hates how good his girlfriend makes me feel. I hope, when he was standing at the bridge, waiting for his chase, that he felt betrayed by the masked stalker.

Someone he doesn't even know is me. It's a sharp reminder that Blaise doesn't give a shit about fucking around with more than one person. He'll mess around with me, fuck his pretty little girlfriend, and get chased down and forced upon by an unidentified person.

He doesn't care about anyone else but himself.

I thrust into Mia's mouth, attacking her throat, her nails digging into my thighs, tearing the skin. She's gagging, moaning, sucking, slurping on my dick while Blaise keeps fucking her ass and smacking her cheek until it's red and raw. Mia's hand slides down my leg, and I tense everywhere, waiting for her reaction when her fingers feel the destroyed skin I keep hidden with tattoos, but her eyes lift to me, as if she's silently telling me it's okay, and then she keeps going.

When I look up at Blaise, he's already watching me. He leans forward, dipping his hand down to Mia's pussy, and she whimpers around my cock as he shoves his fingers inside her, pulling them out to show me how sticky they are. "What do you think has my girlfriend so wet, me in her ass, or your dick in her throat?"

Blaise leans farther over Mia, bringing us closer together, and

I can see how dilated his pupils are, the neediness in his gaze. He's still fucking her back hole when I grab his jaw.

"Open," I order.

His mouth parts, and my balls tighten at the memory of the first time I had him. He groans around my fingers as I slide them between his lips, three fingertips pressing down on his tongue and teeth until he gags.

I push deeper, feeling his throat contract, his pupils dilating even more until they completely take over the green of his eyes.

"Suck," I whisper.

Mia sucks harder, the same time as Blaise's lips close around my three fingers and does as he's told.

While I thrust into Mia's mouth, her tongue curling around my cock, Blaise sucks on my fingers while fucking his girlfriend's ass. Each thrust from him knocks her into me, and I throw my head back on a moan as my balls pull tight and heat rushes up my thighs, barely able to stay steady.

"You'll taste my cum on her lips later," I whisper. "That's as close as you'll ever get to me again."

Mia's screaming around my dick, and I know her ass is gripping Blaise through her orgasm enough that he groans around my fingers and stills completely, his abs going taut as he spills every drop of cum into her hole. The knowledge is enough for me to grab Mia's hair to keep her still and find my own release.

I pull my fingers out of his mouth, freeing my cock from Mia's, and step back. Then step back again. And again. Blaise is still inside Mia, panting over her while watching me retreat. Until I'm out of the cubicle and grabbing a towel and my phone, making a quick exit from the bathroom.

CHAPTER 19.
BLAISE

When he opens the front door, Jackson looks surprised, but then he seems to shake himself off and steps back to let me in. Don't ask me why I'm here because I don't fucking know. We're not friends. This is the last place I should be, but I feel so…broken after what happened in the shower with Cole and Mia.

It's late, and I couldn't sleep. I needed to leave the house and couldn't think of anywhere to go. Jackson… Well, Jackson is the only guy I know, except for Cole, who is into other men. I haven't told my friends about my fucked-up emotions where Cole is concerned.

Jackson walks ahead, and I follow him upstairs to his bedroom. I've never been to the house he shares with a group of other college guys, but it looks like I expected—plain walls, a bed with navy sheets, and clothes strewn on the desk chair. He plops down on the mattress and watches me scan his room.

"Want to talk about it?"

I tense, glancing at him. Why the hell am I here? "I broke up with Mia."

His eyebrows shoot up, but he stays silent.

Shrugging, I walk over to his desk and pick up an empty can of pop to keep my hands busy. "She cheated on me."

"Is that really why you're here?"

I place it back down and lean back against the desk. Jackson studies me beneath his dark lashes, and I stare at my Vans. I should leave.

"Hey," he says, rising to his feet and walking up to me. Up close, he looks worried as he tilts his head to force me to look at him. "What happened?"

Wincing, I try to look away, but he invades my space and cups my chin. I'm not into Jackson like that, but a pang of loneliness strikes me as he drops his eyes to my lips. My heart thuds hard for all the wrong reasons. For once, I want to feel something real instead of this constant ache whenever Cole is nearby. The fury I felt in the bathroom when I saw him with my girlfriend is gone, and now I'm empty. I should have seen it coming. Mia wasn't subtle with her glances in his direction. Fuck, I'm not even upset about that. I couldn't give a flying fuck about Mia or her wandering hands, but Cole... How could he do that to me? I mean, it makes sense... He likes pussy, and I'm a fucking guy.

"You're okay," Jackson says, and I lift my gaze. He must see my inner turmoil because when I try to free my chin, he drops his lips to mine, and for a brief moment, time pauses. Soft fingers stroke my cheekbones as Jackson swipes his tongue across my lips. If it were Cole in his place, I'd open my mouth and heart. But it's not Cole. It'll never be Cole.

I pull my face away, and Jackson sighs with defeat.

"You're that into him, huh?"

I don't ask him who or what he means. My heart is too battered tonight.

Pushing away from me, Jackson walks over to his bed. "Come on," he says as he lies down and cushions his head with his arm. "Lie down with me." He draws his knee up and looks up at the ceiling. "I promise not to touch you."

I stare at him for a beat before chuckles vibrate my chest. I'm being stupid. Shaking my head, I rub my neck as I make my way over to the bed. I feel ridiculous now. Jackson and I aren't friends, so whatever this is...

"What?" he says when I hover by the bedside.

"This is weird, isn't it?"

His lips twitch. "What's weird? You coming over here in the dead of night, me kissing you, or you lying down beside me?" Amused, I slide my hands into my jeans pockets. "All of it."

"Yeah, well, I got kicked off the football team because of you. Consider this your olive branch." He pats the space again, and I crawl in beside him. We stare up at the ceiling as a car drives by outside. "Can I stay here tonight? I don't want to go home."

"Do I get a blowjob, at least?"

My chest tightens, but his eyes twinkle with mischief when I look over at him. This is a side to Jackson I've never seen before. "Relax, I'm messing with you," he says, gazing back up at the ceiling. "Go to sleep."

In the ensuing silence, I study his side profile. "Have you ever been in love with a guy?"

His eyes find mine again, and the mattress squeaks as he turns over on his side. Resting his chin on his palm, he gazes down at me. "I've had sex with guys."

"But have you been in love with one?"

"I don't think I've been in love with anyone," he replies, shrugging.

"Trust me, it's not all it's cracked up to be."

His eyes roam my face, and I fight the urge to squirm beneath all that intensity. He studies me as if I'm a curious specimen. "What's it like?"

"To be in love?"

He nods, and I sigh as I gaze up at the ceiling again. "It aches...right here." I place my hand on my chest and move it in a circle. "And I'm powerless to make it go away. I was curious at first, you know? I noticed him when I didn't notice anyone." I look at Jackson, at the stubble on his cheek and his dark hair. "I didn't know how to handle those emotions."

"What did you do?"

"Annoyed him mostly. I tried to get under his skin. Anything to make him notice me." I stop short of telling him that I drugged my stepbrother and made him fuck my girlfriend while his girl sucked me off. That feels like oversharing.

"Have you done anything with him?"

A trickle of unease travels down my spine, and I peer at Jackson. "Sexual?"

"Yeah."

"No," I lie, feeling oddly protective of Cole. "He won't let me close."

"Do you mind if I ask who the guy is who got you this worked up?"

Breaking eye contact, I stare back up at the ceiling. "It doesn't matter. He doesn't want me anyway."

"That's his loss." Jackson leans over me to switch off the bedside lamp before lying back down. My eyes are slow to adjust to the darkness. It's strange to be in someone else's bedroom and even stranger to smell another guy on the pillows, but I'm too exhausted to care. Within minutes, I'm out like a light.

JACKSON

Blaise sure knows how to sleep like the dead. It's almost ten in the morning, and he's still out cold. He must have been warm in the night because he's removed his T-shirt. Chuckling, I open my camera app and take a quick photograph of him shirtless in my bed. Cole will love this. Fuck me, Blaise makes this too easy. I mean, it would work better for me if he would let me kiss him or fuck him, but a photograph will do nicely.

While Blaise sleeps like a baby, I open my chat with Cole and type out a short message to go with the photograph. The moment I hit send, Blaise stirs, and the muscles shift enticingly in his tanned back as I put my phone on silent. No doubt Cole will blow up my phone with calls and messages soon.

"Fuck, what time is it?" Blaise asks in a sleepy, gruff voice as he lifts his head off the pillow. His dark hair is a crow's nest, and he has pillow streaks on his cheek. I can see what has Cole so worked up. Blaise is sinfully hot. How do I even know about their little dalliance? Well, Cole wasn't exactly subtle at the chase. Anyone could have walked by and seen him take advantage of Blaise. It just so happened I followed him, and the evidence is on my phone. I don't care what it takes or who I have to throw under the bus; I will get my spot back on the team. And in the meantime, why not play with them both? Have a bit of fun.

"It's ten," I reply, and Blaise looks at me, balanced on his elbows. I try not to make it obvious that I'm checking out the bulging muscles in his arms or the kinks in his dark hair at the nape of his neck. He looks freshly fucked.

"Shit… I should get going," he replies, but he makes no move to leave, and my smile grows when my phone vibrates on the nightstand.

Right on cue.

Turning over on my side, I flash Blaise my most charming smile—the one with a dimple and shit. Girls lose their panties every time it comes out to play, much like my cock. His eyes drop to my lips before he can stop it, but then he sits up and leans over to grab his T-shirt off the floor. He's more flighty than a damn virgin, and I find myself wondering if he's ever had a guy pound his ass so hard he couldn't walk the next day. I doubt it. Blaise likes to be in control, and so does that two-faced fucker Cole. No wonder they clash. Until one of them gives in, they'll continue skirting each other.

"Do you want some breakfast?" I ask as I climb out of bed and strip out of my clothes.

Blaise blinks at me, and I grab a towel from the dresser and toss it at his face before I collect one for myself. "I'll catch a quick shower, and then you can have one after me." I don't wait for his response as I enter the bathroom and turn on the shower. Scrubbing down, I soap up and rinse off before stepping out and tying a towel around my waist.

Blaise is where I left him, looking confused as hell. "The shower is all yours," I say, and he walks into the bathroom like an obedient puppy. I stop short of calling out, "Good boy," as the door shuts behind him.

Oh, I love a car crash. Any minute now, Cole will be over, and I can't wait to watch him flip his shit. With that thought in mind, I pull on a pair of jeans and leave them unzipped. Water droplets cover my chest, and my wet hair dampens my neck as hard knocks pound the front door.

This shit is too fucking good. Chuckling under my breath, I jog downstairs, cross the hallway to the front door, and pull it open. Cole looks up when I lean my forearm against the doorframe. "Well, this is unexpected." No sooner have the words left my mouth than his fist slams into my cheek. I've got to give it to him, he has a mean right hook.

"Where the fuck is he?" he seethes, trying to push past me, but I block the doorway.

"He's in the shower. Now fuck off home." Wiping blood from my busted lip, I smirk at him. "I have to say, he has a tight ass, and those sweet fucking moans—"

He goes to swing again, but I shove him away with such force he stumbles down the porch steps and only just manages to grab hold of the railing before he falls on his ass. Jumping to his feet, he storms back up and walks right into me, chest puffed up and all. "I'm gonna kill you, Jackson! You're fucking dead."

"Why are you so worked up?" I mock, squaring up with him. "Are you into your stepbrother?"

Blanching, he stumbles back. You would have thought I punched him. His face drains of color as he looks over my shoulder. My peppermint soap on Blaise's skin hits me before his voice cuts through the tension. "Cole? Why are you here? Is everything okay at home?"

My smirk grows, and Cole swallows as he looks between us. "Yeah…" he says, his voice scratchy. "Your dad is worried about you. He asked me to come and pick you up."

I move away from Blaise, and he sidesteps me while his Cole stares at me with a broken look I wish I could frame and put on my wall. Leaning my shoulder against the doorframe, I wink at him. Swinging around, he follows Blaise to the car, and I wait until the headlights disappear around the corner.

BLAISE

"Blaise... I know you're angry. I'm so sorry. I shouldn't have cheated on you with Cole, but...you were into it. Please, can we talk? Call me back."

Lowering the phone from my ear, I delete Mia's voice message, and then I remove her countless other ones. I don't care for her excuses. I'm done. Why did I even keep up the pretense for so long? I was never in love with her. She was nothing more than a wet hole, and she kept my father off my back. In fact, I thought she was okay, until I caught her in the shower with Cole. The image of them naked together won't fucking leave, and the fury that died down, rises back up when I glance at Cole's hand on the steering wheel. His cracked knuckles grip the steering wheel as though he has a vendetta against it. "What crawled up your ass?" I ask as I pocket my phone.

He snorts, and the sound makes me grit my teeth as I look out the window.

"Why did you do it?"

I swing my eyes back in his direction. "Do what?"

He looks like he's tasted something sour as his hands wring the steering wheel. "You know fucking well what I'm talking about."

Frowning, I stare at his side profile until he finally looks at me, and when those dark eyes lock on mine, my heart thuds hard. I cross my arms and say, "No, I don't. Why don't you fucking tell me what I've done. Enlighten me."

A muscle tics in his jaw, and he scoffs bitterly. "Why Jackson, of all guys?"

"Jackson?"

We drive past boarded-up shops, but the depressing view outside is the last thing I see when Cole slams his hand down on the steering wheel. "You fucked my friend, Blaise."

My mouth opens and closes, but then his words register, and a harsh laugh rips from my throat. I shake my head. "That's fucking rich coming from you. Have you forgotten I found you and Mia together in the shower yesterday."

"So, it was revenge? Is that it?" Sucking on his teeth, he nods. "You fucked Jackson to get back at me."

"Get over yourself," I growl. "I'm so over this."

"Over this?" he spits, but there's an undertone of insecurity in his voice. I know him too well—something he seems to forget.

"You're not into guys, Cole. I get it, okay? You've made your fucking point. You want me to stay away from you. Guess what? That also means you don't get to be jealous."

"I'm not jealo—"

"Shut up, Cole. I'm done with your excuses. I'm done chasing you and hurting because of you. You want me, Cole? I'm right here."

Breathing hard, he pulls over by the roadside, and the car idles in the silence.

"I'm here." My voice breaks. "I'm here, Cole…but you won't look at me." The ache in my chest is back, and now it's multiplied. I struggle to breathe when he stares out the windscreen. "I'm. Here."

When he stays quiet, I grind my teeth. *Please say something. Please look at me.*

Pushing open the door, I climb out.

Cole doesn't follow.

The car stays idling behind me as I kick up the dirt and swipe at my wet cheeks. One thing is becoming clear. I need to get over this stupid crush. Cole's made his point, and I need to claw my heart from my chest and burn it to fucking ashes. Maybe then I'll stop hurting.

CHAPTER 20
COLE

Blaise is still storming through the woods an hour later while I watch him, following, stalking, keeping my eyes on his shadowy form through my mask.

I hear the snap of branches, the muttered words under his breath, and my heart races the closer I get. If he keeps going forward, he'll reach the river. Our town isn't for miles – Jackson lives the farthest away of my friends. Ex friend. I might kill him if I see him again.

My knuckles burn, but I ignore them as I pull my hood up to hide my hair, inhaling the smoke as I slip my mask up to take a drag.

Nothing calms me.

Nothing but the thought of hurting him. Driving my fist into his face like I did with Jackson won't do shit for my temper, yelling at him will make me madder, so this is my next best option.

I'm silent on my feet, careful not to give myself away. Keeping the hoodie and mask in the trunk was a good idea. As soon as he slammed the car door and started walking, then slid into the trees, I let my rage win and I fell into my own little ruse of being the unidentified fucker who can't keep his hands off Blaise.

Adrenaline courses through my veins, the feeling of being so fucking twisted and careless and injected with motivation pushing me forward, making sure I don't lose him.

The outline of him stops, a slow glance over his shoulder in my direction, making me slink behind a thick tree.

"I know you're there," he calls out. "I'm not in the fucking mood for your shit."

He knows it's me or...?

My burner buzzes in my pocket, the faint glow giving my position away. I pull it out, seeing a message on the screen.

Make me forget about him, it reads, and I gulp down the lump in my throat, my hand shaking as I grit my teeth and turn off my screen.

So he wants to play dirty. Go from me to Jackson to this version of myself he doesn't know.

My eyes close as I inhale deeply.

Shoving my phone back into my pocket, I pick up a thick branch, moving from behind the tree to see him turning and running.

"Fuck," I blurt and shoot after him, gripping the branch in my hand and dodging smaller branches, nearly tripping over a fallen trunk.

I can hear him running.

I can hear him breathing heavily.

My cock is too fucking responsive to the chase. It's aching and hard and my balls need to be emptied, preferably down his throat like that first time.

Blaise goes left, jumping over an abandoned, burned-out car, letting out a chain of curse words as he hits the forest floor and pushes himself back to his feet.

I smirk to myself as I slow down, my lungs burning as my chest rises and falls, watching him hopping along and struggling to walk on his twisted ankle.

"Pathetic," I say under my breath.

"Who the fuck are you?" he says through gritted teeth, going onto his back and shuffling away from me, as if that'll stop me.

I tilt my head, lifting the branch and slamming it down on his sore ankle, making him shout out a "fuck" and grab at his foot.

I want to snap his neck. I want to drain every drop of his blood and blind him. To make him feel an ounce of betrayal I feel that he not only went to one of my best friends, but also decided it would be a good idea to have me, the masked guy with no name, chase him.

He's a fucking slut, and I mean nothing to him.

The anger drives me to swing the branch, grazing his cheek and slicing the skin. But before he can fight back, or even blurt some sort of retort, or register the injury, I rush for him, dropping a knee on his chest and forcing his head into the dirt by the throat.

I rob him of breath, cutting off his airways and making sure his lungs feel more suffocated than I've felt my entire life. I want it to hurt, to see him begging with his eyes.

With my free hand, I slide the black material from my pocket, ripped from my shirt, and shove him into the dirt more.

"You gonna fight me?" I mutter, dangling the material in front of him. Even with only the moon lighting up inside the woods, I can see the black of his pupils taking over the green, and my cock gets even harder as he tries to push me off.

I dig my thumb into his neck, and he lets out a painful, barely-there hiss before I yank him up by the throat. He doesn't do shit when I blindfold him with the material, or when I push him back down and slap his cheek hard enough to redden the skin.

Not needing to wait, I rip open his jeans and force my hand under his waistband, groaning under my breath when I feel the hard muscle waiting for me. I fist his cock, my pulse thrashing in my neck when he arches his back ever-so slightly. He wants the release, but hates that he does.

For someone who had his fun not hours ago, he's silently begging for my touch, especially when I free his cock completely and wrap my fingers around it, stroking him while he stays in the mud, his lips parting on little breaths.

Blaise whimpers when I stop touching him and undo the lace

of one of my sneakers. I pull one free and move to his side, grabbing his wrists to tie them together.

He'd be able to easily get out of this and fight me off, or at least pull off his blindfold, but I know he won't.

Sliding off my mask, my hoodie follows, and I drop them both on the ground beside him. I yank his pants off completely, then his briefs, and toss them aside, watching his cock pointing to the canopy of the trees, thick and long and fucking...

My mouth waters to taste the precum on the tip.

I've never put a dick in my mouth before, but I want to try it. I want to make Blaise feel good, yet hate himself for it. To devour each inch and feel my own dick beg for some sort of sensation.

I pull out my cigarettes and light one. "Do you smoke?" I say under my breath, keeping it deep and unidentifiable.

His chest heaves, not gracing me with a reply. That fucks me off more. I inhale deeply and hold the smoke in as I study him, half naked in the dirt, blindfolded and his wrists bound.

My dick loves the sight. I can't help but take it in my hand, freeing my cock and pumping the length of it in my palm. Fuck. It feels good. Watching him tremble with anticipation, his dick thickening, the cold air licking his dirty skin.

I go to him, stroking myself slowly with one hand and feeding my nicotine addiction with the other. I kneel between his legs, lick my lips, and observe him stiffening as I press the head of my cock against his, mixing our precum.

Absently, he moves his hips upwards, and my tip rubs the underside of his cock, which makes us both stop breathing. He does it again and again, until I start moving with him while I fill my lungs with toxic fumes and blow it at him in a cloud of smoke.

He hisses as I press the burning orange ember to his hip to stub it out and throw my cigarette into the roots of the forest floor. The pain doesn't put him off. Blaise's precum gathers at the tip again, and he flinches as I swipe it with my thumb.

Bringing the sticky substance to my face, I fight my anxiety of having one of my firsts by tasting it, slipping my thumb into my mouth and closing my lips, unable to stop the deep groan and the way my eyes close as if I've just tasted the best fucking meal of my life.

"Hmm." I lick at my lips, staring at his mouth, the parted lips and the anticipation for more. I lower my voice. "I think you taste good, but I need more than a teaser."

My nerves pick up when I fist his cock roughly, jerking him a few times, and push through the uneasiness as I take him into my mouth.

The explosion of different senses has me pausing around his thickness. I can taste him. Really taste him, as I swirl my tongue around his head, lapping up more of his precum as I work my hand on his length.

"Fuck," he moans, pushing his hips, forcing another inch into my mouth.

It's foreign, the feeling of doing this instead of being on the receiving end. I had no idea it would make me so painfully hard; I need to grab my own dick as I suck my stepbrother.

He keeps working his hips up, trying to take control even though he's beneath me, so I let go of his length and force my head down more, taking him to the back of my throat and making myself gag. But I do it again and again and again, until he's gasping for air and I'm choking on a dick for the first time in my life.

I can taste him leaking, and I swallow around his head and suck and lick and take more into my throat.

"Cole," he moans, and I pause.

I stop everything.

I don't even breathe, thinking I'm caught.

He chokes out another word, breathing heavily. "Let me… Fuck. Let me call you Cole."

My dick aches as I stare up at him, his little sounds turning me on more.

The idea hits me, and I pull my mouth away and turn

around, lying on my side as I tip him on his, so my cock is at his face and his at mine.

"Open," I order, as I perch on my elbow. Slapping my swollen crown against his cheek, I press it against his mouth. His lips part, and the warmth envelops my dick as he takes me in.

My eyes roll as he starts sucking slowly, licking at what he can until I lie down on my side and copy him. He whimpers around my dick as I suck on his.

Me and Blaise. On the forest floor and sucking each other's dicks. I kind of want his dad to find us, for him to see me fucking his son's throat. It'll teach him a lesson not to mess with me anymore, because I'd just fuck his spawn over and over.

But then again, if he did find us right now, sucking and licking and snapping our hips to make us both gag and choke, he'd know who I was and tell Blaise. I like being unknown right now. I can do what I want to Blaise and not worry about any consequences. I can comfortably grab at his ass cheeks and take him deep into my throat without worrying about my sexuality being questioned, or the fact I'm fully into my little stepbrother.

The thickness of him kind of robs me of air, needing to breathe through my nose, but that's okay. I can handle it.

My fingers dig into his ass, and my middle one accidentally pushes just beside his back hole. Blaise tenses all over and chokes around my dick that's buried to the hilt.

Fuck, I want to feel him do that again, so I tease around the rim, using the wetness of my saliva pouring from the corners of my mouth to soak my finger tip and keep curling around his hole.

He's moaning so loudly against my dick, and I'm close.

I pop his length out my mouth, filling my lungs as I watch my middle finger go around and around, his ass puckering and dying for attention. He flinches as I gather spit in my mouth and aim for his hole, making him moan again, even louder, and fuck me, I nearly come with the way his throat tightens.

Blaise stops sucking as I press the tip of my finger through the tight hole of his ass, his cock pulsing beside my face, dying for another mouth to fill.

For being with Jackson not long ago, he's tight. Really fucking tight. Unless he was the topper?

The thought pisses me off, and I shove my finger to the first knuckle and smirk at the way his muscles all bunch and his groan echoes around us.

I keep my finger there, pulsing it in bit by bit, gentle, slow thrusts as I take his cock back into my mouth and start sucking him off again.

I freeze as he grabs my hip. He must've gotten himself out of the shoelace, but instead of fighting me off, he's tugging my pants fully down to my thighs and matching the way I suck his dick.

We fall into a rhythm while I fuck his throat and finger his ass. He chokes, I choke. He gags, I gag. He thrusts, I thrust.

I nearly blow my load on his tongue as he copies me, not giving me any time to adjust as he thrusts a finger into my ass as he takes me deep into his throat.

I mutter a "fuck" against his dick and silently beg him to push his finger in more, to add another, to suck me harder. So I do it all to him. I pummel his ass with my middle finger, fast and hard, filling the woods with gasps and moans and curses until he tenses all over and explodes into my mouth without any warning.

I drink every drop like I'm a man possessed while he scrapes his teeth on my dick and keeps releasing. It's like coming makes him hornier, and he ravishes my dick, his saliva dripping onto my ass.

His dick pulses until it's spent, and I release it from my mouth and pull my finger free, gritting my teeth with how good his mouth feels. His tongue slides against each inch as he bobs his head.

Blaise pops my cock out of his mouth and replaces his finger with his tongue and...fuck.

Fuck, fuck, fuck.

His tongue slides around my rim and punches the tip into the tight hole, spreading my cheeks to open me for his mouth. He licks at me, forcing his tongue in more, and eats my ass while he adjusts our position. He drags me to my knees and licks and sucks at my ass from behind, until his hands find their way in front, one fisting my dick and the other grabbing my balls and massaging them.

I'm supposed to be the one in charge right now – he should be submitting to me. And now I'm on all fours with someone I claim to hate, who's devouring my ass while making me feel so many different things at once.

"Fuck, Blaise," I groan. "Keep going."

He listens, stroking me faster, massaging my balls while tongue-fucking me until I drop my head into the dirt and give in to my temptations. I let the orgasm wrap around my balls and shoot up my spine, to blur my vision and tighten my ass while my muscles tense all over, and I come like I've never released before.

Blaise cups the head of my dick while I pulse each drop out, burying my forehead into the branches beneath me until I'm completely spent.

Then his tongue vanishes, his touch too, and I turn and push him away, so he falls on his back. I go to hit him, because what else am I supposed to do? But I stop with my fist in the air as Blaise brings his cupped hand to his mouth and rubs it over his mouth, my cum dripping from his lips. "Mmmm," he hums.

I gulp, my mouth growing dry again as I watch him taste me. I love the sight, and it only pushes me to go to him again. Grabbing his jaw, I line our softening cocks together, thrusting against him even though we're far from getting hard again.

My mouth falls on his before I can even think about it, forcing my tongue into his mouth. Instead of refusing, Blaise lets me take his bottom lips between my teeth and rip the skin. He moves his hips up to rub our cocks together as I suck on his tongue, needing more.

I need so much more that I can't have.

He kisses me back, and it turns into a frenzy of tongues and lips and rubbing dicks. His hand flies up to fist the hair at the back of my head, devouring each other like he knows who I am.

He doesn't.

The thought makes me freeze.

Blaise isn't kissing me. He's kissing someone else.

I'm not Cole.

I sink my teeth into his lip one final time, making sure it hurts enough to make him pull away and wipe blood from his mouth.

Getting off him, I pull up my pants and grab the hoodie and mask, quickly sliding them on while Blaise lies there, panting, confused, hard again.

I shake my head at myself and pull out another cigarette, lifting the tree branch I dropped beside him. Blaise would be able to hold up against me in a fist fight. He's not a pussy. So the only way to end this is to swing the branch at his head and knock him out.

And I leave him in the woods for the second time, hating myself for not being able to be me.

As soon as I got that fucking message from Jackson, I ditched my mom's little speech about my anger and barged my way out the front door. I don't even remember driving to his place, or smashing my fist into his face, but fuck, I'm still mad.

I stare at the split skin on my knuckles, flexing my fingers to make the slices open more and feel the pain of the tearing.

There's mud under my nails, and on my knees and legs. I haven't showered yet since I got home. I'm lost in my own head again.

I slide out from under my bed and crack my neck side to side.

Blaise still isn't home. I wish I had stayed and confessed, then yelled at him some more for messing me around, but there's no point.

Because he isn't mine. Plus, I'm not attracted to him.

I laugh bitterly at myself and my denial. It's obvious now that I'm into Blaise, the taste of him on my tongue and the way I wanted more tonight is more than enough evidence. I've never had an orgasm like that. Not with Allie or anyone else I fucked around with.

I wanted more. I still do. But I'm just lost in my head about what this can all mean. It could fuck up my mom's life. It would be my fault again.

Even fucking Jackson knows, and he used it against me by...

My back hits the mattress as I drop and press my palms into my face. "Fuck," I blurt. "Fuck me."

My phone buzzes, and it takes me an entire two seconds to jump for it, seeing it's from an annoying existence.

Mia: Allie knows.

I want to reply and ask if she means Allie knows I sixty-nined her ex an hour ago, but her second message comes through.

Mia: I had to tell her. She was bound to find out eventually what was going on between us.

"What is it with this psycho?" I ask myself, deleting her message and awaiting the storm to blast through the front door. No doubt she'll make my life a living hell if she truly thinks I'd go there with Mia.

I mean, I kind of did? Not because I wanted her, but because it was the closest I could get to Blaise without any confused back and forth shit.

My phone rings, and I frown when I see it's an unknown number.

"Hello?"

There's a hiccup, and then a deep voice booms through the line. "Son!" my dad sings. "My boy! I have been trying to reach you for months!"

My breathing halts. I can feel his hands on me without needing to think about my past. Skin crawling, my stomach turns inside out just as my door opens. The burning in my leg hits me, and I feel the urge to hold my side.

Blaise limps in with his sore ankle, covered in mud, his eyes red, the gash on his cheek deeper than I thought. He stops in the middle of my room.

"What do you want, Dad?" I ask, and Blaise goes deathly pale.

"That asshole brother of yours has been hanging up on me for months." He throws something, and it smashes on the other side of the line. "He made me mad, son. Real fucking mad. You know what happens when I'm mad."

I clench my teeth together. "I didn't know," I say, because as much as I like to think of myself as a hard-ass, this fucker who is half my biology is the scariest man on the planet in my eyes.

He can destroy my entire life.

He can hurt me.

He'll take Mom and hurt her.

"There's a restraining order," I tell him. "You can't do anything."

Blaise doesn't move from his spot, watching me like a hawk, seeing the anger building behind my eyes. If he had just told me my dad had been calling, I could have figured something out. He's only pissed him off and potentially made this way harder for everyone involved. He'll stop at nothing.

"It's too late for any of that. Restraining order or not, you took your mother from me, and he tried to take you away from me too," he slurs, drunk off his ass. "I'm going to take you away from them all."

CHAPTER 21.
BLAISE

The look in Cole's eyes and the tremble in his hands when he lowers the phone scares me more than his silence. He's not looking at me, and I worry that I have lost him for good this time.

What if he won't talk to me? I've really screwed up.

Swallowing thickly, I wait for him to say something. Anything. My cheek stings, and bruises and mud cover every inch of me. In other words, I look like I have been through a war. Cole swallows hard and slides his fingers into his hair, and my battered heart aches. What do I say? *I'm sorry I kept your dad's phone calls from you? I didn't want to see you hurt like you are now? I tried to protect you?* Tears cling to his lashes as he begins to rock on the bed, fisting his hair so damn hard it's bound to hurt.

"Are you okay?" I ask, then wince. Of course, he's not. Nothing about this situation is okay. His father is out to hurt him and his family. Cole still carries the scars from years of abuse, and sure, he hides them well. But every now and then, the mask cracks and I get to see the real Cole.

I take a step toward him. "Cole?"

Hours ago, I was tied up, helpless, and turned on beyond belief by Cole's rough treatment, but now that side of him feels like a distant memory.

When he still doesn't reply, I crouch down in front of him, my heart thudding in the silence. I can't believe that, for once, I wish he would shout at me and throw me out of his room. I'm familiar with Cole's anger and cruel words, but this broken side of him feels as foreign as the lump in my throat or the urge to hold him. The last time I tried to reach him, he pulled away, and I was left feeling confused and hurt.

When did I become so...*soft?* The truth is that I don't know if I'm ready to suffer rejection so soon after our encounter in the forest. I want to hold him, but I'm...scared.

His dark eyes meet mine, swimming with tears that I know won't fall. Not yet, anyway.

"I should have told you about the phone calls," I blurt before I can stop myself, and he continues staring. "I understand that you're angry. Fuck, I would be, too, but please...just..." I reach out to take his hand but pull away and fist mine instead to stop myself from crossing boundaries that will see me crash and burn. "Say something...please."

Lowering his hands from his hair, he stares at his palms and cracked knuckles as though they belong to someone else. "Why?" he asks, his voice barely audible. "My dad... The phone calls."

"I wanted to protect you."

"Protect me," he replies, tasting the foreign words, with that blank look in his eyes. "Why?"

"Why what?" I ask, confused.

He's still not looking at me, transfixed by his cracked knuckles. He mumbles something I don't catch.

I can't hear him, so I lean in closer to catch his eyes. "Talk to me, Cole."

He stares at me for the longest time before he asks, "Why would you want to protect me?"

Is it that hard for him to believe someone could care for him? *Really* care for him? Searching his eyes, I muster up my courage to reach out and take his hand, interlacing our fingers. "I care about you, Cole."

Those dark eyes swim with emotions I wish I could decipher. He flicks his eyes to our fingers, and a crease forms between his brows as I trail my thumb over the top of his hand. I wish I could stay like this forever. Even this small connection with my stepbrother hurts in the best way possible, like the kiss of a blade at my throat. *Cut me open, Cole.* But then he says, "It makes no sense."

My thumb pauses, and he pulls his hand from mine before rising to his feet and walking past me to the bathroom. The door clicks shut behind me, and I stay crouching by his bed while listening to the shower turn on. Does he really think he's that unworthy of something good?

And what the hell is happening to me? I don't recognize myself. It wasn't that long ago I did everything to get underneath my stepbrother's skin—to be the villain in his fairytale.

When did I acquire a white horse and a beating heart?

Fuck me. Rising to my feet, I glance at the bathroom door, and my throat goes dry at the thought of him wet and naked. Fisting my hands at my sides, I fight my emotions. I want to break down the door and hurt him to get at what's hiding beneath his shell. Force him to take my biting kisses and rough touches. Instead, I unclench my hands and admit defeat. Cole needs space.

DISTRACTED, I stab a pasta shell on my plate, but it falls off. I try again, the fork crashing against the porcelain. Cole hasn't come down for dinner, and the silence at the table is stifling. My dad is silently stewing, and Rachel tries her damn hardest to take up as little room as possible when he gets into one of these moods. While he has never hurt her physically, like her ex-husband, he's a moody fucker, who'll take a jab at Cole's personality any chance he gets. I'm sick of it. I'm also sick of his mom trying to placate my father when he gets like this. Someone needs to stand up for Cole.

My dad gives me a questioning look over the rim of his wine glass. "What's wrong?"

Another piece of pasta falls off, and I toss the fork down. Fuck this. I'm restless and unable to stop replaying the moment when Cole pulled his hand from mine. How my heart sank like a rock. "Nothing is wrong."

He chews while watching me. Beside him, Cole's mom offers me a gentle smile, but it falls when Dad mutters, "Did Cole do something to you again? I swear that boy shows no respect in this household."

"Gavin," Cole's mom tries in a quiet voice, "I'm sure there's an expl—"

My father slams his hand down on the table, causing the wine glasses to rattle. "Stop making excuses for him." He nudges his chin to Cole's plate of food next to me. "You spent hours cooking this meal, and he refuses to come downstairs."

My lip curls as I stab another piece of pasta with enough aggression to cause loud clangs.

"It's okay," she says, eyes downcast. "He can eat it lat—"

"Stop making excuses for that boy!"

"Enough!" I bite out, fisting the fork in my hand. "That's fucking enough!"

Dad's eyes slowly skate in my direction, and I meet his glare dead-on. It's not the first time we've clashed like this over Cole, and it sure as hell won't be the last.

"Excuse me?" he asks, and I know I'm in trouble when he wipes his mouth with his napkin before tossing it onto the table.

"You heard me. Leave Cole alone. I'm sick and fucking tired of you treating him and your wife"—I tip my chin in her direction—"like shit."

I swear his eye twitches when he glares at me, but unlike the woman at his side, I don't fear him. Cole's dad might have been physically abusive, but my dad won't win a 'husband-of-the-year award' any time soon either. Scooting my chair back, I rise to my feet and turn to leave but hesitate. Smiling at Cole's mom, I thank her for the meal, which I still haven't touched because of my complicated emotions where her son is concerned, and then make my way upstairs.

I pause outside his door, wondering if this is a good idea. It's not. None of this is a good idea. Why do I break myself open again and again on Cole's blade? Glancing past his door to mine, I debate walking away, but I can't get my feet to move no matter how tempting the thought is. I stay rooted in place with nothing but a thin piece of wood between me and the boy I can't get out of my fucking head.

My own stepbrother. My very *broken* stepbrother. My father would flay me alive if he knew how deep my emotions run for another man—his wife's son.

As my heart thuds, I push down on the handle, and the door creaks open with a soft click. I hold my breath as his navy walls and messy desk come into view. There's no sign of him. His bed is empty. Standing in the doorway, I stare at the creased bedsheets. Where is he? Did he leave the house? No, I would have heard him.

I drop my gaze to the space underneath his bed, my heart squeezing tight. It's the only place in the world where Cole feels safe when the nightmares and haunted memories crawl out from the shadows to torment him. Anyone else would think it's weird that a twenty-year-old man hides under his bed, but I get it.

Crossing the threshold, I shut the door behind me. His smell surrounds me—citrus and leather, as always. I breathe it in. I've never known a scent to calm me like this, and it gives me the courage to step closer to his bed. "Cole?" I ask, swallowing. "It's me…"

When there's no response, I briefly close my eyes as I try to steady my shaky breaths. Why am I here? As the seconds turn into minutes, I come up with a million reasons why I should walk out and leave him alone. *Fuck it.*

Before I can change my mind, I lower myself down and then crawl beneath the bed to find Cole on his back, staring at the slats. He doesn't acknowledge me as I lie beside him and try to go as unnoticeable as I can so that I don't spook him. I've been scared before, sure, but nothing like this, not even close. My heart beats so hard that I struggle to hear his soft breaths. His woodsy scent surrounds me while I think of a thousand things to say, yet come up short.

Thud.

Thud.

Thud.

"I never slept with Jackson," I admit in the ensuing silence.

Thud.

Thud.

"He tried, but...fuck..." I drag a hand down my face before lowering it back down dangerously close to Cole's fingers. "I..." My throat constricts, and I turn my head to look at him. His eyes stay locked on the bed. "All I could think about was you," I whisper. "I wished it was you."

When he shows no sign of listening, I sigh and look up at the slats. I guess it's a good thing he hasn't told me to leave—at least he's allowing me in his sacred space. That accounts for something, right? He could have told me to fuck off by now, but instead, he's letting me see this vulnerable side of him.

I'm torn from my thoughts when his calloused fingers slide through mine. He clasps my hand in his, and my breath catches. It's just something as innocent as hand holding, but my heart is clawing its way out of my chest. I can't breathe. I don't dare to move. Is this real life? Am I dreaming? Is he touching me?

"Cole?"

"Don't talk," he whispers, and I snap my lips shut.

Fuck me. Cole is holding my hand. My heart is too big for my chest. Every nerve ending in my body screams at me to pull him to me and kiss the living daylights out of him, to wrangle his demons and put a fucking end to his torment, but I don't move a muscle as I home in on the feel of his hand in mine. I've kissed and fucked and lost myself in others, but none of those experiences hold a candle to the electric connection between me and Cole.

Is he feeling it too, or is it just me?

He has to feel it, right? I can't be alone in this.

"I know you want me to stay silent, and I will...as soon as I get this off my chest." I swallow hard. "I need you to know, Cole, that I will never let anyone hurt you again." My head rolls on the hard floor, and I gaze at his side profile. "Your father will never come close to you or your mom again. I swear it."

He doesn't reply, but that's fine. I don't need him to. His hand in mine is enough for now. I'd live and die a thousand lifetimes to relive this moment, and if this is his only surrender, I'll take it.

"I'll protect you."

CHAPTER 22
COLE

Puddles scatter across the field as the rain falls. The coach has us running laps, so even though the air is bitter, and I'm soaked right through to the bone, the coldness is a treat to the heat pouring out of me.

Either that or the raging warmth twisting around my spine is from the glimpse of abs I keep seeing whenever Blaise uses his shirt to dry the rain from his face—it's an unintentional glance in his direction that I can't help but fall into. I'm more drawn to him than ever, and my entire body is aware of his proximity when our shoulders brush on the field.

I lost myself for a bit. Blaise stayed with me until our parents called us down to tell us they were going to go on another trip, just the two of them. They want a breather, away from us and life.

I stayed quiet and kept my eyes on the floor, while Blaise did all the talking. Asking where, when, how long, and if they think they can trust their sons not to blow the house up. He meant it in a laughing manner, but I didn't laugh. I didn't acknowledge a word. I dismissed myself and silently retreated back to my room and fell asleep.

I woke four times last night, and I could have sworn Blaise was there two of the times.

It's fucking confusing. The way I feel. It's messing with my head. I should hate him, want to smash his face in for being a pain in my ass since we met. But if I'm going to be honest with myself, in the least pitiful way, I never felt an ounce of peace under my bed until he joined me.

I didn't pull away when our palms pressed together, and my heart slowed to a healthy pace when our fingers entwined, and just... Fuck.

"Any slower and you'll stop, Carter."

I pick up speed since I'm falling behind, catching up with Keith and Samson. "Fuck, man," Samson gasps. "I feel like my lungs are dead."

"Mine are on fire," Keith replies.

"Pair of pussies," I throw in as I overtake them, dodging one of them trying to kick my ankles. I run backwards while giving them the middle finger, getting back into a steady pace as I turn around.

My hair sticks to my forehead as I round the benches and ignore all the bystanders—the usual girlfriends, boyfriends, and wannabe jocks enjoying the view while we nearly die from exhaustion.

It's been an hour, and Coach won't let us stop. It's punishment for the locker room getting trashed last night. It wasn't me, and I don't think it was any of my friends, since I would've heard about it on the group chat, so everyone speculates that it was Allie.

Apparently, she's made it publicly official that we broke up with some huge social media post about betrayal and heartbreak.

I was sent a few screenshots, but I didn't bother reading any of her bullshit. She'll play victim, like she always does, then go spread her legs for her professor again in an attempt to make me jealous.

It explains why she's here, watching with rage in her eyes.

Jackson sits on the bench behind her, with Samson's big brother beside him. I know they're going to party later. They'll be waiting on the guys finishing up so they can head out.

I said no.

The last place I want to be is anywhere near Jackson. He made it out that something happened between him and Blaise. Blaise wouldn't lie about it. He's more the type to rub it in my face to get some sort of reaction from me.

I reacted. I hit my friend, ended said friendship, then let myself spiral.

I breathe heavily when we're eventually allowed to stop. Bending forward, I keep my hands on my knees and cough up a lung. My leg aches like it always does when I exercise, but I learn to get on with life and ignore the constant reminder of my past. Sweat mixed with rain drips from my eyebrow as I glance up to see Allie smiling at me as if she hasn't blasted me all over the internet. Jackson smirks, his head tilting to Blaise, and I follow his gaze to see Blaise talking to Mia.

Mia.

Why the fuck won't these girls leave us alone?

And why is he talking to her?

I watch as they interact. He runs his hand through his hair, his chest rising and falling from the running, while she talks. Then she reaches for his hand, which he pulls away, making her brow furrow.

Good boy.

My nerves crash when Jackson hops down from the bench and walks straight toward Blaise, and before I can stop myself, I aim for them too.

"Practice isn't done," I snap at them, my eyes not daring to look at Mia or Allie. I'm glaring at Jackson. "Fuck off."

"Hmm," Jackson hums, before dragging his eyes to Blaise. "I'll see you at the party tonight."

My heart accelerates, but I don't show it as I stare at my old friend. He backs off, lifting his hands, then swings his arm over Allie's shoulder. "You don't mind if I take a shot of your girl now, do you?"

"Not my girl," I retort, grabbing Blaise by the shoulder and turning him toward the field.

"We have forty minutes left of practice," I say without looking at him. "Then you can go to the party all you want."

Blaise shrugs me off, grabbing his helmet from the side of the tracks just as I take mine and pull it over my head. Keith whistles to hurry us up, and Blaise stops beside me. "If you're jealous, you know what you need to do," he whispers. "If you don't want me to go to the party, all you need to do is say that."

Coach signals for us to get into position. Blaise jogs to his side, since we're on opposite teams for practice, getting into a squat position, ready to catch the ball.

Half an hour into the match, I think I've tackled every single player, imagining they're Jackson. I nearly punched Keith in the gut when he told me to calm down.

The last pass, and I aim for Blaise as soon as he catches the ball and runs up the side of the field. My feet pound the wet ground as I gain on him, throwing my body into his side before he can touchdown.

I hear the air rush from his lungs on impact, slamming him into the ground and pinning him down.

"Shit, Cole," he groans beneath me. "That was fucking personal."

I grab the cage of his helmet and yank him up to me, so our helmets clash. "Stay the fuck away from Jackson," I snap. "If I see you even talking to him, I'll beat your ass and snap your legs and watch him get his spot back on the team. If you want to take that as a threat, good, because it is. Stay. Away. From. Him."

When I let go of him, he headbutts me, cracking our helmets together and shoving me off so I fall onto my back in the mud. He jumps to his feet, panting. "Don't threaten me again." Then he laughs. "Knew you were jealous."

"Rowle," Coach yells. "Carter. Get over here."

Rolling my eyes, I slap Blaise's hand away when he tries to help me to my feet. Coach shakes his head at us both as we approach.

"Your father said you'd both fight during a match, so this is your only warning. Another brawl between you both and I'm benching the pair of you for three games."

He thinks *that* was us fighting? Fuck, he should see what it's like when I'm masked and Blaise is sucking my cock. Or not – I don't want anyone seeing that side of us.

I sigh. "Then you'd lose the games. We're your best players."

"Get out of my sight."

I laugh as I walk by him. Everyone's already inside getting showered and dressed. Blaise follows, muttering something under his breath about being an asshole.

Must be talking about himself.

The stalls in the shower room are empty when we get in, the guys pulling on their clean clothes, some cocks out. I glance at Blaise to see if he's giving them any attention, but he's too busy trying to unfasten the clip on his helmet. Tossing mine down, I yank off my shirt, then my guards, and hike my foot onto a bench to undo my laces.

"I'm not helping you," I say to him when he huffs. "Learn to do it yourself."

"I know how to fucking take off my helmet. I played in high school."

Keith comes over, squirting water into his mouth from his sports bottle. "J will pick us up around seven," he tells Blaise. "Be ready."

He nods, and I feel every fucking nerve snapping as I switch shoes to undo the other lace.

"You sure you're not coming?" he asks me, and I shake my head. "Well, suit yourself. We're gonna play another chase."

Great.

Fucking perfect.

Blaise isn't going.

Keith leaves the locker room, and after a few minutes, everyone else leaves. Blaise finally gets his helmet off and drops it onto a bench. I catch him looking at me while I undress down to my boxer shorts, but he isn't doing the same.

I'm annoyed with him. I'm always annoyed with him, but something inside me likes that it's just the two of us in here. And I want him to fucking take off his clothes so I can at least look at him the way he keeps looking at me.

Instead, I snatch my towel from my bag and head to the shower stalls, resting my towel on the hook on the way in. I remove my boxers and let them splash in the puddle on the floor, catching a glimpse of Blaise glancing in my direction before I vanish into the cubical.

Warm water cascades over my body, washing away all the sweat and dirt from my skin. I drop my head forward, soaking my hair under the spray, facing the wall with my hand on it.

Footsteps sound, and I hear the shower next to me. I turn my head to see Blaise, from his shoulders up, doing the same as me.

I don't hide the fact I'm watching him. Watching him soak his hair and run his fingers through it, dropping his head back and rubbing the dirt from his throat and chest.

My cock hardens. It twitches between my legs, begging for touch. It wants his lips. His mouth. His throat.

Blaise's jaw is clenched as he washes his hair, and my breathing halts as he looks at me from under his wet lashes. We both gulp. He sucks his bottom lip into his mouth, jaw clenched tightly.

Slowly, his eyes close as he releases his lip and parts them both, his head falling back to elongate his throat. His shoulder rises once, twice, three times. And I realize my hand is following his movements. I wrap my fingers around my cock, not daring to break our colliding eyes. Letting out a puff of air, I stroke myself the way he is. Slow. Long. Twisting at the tip and back down.

With my mouth open on a deep whimper, Blaise lets out a "fuck," groaning as we keep the slow, sensual pace of fucking our own hands. "Tell me not to come in there."

I don't speak. I just keep touching myself, feeling the energy of him all over me while I pant for air within the steam-filled room.

Blaise doesn't stop stroking himself as he ditches his shower and rounds mine, and my nerves spark into an inferno when I see him fully naked, his long, thick cock in his hand. I moan as he snatches my throat and slams me into the side of the cubicle, pressing his forehead to mine as we breathe the same air, still stroking up and down.

My tip hits his, mixing our precum, and neither of us bother to turn the shower back on when the timer cuts off. My free hand reaches for his chest, dragging my blunt nails down the muscles there, loving the way he sucks in a rushed breath between his teeth when I reach his abs.

Absently, we move our cocks in sync. He rubs into the side of mine, and we wrap our fingers around them both, thrusting, getting into a rhythm where he thrusts forward as I drag back, watching how good our cocks look together.

I lift my head, staring at him as we keep going, as heat rushes up my spine and makes me dizzy. My gaze drops to his mouth, and I don't hesitate to slam my lips to his. It's feral. It's painful. It's everything I fucking need as he kisses me back. The strokes get faster, deeper, and when we both part our lips and our tongues collide, the world stops spinning, the shower room vanishes around us, and time halts as we devour each other's mouths, deepening the kiss as he snatches my bottom lip between his teeth and nips at me.

Blaise slides his hand up into my hair and tugs, yanking my head to the side. I nearly explode all over him as he kisses along my jaw and down my throat, stopping just under my ear to suck on the sensitive skin there. My cock jumps, and I moan deeply as he bites and licks and kisses while we fuck our hands.

A door opens, and we both pause.

"Cole!" We hear Keith coming in. "You in here? Your car's outside still."

I push Blaise down to his knees just as Keith walks into the shower room. I quickly turn on the spray and pretend to wash my body as Keith stops in the middle of the room.

"Ah, good, found you. Did Coach tell you about the away game in South Carolina?"

I turn and nod once, even though I don't have a clue what he's talking about. I'm too much in a panic that he'll walk around more and see Blaise crouching in front of me.

I don't look down as a hand slides up my thigh while Keith tells me about the trip. My body freezes all over when his lips trace over the scar on my hip, a reminder of my father's abuse. He kisses it and drags his lips lower.

I swallow, my cock twitching as fingers wrap around the base. I fight the groan and how badly I need to screw my eyes shut as Blaise's warm mouth takes the head of my cock. His tongue circles it slowly, so fucking slowly I think I might blow while Keith tells me about the hotel and flights. Not that I'll be going since I have too many assignments for college.

Sneaking a glance down, I stop breathing at how deep he takes my cock into his throat. I absently move my hips forward, bringing my gaze back to Keith still talking away like I'm not in the middle of being sucked off by Blaise.

I flinch when he palms my ass cheeks, spreading them, and I tense all over when a sneaky fingertip presses to my back hole as Blaise swallows my cock.

"Anyway, yeah, I just wanted to check that you were on board. I'll make sure the coach doesn't room you with your brother. We don't want any fights."

I nod once. "Right."

Blaise chuckles silently around my cock, and I fist the hair at the back of his head and force my cock in until it hits the back of his throat. Quietly choking, he gags around the base of my dick.

He returns the favor by pushing his finger into my back hole just as Keith waves himself off and leaves. The locker room door shuts, and I let out a gasp and pant and grab the back of his head and shove in deeper.

"So sneaky on your knees for me," I breathe, my balls tightening as he pushes a second finger into my ass, making my eyes roll.

His eyes are watering from the intrusion while he pulses his finger in and out of my ass, and I move with him. I fuck into his mouth while he finger-fucks me into a frenzy. My vision blurs, and I quicken my pace as his fingers curl in my ass and hit something that blows my fucking head off.

"Fuck," I moan. "Fuck, Blaise."

I empty into his mouth, filling his throat with my cum. I nearly die when he swallows around my cock, his throat tightening around my thickness. He moans, and I realize he's been stroking himself, getting himself off while he pleases me in the college shower room.

He stills completely, and I feel the hot spurts of his release hitting my legs as he whimpers around my dick.

Pulling out, I use his hair to get him to his feet quickly and fist his cock at the same time as I kiss him. He's still coming as I stroke him, squeezing, twisting, fucking swallowing his groans and tasting my cum on his tongue as I bite down on it and suck.

When he's finished, I let go of his dick, and instead of pulling away completely, I take his face in my hands and kiss him harder. Our chests press together, hands everywhere, as I taste and bite and lick and fucking feel Blaise all over me.

"We're really doing this?" I ask between kisses, both our hands in each other's hair and pulling, the muscles on our chests and abs rubbing together, even though we've already gotten off and our cocks are flaccid.

"Just don't make it obvious and we won't give our parents a heart attack," Blaise replies, nudging my nose with his before slowly kissing me again. "We still hate each other, remember?"

"And you'll stay away from Jackson?"

He grins against my mouth, the smile making me feel warm as it lights up his green eyes. "I knew you were jealous."

I laugh and shove away from him. "Fuck you."

CHAPTER 23
BLAISE

Cole cuts the engine and looks out the windshield as silence falls on the car. Our parents have gone away for the weekend. Now, as he flicks his eyes in my direction and swallows, the weight of what that means for us thickens the tension in the car. I smirk, wetting my lips. I can still taste him on my tongue.

He pushes open the door and steps out into the rain. It soaks through his clothes in seconds, making the gray fabric mold to his muscles. Fuck me, he'll be the death of me. Climbing out of the car, I jog up the driveway with my eyes on the prize. Cole enters the house, tosses his keys into the crystal bowl on the console table, and then hesitates with his back to me.

"Do you know what I love?" I ask as I close the door behind us and turn the lock to heighten the anticipation. His shoulders stiffen at the soft click, and my eyes fall down his body as I approach him from behind. "You talked a big game back there, and you grew hard as a fucking rock in my mouth when Keith walked in on us." The floorboards creak with my next step. I can smell the rain on his skin, and fuck me, if that doesn't do dangerous things to my heart. I'm screwed. My fingers tingle with the urge to fist his hair and pull until he hisses. "But there's fear beneath the desire, too." I'm close to him now. Close enough to touch. "There's something about the hitch in your breath that makes me want to hurt you."

He doesn't move a muscle as I step close enough to feel his

heat through his clothes. Raindrops cling to the ends of his hair, and more dot his skin. I stifle a groan when my dick jumps behind my fly. "You like the thrill, don't you?" I ask.

"You want to hurt me?" His eyes find mine over his shoulder, and mine drop to his tempting mouth. "What's holding you back?"

Giving in to the urge to touch his wet hair, I grab the strands and yank his head back. "I can think of better ways to hurt you."

"Fuck—" he grunts as I shove him up against the wall, but the sound is cut off when I crush my lips to his.

This moment right here...

I bite his lip hard until the taste of his coppery blood floods my mouth, and he fists my T-shirt and hauls me close. We're a clash of teeth and tongues and bumping noses. It's messy, sloppy, and everything I've ever imagined late at night with my hand in my boxers. Now that I can kiss him any time I want behind closed doors, I'm sure as fuck going to get my fill of these enticing lips.

"Fuck, you make me feel things I've never felt," I growl, lifting him away from the wall and slamming him back against it. He gives as good as he gets, and I wrench my mouth away when he sinks his teeth into my lip. "What the..." I growl, my cock straining inside my jeans. His eyes follow the blood dripping down my chin, his panting breaths coming hard and fast.

"You like to see me bleed?"

He wets his lips, and the move is so seductive that I groan. Grabbing him by the throat, I slam my mouth to his again. "Fuck me," I whisper against his lips. "I could kiss you for-fucking-ever." His wandering fingers slip beneath my wet T-shirt, making my abs contract. "What do you want to happen now?" I ask and kiss him deeper, slower. These fucking sweet lips. I'm in heaven. "You call the shots, big brother."

"Stop fucking calling me that," he growls, shoving me back, and a chuckle rips from my chest at the heated look in his eyes. Walking past me, his fine ass disappears upstairs. My lungs expand as I inhale a steadying breath. I don't want to hurt him, but I want to hurt him. I'm a mess.

Making my way to the kitchen, I slide a knife from the wooden block and glance at the doorway. "I'm coming for you. You better run," I call out before smiling so wide my cheeks cramp. It's so damn exhilarating and freeing not to have to hide how crazy and out of control I feel around him.

Twirling the knife in my hand like I'm a pro, I set off to hunt him down. "I don't think you quite understand what the hell you've agreed to," I say as I ascend the carpeted stairs. My heart thuds as I reach the top and his closed bedroom door comes into view. I wonder what awaits me on the other side. Is he jacking off? Naked already? Even better, is he hiding? Is it my turn to chase him? Tossing the knife into the air, I catch it by the handle. Hell yes. Cole may not know the extent of my obsession, but I've chased him for months, and it's time for me to claim my prize. Without a preamble, I stride across the hallway and drive my boot into the door.

"What the fuck—" Cole blurts as the door slams into the wall, but his words die when he drops his eyes to the knife in my hand. "Blaise?"

"Why are you not naked?" I casually close the door behind me. "I'm disappointed."

"What's with the knife?" he asks, notes of fear bleeding into his voice.

"You like to see me bleed." I point the blade at him, then the bed. "Lie down."

Swallowing, he hesitates, and I raise a brow. "I thought you said we're doing this—you and me. Are you scared?"

Cole looks down at the knife, uncertain. My chest swells with satisfaction when he walks to the bed and crawls on. Approaching the bed, my eyes roam over his body. "You trust me." My hungry gaze lingers on the outline of his hard cock. "Maybe you shouldn't," I whisper, the mattress dipping beneath my weight as I climb on. Straddling his lap, I pull my T-shirt over the back of my head before tossing it to the floor and reaching for his hands. I place one over my heart and curl the fingers of his free hand around the handle.

"What are you doing, Blaise?" he asks, his eyes growing wide.

Guiding the blade to my collarbone, I drag my tongue across my bottom lip as we drown in each other. "I will always bleed for you."

His fingers tremble on the handle, but he makes no move to hurt me, and suddenly, I've never wished for anything more. When he looks up at me, his throat jumps. It's the sexiest thing I've ever seen. "Cut me."

I expect him to fight me or to say he doesn't want to hurt me, but instead, he looks into my eyes, speaking a thousand soundless words while dragging the knife down my chest. A sharp sting has me sucking in a breath.

"Fuck," he breathes and pushes up on his elbows. Blood rushes to the surface, stark red against my pale skin. Dragging a thumb through a trickle of crimson, I trace his bottom lip. He sucks it into his mouth. "Do you have any idea of how fucking perfect you are?" I ask, and he forces me back as he sits up and trails his tongue through the blood. His eyes find mine, his mouth and chin smeared with red. I've never seen him this... undone before. I almost come in my fucking pants at the need in his heated look. How can I ever deny him anything?

Still, I like to play with my prize. Grabbing his stubbly jaw, I nip at his bottom lip. "Admit that you were jealous earlier."

A sharp sting in my abdomen has a smile pulling at my mouth. Cole is brave, digging the blade into my stomach. "One wrong move on my end, and you'll gut me. Maybe that's what you want?" I ask, reaching down to unbuckle his belt. "Does the thought turn you on?"

"Are you always this fucking crazy?" he snips.

Chuckling, I reach into his boxers. "Forgive me, but I'm not the one with a knife in my hand." My fingers curl around his hard shaft, feeling it throb. "I'll make you come if you admit that you were jealous."

"I wasn't fucking jealous," he sneers, but the tremble in his voice gives him away.

"No? So you don't mind if I hang out with Jackson again?" It's the wrong thing to say, or the right thing, depending on how you look at it. I quite like violence, so when Cole tosses the knife aside and tackles me to the bed, my fucking toes curl. Reaching for the knife, he rests it against my throat while yanking my belt open. "Say his name one more fucking time. I dare you!"

My lips spread into a wide smile. "Oh, I like a challenge."

He snarls, digging the knife into my throat. Blinded by fury, he frees my cock and strokes my length until I'm squirming beneath all that pent-up anger.

"I want to fuck you," I say, wringing the sheets, my cock growing even harder in his firm grip. "Dammit, I want to fuck you so badly."

"Yeah?" he mocks, forgetting the knife at my throat, and I wince when he cuts me. "Fuck," he says, rearing back. "Did I hurt you?"

"Shut up." I fist his hair and pull him to my lips. The knife falls to the floor with a loud clatter, and then it's just us and our wildfire desire burning through our souls while we claw at each other's clothes. Somehow, in the commotion, Cole knocks the lamp to the floor, and we break into laughter. "You're so fucking beautiful," I say, pausing with my fingers in his hair as he hovers above me.

"Can dudes be called beautiful?"

"I don't fucking care." I swallow down the lump in my throat. "You're perfect in every fucking way...and your smile. It lights up the room. I only see you."

Cole stares at me for a beat before silencing the words on my tongue with another heated kiss. But this one is different. The anger is gone. His touches are softer, but if anything, they hurt more. Every stroke of his calloused fingers burns like a cut of his blade, and I love it.

I love him.

Pausing, I breathe heavily. Cole's weight on top of me, his parted lips, and the way his hair falls over his brow have my heart rate accelerating. I can't think about anything except how badly I want to make him feel good, to make him fall apart at my touch. I roll us over until I'm on top and stroke his hair away from his forehead. His cock rests against his stomach, hard and leaking precum. "I won't fuck you yet."

I see the question he wants to ask as his brow furrows. "You're not ready," I whisper instead, knowing Cole is still wrestling with himself on a deeper level, and until he begs me to, I won't cross that line. Holding his gaze, I kiss a line down his body, my lips grazing his contracting abs. I dip my tongue into his belly button. "Keep your eyes on me," I say and stroke his dick in a long, slow pull. "Don't look away."

His throat jumps. "I won't."

"Good boy," I tease, and his eyes narrow. I swirl my tongue over a bulging vein before he can complain. He sucks in a breath, and I decide there and then that it's the best sound in the entire world. "You trusted me earlier when I barged in here with a knife. Do you trust me now, Cole?"

The question might seem crazy, but this is us, baring ourselves wholly after sparring back and forth for weeks—months, even. What I'm asking him is more profound than I could ever voice, and I know he feels it, too, when he strokes his fingers through my hair. "I trust you."

My smile rivals his before I take him in my mouth. His cock jumps, and he pulls my hair to the point of pain. I suck him deep, bobbing in time with my thrashing heart. As I reach up to palm his balls, my phone rings in my pocket—it's my dad's ringtone. Maybe I should feel bad for sucking off his wife's son, but every-fucking-thing about this moment feels right. I'm too drunk on Cole's moans and groans to even contemplate how this could tear our family apart. I reach up and drag my fingers over his abs, feeling the muscles shift and bunch beneath my touch. He shivers and throws his head back. I love the veins in his elongating neck and how he traps his lip between his teeth. "Blaise... Jesus..." he groans.

I release him with a pop. "Jesus? No, he can't make you feel this way." Releasing his balls, I spit on my fingers before reaching down to circle his tight exit. More precum leaks from his dick. Licking him from root to tip, I swirl my tongue through the beads, tasting his saltiness. "You're an addiction."

"Do you always talk this much?" he pants, and I chuckle before shifting onto my knees and pulling him to his. Grabbing him by the back of the neck, I press my forehead to his and palm his big cock. A hiss escapes me when his warm hand closes around my length, and we stare at each other's mouths while stroking each other's dicks.

Cole wets his lips and frowns like he's in pain. I pick up the pace, my chest heaving with shuddering breaths. "It feels so damn good," he whispers.

My fingers slide into the damp hair at his nape, and he mirrors the movement. Fisting the strands tight, I smile. "Good. I want us to come together."

"I want you to fuck me," he admits.

My lips pull to the side. "No, you don't."

His breathy chuckle wafts across my parted lips. "Oh, I fucking do."

"Then beg me to fuck you, Cole. Beg me to fill you up with my cock. Beg me, and I might give it to you."

"Fuck," he grunts, briefly closing his eyes. "You're killing me."

"Are you close?" I ask, staring at his tempting lips. "Please tell me you're close. I need to feel you come all over my hand."

"Please, Blaise." His throat jumps. "Fuck me."

"Soon," I reply as I tease the tip of his dick with my thumb. The moment his muscles stiffen and cum rains from our cocks simultaneously, I crush my mouth to his and devour his swollen lips. "That's it," I praise between kisses. "You're coming so hard for me, big brother." A jet of cum hits me on the throat, and I drive my tongue into his mouth. "You're delicious. Come all over me, Cole. Fuck me up."

"Christ," he groans, his fingers twitching in my hair. "Fuck, I can't..." His hips stutter. More cum rains over my chin, and I relish it. We breathe hard, staring at each other. Glancing down at my cum-covered chest, I snigger. Cole is no better off. Cum drips down his chest and abs, and some has even made it to his collarbone.

I see the mischief in his eyes before he launches himself at me. "Come here, you fucker. You know you want a hug." And just like that, we're laughing and wrestling on the bed. Cole soon gets the upper hand, but not because he is stronger than me. No, I love the victorious glint in his eyes as he pins me to the bed with my hands on the pillow beneath my head.

"I surrender," I say, swallowing and staring at the racing pulse in his neck. "You win."

Cole blinds me with his smile as his hair flops over his eyes. I feast my eyes on Cole Carter, naked on top of me, his muscles straining in his arms.

"How come you won't go to the party tonight?" I ask and regret it the moment the words leave my lips.

Cole's smile falls, and he climbs off me and flops onto his back. "I'm not in the mood."

"Is that the only reason?" I ask.

With his arm behind his head, he stares up at the ceiling. I turn over onto my side and push up on my elbow.

"Why are you going?" he asks, not looking at me. "They're not your friends."

I have to go to this party for personal reasons. Jackson has flirted with me on multiple occasions, and I know it makes Cole uncomfortable. Something happened between them the morning when Cole picked me up. I'm not sure what exactly, but Jackson's busted lip tells me everything I need to know.

"I'm gonna talk to Jackson," I say, and Cole whips his eyes in my direction.

"Why the hell would you do that?"

I can feel him pull away even before he sits up and reaches for his clothes on the floor.

"Dammit, Cole," I breathe, dragging my hands down my face. "You're so quick to run away. Just hear me out."

"Then talk. I'm not stopping you." He pulls his top on with jerky movements.

I sigh. "This is exactly why I need to talk to him. Don't you get it? I don't want to come between the two of you. He's your friend."

"Some fucking friend," Cole mutters, swiping up his pants off the floor.

Sitting up, I place my hand on his shoulder, and he stiffens. That hurts more than the hard look in his eyes. "I'm going to smooth things out with him. It upsets you when I hang out with him, so I won't do that anymore. But I can't just ignore him either. I need to have this conversation."

Cole snorts and rises to his feet, hopping on one leg while he pulls his socks on. "Do whatever the fuck you want."

"What happened to the threats on the football field? I thought you were gonna snap my legs." I say it as a joke, but my voice trembles too much, and Cole inhales a ragged breath. "I thought you said you trusted me."

"I do trust you."

"No, you don't." My jaw clenches tight. "Why are you walking away if you trust me? What is it that has you so worked up? Are you scared I'll do something with him? You have nothing to worry about. I only want you. It's okay if you're jealous, but please talk—"

"I'm not fucking jealous," he spits.

"Fine..." I climb out of bed and stomp up to him. We're toe to toe, just like before, but it feels like we're oceans apart. "If the roles were reversed, I'd be jealous as hell. But I get it... You don't feel the same way about me." I turn to leave, but he grabs my arm. As his heat warms my back, I stare at the door.

"I do feel the same way. I'm just...scared."

How can I not soften when he presses his lips to my bare shoulder? "I've never felt like this, and I don't know how to handle these emotions."

"What are you scared of?"

His breath drifts over my skin, and he kisses me again, higher up on my shoulder, closer to the curve where it meets my neck. "I'm scared of losing you. That maybe...you'll figure out I'm not good enough."

My heart squeezes. "You are good enough, Cole."

More kisses.

More gentle touches.

"Come with me," I plead.

He shakes his head and steps back. "No, it's too risky."

"Risky?"

Cole walks to the bedroom door and opens it before looking at me over his shoulder. I'm still naked, my dick flaccid. "I might kill him if I see him anywhere near you." Looking past me to the window, he continues. "You're right. I need to trust you, but what good does it do when I don't trust myself around you?"

"So you won't come?" My shoulders slump with disappointment, and I don't know why. But a part of me had really hoped he would come with me.

His smile doesn't reach his eyes. "I'll see you tomorrow." Then he slips from my room, and something breaks inside me. Walking up to the door, I slam it shut with enough force to make the picture frames rattle. My eyes land on the creased bedsheets and bloodstains.

Every moment with Cole feels very much like one step forward and two back.

> Tiago: Are you coming over tonight? Mia and Allie won't be around.

> Me: I can't, sorry.

> Tiago: You never spend time with us anymore.

> Ronnie: He's too busy sucking up to Cole's friends.

> Me: Leave him out of it. I have things I need to take care of tonight.

> Tiago: You're defending him? Who are you, and what did you do to my friend? Are you best buddies now?

MUSIC BLASTS in the background as I tap the side of my phone. My stomach churns with unease as I shift on the couch. I've been distracted lately by Mia's bullshit and my complicated emotions where Cole is concerned, and now the cracks are starting to show in my friendships. Ignoring the messages, I pocket my phone when Jackson flops down beside me. He rests his arm behind me on the couch and spreads his legs obnoxiously wide as though he owns the place. His eyes sparkle in the dim light as he flashes a side smirk. "Where's your brother?"

"He couldn't make it."

He smiles and flicks his eyes to my mouth. "I'm glad you came."

My teeth grind at the hidden meaning beneath those words. If he thinks I'll fall for his blatant flirting, he's dead wrong. Something about Jackson feels off, and I can't put my finger on it. I sought him out the other day because I was in emotional pain and had nowhere else to turn. My bullshit radar was broken. But tonight, as he presses his thigh against mine, a shiver runs through me. It's not a pleasant one. "Are you having a good time?"

A good time? I've sat on this couch alone for the last hour. Mia tried to speak to me earlier, but I brushed off her attempts, not in the mood. This isn't my crowd. "Sure," I reply instead.

"We're doing another chase in a bit. You in?"

Frowning, I glance away from the busy dance floor—and by the dance floor, I mean the empty space in the living room where scantily clad girls hop around like Duracell bunnies on speed. "Another chase?"

"Yeah." I stiffen when he grazes his fingers over my shoulder. "Like the other time when we broke up into teams."

Something is definitely off. "Sure." I open my mouth to talk to him about his flirting and how it needs to stop, when he jumps to his feet the moment Allie enters the room.

My brows knit together as he plants his lips on hers and shoves his tongue into her mouth. What is he playing at? And not only him. When he's done eating her face, he whispers in her ear, and her eyes flick my way. I swear she's smirking.

"Sup, man." Samson slams his hand down on my shoulder, tearing me from my thoughts. Jumping over the back of the couch, he sits beside me. "See a pussy you like?"

I pretend to scan the crowd. Girls no longer interest me, but neither do guys. I have tunnel vision for Cole. "That one?" Samson asks, following my line of sight to a girl on the dance floor. Her short skirt swishes around her tanned thighs. Samson whistles, shoving a beer bottle at me. "I'm up for sharing if you're into that stuff. A good old spit roast."

I stare at the beer, trying to determine if Samson has slobbered over it, then pretend to take a sip. I don't trust anyone anymore. "You can have her."

He licks his lips like he is eyeing up a chopstick. "Thanks, man. I'll ride her hard tonight. What do you think she's into? Reverse cowgirl or doggy?"

"Doggy," I reply absentmindedly, watching Jackson talk to some of the other guys. Why do I have such a bad feeling about tonight? It makes no sense.

"I think you're right. She looks like an 'ass in the air and face shoved into the pillow' kinda girl. Those are my favorites. Nasty girls who like to be fucked hard."

Chuckling, I shake my head. "Whatever you say."

Samson smacks his knees before standing up. "I'm going in. You partaking in the chase later?"

I nod. "Sure am."

"Good, man." Samson claps me on the shoulder, his eyes on the girl. "Later."

"Later." As he walks away, I scan the room for Jackson, but he's nowhere to be seen. Fucking typical. I don't know when I'll get to speak to him at this rate. Fishing my phone out of my pocket, I check for the hundredth time if Cole has messaged. He hasn't.

My heart sinks. I type out a quick message, but delete it. Then I type another one, my thumb hovering over the 'send' button.

> Me: I wish you were here.

I delete that one, too.

CHAPTER 24
COLE

Blaise is at the party.

There are photos already on social media. He's in the background in a few, drinking a beer, and one of them has him talking to Mia. She's close, sitting beside him on the sofa, her thigh pressed to his.

At least he's keeping his hands off her.

I swipe to the next photo, and my blood runs cold when I see Jackson leaning over the back of the sofa, saying something to Blaise. He's not looking at him, though, his eyes on the beer bottle in his hand as he peels the label.

The next swipe, Samson and Keith are taking a selfie with Allie, and Blaise is no longer on the sofa, and there's no sign of Jackson.

He's with my fucking friends, our ex-girlfriends, and Jackson, and I've not had a single message from him. My nerves have been acting up all night. A bad batch of butterflies in my gut when I think of all the ways he might be fucking around. He's probably drunk and forgetting I exist.

I should trust him, but why? He fucked Mia only a few days ago, went to Jackson's place, and then got chased by me without knowing it was me. And then earlier, we…

Every insecurity I have is valid.

I grind my teeth together as I cut off my phone screen and toss it aside, anxiety bubbling in my chest, heart pounding.

Maybe I should go. Maybe I should get dressed and go lay claim on him, once and for all.

The shrill of my phone has me grabbing it and bringing it to my ear without looking. "Hello?"

"Son," my dad says, hiccupping. "Don't hang up on me again."

With a sigh, I pinch the bridge of my nose, dropping my head back on the couch. "What do you want? Calling to threaten me again? Seeing if no one is home so you can wreck the place again? Oh, wait, you want to scare my mom into leaving town and kidnap me?"

He sniggers, tsking. "You know me so well."

I roll my eyes and shake my head. There's silence, and my heart races at the possibility of him crashing into my life and making it hell.

"She's mine," he says, snarling the two possessive words.

"Who?"

"Rachel," he replies, hiccupping again. "He has no claim on her, she belongs to me. I married her first. I loved her first. She's been mine since we were fifteen years old."

"You beat her and abused your title as a parent," I say, laughing bitterly. "The only reason you're not in prison is because of your badge. I hope loneliness feels good and worth all the shit you put us through."

"You little asshole—"

Hanging up, I let out the heaviest, most audible breath ever. I lean forward, head dropped between my knees, needing this anxiety to fuck off already. Between my dad and Blaise, and Jackson being an asshole, I feel like the world is closing in on me and I don't know how to stop it.

My phone rings again, but I ignore it, rocking back and forth on the seat. I'm dizzy, and my eyes burn. I stay like this through five missed calls and message pings. The sound of the vibrations nearly drowns out my deep, rushed breaths.

I eventually sit up, just as the next call ends, and I catch the number I still haven't saved, but I recognize it. Grabbing my phone, I see I have ten missed calls from Mia and multiple messages begging me to call her back.

I swipe away from each notification with a groan. She's probably drunk and thinking we're in love – or maybe she wants round two without the third person involved. How the fuck do I get her to leave me the hell alone? Tell her I'm into her ex and that I'd rather fuck him?

Then another message pops up.

It's about Blaise, it reads. *I think Jackson and your friends are up to something.*

Quickly getting to my feet, I throw on my hoodie and shove my feet in my sneakers, grabbing my keys on the way out of the front door. I call her back, but of course, the idiot doesn't pick up.

It starts ringing ten minutes into me driving to the house. "What's going on?" I skip the introductions and manners. "Where's Blaise?"

Music blares in the background, then it grows faint. She must be trying to get somewhere to hear me. A door closes. "Cole?"

"What's wrong?"

"They're about to play that chasing game again, but something doesn't feel right. Allie was making out with Jackson in the bathroom, and I walked in. I overheard them ask if the plan was set and if Blaise was taking part. They're putting him in the runners and they're the chasers."

I frown. "I don't understand." It doesn't help that she's drunk and falling over her words. "Where is Blaise now?"

"I don't know," she replies. "Are you coming here? Can you pick me up?"

"I'm coming for Blaise," I tell her. "I'll drop you off at the dorm."

"Can I come to your place? Allie will go there with her professor again."

I blink a few times, trying to think of a response.

It's the least I can do. She obviously isn't comfortable where she is, and I'm not a complete and total asshole. But then again, she'll be expecting something, especially after what happened between the three of us.

"Go grab Blaise. Tell him I'm coming for you both."

"Okay," she says quietly. "I know, by the way. I won't say anything."

I pause my breathing, staring at the road as I turn a corner, five minutes from the house. "What do you mean?"

"I love him too."

She hangs up on me, and my Bluetooth reconnects and music starts playing, filling the silence.

Fuck.

How the hell does she know?

The rest of the drive is a blur, until I reach the house. Parking, I narrow my eyes on all the people standing outside.

Keith walks out the house and closes the front door, locking it, and I go straight to him. "What's going on?"

He grins and shows me the iPad screen, red and green lights dotted around what looks like the digital blueprints of his house. "I have trackers in all the masks now. Was part of a project I was doing for school, but thought it would be a great idea to use them for this game. Neat, right?"

My eyes flicker around the screen. "The initials are their names?"

"Yeah. Here, there's your little bro." He points at a red dot on the screen. It's moving quickly through the kitchen area and into the dining room. Four green dots are gaining on him.

I spot the initials on one of them. "Allie is playing?"

"Yeah, man. Is that alright? She's been all over J all night. He said you were good with them."

I don't give a fuck about them. I'm not surprised either.

But then I see another two green dots join them, and they follow Blaise.

"J said he wants payback for Blaise taking his spot on the team. You ready to see your baby bro get fucked up?"

I'm shouldering past him before he can finish his shitty question. "Unlock the door."

"What?"

"Unlock the fucking door!"

Keith laughs. "You're kidding? You hate the prick as much as we all do. He deserves this."

I grab his collar and yank him to me, so my forehead slams into his. "Unlock. The fucking. Door."

"Blaise Rowle stole our friend's spot on the team because he spiraled. You're going to stand there and watch him get beaten to a pulp, because you hate him too."

I grit my teeth and shove him. Backing away, I shake my head at my supposed friend, and turn, looking at the windows and how thick they are. Music pounds from inside the house. Blaise probably can't hear himself think, never mind the fact the entire opposite team is hunting for him.

Mia grabs my arm. "I found a way in. Follow me."

She runs in her heels and short dress around the side of the house, and I stay on her tail. No one comes with us. Keith is too busy drinking his beer and cheering when another red dot gets eliminated.

She slides on a flowerbed, and I grab her hips to keep her up. Snatching my wrist, she pulls me along. "Right over here. One of the windows on the first floor is open."

We reach a drainpipe, and she looks up. I follow her gaze and see the partially cracked open window. "Can you climb up there?"

I nod. "Yeah. Go back to my car and wait for us." I hand her my keys, and she takes them, hesitating. I glance down at her when she doesn't move. "What happened the other day..." She chews her lip. "You only let it happen because it was with Blaise, right?"

I stay silent.

She nods a few times. "Does he feel the same way?"

"I don't know."

Her eyes glaze over, and she wipes under them. "I hope it works out."

Me too. Me fucking too.

She gives me a flat smile and vanishes back to the front of the house.

By the time I climb up and manage to slip through the window into the pitch-black house, I wince with how loud the music is. It's intentional. I remember Keith saying he wanted to set up some amusement park for this type of stuff. To have music so loud, you can't hear your pulse throbbing in your ears, and the fear mixes with the adrenaline as the heavy beats of the songs play.

I faintly see from the moon and streetlights shining into the house. I listen for the running feet, but I can't hear anything but Sleep Token nearly blowing my eardrums.

Making my way through Keith's bedroom, I check the other rooms on this floor, swearing to myself when I realize it's been twenty minutes since the game started, and they could've easily have caught Blaise by now. I know he can hold himself in a fight. He's solid, and it fucking hurts when he hits me, but when there's multiple people after him?

I run up the stairway before I'm thrown to the side by someone tackling into my ribs, knocking me onto the ground. They get to their feet, and I grab their ankle so they fall. I crawl over them, groaning when I see long blonde hair. I tug off the black mask to see some chick nearly crying beneath me.

"They have bats, and one has a gun," she cries. "Please help me."

"Go hide," I snarl and drag us both off the ground. "Stay out of sight."

She nods erratically and runs down the hallway. I brush my

hands through my hair, sweat clinging to my skin as I look left and right. One of them has a gun? What the fuck?

And bats.

Blaise.

I rush down the staircase, then down again to the ground floor, tripping over someone lying unconscious on the ground. They're covered in blood, gasping for breath. I don't breathe until I yank off the mask and see it's not Blaise. One of the guys from college. He's in Blaise's business class. He's just busted up, not dying.

Turning a corner, I stop in the dining area to see Jackson and Allie. He's bending her over the table and fucking her from behind, grabbing her hair and holding the barrel of the gun to her temple. Three others are behind him. As if they're waiting for their turn.

In another world, I'd get jealous and run at him. I'd rip him off my ex and beat the living shit out of him. But instead, I back away, let her get the railing she obviously wants.

Bypassing the downstairs bathroom, I see someone running, but they have brown hair down their back, so I know it isn't Blaise.

Another runner, and I shake my head. Where the fuck is he?

I shove open a door and the fist that snaps into my face knocks me back on my ass, momentarily dazed as the person crouches through my blurry vision.

He slides off the mask, tousled hair falling on his forehead.

"Cole?" I think he says, going by the way his lips move. "What the fuck are you doing?"

He grabs my arm and drags me into the room, slamming the door shut. Crouching again, he slaps my face so I focus.

I blink away the haziness and scowl at him.

"You fucking hit me," I grit.

I want to yell at him, but I pause at the blood on his face, the busted-up lip and swollen eye.

"Who the fuck did that?"

"It doesn't matter. Why are you here? How did you get in?"

"Mia," I say, breathless from running around the house for the last half an hour. "She called me. She knows I love you."

Blaise goes to speak, and his lips slam shut. His brows furrow.

"I must've hit you pretty hard," he laughs. "What's the plan, then? One has a gun and the others have weapons, and I don't think this is a case of runners and chasers. This is serious."

But we're out of time, because there's a bang on the door, and we know we've been caught when Jackson's voice faintly filters through the wood, even over the ear-bursting music.

"Keith says he's in here."

"The window," I say, nodding to it. "We're on the ground floor."

Blaise doesn't hesitate to grab the hardest object and launch it at the window, just as something hits against the door. Luckily, the door doesn't crack the way the window blows out.

I tell Blaise to go out first, and he flinches when his palm cuts on the glass. He jumps down, and when I go to climb out, the door is kicked open, and someone snatches my hair and yanks me back in.

"Wait, no, that's Cole!" Allie cries over the music, just as a bat swings into my gut and winds me. "Don't hurt him!"

Blaise can't get back in. Although we're on the ground floor, there's still a jump to the grass from the window, and I can't hear him over the music if he's saying shit.

Jackson goes to say something against my ear, but I slam the back of my head against his face, turning in his hold and punching him in the throat. He gags, and one of his little friends catches the gun he drops, but Allie stands in front of me.

"Don't you dare hurt him. We didn't agree to this. You said you'd beat up Blaise. No one mentioned Cole."

"You're still defending him?" Jackson spits. "He's been

screwing his brother behind your back. You saw the video of them on the first chase night."

I frown and move Allie from standing in front of me. "What the fuck are you talking about?"

He grins. "Did you think no one would notice you hiding your identity so you can force him to blow you?"

I glance over my shoulder. The music is too loud for Blaise to hear, but still. "I don't know what you're talking about."

"And the second time in the classroom. You wanked him off, still hiding who you were."

Allie crosses her arms. "You didn't mention that time," she says to him.

"That's why he has no interest in you. He's gay."

The term doesn't make me uncomfortable. Before, I was in denial, but now? Yeah, I am fucking gay, and I don't wait around to hear another word from this asshole's mouth. My knuckles burn as I punch him again, again, and a third time to throw him on his ass. I climb on him and grab his throat. No one stops me, They watch as I slam the back of Jackson's head into the ground.

"Stay the fuck away from Blaise," I snap, cutting off his oxygen. Squeezing, I pull him to me, so only he can hear my next words. "Or I'll sneak into your room at night, tie you to your bed, and I'll carve his name into your skin. I'll cut you. I'll snap your fucking bones one by one with pliers and make you drink your own piss. And when you're still alive and begging me to stop, I'll silence you by cutting off your cock and making you choke on it until your body is found weeks later, because no one cares about you enough to check in."

Not that I would lower myself to getting into trouble with the law for this asshole, but with how pale he goes, I've driven my point home. I release his throat and stand, glancing over at Allie.

"Unlock the fucking door."

She nods a few times and runs out of the room. I wait for someone to hit me, to feel a fist or a bat or even a bullet penetrate my skin, but they all stand back as I step over Jackson and leave them there.

"You'll regret threatening me," I hear Jackson call out. Yeah, probably. But I'm not caring.

As soon as Allie unlocks the door and I step out, Blaise barges through the crowd and runs straight for me.

CHAPTER 25
BLAISE

My hair tickles my brow as I watch Cole from beneath my lashes. He puts a bottle of antiseptic and a cloth on the bathroom sink before reaching for my cut hand. His touch is gentle as his blue eyes flick up to mine, and my heart thuds harder. While the thought of being in love with him should scare me, it doesn't anymore. I feel safe around Cole.

Even when we dropped Mia off at her friend's house, I couldn't stop looking at him.

"Are you sure your nose is okay?" I ask, feeling uncharacteristically nervous. He's different tonight, touching me as though he's worried he might hurt me.

His fingers ghost the deep gash, and his brows furrow. "Does it hurt?"

"No," I whisper, and his fingers pause.

"Don't lie to me, Blaise." A muscle tics in his jaw as his touch resumes its journey across my palm. "Always be honest with me."

I wince when he applies pressure with his thumb, and I try to pull away, but he tightens his grip and drags me from the edge of the bathtub. Rising to my feet, I let him pull me close.

"I could have killed Jackson tonight," he admits, holding my gaze and stroking his thumb back and forth across my wrist. "I saw fucking red when I realized he was planning to hurt you."

"I can handle myself," I tease, but Cole looks away and

grinds his teeth. "Hey," I say, trying to coax him to look at me. "I'm okay. You don't have to worry about me."

"I don't have to worry about you? Really?" His eyes flash with anger, and he steps away to create space between us. I grab his hand, ignoring the sharp sting in my palm. "I'm okay, Cole."

Looking down at our interlaced, bloodied fingers, he nods once and swallows. "If I hadn't arrived... What then?"

"I would have taken them all on, like John Wick."

Cole's lips twitch, and fuck me, it feels like I've won the lottery. I pull him closer, my chest swelling when he finally meets my gaze.

"No one is allowed to hurt you."

I sink my teeth into my bottom lip to contain my smile. "You sound like me. There's no room for two psychopaths in this relationship."

His eyes flick to my mouth. "You're not a psychopath."

"You have no idea the lengths I'll go for you or the things I've done..." I reply, and Cole stares at my mouth for all of two seconds before fisting my T-shirt and crushing his mouth to mine. His biting kisses hurt in the best way possible, and I groan into his mouth.

"Jackson is dead if he ever tries to hurt you again," he warns as I fist the hairs at his nape. A part of me secretly enjoys his threats and how possessive he is. The feeling is mutual. If anyone ever hurts him or tries to steal him from me, I'll burn them alive. I deepen the kiss, my tongue invading his mouth, and he slips his hands underneath my T-shirt to explore my muscled chest. I break away from his lips to catch my breath, and we gaze at each other as the seconds turn into minutes.

"Thank you for turning up tonight." I capture his lips and taste him again. It's official—I'm addicted to Cole's kisses and trembling touches.

Pulling away, he reaches for the bottle of antiseptic, and I keep my eyes locked on his face while he uncaps the lid and soaks the cloth. I doubt he knows how unbelievably perfect he is or how my heart skips a beat every time he lifts those dark eyes to mine.

"This will hurt," he warns as he puts the bottle back on the sink. I swallow as he reaches for my hand and turns it over. His thumb skims the gash. At the same time, his brows knit together, and he looks pained.

"I can do it myself," I offer, but he shakes his head.

"No... It's my fault."

I hiss as he presses the cloth to my hand. *Fuck me, that stings.*

"None of this is your fault."

"Jackson blames me for getting kicked off the team," Cole says. "He knows how I feel about you, and he'll use you to get at me."

"But that's bullshit," I reply. "Jackson got kicked off the team because of my dad." I hiss again, trying to pull my hand back, but he tightens his grip and gives me a warning look.

"Stay still."

"I can leave the team," I offer. "I never wanted to be on the team anyway—"

"Shut up," Cole growls, a muscle working madly in his jaw while he cleans my wounded palm. "Jackson is off the team because he's slacking. He has no one to blame but himself."

"Even so, I'll quit."

"Say that one more time, and I'll punch you."

I smile, and he looks up from beneath his messy mop of hair. "I would rather fuck you," I admit. "But if you'd rather fight..."

Cole smiles, too, and my heart flutters—fucking flutters. I look down at my hand and will my stirring dick to go down. Now isn't the time to touch him.

"Jackson knows about us?"

Cole stiffens before reaching for my other hand. "He knows I'm gay."

"You're gay?" I ask, curious about his sexuality. I assumed he was bisexual.

Shrugging, Cole pours more antiseptic on the cloth and

proceeds to cut me open with his careful touches. "So what if I am?"

"I like it," I reply, and he looks at me questioningly.

"I mean… At least I don't have to worry about killing all the women who flirt with you."

He snorts, amused, and my cheeks hurt from smiling.

"Now I just have to beat the men off with a stick. No, screw that. Any man who flirts with you will regret ever being born."

Cole chuckles, and I sober. "I'm sorry I punched you back there."

"You had no way of knowing it was me."

"I know," I reply, "but the thought of ever hurting you…"

"You won't hurt me," Cole says as he wraps my hands in bandages.

I wish I could feel as confident as he sounds, but sometimes, I fear myself and the lengths I'll go to protect him. Sometimes, I worry he'll get caught in the crossfire. And someday, the people we care about will find out about us. Someday, we'll tear our families apart.

In the end, I will hurt him. It's inevitable.

COLD AIR SAWS through my battered lungs, and twigs break underfoot. I weave through spindly trees, pumping my legs harder, pushing my body to the limit to get away from the masked man. Excitement quickens my breath as I glance behind me. He's gaining on me, and my body flushes hot. I want him to catch me, but I also want to draw out the chase. This unhinged side of Cole makes me so damn hard. It's as if someone unchained his dark, starving side and let it lose in the forest.

Branches slap me in the face, but I can barely feel the stinging pain because I'm too high on adrenaline and the rush of the chase. Jumping over a fallen log, I land in a stream of icy water, which quickly soaks through my shoes and socks. I spin around, only to see the masked man step over the log as though he has all the time in the world to hunt me, and I realize, as he rests the baseball bat on his shoulder, that he's dragging it out on purpose for the same reason as me. He enjoys the chase, too.

Stumbling back, my foot catches on an exposed root, and I fall to the damp ground. My heart threatens to beat out of my chest as I glance around for a stick or a rock to use as a weapon, but there's nothing within reach. He tilts his head sideways to study me, and pinecones sink into the mossy ground as he stalks me.

Crawling backward like a crab, I spin around and launch myself to my feet. There's no time to think and no time to strategize. I run like my life depends on it, and the faster I run, the harder my dick gets. Raising my arms to protect my face, I barrel through the branches of two fir trees. The forest is denser here, and the moss is wetter. I've lost track of time since my stepbrother caught my scent like a predator in the night, but I'd lie if I said I didn't enjoy playing the role of the helpless prey.

I make the swift decision to grab a broken branch off the forest floor. It's heavy in my hands and takes effort to hold upright, but it'll do just fine. When Cole emerges, slapping the fir branches out of the way with his bat, I swing at him and knock him off his feet, but the victory is short-lived.

"Fuck," he growls underneath his mask and rises to stand, unfolding to his full height like something out of a horror flick. I swear I almost come in my pants when he snarls at me. "You'll regret that."

Dropping the heavy branch, I bolt.

My T-shirt is soaked with sweat, and my thigh muscles burn. I can't remember the last time I put this much effort into running. I play football, sure, but this is different. Thank fuck, I'm in good shape, or I would have collapsed by now. Behind me, Cole's boots pound the forest floor, crushing red-capped mushrooms beneath his rubber soles. Pine needles stick to my jeans from my fall earlier, and I'm sure my hands are covered in grime, but the eerie setting is perfect.

Darkness soon settles over the forest, and an owl's hoot penetrates the sound of my heavy pants.

I emerge into a clearing and pause at the sight of a derelict old building. Shivers race down my spine as I take in the broken windows and the vines crawling across the weathered brick. The door is long gone, and now the entryway gapes like a dark void.

"Fuck," I breathe, then glance behind me. There's no sign of Cole. Only silence surrounds me now. Even the owl has stopped hooting.

Turning around to scan the tree line, I inch closer to the house, deciding that the creepy house is less of a threat than my chaser with his bat. But that's a lie. My dick tells me as much when it jumps at the thought of seeing him enter the clearing.

Something breaks through the branches to my left, making my heart stutter, and I look down in time to see a large rock roll close to my shoes.

Fuck...

Inhaling a steadying breath, I will the organ in my chest to get a grip. He's trying to psyche me out, and it's working.

I lift my gaze and stiffen. Shadowed by the fir trees, his mask peers at me from behind the spindly branches. He shifts, and something else catches my eye. There's no sign of the bat, his previous weapon of choice.

"Fuck me," I choke, staring at the carved hunting knife in his hand. My throat jumps as he tilts his head, and I swear he smiles underneath the mask. A trickle of fear licks my spine and mixes with the growing thrill. I don't know how to feel, and it makes me dizzy.

Before I can explore the heady concoction of emotions, instinct takes over. I whirl around and dart for the house. There's no time to think and no time to process what the hell is happening, or why he's armed with a knife, or what he plans to do with it.

I enter through the doorway, kicking up dried leaves as I run down the dark hall. How this building still stands is a mystery. It reeks of rot and decay. Covering my nose with my hand, I come to a stop at the bottom of the staircase. I could escape upstairs, but the steps are wooden, and there's no telling if they'll collapse beneath my weight, though judging by the foul smell, it's not worth the risk.

"Blaaaiiiise." His voice booms behind me, and I curse under my breath and escape into the nearest room.

An overturned couch in the middle of the small space and a mannequin by the window are the only items here. There's nowhere to hide.

"Shit," I whisper, my head whipping from left and right in search of something to use to fight him off, but there's nothing. When his heavy footsteps fall silent in the doorway, I know my time is up. Short of launching myself at the broken window at my back, there's nowhere to go.

My breath catches when he crosses the threshold. This is it. I watch, unmoving, as he makes a show of rounding the couch to get to me. Maybe I should take my chances with the shards of glass lining the window frame, after all.

At the memory of escaping through the window at Jackson's party, my wounded palms throb.

"I bet your dick is leaking for me," Cole taunts, the rotten floorboards creaking beneath his weight.

His raspy voice is my undoing. I almost groan out loud at the ominous undertones.

"I bet you're throbbing."

My eyes fall to the gleaming knife, and my stomach tightens in response. I shouldn't want him to use it on me, but I can't deny the thrill.

He takes another step, and the complaining wood causes a spike of anxiety to rush through me. I throw myself over the couch and tumble to the floor, rolling through debris and dried leaves. I'm up on my feet in the next second, propelled forward by adrenaline. As I run for the doorway, something hits my back. I fall again. My chin smacks off the hard floor, and it takes a few seconds for the pain to register, but then it blooms across my shoulder blades.

What the hell?

What was nothing more than a trickle of fear before is now a burst dam that destroys everything in its path. I can't get away. I'm wounded and unable to run. As his footsteps sound behind me, I try to crawl forward, my nails catching in the ridges. I cough, and blood splutters from my mouth.

He yanks the knife from my back and wipes the bloodied blade on his jeans while I continue to army crawl toward the door. It's useless, I know it, but my brain still urges me to fight.

"Where are you going?" he asks, his voice morphing and twisting. "Are you in a hurry somewhere, *little brother?*"

A choked sob escapes me as he grabs my hair and hauls me up. Grappling with his wrists, I scratch and claw. Nothing works to dislodge him. I even try to kick out at him, but I'm weak, and blood is quickly soaking my T-shirt.

"On your fucking knees where you belong," he snarls, pressing the knife to the underside of my chin when I continue to fight. "Maybe you should have checked if it was really Cole before you let a masked man chase you down like an injured rabbit." He tears off his mask and tosses it to the side before flicking his blond hair out of his eyes. "But you don't really care who hunts you, do you? As long as you get off on this little... kink of yours."

Swaying on my knees, I glare at Jackson.

I should have known he wouldn't let last night go. His ego was wounded at the party, and now it's no longer about Cole— it's personal.

"You want cock, is that it?" He laughs, cupping his junk.

I open my mouth to snarl at him, when a familiar voice says, "You should force it down his throat while I record it on my phone."

Allie leans against the doorframe, with Jackson's discarded baseball bat resting against her shoulder and a mask dangling from her fingers. She flashes me a cold smile. "It would make a perfect parting gift for Cole." Pushing off the doorframe, her heels click on the floorboards. "Did you really think you could get away? You stole what's mine, Blaise."

"Fuck you," I growl, and Jackson whacks me with the knife's handle. My head whips to the side, and pain radiates through my skull. I bite down hard on my tongue to keep from whimpering. Fuck that. I refuse to show weakness.

While my head pounds, I'm vaguely aware of Jackson securing my wrists behind me with a zip tie. Allie keeps talking, but I struggle to make sense of her distorted words. She's blurring before my eyes. One minute, there's one of her, and then there's two. Laughter bubbles from my lips, my face wet with blood. Jackson must have split my brow when he hit me with the knife's handle.

"Shut the fuck up," Jackson snarls, fisting my hair and exposing my throat with a hard pull on the matted strands. A sharp sting follows as the blade nicks my skin.

Allie's heels sound on the floor, and she slows to a stop in front of me. "Did you really think Cole could want someone like you? I'll let you in on a secret." She crouches down in her too-tight jeans and tries to cup my cheek, but I pull away.

If only I could strangle her with my bare hands. I'd love to watch the terror in her eyes as I squeeze the breath from her lungs. I bet she's pretty when she's dead.

Undeterred, she digs her sharp nails into my chin. "He likes a wet pussy."

I bare my teeth. "I'm going to kill you."

"The only one who will die here tonight is you." Patting my cheek, she stands up and nods to Jackson behind me. It's all the warning I get before a piercing pain trails a hot path across my throat, and I choke as blood pours from the deep gash.

Allie pretends to pout. "Don't worry about Cole. I'll be his shoulder to cry on."

"And his cum bucket." Jackson chuckles, shoving me forward. My head hits the grimy floor as I topple over. I drown in my own blood, my body jerking as a sharp heel digs into my cheek. Allie peers down at me through the strands of her cascading hair. "I'll see you in Hell, Blaise—"

I startle awake with a gasp and clutch the quilt to my sweaty chest. *Fuck...* The nightmare is still vivid in my mind, and it takes me a couple of seconds, or maybe minutes, to gain my bearings. I'm in Cole's bed. His side is empty.

"Fuck me," I breathe, scrubbing at my face. What the hell was that dream? It seemed so fucking real.

I drop my hand and check the time on Cole's nightstand. It's still early hours. Where is he? How is he awake already after letting me paint him in cum not once but three times last night?

Flopping onto my back, I drag my hands down my face but pause when the door opens. I peek between my fingers to see Cole, dressed in only his black boxers, enter the room with a tray of...breakfast. He must see the look on my face when I lower my hands because he sniggers as he takes a seat on the mattress. "Don't look so shocked. I figured you would be hungry after last night."

And just like that, I'm hard again. I swear he's a drug. One fix was all it took, and now I'll never get enough.

I sit up, and he puts the tray on my lap.

Cole shrugs, looking anywhere but in my direction.

He's nervous.

The thought makes me smile, and I reach for a slice of buttered toast, moaning as I take a bite.

Cole rests his elbows on his thighs and pretends to be very interested in his hands. It's cute how he can let go of his inhibitions and choke me with his dick, but something as simple as making someone else breakfast is uncharted territory. I like that. It makes me think that maybe he never did this for Allie.

"Is it okay?" he asks, peering at me over his shoulder. "I... You like bacon."

"I do," I confirm, picking up a slice and taking a bite. It's crispy, just how I like it. "This is the best breakfast I've ever had."

He snorts, shaking his head, and I can't help but smile too. Cole thinks I'm lying, but I'm not. If only he knew the butterflies he lets loose in my stomach like I'm a teenage girl with a crush.

"Are you okay?" he asks, turning his body to face me. "You're sweaty."

I take another bite of the bacon, my stomach churning at the memory of my nightmare, and lift a shoulder in a shrug. "I had a bad dream, is all."

"About last night?"

My chewing slows. I'm not hungry now that I'm remembering the feel of Allie's heel on my cheek.

"Can I take you somewhere today?" he asks in a scratchy voice, then clears his throat. I study him, my heart beating harder when he meets my gaze. I've never seen him this nervous before. "Of course."

He nods as if my confirmation settles it, whatever *it* is.

His eyes fall to my almost empty plate, and the tips of his ears redden. It's the most endearing thing I've seen. The mighty Cole blushing? I never thought I'd see the day.

I place the tray beside me on the mattress. "I need a shower first."

"Sure," Cole replies, wetting his lips, but he makes no move to stand up, and I don't either. We stare at each other, exploring this new uncharted territory between us. I want to hold him. It sounds like such a small thing, but it's not. I've woken up next to Mia for months, and not once did my heart hammer like it does in Cole's presence. I want to make him happy. I want to see him smile.

His eyes roam my face before falling to my lips, and he crawls forward, never taking his eyes off my mouth. I hold my breath when he's close enough for our noses to brush. He keeps staring at my mouth like he wants to devour me, and it's all I can do not to launch myself off the bed.

"What are you doing to me?" he asks, his breath skating across my lips like a whispered kiss.

"What are *you* doing to me?" I counter, and he smiles, his eyes clashing with mine.

Fuck... He has the most breathtaking smile—a smile with the power to soften the most hardened hearts.

Leaning in slowly, he trails his warm hand up my bare chest. "Keep looking at me like that." His fingers explore each ridge of muscle, and I shudder with pleasure at the feel of his ghosting touch. Circling each nipple, he skims his fingers higher in a teasing caress. I'm panting by the time he trails across my collarbones. How can he hold this power over me when no one else has come close? He pauses at my pulse point, and I shiver.

I'm hard and putty in his hands all at once. I'm feral yet tamed. I'm...his.

"Come," he whispers against my lips before easing back. I'm left reeling, my mouth dry. "Let's take a shower," he says and pulls me to my feet. I would follow him off a cliff. I'd jump so fucking fast if he asked. The realization hits me like a wrecking ball.

He guides me into the bathroom and, with his eyes locked on mine, shuts the door behind us. "You make me feel seen," he says, pulling me toward the shower. "I like the way you look at me."

I gulp as we step behind the frosted glass. Cole blinks as the water beats down on him, and droplets cling to his dark lashes as his hair sticks to his forehead. I pull him to me by his hips, feeling the wet fabric of his boxers beneath my fingers. "I see you," I confirm and drop my lips to his. As the water soaks our hair, we kiss like it'll be our last. Cole's kisses are ravenous and desperate, and so are mine. We claw at each other, our tongues battling for dominance.

I'm in love with you, Cole.

Breaking away, I pant to catch my breath. Cole caresses my cheek, his forehead pressed to mine. I don't want to ruin this moment with words, so I keep them locked away.

Switching off the shower, he reaches for the bottle of mint-scented shampoo and squirts some onto his palm. Then he sets to work washing my hair, and the pleasurable sensation of his fingers on my scalp sends a groan through my chest.

"If you tell anyone on the football team that I made you breakfast and washed your hair, I will kill you," he teases, and I can't help but laugh. "I have a reputation to uphold."

I groan again as his fingers slide across my scalp. "Your secret is safe with me."

Chuckling, he spikes my hair up before stepping back to inspect his handiwork.

"Do you like what you see?" I ask suggestively and wiggle my eyebrows. He hums, looking pleased with his efforts. I'm too distracted by his mischievous smile and wet hair to see him place his hand on the shower tap. Cold water pours down on me, and I squeal like a pig while he laughs like the fucking devil that he is.

My teeth chatter and my usually impressive dick has fled for warmer pastures. I point a finger in his direction. "You'll regret that."

Chuckling to himself, he exits the shower. "You sure know how to sing some high notes, asshole."

CHAPTER 26
BLAISE

I stare out the passenger window at the passing houses and trees. A dog barks behind a wire fence, and a bike lies abandoned on the sidewalk. It's a rundown street in a shady neighborhood. I don't ask questions. Cole is unusually silent, his grip tight on the steering wheel. The window is down, and a mild breeze rustles my hair as I turn my head in his direction. A muscle clenches in his jaw as he focuses on the road.

Sensing that he's hurting, I reach for his free hand on his thigh and interlace our fingers. I want him to talk to me, but I know I can't force Cole to open up. He has to do it in his own time.

Stroking my thumb over the silver rings on his fingers, I squeeze softly before looking out the window. We pass a series of boarded-up buildings with colorful graffiti—a sign of bored youth with little hope for the future. I've never been to this part of town. My dad has a good job. Expensive cars and enough Christmas gifts to sink a ship are all I've ever known. It's easy to forget that Cole's life would look very different today if his mother hadn't left his father and married mine.

We pass a house that resembles a shoe box, and shame burns my chest. All the times I gave Cole grief, and not once did I stop to think about his past or the memories he's forced to relive every time his dad makes contact despite the restraining order.

He pulls up by the sidewalk and cuts the engine. My eyes

sweep over the houses. It's another rundown street with rusty cars, littered, overgrown yards, and sagging porches.

With his hand hanging over the steering wheel, Cole points a finger at one of the shoe boxes farther down the road. "See that house?"

I peer through the windshield at the tiny white house with a broken wire fence and a yard that's smaller than my bedroom. The screen door flaps in the wind.

"That's where I grew up. Home sweet fucking home."

My throat jumps, but I don't know what to say, so I stay silent, sensing that Cole wants to share a small part of himself that no one else gets to see.

"When my dad came home drunk, Mom would make me hide under the bed to keep me safe."

I tighten my grip on him in response, but he doesn't seem to notice, lost in his painful memories. I wish I could reach him somehow.

"I could hear her cry while he hurt her. At first, I was scared, but then as I grew older, I felt..." His jaw tightens, and his chest expands on a ragged inhale. "I felt angry at him and myself. I hated that I was too small to protect Mom." Looking away from the house, his hair flops over his forehead as he gazes down at our clasped hands. When he continues speaking, his raspy voice squeezes my heart in a vise. "I eventually built up the courage to crawl out from beneath my bed. I still remember how fucking scared I was when I told him in a shaky voice to stop hurting her. My body trembled as I fisted my hands." Shaking his head as if to rid himself of the haunted memories, he stares out the window with a faraway look. "He laid into me like I was a fucking punching bag while my mom threw herself at him to get him to stop. She was too weak, but I still remember her beating his back."

Tears glaze his eyes when he pulls his hand from mine and stares at his palms. "I pissed myself. That's how scared I was."

I suck in a breath, wishing I could go back in time to murder his fucking dad. Hell, I might just do it anyway, but it won't wipe the pain from Cole's eyes. Nothing will.

"That only made him even more angry, and he called me a pathetic coward before punching me so hard I flew into the wall and knocked a framed photograph to the floor. Guess what?" He looks at me, and I hold my breath. "It was a photograph of the three of us. We looked so fucking happy, smiling like the perfect family." He laughs, but it's a bitter, cold sound. "Such a fucking lie."

His brows furrow as he reaches for my hand again, and he looks down as he slides his fingers across the lines on my palm. "He basically stabbed me when I fought back, and it got worse." He gestures to his right leg, the tattoos covering the scars.

I can only stare at him, my heart breaking at the trauma.

"I'm sorry… I shouldn't have unloaded all this crap on you."

"Fuck… Cole." I sit up straight. "Don't apologize. I'm glad you brought me here."

Those dark brows knit together, but he still won't look at me. He's embarrassed. I get it… It took him a lot to be vulnerable with me, and if there's one thing Cole isn't good at, it's communicating. Somewhere in the back of that troubled mind of his, he thought the best way to let me in was to bring me here. Sometimes, actions speak louder than words, and now that I've been here and seen this sliver of his past, I feel like I know him more than anyone except for his mom.

I bring his hand to my lips and kiss his knuckles. Cole tracks my every move, holding himself back like he thinks I might strike. I want to scream, 'You're safe with me,' from the fucking rooftops, but I communicate better through actions, too. We have that in common.

Grabbing the back of his neck, I pull him to me and pry his lips open with my tongue. We kiss out in the open for the first time, but Cole doesn't seem to care that anyone could walk past and see us silencing his demons.

It's not like any of our friends would see us here on this

rundown street in these shady parts of town, but my heart still rejoices.

Breaking away, I nip at his kiss-swollen lips before exiting the car and sliding across the hood. My grin hurts my cheeks as I open his door. "Get out."

He blinks at me and then scans the street.

"It's my turn to take you somewhere," I say, and Cole looks back at me. My smile grows impossibly wide. I rest my arm on the roof and lean into the car. Fuck me, I want to kiss him again, but I let my dimples out to play instead. "Scoot over, princess."

That makes him laugh, and he unbuckles his belt and forces me back as he unfolds from the car. "Call me a princess one more time, and I'll make you my bitch in the backseat of the car."

"Woah," I laugh as he rounds the front of the car. "Now that sounds like a promise, *princess.*"

Cole flips me off, then climbs in, and I can't stop more chuckles from shaking my diaphragm. My gaze snags on the white house, and my laughter dies in my throat. This is the shadow his past casts on his reality, like a cloud in the blue sky, and one of these days, I'm going to make his father pay for the shit he put his son through. I swear to fucking god, I'll make him beg for his life.

COLE LOOKS CONFUSED as I drive us through a remote village. It's the 'blink and you miss it' type of town. My dad drove us here once to drop something off for someone, and I've come here since.

I pull up in a small parking lot, big enough to fit four cars and exit the vehicle. Cole climbs out, too, and looks around like he expects me to drag him into the bushes and strangle him. "Where the fuck are we?"

"You'll see," I say, walking toward an opening in the cliffs. The sandy path crunches beneath our soles, and a warm breeze ruffles our hair from the sea to our left. A seagull screeches as I shove my hands into my jeans pockets to stop myself from reaching his hand.

The cliffs part and the small rocks beneath our feet shift to soft sand. We step onto the beach, which is this village's hidden gem. Very few people know about this place.

Walking ahead, the sun heats my shoulders through my T-shirt as I pick out a dry spot of sand. Kicking off my shoes and socks, I sit down.

Cole comes to a stop beside me, and I shield my face from the sun as I peer up at him. "Join me."

A small smile plays the corner of his lips, and he looks out at the crashing waves. The wind shifts his dark hair as I feel my heart beating harder. Reaching for his hand, I pull his attention back to me. "Please."

He lowers himself, and we sit in silence while watching a seagull ride the breeze.

"The space beneath your bed is your safe place," I say, and Cole looks at me. I lift a shoulder in a shrug. "This is mine."

Resting my arms on my knees, I let my eyes drift over an incoming wave. It builds in strength, much like my emotions where Cole is concerned and, with a ferocity that's both terrifying and exciting, it crashes against the shore. "You've met my dad," I reply, staring at the white sea foam as the wave retreats out to sea. "While your father abused you both, my father..." I drift off, unsure how to express myself. Scratching at my temple, I try again. "My dad is cold. He provides for your mom, takes her on holidays, and makes sure she has everything she needs. On the flip side, when it comes to her emotional needs, he's completely clueless. You're her son, the most prized possession she has, and he won't even try with you. It's emotional abuse, Cole."

Cole listens without interrupting, and I appreciate that he lets me stumble over my words.

"I like you, Cole. Fuck, I'm falling for you." Reaching for his hand, I squeeze his fingers. "I want this for us, but I share my dad's blood and fear that maybe—"

Cole kisses me before I can finish that sentence, his lips pressing against mine. "Shut up," he whispers and nips my bottom lip. "You're not your dad."

"And you're not yours," I remind him, making him pull away and bounce his eyes between mine.

"This is all very new to me." Scooping up sand, I feel it pour through my fingers. "For the longest time, I thought I was incapable of feeling. I was fine with it."

"What are you saying?"

Another wave crashes against the shore.

"I've done some things... You might not look at me the way you do now when you find out."

"What have you done?"

I should tell him about the time I drugged him and recorded him fucking Mia while his girlfriend blew me, all because I wanted blackmail material to hold over his head. I should also tell him I know he's the masked man and that he's the only one I want.

There are a lot of things I *should* say.

But I don't because I'm scared of losing him. I'd rather keep him in the dark, regardless of how selfish that makes me. But maybe I deserve to be selfish for once. I've always lived up to my dad's high expectations of me, and sometimes—no, a lot of times —it forced me to be someone else.

Dad wanted me to get a girlfriend from a high-standing family, so I brought Mia home.

Dad wanted me to play football, so I joined the team.

Dad wanted me to follow in his footsteps, so I took up majoring in business.

If Dad wanted me to jump, I asked how high.

As long as I did as he asked, he clapped me on the back in passing. If I disobeyed him, he gave me the cold shoulder.

Instead of answering Cole's question, I do what I do best. I distract him with a blinding smile before rising to my feet and pulling my T-shirt over the back of my head.

Cole catches it mid-air when I toss it at him. "What are you doing?"

Unbuckling my belt, I pull down my zipper. Cole's eyes widen, and he whips his head around to scan the beach.

"There's no one here," I say, stepping out of my jeans.

"What are you doing?"

"What does it look like I'm doing? I'm going for a swim."

He opens his mouth to speak, but snaps it shut as I hook my thumbs in my boxers. My cock springs free, and the knowledge that someone could come walking through the opening in the cliffs quickens my heartbeat. "Do you like what you see, *princess?*"

His eyes fly up to my face, and he growls, making me laugh. I kick off my boxers, cup my junk, and look at him from beneath my dark lashes. "First to the water wins a blowjob."

"Oi!" he shouts, shooting to his feet when I run for the water. "You fucking cheat, I'm still clothed."

"Tough luck, *princess.*"

Kicking up sand, I'm just about to enter the cold water, when Cole darts past me fully dressed, not giving a shit about soaking his clothes. He dives into the waves as I come to a skidding halt ankle-deep. His head pops up, and he spits out water and whips his wet hair out of his eyes. "What are you waiting for, princess?" he calls out, his eyes sparkling with amusement. "Looks like you owe me a blowjob, after all."

I raise a brow as laughter rumbles in my chest.

If this is what happiness feels like, I want more.

Cole curls a finger at me. "Come here."

Wading into the water, I allow myself to be called forward by the darkening look in his eyes, knowing far too well that at some point, my lies will blow up in my face. Secrets can only stay buried in the murky waters for so long, but who can deny the siren's call when he's smirking like my tailor-made devil?

CHAPTER 27.
COLE

Blaise sleeps on my chest, his legs tangled in mine. Soft, slow breaths fall from his lips, and his hair goes in all directions.

He went out with his friends last night and woke me up by sliding under my covers, still fully clothed, and passed out before I could even ask him what he was doing. Like it was normal to just…sleep beside each other.

I like it.

I shouldn't like it.

Because our parents are married. And when they find out—*if* they find out—shit will hit the fan. I'll get the blame. I manipulated him, coerced him into bed with me. I forced myself on him. The big brother who was supposed to protect him, preferred to chase him through the woods and make him submit, at the same time as doing this…

His arms are wrapped around my body while I run my fingers through his sweaty hair. The scent of him keeps me in place. Feeling him against me, around me, makes me refuse to get up and take a piss or decide to make breakfast again.

I told him the minor details about my life before meeting him. I even showed him the shitty house I grew up in, and he didn't grimace or judge or run away from me. He took me to his safe place, kissed me in the sea, and then we stayed on the beach until the sun dropped into darkness.

I came back to loads of missed calls from my mom, telling me they're staying at their hotel for a few more days and to make sure I tidy my room, do my laundry, make things right with Allie—which I definitely won't—and to ensure Blaise gets to college and practice on time.

I think she forgets I'm only twenty.

As if he's not eighteen and waking up in my arms.

He lifts his head a little, blinking up at me, then groans and buries his head back down into my chest. "It's too early for you to be looking at me like that."

I snort. "It's one in the afternoon."

He groans again. Then falls back to sleep.

I don't realize I fall back to sleep too until I blink awake and I'm pinned beneath Blaise's large, muscular body. His thigh is between mine, chest to chest, with his face pressed to my throat.

Trying to slide from under him so I can get to the bathroom, he tightens around me. With a shake of his head, he kisses the side of my neck. "Don't move."

"I'm seconds from pissing all over you. If that's not a kink of yours, then I highly suggest you let me go."

His head lifts, staring down at me. "Come straight back to bed."

Shifting from under him until I'm sitting on the edge of the bed, I breathe, needing to cool down. The room is hot as hell and being glued to him has me feeling like a furnace.

Once I relieve myself and turn on the shower, I stick my head out to see Blaise sitting up against the headboard, only in his boxers, and checking his phone. His brows are knitting together, and I wonder if it's Mia.

She told me she loved Blaise too. Will she try to get back with him? Will she worm her way back into his heart?

It's not as if she did anything wrong. Her and Blaise were good together before she magically had this weird fascination with me, which I only made worse by fucking her mouth while Blaise took her from behind.

I keep the thoughts at bay while I shower, coming out of the bathroom in a towel to see Blaise still frowning at his phone.

"Everything okay?"

He quickly shuts off his phone and glances up at me. "Yeah. Just some of the guys wanting to head out again tonight. I said I was busy."

I step forward. "Are you busy?"

"I could be," he says quietly. "What are your plans?"

I shrug, making my way to the dresser to grab boxers and sweats. Dropping the towel, I give him a view of my ass, and then conceal it within my clothes. I turn to see his eyes lowered.

"Stop checking me out."

He scoffs and shakes his head, sliding off the bed and kind of hovering for a bit. Running his hand through his hair, he then glances between the bed and the door. "I better..." He gulps, looking at me. "I'm gonna shower and get dressed."

I nod once, and he's out of the room like a fire lit under his ass.

Nervous Blaise makes butterflies go nuts inside of me. Seeing him all flustered, all anxious, fidgety, and unsure of his next steps, brings me joy in the best way.

Once I'm fully dressed and downstairs, I clean up and fill the dishwasher. Transferring wet laundry to the dryer and grabbing the vacuum. Mom got some workers over to fix the house, and as much as she cleaned and cleaned, sawdust and flakes from the plastering are still sitting around. I try to get most of it, ending up throwing off my shirt from sweating.

I turn off the vacuum and drop onto the sofa. How the fuck does my mom do this every damn day? I'm two hours in and feel like I could sleep for weeks.

Blaise comes downstairs, freshly washed and wearing jeans and a sweater. He's fixed his unruly hair, and the shirt he has under his sweater nearly covers the hickey I gave him. Nearly.

I smirk at my work of art as he drops onto the sofa in front of me.

"I told my friends I'd meet them at eight. It's been a while."
Staring at him, I don't grace him with a reply. He shouldn't
feel the need to explain to me if he wants to see his friends. I'll
just do the same. I need to talk to them all anyway about Jackson
and the position I'm now in with them all. Samson and Keith are
talking to me as normal, some of the jocks sending me memes or
screenshots of shit Jackson has been saying, so I know there's no
bad blood against me for smashing the window to get me and
Blaise out of Keith's house.

I want to ask him if he plans on telling his friends about us.
That we're…messing around? Seeing how it goes? Testing the
line to see where we can cross despite our family ties?

Is he my boyfriend? Fuck toy?

"I have a question," I say, and I see all the color drain from
his pretty face. He straightens his spine, grabbing his knees,
waiting for me to keep going.

"How many times has my dad called?"

He chews his lip and drops his gaze, thinking to himself.
Maybe he'll make up a lie, or he'll be honest. Who knows. But
his silence is deafening.

"Tell me, Blaise," I say. "I deserve to know."

"He just wanted to talk to you."

I tilt my head. "That's all? He never said anything else?"

"He doesn't like me very much, or my dad," he replies. "I
think I probably made him angrier, but I didn't want him getting
anywhere near you. If he hurt you again, I would end up behind
bars."

"I don't need you to protect me."

"I know. That doesn't mean I won't."

My nostrils flare, and my jaw tics as I sit forward, leaning my
elbows on my knees. "Going forward, don't you dare put yourself in his firing line. He'll come for you if you try to stop him.
I'll deal with him. He's all talk anyway."

The invisible scars on my mentality are screaming that I'm a
liar. The physical damage to my skin is burning. He's not all talk.

He's all fists and words and laughing at the way he hurts everyone around him. I can still see him grabbing Mom's hair and smashing her into the wall. And how I laid beside her for hours until she woke back up and acted like nothing had happened.

I can feel the sharpness of the blade hacking my leg. How I didn't get muscle or nerve damage is a damn miracle.

Blaise nods in agreement, but I know he isn't listening to a word I'm saying. I swear, if Dad hurts him, I'll lose my shit and kill both him and Jackson.

"I'm heading out now," he says, but doesn't move.

"Right."

His eyes flicker around the room, back to me, then to his fidgeting hands.

I try not to smile and have to suppress it by biting on my lip. He stays still as I shift off the sofa and shuffle over on my knees until I'm between his legs. I grab his chin and jerk him to me, pressing my mouth to his.

"Behave," I say against his lips as I snatch them between my teeth, sucking while he whimpers deeply. Releasing him, I stand, adjusting myself by shoving my hand down my sweats to hide my boner. He's a little breathless as he looks up at me with expanding pupils. So fucking hot and delicious. I want him, in ways I've never thought before.

Smirking and backing away, I grab the vacuum and take it to the cleaning closet, only hearing the front door closing a few minutes later.

CHAPTER 28
COLE

Samson whistles to a tune I've never heard as we walk down the sidewalk. Keith and a few other lads from the team are here too. We've gone to a few bars, only getting into two of them with our fake IDs.

Keith is drunk because he has no idea how to stop at two shots. I think he downed a full bottle of tequila before the dude behind the bar said he wasn't serving him any more. Samson is of age, though – he's the one who's been going to the bar for us.

I check my phone, feeling uneasy that I haven't heard a word from Blaise. On social media, he's tagged in photos in Shingles, a bar just down the street that I may or may not have tricked my group into going to.

His friend has his arm over his shoulders as he smiles for a group photograph.

It's tagged as "Dream Team," and it annoys me enough that I change the settings to hide any further posts from his friends. Petty, but I don't care. He can happily sit with his friends and talk to them, but he can't spare a second to ask me what I'm doing, or if I'm missing him?

He doesn't even know I'm out.

When we reach the bar, I stand outside and light a cigarette, pressing my foot into the wall. Keith hovers before he checks his surroundings and lights one too.

"Why are you acting sketchy?"

"I told my new girl I'd quit smoking."

"I thought she was out of town?"

"She is," he replies, checking around us again between each draw. "But her folks or friends might catch me."

I chuckle and inhale, filling my lungs with the toxic smoke while I slide my phone out again and spot a new message that has my heart accelerating.

Blaise: Your friends are here.

Well, well, well. He remembers I exist. I put the smoke between my lips and type out a reply, but then I pause. It hasn't even been a full minute since the message has been received. Will I look desperate if I reply right away?

Tucking my phone back in, I listen to Keith talking about his new girlfriend, and how his parents nearly kicked his ass for the broken window. I offered to pay a few days ago, but he refused and said it was his fault since he was the one who made up the game in the house and locked everyone in. He didn't know Jackson had a gun, or that he was fucking Allie.

Not that I care. Allie has become nothing but a faint memory in my mind. The ex who cheated constantly, who never made me happy, and the more I think about her, I hated the bitch for the way she thought she could manipulate me on a daily basis.

Imagine I actually liked her?

Keith follows me inside, and I try not to hunt the place for Blaise. I know he's sitting at a booth, right in front of the dance-floor, to the left of the bar. There's an Elvis poster above his head, and he's beside that moron.

I reach the bar, and Samson orders us all drinks while one of the guys finds us our own booth. The music isn't too loud, so I can hear Tiago talking. I follow the voice, and my gaze clashes with a green one, staring at me from the other side of the bar.

Blaise and his friends must have fakes too as they order more booze, but he's staring at me while his lips move, talking to the waitress.

For a long moment, I'm trapped here. It's like I'm entering a subspace without the push. He's watching me, hunger in his eyes, possessive, and I have the urge to grab him by the throat, pin him to the bar, and claim him in front of everyone.

To make sure everyone here knows he's fucking mine.

Someone shoulders me. "Hey, man. Stop growling at your little bro and come sit down."

My annoyance is short-lived when Keith is summoned by one of Blaise's friends – they're in the same study group, if I remember correctly. They invite us to sit with them, and as we close in, Blaise walks toward his booth from the opposite direction. The closer our proximity gets, my heart races powerfully. It's stupid, getting all wound up because he's close to me. Closer. Closer. Fucking closer.

He slips into the booth when I reach it, and his friend drops in beside him, but I place my beer on the table and jut my chin to the side. "Move."

Blaise goes ramrod beside him. His friend narrows his eyes. "Me?"

I tilt my head. "I'm looking at you. Move."

Finding his words through a chortle and a disdained look, he looks flabbergasted. "Excuse me?"

"Just fucking move."

My friends are silent, probably wondering what the fuck is going on.

Hesitantly, he takes his cocktail and slides out, giving me a strange look while I take his place. My thigh presses to Blaise's, and my blood thrums hot in my veins. There's adrenaline fucking pumping so fast that I can hear it roaring in my ears. My eye twitches, and I pause when I feel Blaise's lips against my ear. "What's wrong?"

I shake my head and take a drink, gulping down half the bottle. I have no idea what's wrong with me. Everyone's just sitting around, chatting shit, bobbing their heads to music or flirting, and I'm hitting a rager.

"Cole," he whispers, secretly grabbing my thigh under the table – no one can see, because I'm his little secret. He doesn't want anyone to know about us, or he would have smiled when he saw me, kissed me, or some other romantic shit.

I hold my breath at the pain in my chest. It burns. Everything burns, especially when I down another five gulps of my beer and finish the bottle.

"Jackson called any of you?" Samson asks, and it catches my attention enough that I can fill my lungs. "The asshole has been extra quiet lately. Ever since that mess at your place."

Keith shrugs. "I told him to pay for damages. The dickhead smashed the house up and left cum on my dining table, not to mention all the shit he did to Blaise." He looks at him. "I'm sorry, man. That wasn't the plan. We just wanted us all to hang out. We thought you'd bring your friends too."

"He didn't even ask us!" one says. "He's been too busy with Mia to know we exist the last few weeks."

My eyes snap to him. "They don't know you broke up with her?"

"You *what*?" all of his friends retort at the same time.

Blaise shrugs and takes a drink of beer. "It's not a huge thing."

"Mia and Blaise, set to be the epic lovers. You seriously want us to believe that's it?"

My eye twitches again, and I grit my teeth and look down at Blaise's hand still on my thigh. He's squeezing it so hard, trying to get my attention, but I fist my hands instead and pretend I'm not losing it while they talk about how good they were together.

"What about you and Allie?" Samson asks me. "You two done?"

"Yeah," I reply sternly, trying to stay calm.

"What happened there? You finally accepted she was a cheat and saw you deserved better?"

I shake my head, and the words slip out without needing to think. "I broke up with her because I'm not into girls."

They all stop and stare at me.

Why are they acting like it's a big thing?

"Is there an issue with me being gay?"

They all shake their heads, and Samson grins like the Cheshire Cat before toasting. "To Cole leaving the closet!"

For some reason, I smile, chuckling at how happy he is. Something settles within me, and instead of taking Blaise's hand under the table, I throw it over the back of him, resting it on the booth. The position presses me up against him, and I watch them all connect the dots.

Blaise is still as a statue, except his breathing has become heavy and forced through his nostrils. His fingers press into my thigh more, and I can feel myself growing excited at his anxiety.

"You two?" Blaise's friend says. "You two are...together?"

Blaise grabs his beer and downs it. "Is that a problem?"

"Wow," Keith blurts. "I didn't see that coming. Not gonna lie. Wow. Aren't you, like, underage?" he says to Blaise.

I frown. "He's just about to turn nineteen, you asshole. I'm twenty."

Samson is grinning. "Your parents are gonna lose their shit."

Blaise stiffens beside me, but I drop my arm over his shoulder and squeeze it, pressing my thigh up against his. I'm claiming him, officially. Everyone here now knows that I own him, and he owns me. Why does that make me feel so giddy?

I order another beer, and two hours later, we're all laughing at Tiago dancing on the table as others around us cheer him on. Keith is on the phone, the other guys are either flirting with someone or drunk and dancing, and Blaise and I are still sitting in the booth.

"Let's go home," he whispers in my ear. "I want to be alone with you."

Fuck. His words make my balls tingle, and I turn to him and grin. "Getting all desperate?"

"If I say yes, can we leave?"

"One more drink," I say, my nose bumping off his, in public, where everyone can see. His eyes flicker down to my mouth, and I close the distance, kissing him softly, briefly enough to drive him insane, before I yank myself away and hop over the back of the booth to get us more drinks.

BLAISE SLAMS me against the door as soon as it closes behind me. He's devouring my mouth like he's a starved animal, sucking and kissing and pulling off my shirt and messing my hair.

He fists the strands at the back of my head and presses our bodies together, sliding his tongue against mine and grinding his thick cock into my own.

Fuck. He's killing me. I keep trying to get his sweater off but he's pinning my hands to the wall and robbing me of air while strangling the living fucking life out of me.

Pulling me away from the front door by the throat, we nearly break my mom's favorite vase as we hit the tabletop. Blaise drags me along the entrance way, not stopping devouring my mouth as he demands everything. We barely make it halfway up the stairs before he unfastens the buttons on my jeans and shoves his hand down them to fist my cock.

I let out a deep groan and drop my head back onto the stair while he strokes me. He's squeezing and twisting at the tip, making me even harder than humanly possible.

"I want to fuck you," he says against my mouth, sliding his tongue against mine and snatching my bottom lip between his teeth, pulling it back until it's painfully snapping into place. Copper fills my mouth, and I kiss him harder. As if I might die if I stop.

Blaise pulls away from my mouth and looks down between our bodies, watching the way he fucks me with his hand. The precum beads at the tip, begging for more.

"My room or yours?"

"Yours is closer," I say, panting as he strokes faster. "Fuck, Blaise. You're gonna make me come."

He lets go, and I feel like murdering the dickhead.

"Not yet," is all he says as he pulls me up and drags me to his bedroom. He slams his door shut and pushes me, taking full control of my body as I drop onto the mattress. Curling his fingers into the waistband of both my jeans and boxers, he slides them down my legs to free my cock.

I can see how much he wants me. His eyes, the starved look, how much his pants are tenting, the way he kisses me as he lowers onto me and sucks on my tongue while simultaneously grinding against my bare dick.

Blaise leaves my mouth, kissing along my jaw while nipping with his teeth. The sensation rushing through me has me squirming under him. Why the fuck is he still fully dressed?

I groan as he sucks the skin on the side of my throat, marking me – his claim. Then he kisses down farther, my collarbone, his hands everywhere but on my dick while he kisses down my heaving chest.

His eyes flick up just as his tongue circles my nipple, and fuck, I hold my breath and feel the solid slam inside my balls with how good it feels. He captures it with his teeth, and I pulse between my legs, my spine twisting and making me arch my chest into his mouth more as he sucks and licks and bites and scrapes his blunt nails down my side.

"Fuck," I breathe.

Grinning against my skin, he travels down until he's sucking on my ribs, my hips, making me tense every single muscle as he grabs my cock with both hands and pumps while he stares at how much I'm leaking.

"You're making a mess of my bed, Cole," he says, his eyes on mine as he drags his tongue up the underside of my dick, dodging the sensitive area of my tip.

"If you don't suck my dick right now, I'll beat your ass."

He laughs and shakes his head. "You seem to forget who is in control here."

Blaise flips me over so damn easily, I barely register my new position as he palms at my ass cheeks and spreads them, and when something wet and warm touches my tight hole, I press my face into his pillow and moan.

"You love getting your ass eaten, don't you?"

I don't reply. I can't. He's sinking his tongue as far as he can, and I'm pushing back against his face, thrusting my cock against his sheets while he fucks me with his tongue. It feels too good. I'm gonna explode soon if he keeps going.

"Fuck," I moan, since it seems to be the only word left in my vocabulary at the moment. I repeatedly mutter it into the pillow while Blaise spreads my cheeks more and slaps me hard enough to hurt, but I clench around his tongue, nearly finding my release before he stops altogether and turns me. He steps off the bed, panting, his cock almost breaking through as he tosses off his sweater and shirt, then gets entirely naked.

"In the drawer," he says, nodding beside me. "Lube. Grab it."

I do as he says, happy to see it's unopened. He climbs on top of me again, his arms straight so he can watch me pump it a few times until the wet, cold liquid comes out.

Blaise coats his fingers with it, and I do the same, like we know what we both need. To be filled. To be fucked. To rub our cocks together. His mouth smashes on mine, thrusting into my cock as he reaches under me and presses his sticky fingers to my back hole. I do the same, spreading him with one hand while the other positions where he needs me.

We thrust together, our fingers and cocks, and Blaise swears against my mouth and kisses me harder. All that can be heard in his bedroom is our moans, the wet, slippery sounds of our fingers, and the way Blaise pants and rubs his cock into mine faster.

His precum is everywhere, and so is mine. Mixed together.

My balls ache for release as his fingers go deeper, but I want more. I need more.

"Do it," I demand.

Blaise freezes. "What?"

"I want you to fuck me, Blaise. Do it. Just fucking do it."

Hesitantly, he slips his fingers out of my ass and straightens his arms to look down at me. "You're sure?"

Nodding desperately, I move my cock against his, my fingers slipping away and grabbing at his hips. I chase his mouth and kiss him. "Do it."

Blaise pulses against me as he searches my face, then he pulls away enough to flip me over. "If it hurts, I'll stop. Don't you fucking dare let me do this if it's hurting you."

He's saying all these words while he squirts more lube, and I whimper as some drops onto my back. Everything is sensitive, and I think I might die if he doesn't hurry up.

Lying down on top of me, he settles his cock between my ass cheeks as his hand slides up my side, under my chest, and snatches at my throat. He yanks my head up, tilting me enough to kiss me, his tongue playing with mine. It's a soft and slow kiss, distracting me as he thrusts faintly against my ass.

His hips pull right back, and he positions himself so the tip is nudging at my tight hole. It throbs, my dick throbs, my balls throbs, my fucking heart throbs as he kisses me deeply and eases in. The tightness and burn have me choking, but he keeps kissing me with each inch.

"Relax," he orders as he slides another inch inside, gradually thrusting, more like pulsing his hips to get me used to it. It's different. A little sore, but fuck, it's good. I absently rock my hips with him, forcing him deeper. He gasps and pauses, groaning as I move against him and he stays still.

"Fuck me," I grit through my teeth. "Fucking fuck me like you hate me."

His jaw tenses, and he opens his eyes. The green is gone, overtaken by the darkness. I choke on air as he pulls back so just the head is in and slams deep. His eyelids fall closed again, and he groans as he does it over and over.

He arches me up by the throat, dives into the sensitive skin under my ear, and bites and sucks as he fucks into my ass.

His fingers wrap around my cock, stroking me while his thrusts get harder, faster, more fucking erratic as I struggle for breath from how good it feels.

Hitting something deep, my insides light up like fireworks, and my eyes ping open at the intense feeling, the sensation ripping through me with my orgasm.

"Blaise," I moan. "Fuck. Fuck, fuck, fuck."

I paint cum all over his sheets as he strokes and keeps pummeling. He doesn't slow down or give me a second to realign with reality; he loses his control and pulls me fully onto all fours and grabs my hips.

Each thrust feels like I'm freefalling into something magical. Each time he groans, there's a thump in my balls, and I force myself back into him.

As his hand slams down on my cheek, and the deep tunnel of my ass tightens around him, I feel him getting even harder. He fists the hair at the back of my head and uses it to control me, fucking faster, thrusting longer, slapping the side of my ass, then fisting my cock that refuses to go soft.

Stopping mid-thrust, he lets out the most addictive sound as his cock pulses inside me, pumping me full of his cum that feels so fucking good. I think more cum leaks from me too, dripping down my thigh.

He collapses on top of me, both of us panting and gasping for air. Grabbing my chin, he turns me to look at him. "You good?"

I nod once and he kisses my forehead—something I never thought would make me fight a grin, but here I am. I kiss him fully, layering my mouth on his softly.

"I love you," I say, still trying to breathe properly as his cock softens and slips out of me. "When the fuck did that happen?"

He laughs and rolls onto his back beside me, his chest rising and falling as he comes down from the high.

The knock at the door and a deep voice make me jump. Blaise shoves me off the bed and out of sight, pulling a blanket over himself, just in time for his dad to open the door.

"Blaise," he says, and my eyes widen. "What happened downstairs? The place is wrecked, and Cole's clothes are on the floor."

"No idea. Why are you home? Rachel said you were going to be staying away a while longer."

"Oh, she's staying there. She needs space."

My brows knit together. He doesn't even sound like he cares. "Are you and Rachel okay?"

"No, son. But it's fine. Can you find your brother and tell him to clean up his mess?"

The door closes, and I get to my knees and look over at Blaise. He gathers my cum on his sheets. "What he said." He sticks his fingers in his mouth, tasting me. "You wanna clean up your mess?"

CHAPTER 29
BLAISE

I smirk as I peer out the windshield at the house at the end of the dark street. The lights are out, but Jackson's car is in the driveway.

"I don't like this," Ronnie says, getting on my last nerve. The guy is always nervous and goes to great lengths to avoid conflict.

I, on the other hand, like to instigate chaos. Admittedly, my methods are usually more subtle, but now I'm pissed and want to make a point.

"Relax," I reply, squeezing his shoulder. "It's just a friendly talk."

Tiago snorts a laugh, and Ronnie looks unconvinced. I flash them my widest smile before exiting the vehicle and opening the trunk. The car doors open and shut, and Ronnie makes a strangled noise in his throat as they join me. "I thought you said a 'friendly talk.'"

I hold out the baseball bat for him, and he looks at it like it's an alien lifeform. He makes no move to take it, so I hand it to Tiago instead. "Like I said…" I reach in for the two other bats and the masks, then shut the trunk. "It's just a friendly talk."

Ronnie reluctantly accepts the bat, and I toss him the Scream mask. He barely manages to catch it mid-air. I hold the other one out for Tiago. "Ready to teach Jackson a lesson?"

"Nací preparado," Tiago says and practices a swing with the bat like he's playing golf. "That's Spanish for 'I was born ready.'

Chuckling, I slip my mask from my back pocket and slide it over my head. Jackson lives on a dark street with only one lamp-post. The dim orange glow doesn't reach this far, but I still pull my hood up to hide my hair. Better safe than sorry.

"C'mon," I say, setting off down the road with the bat resting on my shoulder. I've got to admit that I feel like a badass vigilante with my choice of weapon and mask. The thought makes me snigger.

Tiago is right behind me, and Ronnie jogs to catch up with us.

"What if his parents are home?"

"They're not."

"How do you know?"

I roll my eyes behind the mask. "We didn't come here blindly, Ronnie. I did some research first."

"Fuck, Ron," Tiago says, "it's been ages since we spent quality time with our boy here." He wraps his arm around my neck and chokes me. "He didn't fucking tell us he is loved up. We thought he'd abandoned us for Cole's friends." When he releases me, I try to grab him. He dances out of the way and speeds ahead before turning around and walking backward. "Let's have fun tonight."

"Parties are fun. Holidays abroad are fun. Those sweets where some taste of candy and some are weird flavors, like sick and snot—that's fun. I doubt the definition of the word fun covers threatening people with baseball bats."

"Actually," I reply, pointing my bat at him, "that's the definition of fun to some."

"Break some bones, crack some skulls," Tiago says, and Ronnie slows to a stop.

"We're not hurting him, right? Please tell me we're not. My mom will kill me if she finds out about this."

Draping my arm around his shoulder, I jostle him. "Relax. You're overthinking it. No one is dying tonight."

Ronnie grumbles under his breath as we near the house. I lift a finger to my lips. The lights are out, except for a lamp in the upstairs bedroom window. Jackson is home alone. His parents are away overnight at a charity event to raise money for some obscure cause.

Our shoes disturb the glistening dew on the damp grass as we cross the front lawn. Tiago raises the flag on the mailbox, making me snigger. Jackson's brand-new black Jeep Wrangler sits in the drive, which is his pride and joy and a total showpiece.

I raise the bat and bring it down full force on the shiny hood, leaving behind a large dent. "Oops," I chuckle before smashing the headlights. It's a lot of fun to go psycho and a great way to dispel all that anger. My therapist—if I had one—would approve. Tiago laughs, then joins in with the chaos. Glass explodes everywhere as he slams the bat into the passenger windows. He rounds the vehicle to take out the taillights, the shattered glass crunching beneath his boots.

"What the fuck?" Jackson blurts as he exits the house. Moths flap their wings against the porch light at his back while he gapes at us like he can't believe what he sees. "You... I... My car."

The others snigger behind their masks. I slide mine up to smile at him, and his eyes widen. "I don't take well to threats, Jackson." As I step closer, he stumbles away from the door. I always knew he was all bark and no bite. Guys like Jackson are cowards with mommy issues beneath the cocky attitude. "What did you plan on doing at the party? Beat me up? Break a bone or two so that I can't play football? Send a message to Cole?" My teeth grind together. I hate the thought of someone hurting Cole. But one thing that enrages me even more is the thought of someone using me against him.

Jackson's throat jumps, his eyes falling to the bat in my hand. "Blaise, man...let's talk about this."

"Talk about what?" I ask. "How you and your friends targeted me at the party?"

Nervous laughter bubbles up from his chest. "It was just a bit of fun."

I hum as I drag the bat through the shattered glass on the ground. Jackson's fear is palpable in the air, like a sweet aroma I can't help but breathe in—a crackling fire on a summer's evening, popcorn at the movies. "I'm all for fun, too, as you can see."

Jackson skates his gaze to his car behind me, and I jerk forward with a "Boo."

He falls onto his ass, like the scaredy cat he is, then jumps to his feet and runs to the edge of the porch, where he leaps over the railing like Spiderman.

I fucking love a good chase.

Cracking my neck, I let out a loud holler before setting off after him. Leaping over the railing, I land with a hard thud and laugh with glee. When was the last time I felt this thrilled, well, except for when I was balls deep in Cole? I force the memory aside. Now isn't the time to remember how he felt, smelled, or how he groaned when I pounded him.

Tiago and Ronnie are hot on my heels. We run down the side of the property and catch sight of Jackson escaping into the forest at the edge of the yard.

If he thinks I'll let him get away, he's got another thing coming. While the plan was never to hurt him, I'm tempted to break his skull.

Sprinting across the lawn, we enter the forest, slapping branches out of the way. We catch up to him as he climbs up a tree, like that will keep him safe.

We pace around the trunk like a pack of starved lions. Tiago turns back, leaving me with Ronnie. I jerk my chin at him. "Go get him."

Ronnie gawks at me behind his mask before glancing up at the tree. "I can't climb up there."

"Why not? Jackson did it."

"What if he kicks me, and I fall?"

"You won't fall."

"The likelihood is that I will," he argues. "It's not so easy to 'retrieve'"—he makes quotation marks—"a six-foot football player from a tree. He's not a baby kitten."

Snorting, I direct my attention to the fucker quivering on a thick branch near the top of the tree. "Maybe that should be your nickname moving forward? What do you say, kitten?"

"*Baby* kitten," Ronnie corrects, and I wave him off.

"Kitten. Baby kitten. Whatever. Why don't you come down and play with us?"

"Has anyone ever told you that you're sick in the head?" Jackson spits.

I screw my eyes into slits before ramming my foot into the trunk and whacking my baseball bat against it as though I'm Superman. Of course, nothing happens, but I'm sure Jackson nearly pisses himself. "Don't make me come and get you, baby kitten."

"Fuck you!"

"You already tried that, remember? I wasn't interested then, and I'm certainly not interested now."

"I'll make you regret this," he snarls.

"Oh?" I laugh. It starts out softly before gaining strength, like an incoming wave. I have to brace my hand on my trunk because I'm laughing so hard. "Are you threatening me, kitten?"

"You're dead. So fucking dead!"

"You're pretty ballsy for a guy who's stuck up a tree. Want me to phone the fire brigade for you? I hear they rescue cats. We can get a man in uniform to help you down."

Ronnie makes a strangled noise beside me, turns to face Tiago, and asks, "Where did you find those?"

Tiago sets a heavy plastic container on the leafy ground and holds up the saw in his hand. "I found it in their basement," he says.

"It'll take you hours to fell the tree with that," says Ronnie, gawking. I roll my eyes and reach for the saw. Sometimes, he really is a fucking bore.

"Ready to come down yet?" I ask Jackson and rest the serrated blade against the trunk. "Or do we have to help you down?"

"Fuck off," he snarls, his lips thinning over his teeth.

"Have it your way," I reply, applying pressure to the saw. The blade cuts through the bark, and my dark smile grows until my cheeks hurt. I bet he's trembling like the leaves surrounding him. "Scared yet, kitten?"

He curses, and I toss the saw to the ground, my muscles burning from the exertion of sawing through such a thick trunk. Ronnie was right—we would be here all night. I reach for the container and uncap the lid. Jackson shifts on the branch while I douse the trunk in gasoline. The pungent stench pricks my nose, reminding me of late afternoon trips with my dad to the garage when he needed his tires replaced. The lanky man behind the counter, with scraggly hair and yellowed teeth, used to wink at me while wiping his oil-stained hands on a dirty rag he pulled from his back pocket. I used to like those trips because I always got to pick a lolly from the jar the man kept behind the counter.

"What the fuck are you doing? Are you insane?" Jackson asks frantically. The liquid splashes against the trunk. I keep going until the container is empty, then toss it aside. Tiago throws me a small box of match sticks, which I catch mid-air. Anticipation hums in my veins. I strike a flame, watching it flicker menacingly in the darkness.

"Blaise?" Ronnie asks shakily.

"You fucked not only with me," I tell Jackson, "but with what's mine, too. Do you think what we did to your car is bad? Trust me, you've seen nothing yet."

"Blaise," Ronnie pleads. "Think about this… You'll set the tree on fire. He'll pass out from smoke inhalation and…" His unspoken words hang like whispered promises in the air. Jackson trembles visibly on the branch.

"Consider this a warning," I say, blowing out the flame and winking at him.

IT'S LATE when I return. The TV flickers in the living room. Dad nurses a beer on the couch while watching an old western. His wife is still nowhere in sight.

I sneak by, careful to avoid the creaky floorboards. I'll be in deep shit if he spots me now. Sure, I'm eighteen and allowed to stay out late, but sneaking home past midnight, covered from head to toe in filth and sweat, is not my best look. It also raises questions. Dad won't take well to me smashing up Jackson's car, even if the fucker deserved it. My lips pull up at the thought.

When I enter the room, Cole is asleep. I close the door softly before crossing the floor and climbing into bed. The sheets smell of him, reminding me of the first time I met Cole.

Dust flecks dance in the air as a guy sidles past me in the kitchen doorway. A muscled arm brushes against my chest, and I catch a whiff of his cologne—he smells of citrus and late summer evenings.

I look up from my phone and frown.

Who are you, and why are you in our kitchen?

Tufts of his dark hair peek out from beneath his backward red cap, a black T-shirt stretching across his broad shoulders, and his shorts hung low on his narrow hips. The bored expression on his face screams, 'Don't fuck with me.'

I'm immediately intrigued.

Dad stands by the table with his arm draped around a dark-haired woman. His smile does little to hide his disapproval when he glances at the boy, who's undoubtedly the woman's son. The resemblance is striking.

Pocketing my phone, I enter the room, treading carefully like a soldier avoiding landmines. My dad is away on business a lot, so the truth that stares me in the face blindsides me—he had met a woman and failed to give me the heads-up.

I study the tall teenage boy by her side. His dark eyes lock on mine and harden. I can already tell that he doesn't like me, and that makes me want to find out more. I raise a brow, and his jaw tightens. "This is Rachel, your new stepmom," Dad says. "And this young man is her son, Cole."

The mattress shifts beneath my weight as I climb on top of him like a lion on the prowl. He looks so damn irresistible asleep on his front with his arms beneath the pillow. Trailing my nose up his spine, I breathe him in, and he stirs when I slide my fingers through his bed hair to twist the short strands. At the same time, I grind my hard dick against his ass—a crash wave colliding with the shore.

"Blaise?" he whispers sleepily. I decide then and there that it's my new favorite sound in the whole fucking universe. Sinking my teeth into the crook of his neck, I pull hard on his hair.

"Why do you smell of gasoline?" he asks as he shifts beneath my weight. I capture his wrists with one hand and trap them on the pillow. "I need to be inside you," I whisper in his ear, ignoring his question. "Fill you up with cum. I want it to leak out of you tomorrow when you're with your friends."

"Fuck," he groans, shuddering.

My lips spread into a smile, and I release his hair to shove his boxers down his legs. "Tell me you missed me tonight." Ripping open my belt, I nip his ear while freeing my cock. "Tell me you thought about my dick tearing through your tight hole." Cole squirms against my grip on his wrists, but there's no real struggle behind it. I smack the hard length against his ass cheeks and peer down between our bodies, lip trapped between my teeth. "Tell me you want me."

"I want you," he replies, jutting his ass out. "Fuck, I want you."

"Yeah?" I squeeze his smooth skin. "You want me to fuck this ass?"

"Yes..." he groans, the sound muffled in the pillow.

Reaching across the bed, I root through the nightstand for the lube to prep him. "Remember the first time we met?" I ask as I squeeze a healthy dose of lube onto my fingers.

The slippery liquid threatens to drip onto the bedsheet. I smooth my fingers over his tight ring of muscles, my dick twitching. "Answer me, or I will stop."

"I remember," he says in a breathy voice, humping the mattress and wringing the creased sheet.

I press a finger into him. "What did you think about me that first day when you stared at me from across the kitchen?"

"I thought..." He grunts as I work a second finger inside his tight hole. "I wanted to punch the smug look off your face."

My breathy chuckle dances across his bare shoulder. I hum as I work my fingers in and out of him. "You intrigued me that day," I admit, then hiss. "Fuck, you're tight. I can't wait to stretch you with my dick."

"Intrigued you?" he asks, unable to leash his curiosity. "Intrigued you how?"

Slipping my digits out, I squirt more lube onto my hand. Cole sucks in a breath as I fill him up with three fingers. My dick throbs at the snug fit. I can't wait to feel him squeeze the cum from my balls.

"You looked at me like you were a cornered snake, and I liked that." Sucking on his earlobe, I graze it with my teeth. "The threat was clear in your eyes."

"What threat?"

I remove my fingers to lube up my throbbing cock. "You would strike if I got too close. Unless you haven't noticed," I whisper and nip his shoulder with my teeth before flipping him over onto his back and palming his weeping dick, "I like a challenge."

Cole throws his head back on the pillow. "Fuck..."

"You like that, huh?" I goad, stroking his veiny cock. "You gonna come for me? Make a mess on my hand?"

"Blaise," he groans as he wrings the sheets.

Releasing his cock, I palm his balls and massage them between my fingers before rearing up on my knees and spreading his legs. His dick leaks all over his taut stomach. I swipe my fingers through it and suck them clean. A groan rumbles in my chest at the salty taste and the drunk look in his eyes. I want more. So much more. Lining my dick up with his back hole, I sink inside him slowly, careful not to hurt him. My heart races, and my T-shirt sticks to my skin as sweat beads on my back. Cole is naked while I'm fully dressed. Something about that power dynamic turns me on.

"Blaise," he chokes as I palm his hard length and give it a firm stroke. Thrusting shallowly, I work my dick deeper until I finally bottom out. The feeling is unlike anything I've ever felt. He's tight and warm and fucking perfect.

My dick twitches inside him as I tip my head back with a groan. "Jesus, Cole," I moan, spreading him wider with my hands on his knees, wishing I had switched on the overhead light so I could see my dick buried deep in his ass. "You're killing me."

I pull out to the tip, and then sink back inside him—the feeling is exquisite. Collapsing forward, I capture his lips and wrap my fingers around his throat. "Do you have any idea how good you feel?" I breathe into the kiss before delving my tongue into his mouth and tasting his choppy breaths. I kiss him deeper. Cole's fingers are everywhere—on my back, threaded through my hair, and squeezing my ass. We're a tangle of sweaty limbs. He groans into the kiss and pulls on the hair at my nape.

"Cole..." I break away to catch my breath. "I can't..." I swallow, kissing him roughly before trailing my lips across his defined jaw and whispering in his ear, "I'm gonna fuck you hard now."

Before he has a chance to reply, I dig my fingers into his neck and sink my teeth into his bottom lip, assaulting the kiss-swollen flesh by pulling it away from his teeth and biting down until coppery blood rushes to the surface. Cole grunts and tries to pull away, so I grip his jaw to keep him in place while I feast on his mouth.

When I slide out to the crown, only to drive in hard, he claws his short nails down my back and palms my ass. I make true to my promise to fuck him senseless. The headboard knocks against the wall with my next thrust. It's reckless, the thrill of knowing my dad is downstairs while I'm balls deep in his wife's son. But I can't stop myself from doing it again. Especially when Cole lets out such a loud groan that I'm forced to clamp my hand over his mouth to muffle the sound. Fuck me, we'll get caught if I don't calm myself the fuck down.

"You need to be quiet," I instruct, and Cole tries to shake my hand off his mouth. Instead of easing my grip, I tighten it to lock him in place. "Touch your dick. Make yourself come."

Cole's nostrils flare as his hand disappears between our bodies, and I feel him stroke his dick.

"Good boy," I praise, slowing my thrusts. "You feel so damn good... So tight. You drive me insane."

He makes a strangled noise beneath my palm. I'm on the edge—a thin layer of sweat beading on my back from the pressure of holding back. "I need to come inside you."

Cole, the fucking asshole, sinks his teeth into my palm, and I rip my hand away with a hiss. My palm throbs painfully in the aftermath as I shake out my hand. I don't have to turn on the lights to know I'm bleeding.

I grip his stubbly chin with a snarl, smearing his skin with blood, and bite his lip hard enough to cause him to flinch. He must like pain because, in the next second, cum erupts from his cock.

"That's it," I coax, feeling it soak through my T-shirt. "Come all over me, big brother. Show me how good I make you feel."

Seeing him fall apart tips me over the edge, and my own thrusts become erratic. My hips roll into him again as my balls draw up tight. I lock my jaw and push up onto my hands as every muscle tenses in my body just before my dick pulses inside him. Cole rears up on his elbows to dip his fingers beneath my T-shirt and tease my contracting abs—the dark happy trail. I'm still shuddering through my orgasm, my cock emptying inside him.

"You're so fucking hot when you come," he says, trailing his hand higher to pinch and roll my nipples. "But you better stop calling me your big brother, especially while inside me."

My chin meets my chest, and I chuckle. I'm too exhausted to hold myself up, so I collapse on top of him and bury my face in his neck, where his pulse thrums like the wings of a humming-bird. Even now, coated in sweat and cum, he smells delicious. As he strokes his fingers through my damp hair, a sense of content-ment washes over me. My dick is slowly softening inside him, but I make no move to shift my weight off him. If I had my way, I'd stay wrapped up in him forever.

"I should have punched the smug look off your face the first time I saw you," he whispers into the darkness, making me laugh.

I lift my head from his damp neck. "Yeah, you should have."

"It's not too late to do it now."

"I like it when you talk dirty to me," I tease and kiss him softly before rolling off him and stripping out of my clothes. There is no chance in hell I am sleeping in my jeans.

After plugging in my phone to charge on the nightstand and ignoring a text message from Jackson, in which he threatens to take revenge, I roll back over, pull Cole close, and do something I've never done—not even with Mia.

I fall asleep cuddling someone.

CHAPTER 30
COLE

Blaise is showering when I wake up in my bed, no clothes on, a cloth on the ground beside me where he must've cleaned me up after I painted myself with my own cum.

I'm not as sore this morning as I was the first time we fucked. My thighs are a little tender from the way he was grabbing them, but other than that, I just feel...empty. I've been waking up on my own for years, but now, I have someone to wake up to, and I need Blaise to come back to bed already.

His phone buzzes on the bedside table, and I yawn and close my eyes again, pulling the throw back over my naked body.

I hate lying around too. I'm usually waking up and getting to my feet and hurrying with my morning. What the fuck am I doing?

My own phone buzzes, and I glance over to see Jackson is calling me. I roll my eyes and hang up, but he starts calling again instantly. I ignore it a second time, and a message comes through.

> Jackson: This is important. Answer, and you'll never need to hear from me again.

Right away, he rings again, and I flatten my lips, glancing at the door, knowing Blaise is still showering in our adjoining bathroom.

I answer and stay silent.

After a second, Jackson chuckles. "Right. No 'hello' or 'good morning.' Just straight to it?"

"What do you want?" I snap, already losing my patience. His voice irks me.

"You need to check your brother's phone. Pin to unlock it is your date of birth. He has a video saved in a folder on its own, but don't try to watch it when he's there. Call this my last piece of niceness before I leave you both alone. Good luck, the guy is a fucking lunatic."

He hangs up, and I frown, pulling the phone away from my ear.

The fuck?

Blaise is still in the bathroom as I look over at his phone.

Jackson could be fucking with me, but he was so specific with password pins, folders, videos. I bite my lip and shift toward his side and pull out the charger.

My heart hammers, eyes flipping between the phone and door as I input my date of birth, my chest caving when it opens to his main screen. I'm not really expecting much. The usual apps installed to an iPhone, unopened emails, and messages.

I gulp and open his social media, but he's logged out of all the platforms.

I go to his pictures and hunt all the folders until I find the one that has only one file in it. My eyes lift to the door again, and my nerves catch fire when I click on the folder to see a thumbnail of a video.

It's six minutes long.

Clenching my jaw with butterflies already gathering in my gut, I play the video. My eyes zero in on the room—it's where I woke up with Allie at Samson's birthday party. I was so fucked up and had no idea how I got there.

The phone is set up on a stand, or maybe against something. A mask appears in front, tilting its head and staring right into the lens.

My insides turn upside down when I realize it's the mask I wore to the party, but I know it isn't me. And Mia and someone else are kissing and laughing on the bed the phone is aiming at, Allie dancing off to the side.

When I pause and zoom in, my eyes fucking widen when I stare at myself with my hands on Mia's face, my mouth on her throat.

What the fuck?

Me and Mia?

The person in my mask has his back to the bed, staring at the camera, as if he's staring right at me, mentally laughing as I kiss Blaise's girlfriend while my ex dances like she's on acid.

The person's hands fist at his sides.

But they're interrupted by arms wrapping around their waist by my ex. She grins up at him, her eyes telling me how fucked up she was that night. But then she says, "Why so serious, Cole?"

He tucks hair behind her ear while I'm still kissing and rolling around the bed with Mia, my hands all over her fucking body. I'm certain the phone is about to drop from my grip with how much my hand is shaking, trying to keep it upright while Allie drops to her knees and starts pulling off the person's belt.

I'm not surprised about her behavior. I've been sent more than enough videos of her fucking around, but this is different. She's cheating on me in the same room as me and Mia are kissing and—what the fuck am I doing now?

I'm pushing Mia's legs apart, spreading her wide on the bed while I...

She's moaning, arching her back while I bury my face between her legs.

A groan sounds from the other guy, and his hand tightens on Allie's hair while he watches me, like it excites him to watch me while he grunts and forces her to take more of his cock to make her gag.

I'm sweating as I keep my eyes on the screen. Why does

Blaise have this? Who sent him it? He should've beat me up for fucking around with Mia.

The shower is still running while I watch the guy pull his dick from Allie's mouth, and he's stroking himself while watching Mia screaming as she hits an orgasm against my mouth.

Then I'm climbing up her body and pulling out my cock, and my head is fucking spinning, because I have no recollection of this. As I thrust into Mia, the other person shoves Allie from his cock, keeping his attention on the way I'm fucking Mia into the mattress.

When Allie grabs at his thighs again, he snatches her chin and pulls her lip with his thumb. "You want to suck Cole's dick?"

I drop the phone and stare at it, wide-eyed, my heart stopping completely as Blaise's voice echoes in my head over and over and over again.

I close my eyes and cover my face with my hands as I hear, "Call me Cole."

Then there's slurping and gagging and Allie moaning. "Choke me, Cole. Fuck my throat, Cole. I'm your whore, Cole."

I cut it off, refusing to hear or see anymore. My chest is tight, and I think I might be sick. Swiping off the video, I exit the folder, and plug his phone back on charge while I hurry to dress.

I won't fucking cry, no matter how much my eyes are burning. He doesn't deserve my emotions. What the fuck? What the fucking fuck?

The bathroom door opens, hot steam instantly hitting me as Blaise walks out, rubbing a towel into his wet hair, another towel around his waist.

"What's wrong?" He must notice the way I'm dying a slow and heart-breaking death.

I manage to shake my head and swallow a lump threatening to suffocate me. Shaking it again, I pull on my shirt. "I need to go to see Samson about something."

"You want me to come?"

"No," I say a bit too quickly. "I mean, it's about our coursework. He's in the same class as me."

Blaise tilts his head. "You're pale. Did your dad call you?"

I shake my head, nearly vomiting all over the place with how ill I feel. "I'll catch up with you later?"

I try to pass him, and he grabs my chin, stopping me. "Do you promise you're okay?"

His touch feels like poison on my skin as I nod once. His eyes search my face, his brows furrowing. "I think we should talk to our parents tonight."

Fuck. Just fucking let me go. Let me leave before I pass out.

Blaise presses his lips to mine, and the weak part of me allows him to kiss me. My blunt nails dig into his collarbone as he nips my bottom lip and pulls back.

As soon as I get out of the room, before the door closes, I hear three words from the guy I thought I knew.

"I love you."

My heart completely shatters.

CHAPTER 31.
BLAISE

Cole is gone. I don't think much of it at first, but when he fails to respond to my third message, my stomach churns with unease. I can't put my finger on the emotion. It's eating me up from the inside, like a parasitic invader.

Toxic thoughts whisper, *'Something is wrong.'*

Seated on my bed with my elbows on my knees and the phone in my hand, I stare at the screen. Stare and fucking stare.

Unread.

Why won't the two ticks turn blue? Where the hell is he? I think back to this morning when I exited the shower. He looked spooked, pale as a ghost. Something is wrong. I knew it then. I sure as hell know it now. His silence drives the feeling home further, a nail in the coffin.

I shoot to my feet and pace the room. Rain splatters on the window to my left, but I barely notice the soothing sound. My heart is thudding too hard. I want to crawl out of my skin or climb the fucking walls. Where is he? Is he with Samson?

Chewing on my thumbnail, I bring up Cole's number and try to call him again. It rings and rings and fucking rings. I'm trembling by the time I lower the phone before tossing it on the bed and pulling at my hair. My scalp prickles, but the sharp pain does little to soothe this raging storm.

Why won't he talk to me?

Fuck this. I can't wait around all day to hear from him. I'll go insane, tormented by my destructive thoughts until I'm rocking in a corner, ready to be shipped off in a straitjacket.

Snatching up my phone and my jacket, I exit the house. The drive to Tiago's is a blur. The wipers *swish, swish, swish*. My thoughts are a jumble of fucked up, and by the time I pull up in Tiago's driveway, I'm sure I've aged ten years.

Cutting the engine, I stare out the windshield. Tiago's five-year-old sister waves at me on the porch, her dark piggy tails swaying in the wind, her flowery red dress whirling around her ankles. She calls me her 'superhéroe.' It's nice to be a hero in someone's story.

My smile is weak when I exit the car and shut the door. The little girl runs down the steps, and I swoop her up in my arms and spin her around like I always do before setting her on her feet and patting her little head. I'm cold in many ways, but it would take a heart of stone not to smile around Lucía. "Run back inside. It's raining."

"Want to play Café with me?"

"Some other time. I'm here to see your brother."

She takes my hand in her small one and leads me inside. The moment we enter the hallway, I'm greeted by the mouth-watering scent of freshly baked bread. Tiago's mom, Camila, shuts the oven door and looks up as we pass the kitchen. Her face brightens with one of her signature smiles, which highlights the crow's feet around her eyes. "How lovely to see you, Blaise. It's been too long."

She hugs me, too. They're big on them in this household. No one escapes Camila's warm hugs or affectionate smiles. She rustles my hair like I'm still a kid, and the niggling sensation in my chest eases a little. I can finally breathe easier. "Tiago is in his room."

"Are you sure you don't want to play Café with me?" Lucía asks, batting her long lashes.

Tiago's mom ushers her into the kitchen. "Vamos, cariño. Blaise vino aquí para ver a su amigo."

"Some other time," I say to the girl before heading upstairs. Tiago looks over his shoulder, pausing the game on the fifty-inch TV as I enter his room. Tossing the controller beside him on the couch, he removes his headphones and smiles. I plop down on the armchair and waste no time pressing the little button that makes the chair recline.

It whirrs, and I wait. And wait.

When I'm finally lying flat on my back, staring at the ceiling, Tiago covers a laugh with a cough and gets into character. "What brings you here today?"

"If you text someone and they don't text you back...it's bad news, right?"

"Maybe the person is busy?"

"The person lives on his phone. I've texted three times. No response."

"Are you sure you're not overly clingy?"

"Of course, I'm fucking clingy." Frustration bleeds into my tone. "He always responds... Well, not always. But most of the time."

"Most of the time?"

"Okay, so maybe he's terrible at responding on time. Something is different this time. I can feel it in my fucking gut."

"Did something happen?"

I shake my head. There's a stain on the ceiling from the time we shook a bottle of pop, underestimating how high it would spray when we uncapped it. I don't remember ever laughing so hard. "I don't know. We were good this morning. I had a shower, and when I walked back into the bedroom, he looked like he'd seen a ghost."

"Did you ask him if he was okay?"

I roll my head and look at Tiago. "You're a shit therapist. Of course, I did."

"Ask him again."

"I don't know where he is."

Tiago smiles as he rubs his chin, and I frown as I sit up. "What's so funny?"

"I've never seen you so hung up on someone before."

"I'm not fucking hung up on him."

His lips twitch as he lowers his hand. "Are you kidding? Look at you."

I peer down at myself as if my clothing will magically give me the answers I need. Tiago chuckles and reaches for the controller. The game starts back up. He puts his sock-clad feet on the table, crossing them at the ankle. "Mia wasn't right for you."

Pressing the button again, I wait a millennia for the chair to return to a seating position.

Whiiiir.

"I'm scared," I admit, and Tiago sits forward as the race on the screen gets intense.

"Why are you scared?"

"I don't know how to handle these emotions. I want to punch him one minute and fuck him the next."

Tiago barks a laugh.

"I love his smart mouth and his prickly attitude, but I fucking hate how he's so quick to retreat and hide behind his fucking walls." I flop back and release a frustrated groan as I sink lower on the couch. "Why the fuck won't he answer my texts? What the hell did I do?"

"Welcome to the world of chicks." As if he realizes what he just said, he pauses, then shrugs. "I mean, he's a guy... I have no experience with men, but it can't be that different, right? Relationships are relationships. It's like walking on eggshells. One minute, they're happy, and you're the man of their dreams. Then, the next, they're screaming in your face, and you're apologizing for shit you haven't done."

"He's not screaming, though. And I don't know what I've done wrong. I would prefer it if he yelled at me. At least then, I could fix...this. Whatever this is..."

Tiago curses at the game, then looks at me, but his attention soon gets diverted back to the action on the screen. I blow out a breath and stare up at the ceiling, half lying on his armchair. The T-shirt has ridden halfway up my back—that's how far down I've slid on this piece of furniture. Fuck my life. Why can't he return home so I can fuck it better? I bet if I suck him off, he'll smile at me again.

"How do you handle emotions?" I ask Tiago, and he frowns, sparing me a brief glance. Another car rams into him from behind, and he lets out a string of expletives. "You just learn to handle them with time." Giving up on the game, he tosses the controller beside him. "Look...I get it. You haven't been in love before, and it's frustrating and scary as fuck. Remember Amber?"

I wrack my brain. "High school?"

"That's the one. She had big tits and braces."

"I vaguely remember."

"You're a shit friend..." Tiago chuckles. "She was my girl-friend for seven months."

My lips spread into a smile, and I snicker too. "Sorry, I'm a mess."

"My point is that I was crazy about her. She was the first girl I ever fell in love with. We're talking cheesy shit like butterflies and all that stuff guys don't talk about."

I hum an agreeing sound.

"I didn't know how to behave around her. It was scary as hell." He sits straighter. "But I knew one thing. Whatever you do, Blaise, you can't force Cole."

"What do you mean?" I ask, and he gives me a pointed look.

"You can be very...full on when you want something."

His comment makes me bristle. I scoff and shake my head, ignoring the niggling voice that knows he's right. "Don't you think I've tried to be...better? This is who I am, Tiago."

"I'm not attacking you. I'm just saying. Give him space. Don't blow up his phone. Wait for him to come to you, and then ask him what's wrong."

My heart squeezes uncomfortably, and I have to clear my throat. "What if he doesn't come to me?"

Tiago's eyes soften. He feels sorry for me. I'm too vulnerable to take offense. Normally, I don't like to show weakness or even admit that I have any. But this need, this desire to own and possess someone while also making them happy, is new to me. I don't know how to handle it. I don't have any previous experience to draw from. It was so much easier when I just wanted to ruin Cole and watch him squirm like a dying worm. Not buy him chocolates to make him smile and cuddle him like a koala bear at night so I can listen to his heartbeat beneath my ear.

"If he loves you, he'll come to you."

I stare at him until my eyes water, either from not blinking enough or from the strange ache in my chest. Whatever it is, I don't like it. A damaged car can be fixed. A broken leg can be put in a cast. But this... I don't know what the hell to do.

"I don't know what I've done wrong." I sound whiny.

I hate that, too.

Tiago hands me the controller. "Want to race?"

Clenching my jaw, I wiggle the stick with my thumb, then nod before sitting up properly in the chair. "Okay..."

"Okay?"

The lump is back in my throat, and it's so damn hard to dislodge. I swallow and then swallow again, but nothing fucking happens. I rub my wet eyes, then sniffle and attempt a shaky, fake as fuck smile. "Let's race."

Leaning over the side of the couch, Tiago affectionately jostles my shoulder. "You'll be fine. Trust me."

I can't sleep. I keep staring at the streetlight outside the window. I'm on my front with my arms beneath the pillow. My joints ache from how long I've laid like this, waiting and waiting and waiting for Cole to come home. Is he cheating on me? Is that why he's not responding to my messages? Did he find someone else?

A car drives by outside, its headlights briefly lighting up the room before darkness settles over my soul once more. I can't remember the last time I felt this empty, this…broken. I thought he cared for me. I thought we had something.

Just then, the door creaks open, and every muscle in my body stiffens. My heart is in my throat as the bed shifts behind me. The urge is there to turn around and ask him where he's been or why he hasn't responded to a single message. But fear latches my heart, so I close my eyes and pretend to sleep instead.

Cole's warm body settles behind me, bringing with it the scents of late night and citrusy cologne. I can feel him watching me, propped up on his elbow, staring at the side of my face.

I wait…

Soft fingers brush strands of my hair away, and my heart jolts like a spark plug at the sudden contact. Then he's gone, and a tidal wave of hurt floods my chest. Why is fear so crippling? I'm just about to hurt him to get a fucking reaction out of him when he rolls back over and buries his nose in my neck. It's gentle and soft so as not to wake me.

Why doesn't he want to wake me? What is he doing? This isn't Cole. He's abrupt and forceful, yet sweet and… Fuck…I need to get myself together.

"Why can't I stay away?" he whispers so silently I would have missed it if I wasn't already hypertuned to his every breath.

The throb in my chest intensifies. Cole shifts behind me, getting comfortable. His breaths soon even out, but I can't sleep, and when my father bangs on the door early in the morning hours, I haven't slept a wink.

"Blaise, are you awake?" He tries the handle, and I scramble out of bed while Cole stirs.

Fuck, fuck, fuck.

I throw on a T-shirt and stumble across the room. Dad tries to peer past me when I open the door, taking up as much space as possible in the small crack. I'm acting suspiciously, but I don't know how else to behave. My head is a mess.

"I'm awake." I rub the crusty sleep from my eyes and fake a yawn.

Dad frowns, eyeing me with distaste like he only just noticed what are undoubtedly dark shadows under my bloodshot eyes. "You look like shit."

"Thanks, Dad. Love you, too."

"I'm going away for a few days for work. There's food in the fridge and money on the counter if you need to buy anything else."

He looks past me again, and I will my heart to stop thrashing like it's trying to claw its way out of my chest to attack his face like one of the monsters in the movie *Alien*. I can imagine it now — my heart leaping from my chest and latching onto his face, sucking his brain out of his nostrils like slimy goo, or maybe the monsters in *Alien* laid eggs? I can't fucking remember. All I know is that I need him gone.

"Don't get into trouble," my dad says, and I smile politely.

The moment he disappears around the corner, I shut the door and blow out the breath I didn't know I was holding.

Fuck, that was close.

I turn to look at Cole, who sits up in bed. His gaze is shifty, and I don't like that one bit. When he slides his legs out of bed, I stomp across the room like I'm mad, but I'm not. I'm just... I don't even know what I am. But I'm determined to wipe that uneasy look off his face.

Cole tries to rise to his feet when I near him, so I fist his T-shirt and shove him back down. "Where the fuck were you? I was worried."

"I was out with Samson."

"Not answering your calls?" Dropping to my knees, I work his belt, ignoring the way he tries to shove my hands away. My brain runs on a loop, '*Suck him, and he will smile at you again. Suck him, it'll make it all better.*'

The difference between now and the other times is that he didn't fight me back then—not really. But now he's pushing me off. I fall back onto my ass and come right back, throat clogged with emotions I don't even know how to decipher. All I know is that I need to fix this—the broken look in his eyes. The distrust.

"Stop it," he says forcefully, and I rear up and slam my lips to his. We topple back onto the bed, me on top of Cole, pinning his wrists above his head and forcing my tongue into his mouth. He's not kissing me back. It doesn't matter what I do, he won't respond.

He. Won't. Fucking. Respond.

I rip his belt open and slip my hand inside his jeans and boxers. Despite the empty look in his eyes, he's hard. Very fucking hard.

A breath whooshes from my lips as my forehead descends on his. His dick twitches in my grip, and I squeeze my eyes shut as I work his hard length, savoring each labored, harsh breath.

"Please," I breathe, my voice cracking. "Let me touch you."

Tiago's voice comes back to me, whispering in the recesses of my fragmented mind, *"Whatever you do, Blaise, you can't force Cole."*

I frown, trying to shut it out, but the voice grows louder and louder until it's screaming at me. Ripping my hand out of his jeans, I fall back, breathing hard as he sits up and scoots back on the mattress. Shame eats me up from the inside. I don't like the way he looks at me. I've never been one to care about others' feelings, but I do care about Cole. I care about him so much that it eats me up inside. I would do anything to get him to stop avoiding my gaze.

He climbs off the bed and walks out without another word, leaving me alone with the mess of emotions inside me. I suck in a breath and count to three. I try so hard to listen to Tiago's advice: Don't be clingy. Let him come to you.

But I can't. My body defeats my brain, and I'm up on my feet, running after him.

I slam him up against the wall outside my room. Cole's eyes widen at the look of sheer desperation I'm sure is painted on my face. When I try to cup his chin, he turns his head. Fuck me, he could just as well cut me with a knife.

"Please tell me what's wrong," I plead.

A muscle tics madly in his jaw. "Nothing is wrong."

"Nothing is wrong?" I parrot, flicking my eyes between his, searching and hunting for the truth.

"That's what I said."

Tiago didn't offer me any advice on how to deal with a situation like this. He made it sound so easy: ask what's wrong. But what do I do when I ask what's wrong and Cole won't tell me? Like now. What then?

I try to kiss him, but he applies pressure to my chest and moves away. My brows knit together. "Nothing is wrong, huh?"

His jaw tics again, grating on my fucking nerves. Why won't he just tell me why he's angry?

He starts to walk away, and I tear at my hair. The fear inside me is quickly morphing and shifting into anger. It takes everything in me not to tackle him to the floor like we're on the fucking football field. "Why do you always run away?"

Spinning around, his eyes flash with anger. "Now isn't the fucking time, Blaise. Leave it alone."

"No, I fucking won't." I storm up to him and shove him back. "You won't talk to me. You say everything is fine. It's clearly not fine."

"You're being paranoid!" he roars, and I stumble back a step.

"Just..." He sounds defeated, his eyes pained. "I'll see you later, okay."

This time, when he walks away, I let him.

If he loves me, he'll come back... That's what Tiago said.

And if he doesn't...

I can't let my thoughts go there.

✕

Two days pass. Cole sleeps in my bed, and then he leaves. What do I do with that? I'm not familiar with the rulebook. We're back at college. I'm a zombie at the table in the cafeteria, picking at my food, but not eating. I've spent the last ten minutes rolling a piece of pasta around the plate.

Tiago winces when he looks at me. I haven't slept more than an hour here and there. I look like shit.

Glancing behind him when Cole enters the cafeteria with his friends, Tiago communicates silently with Ronnie. An entire conversation passes between them before Ronnie grits his teeth and slides his chair closer. The metal frame scrapes on the floor, and the scent of his clean clothes invades my senses. He rests his arm on the back of my chair. I pause with my fork on the plate, looking at him questioningly, but it's half-assed. I don't have it in me to care anymore.

Ronnie glares at Tiago, who gestures widely with his hands. Leaning forward, Ronnie hisses, "I don't want to get beaten the fuck up, okay. Why don't you sacrifice yourself for the greater good?"

"Because," Tiago says, looking past us as he leans across the table, "it's more believable if it's you."

Ronnie looks confused. "Why?"

"I'm too close to Blaise. Best friends."

"I am, too," Ronnie argues.

"Are you his therapist? I have the seat and everything."

Ronnie blinks, and Tiago sighs tiredly as though the world weighs on his shoulder. He pushes his chair back, rounds the table, and pulls me to my feet. "You're paying for my medical bill if I end up in hospital." That's the only warning I get before he crushes his lips to mine, right there, in the cafeteria for everyone to see.

I'm too shocked to react. I stand frozen for all of two seconds, feeling confused as fuck, before Tiago is pulled off me like he's a sack of potatoes. Cole shoves him with such force, he crashes into the nearest table, causing a group of girls to scream. Then he punches him square in the face, and blood sprays everywhere.

Cole breathes like a bull. I don't remember ever seeing him quite this...provoked. Not even when he picked me up from Jackson's. Ronnie and Luke fly from the table to help Tiago, but I stay rooted to the ground.

Cole stalks away, and my feet become unglued. I run after him and pull him to a stop in the hallway. "What was that? Why did you punch him?"

"Why do you think?" he asks, pacing on the spot.

"I don't fucking know." I'm sarcastic, but I think Cole is too angry to catch on because he glares at me like he wants to incinerate me on the spot. "Okay, fine. Tiago kissed me. It's not like you care, right? You won't let me kiss *you.*"

He sneers, resuming his pacing.

"I've tried. Numerous fucking times. I'm paranoid, right? Everything is fine. That's what you say." I motion between us. "This isn't fine, Cole. You won't let me touch you. You won't talk to me." I lower my voice as a student walks by. "I'm not paranoid, Cole."

The air escapes his lungs as he leans back against the wall. He looks exhausted. His chest expands with a ragged inhale. He stares up at the ceiling, his hands in his pockets.

How do you get someone to talk who doesn't want to talk?

Instead of trying, I run a hand down my face. I'm tired, too. We're both fucking tired. "I'm done."

As I walk away, shoulders hunched, he calls out, "Remember at the beach when you said you've done some things you regret?"

I draw to a halt, but don't turn to face him—not now when my heart is racing.

His voice is closer now, caressing my nape. "What is it that you've done?"

The video of Cole fucking Mia after I drugged them flashes before my eyes. And the mask I found under his bed... I can't tell him. He won't understand. I'll lose him for good. Haven't I already lost him?

Wetting my lips, I reply, "I haven't done anything for you to worry about."

"Is that so?"

His whispered words crawl down my spine, and I shiver.

"I've told lies, Cole." I slowly spin around. "We both have."

Cole flicks his hard eyes between mine.

I round him, walking back toward the cafeteria. "I'm gonna check on my friend."

CHAPTER 32
COLE

Samson passes me the joint while Keith pays the pizza delivery guy and sets all four boxes on the table. We're all sitting around it, music playing lightly in the background, bottles of beer littered everywhere, with a pack of cards waiting to be dealt.

We've been at this for what feels like days, but it's only been three hours. I came over as soon as I packed enough clothes for the weekend. I couldn't be in that house with Blaise. I'm so fucking lost and confused about what I'm supposed to do.

One thing my mom always told me was to take a breather before reacting, and since I've never taken her advice before, I'm taking it now. I'm having a breather, which also feels like a three-day-long panic attack.

Samson kicks my shin. "Stop zoning out when I'm talking to you."

I blink and shake my head, taking a draw, filling my lungs with poisonous smoke and handing the joint to Keith. Grabbing the stack of cards, I shuffle them and deal.

"Did you sleep last night?"

I nod and continue dealing, setting aside the rest, and checking my cards without them being able to see. Shitty hand. Shitty day. Shitty week. Shitty fucking emotions.

Keith plates us up some pizza and shoves dip in the middle, and we start playing while simultaneously passing joint after joint, until I'm less anxious and more stoned out of my mind. He hasn't sent any messages today, and for some reason, that makes me feel worse.

All I need to do is talk to him, I know, but what the fuck do I say? Yeah, you drugged me and made me fuck your girlfriend while my girlfriend sucked you off? That you've been lying to me the entire time? That Mia was right?

He tricked me, and I don't know what to do.

"What would you do if someone drugged you and made you fuck their girlfriend?"

Samson and Keith freeze, the joint nearly slipping from the former's mouth. "What?"

"Hypothetically," I clarify. "If Keith drugged you, and made you sleep with his girl, while you got his girl to blow you, and he never told you. What would you do?"

Samson's eyes widen. "I... I don't know."

"Blaise did that?"

I sneer. "No. I said hypothetically."

"Do you plan on doing that to someone?"

I roll my eyes and throw down an Ace of Spades. "No."

"Because if you are, that's pretty fucked up, man. Don't you kind of have a boyfriend?"

I grind my teeth together. "It's your turn." I gesture to his cards hanging loosely between his fingers, not even attempting to hide them anymore.

For the next hour, they're being unnaturally quiet, sharing glances here and there, and they keep going on their phones. Mine is in my bag upstairs in the guest room. The idea of checking it every two seconds feels like a painful way to make myself even more ill.

I finish my next joint and stub it out, getting to my feet. "Going to the bathroom."

They both hum and keep playing the game. I'm already out, so they can continue without me.

Taking two steps at a time to get to the guest room, I make my way in and snatch up my bag. I sit on the edge of the bed and pull out my phone to see only one message from Allie's new number. The usuals of her asking me what I'm doing and how I am.

I ignore her, like I do with all her messages, and open a new message box, hunting for the number I'm yet to save.

Clocking it, I type without fighting with myself about reaching out to Mia.

> **Me:** Did you know?

The response is strangely instant.

> **Mia:** About what?

> **Me:** That Blaise drugged me that night.

> **Mia:** He drugged me too, I think. I only remember some moments, but I don't think I drank enough to be like that. Are you finally telling me you remember what happened between us?

> **Me:** I didn't know.

> **Mia:** Do you want to come over? We can talk about it? I won't tell Blaise, I promise. I know you two are together now.

I frown at the screen. Why the hell would I want to go there and talk about it? What's there to discuss? Blaise drugged us, made us fuck, and the damage is done. The damage is... I don't even know if it can be fixed.

Shaking my head, I pinch the bridge of my nose as another message comes in from her.

> Mia: We were sober that day in the shower. You know there is a connection between us. Why not explore it? We don't need to tell anyone until we know we'd work out.

Instead of replying, I narrow my eyes and click off her chat box. Did I just give her mixed signals? Did I just reawaken this fucking fascination she has with me?

Fuck.

I toss aside my phone when she starts calling me.

The other phone is in my bag, along with my cracked mask and hoodie. It takes me a few moments to think, trying to talk myself out of what I'm about to do, but I'm too mad at Blaise.

He needs to be punished and this is the only way I know how.

I open our chat – the masked, unidentified guy and Blaise. There hasn't been any communication since we technically made it official, so my fingers tremble as I type out a location. The middle of the football field at our college.

Two hours from now.

When he sends a thumbs up emoji barely a minute later, I drop the phone on the ground between my feet and stare at it.

And stare and stare and stare.

Until my eyes burn, and my lungs threaten to blow.

Something wet hits my cheek. A tear slides down, met with another, dripping from my chin and onto the offending phone with the message that shows just how little Blaise thinks of me.

Did I push him away, distance us too far?

If I spoke to him, would he have agreed so easily?

Regardless, this motherfucker just confirmed my suspicions.

Piece of shit.

By the time I get back downstairs and smoke another joint, I drink one more beer and quickly slip away, snatching my bag I left at the side of the door. I empty the contents in my car's passenger seat, pull on the black hoodie and stare at the mask.

Nostrils flaring, I turn up the radio and speed out of the driveway, onto the road, and straight to the destination.

My ears are ringing from how loud the music is. I don't even know what's playing. I'm going too fast, my wheels skid on the road when I turn a corner, and another, and when I see a sign for the school, my adrenaline turns dangerous, and I grip the steering wheel until it hurts.

A lash of pain mixes with betrayal as I try to breathe through my rage. It's taking over me, like a fucking thrashing monster inside me is trying to get out.

I stop at the empty, dark parking lot, grab my bat from the trunk. Slamming it shut, I slide on the mask and head for the field.

Everything around me vanishes—time stops, the world crumbling as I see Blaise standing in the middle of the pitch, his hands in the pockets of his jeans. He's bouncing on his heels, impatiently looking around until he glances over his shoulder and sees me. I lift the bat from my shoulder and grip it until the wood feels like it might crack under my hold.

Blaise pulls his hands from his pockets. Nervously, he gulps, and instead of coming toward me, he turns on his heels and runs toward the small building – where we go to get changed and showered.

He doesn't make it that far, though, because I launch the bat at him, smacking him in the back, making him falter enough for me to grab the back of his neck and throw him to the ground.

He lets out a groan when I swing my leg and kick him in the ribs. Once. Twice. Three times. My cheeks are soaked with angry tears as I grit my teeth and kick him again. Until my foot hurts and he's panting on the ground. I want to mess up his fucking face, smash his teeth in, and break his nose. I want to take his looks, since that's all I can do.

The heel of my shoe crushes into his chest, and I tumble back from the force of it.

"Fuck," he groans out, holding himself.

I regain my balance and fist my hand, grabbing his shirt and pulling him up enough to punch him in the face, blood splattering from his nose and hitting the mask.

His head knocks into the ground when I hit him again, his face crimson. He's not even fighting me back – he probably thinks I'll suck his cock or something. That this is part of our *thing*.

I'm not fucking touching him, and he'll never get anywhere near me again.

Fury gets the best of me. I want to kill this motherfucker. I stand tall, glaring down at him screwing his eyes shut and wincing from his injuries.

Pulling off the mask, I toss it at him. He can see my heartbreak, the look of deep betrayal in my wet eyes. His lips part, as if he's going to say something, but I rush forward and punch him again, cracking his skull into the ground once more.

"We're done," I spit, grabbing his bloody jaw, stopping him from talking. "You ever come anywhere near me again, and I won't hesitate to fucking kill you."

Releasing him, I turn around and walk toward my car, wiping tears with my sleeve.

"Cole!" he yells. "Wait!"

I jump into my car, seeing him sprinting toward me as I turn on the engine and shove the gear into reverse. His bloody palm slaps into my window, but I'm already gone.

He's trying to chase the car, but fails as I speed off.

My heart races so fast, pounds so hard, I think it might explode out of my chest cavity. From tensing up so much, my ribs ache, and I think I might be sick.

I drive to the dorm I haven't been in for weeks now. Dragging myself out of the car, I ignore the two guys smoking outside as I throw the entrance door open and head to the third floor.

Mia opens the door in her PJs, her eyes wide. "Cole?"

I barge past her and into the dorm room, pacing in the

middle of the open-planned kitchen. I tug at my hair as she closes the door, rubbing her arm.

"What's wrong? Why do you have blood on you?"

"I beat up Blaise," I say, needing to try to calm down. I'm getting lightheaded and I think I might pass out. "Can we go to your room?"

She tilts her head, then nods, and I follow her. Her PJ shorts are basically up her crack, and her top is barely covering her skin. Blaise used to fuck her, Blaise used to love her and care for her. He once told his dad that he might marry her one day, but I had a feeling it was just to make himself look like the good guy, because he never truly wanted Mia.

Yet he made me fuck her.

I should fuck her again for revenge.

Mia glances over her shoulder at me, and I don't shy away as her tentative fingers curl around mine, pulling me in as she opens her room door. The lamp is on, giving it a soft glow. Her fingers slip from mine as she closes the door behind us.

I think my intentions are clear, and she knows it too. But I don't actually want to be here. I want to be with Blaise, in bed, exploring his body while learning shit about him I don't already know.

I don't leave, though. Mia watches me walk around her room.

"I didn't tell Blaise I cheated on him with you because I thought it was our secret. I thought you knew."

"I didn't."

"Why are you here now?"

I shrug, my heart hammering. "I just drove here." Without thinking, my car brought me here. Like my conscience knew I needed to get back at Blaise.

Mia's room is the same layout as Allie's. But more pink, with a book opened in the middle of the bed. I pick it up, dog-ear the corner, and toss it on her dresser before dropping onto my back on her mattress.

I should leave.

This is a terrible idea. I feel nothing for her.

She stares at her book, then looks at me. "Are you okay?"

I sit up and grab her hand, pulling her between my parted legs. "No."

She doesn't pull away when my fingers grip her thigh. Her hands rest on my shoulders. "Is Blaise okay? If you said you beat him up?"

A shaky hand lifts to my face, and I don't even realize it's my own. I rub my eyes, seeing the cracked, torn flesh of my knuckles. I study it, checking my other hand, then putting both of them on her hips.

"I need you to make me forget," I say, hating myself, but needing to do something to get back at Blaise. "Without it meaning anything."

Mia frowns, her hand sliding up the side of my neck and into my hair. She leans down to kiss me, but I tilt my face to the side.

"No," I say. "Don't kiss me."

Nibbling her bottom lip, she teases her fingers at the seam of her sleep shirt, then pulls it up and over her head.

My cock doesn't get hard, or even twitch. I don't even want to palm her tits. I force my hand onto her chest, but freeze all over.

I don't want to do this.

I can't.

My hands slip away, and I stare up at her. "I love Blaise," I say. "I can't do this with you."

"He doesn't need to know." She grabs my wrists and pulls them back to her chest at the same time as she climbs into my lap. "We can do this. I'll make you forget."

I gulp, shaking my head, but she fists my hair behind my head and forces her mouth on mine. The mixture of being stoned, drunk, and heartbroken, I struggle to fight her off as she pushes her tongue into my mouth.

In half a second, Mia is pulled off me, and a fist slams into my face so hard, I see stars in my vision.

I groan and squint up to see Blaise with a deathly look in his eyes. They flicker between a topless Mia and me on her bed, and he grabs Mia by the throat and throws her toward the door.

"Get the fuck out," he orders, watching as she covers herself and runs out of the dorm.

He turns to me, dried blood on his face, grinding his teeth together.

And punches me again.

CHAPTER 33
BLAISE

"**M**ia? Really?" I punch him again, if only to see his face snap to the side. "You were going to fuck my ex?" One more hard hit. My knuckles bleed. I don't fucking care. What's a little more blood at this point? I'm pretty sure my nose is busted and that I have a cracked rib or two. "You left me on the fucking football field. You beat me up, and you fucking left me there."

Cole flies off the bed and shoves me back. "You were going to cheat on me," he shouts, fisting my T-shirt before pushing me back again.

"Cheat on you?" I stare at him in disbelief. Cole starts pacing, tearing at his hair and kicking random items out of the way, like Mia's bunny slippers.

"I mean nothing to you," he snarls, his eyes flashing with hurt.

"You mean everything to me. *Everything!*" My voice breaks. Fighting with Cole is exhausting. It doesn't matter what the fuck I do; I can't win.

I can't fucking win...

Cole puts his hands on his hips and shakes his head. He laughs bitterly and lifts his eyes to the ceiling. "I mean everything to you, huh?" He glares at me. "Is that why you were meeting up with a masked stranger and letting him fuck you? I must be really special to you."

"What the fuck are you talking about?"

Sucking on his teeth, Cole continues pacing back and forth. "You know exactly what I'm talking about. You were supposed to be with me, but you were more than fucking happy to meet up with a masked stranger."

"But it was you—"

"You didn't know that!" he shouts, shoving me. "You didn't know it was me. No, you thought it was someone else, and you were more than fucking happy to screw around on me. Who did you think it was? Did you imagine Jackson? Samson?" He shoves me again, and I stumble against the vanity desk, knocking over a lotion bottle and a tub of makeup brushes. "Did you hope it was Keith?"

Fury rises inside me, and before I know what I'm doing, I shove him hard, making him fall to the floor. "I knew it was you all along, asshole," I spit. "I found the fucking mask in your bag during the ski trip!"

Cole stills, but the damage is done. He doesn't trust me, and he never will. We're a toxic mess, and we'll never be good for each other. Cole must see the defeated look in my eyes. When I turn for the door, he scrambles to his feet and intercepts me before I can leave the room.

He blocks the doorway, and I come to a sudden stop. His chest rises and falls rapidly, his hair standing in all directions.

"Step out of the way."

"No," he says, bruises forming on his jaw. "I won't let you walk out."

My heart thuds hard as I pause. "Excuse me?"

"I said I won't let you go."

I've never seen Cole this unhinged. The way he stares at me from beneath his dark lashes has my pulse quickening. "Please," I beg, my shoulders slumping. "Let me out."

When he continues breathing hard, I wince.

I clearly have no choice but to force him out of the way.

Cole grunts when I grip his T-shirt and haul him away from the door. He stumbles back several steps. I've never seen him this heartbroken. The sheen in his eyes is one of pure desperation.

I go to open the door, but he tackles me to the floor, and I crash against the fluffy white rug with an "oomph," staining it red with blood. We're fighting now. Cole is on top of me, surprisingly strong now that he's running on pure adrenaline and aggression while desperately trying to secure my wrists. I won't let him. How the tables have turned. Days ago, it was me who tried to stop him from leaving.

"Fuck," I grunt, briefly managing to knock him off me. He throws himself at my ankles, and I fall right back down. I kick out at him, and he manages to dampen the force behind the blows by using his weight. He's a heavy fucker. "What the fuck are you doing?" I growl when he tries to grab my arms again. "Get the fuck off me!"

"Calm the fuck down," Cole says, his voice strained as he pins me to the floor. I'm on my front with my cheek pressed against the rug. I don't know how the fuck he does it—and I don't fucking like it—but he somehow gets the upper hand, trapping my wrists between our bodies, his breath hot on my ear.

"You're not going anywhere," he growls, bearing down on me with all his weight until my fight begins to wane. "You and I are not done."

"Fuck, just let me go," I plead, choking on what sounds suspiciously like a sob. I've been through hell this last week. And when he walked away from that football field—when I saw the look of pure devastation in his eyes—my heart splintered, and fear clutched at the bruised organ. I can't go through that again. I can't keep doing this anymore.

"I told you," he says as he fists my hair. "I'm not letting you go."

"Will you at least tell me what I did wrong and why you didn't want me touching you this week?"

Cole stiffens behind me, and I stare at the closed door, the legs of the vanity table, an abandoned slipper Cole kicked out of the way earlier.

When he speaks, my eyes fall shut as tears threaten to fall. "I know what you did, Blaise. I know you drugged me and filmed me fucking your girlfriend. I know everything." A heavy exhale fans my ear, and then his weight disappears. He climbs to his feet as though he needs distance from me.

I've ruined everything.

Turning my head, I let the rug soak up my tears. I don't stand up. What's the fucking point? My chest throbs. I struggle to breathe. Curling in on myself, I grit my teeth and fist my hands. I want to scream. Release a roar and never stop until my lungs are shredded, but I don't.

"Why would you do something as sick and twisted as that?" he asks behind me, his voice thick with disgust.

The throb in my chest intensifies. I slowly push myself to my feet, feeling broken beyond repair. Every muscle in my body aches, especially my ribs, and I clutch my midriff as I glance at Cole. I'm unable to look him in the eye, so I focus on his throat, seeing it jump when my bottom lip trembles. I open my mouth to speak, to say something, anything. Nothing comes out. What's there to say? He's right… I'm sick, twisted, evil. Other people get their happy ending. Not guys like me.

I wet my busted lip, tasting the tangy blood. The door looks inviting right now. It would be so easy to walk out. I try so fucking hard to meet his gaze, but I can't. I don't want to see the damage I've caused.

"I'm sorry," I whisper, my chin trembling. "I'm sorry I hurt you."

When Cole remains quiet, I drop my eyes to the floor and nod in defeat. I deserved the beating I received on the football field. "I'll get out of your way," I say, my voice cracking. Then I walk away, limping and holding on to my bruised stomach. There's blood everywhere. I should go to the hospital, but fuck that. I just want to be alone.

The moment I open the door, Cole appears behind me and presses his hand to the wood. It shuts again with a soft click. I wait for him to talk, to chew me out, to tell me how much I disgust him, but he does neither. His breath caresses my nape for endless moments as though he's warring with himself.

"When I think of you touching anyone else, I want to commit murder," he whispers, close enough for me to feel his breath against my nape.

"I would never let anyone touch me but you," I admit, swallowing hard. "You're the only one I want."

"Why did you do it?"

Why did I drug him? It all seems so far away, like it happened to someone else in a different lifetime. "I don't know."

"Not good enough," he says and grips my hip.

My hands clench at my sides as my chin meets my chest. "I wanted to bury under your skin, but all along, you were under mine."

"You made me fuck your girlfriend because you wanted to bury under my skin?"

"I wanted blackmail to use against you after you threatened me. I wanted to take back control. At least that's what I thought," I reply, my admittance floating between us. Cole puts his other hand on my hip, and I tremble beneath his touch. "I was intrigued. That's why I took it so far."

"Intrigued?" he asks, lifting my T-shirt to skim his fingers over my bare skin near my belt. "Why were you intrigued?"

"I was jealous."

"I was fucking your girlfriend. Of course, you were jealous of me fucking your girl."

His fingers trail over my contracting abs as I whisper a

choked "No..." and inhale a trembling breath. "I was jealous that she was fucking *you*." He grows still. I'm not even sure if he's breathing anymore. "I let it go that far because my own emotions intrigued me. What you don't see in that video is that I kissed you afterward."

"You kissed me?" He sounds haunted.

"I've wanted to kiss you for so fucking long," I admit. "Even before I realized it myself. I'm crazy about you, Cole." I slowly turn around, the door at my back. "But I get it... I wouldn't forgive me either."

A muscle clenches in Cole's stubbled jaw as I turn to open the door. I need to get out of here, or I'll try to touch him again. We both need space.

"Where are you going?" His voice stops me in my tracks.

"I'm going home."

"The fuck you are!"

I frown, but before I can turn around, he grabs the back of my neck and shoves me hard against the door. "Now, who the fuck is running away?" he asks, reaching around me to tear my belt open. "Who is hiding behind their walls?" His hand slips inside my briefs, and he palms my dick. My cheek squishes painfully against the door. I press back against the wood with my hands, and it's all I can do not to turn around and take control.

Cole's touch is different—more forceful, which is exciting and a little scary. He needs this.

He yanks my jeans and briefs down my legs. Cool air licks at my exposed ass. I hold my breath, my dick twitching against my T-shirt. Holding his body flush against my back, he strokes my cock in languid, mind-blowing pulls. Before long, I'm thrusting into his hand while he unbuckles his belt one-handed.

"Why do you have to drive me so fucking insane?" he growls, angry and turned on.

"Cole?" I ask uncertainly, trembling when he spits on his fingers and applies pressure to my back hole. My entire body tenses up.

"Tell me no one has had this ass before. Tell me all of you is mine."

Fuck, his dirty words make me throb all over.

Cole isn't done. He fists my hair and pulls tight on the short strands, snarling in my ear, "Tell me you want my fat cock to fill your ass with cum."

Jesus...

"You're bleeding," he taunts, removing his fingers and dragging them over a sore cut on my eyebrow. They come away slick with blood. He chuckles. "I fucked you up real good back there, didn't I? You'll need stitches."

I suck in a breath when he circles my tight exit before reaching around me to jerk my cock with his free hand. He presses two slick fingers inside me, using my own blood as lube. I choke on my breath, my toes curling at the burn. My body hums with anticipation.

"Feel that?" he taunts. "Feel how tight you are." He removes his hand to pull down his zipper. My heart rate spikes when he smacks his dick against my ass—once, then twice. His hard length prods my back hole, and I hold my breath. I'm not prepped enough. This will hurt. But if anything, my cock hardens even more at the thought of having Cole inside me. I want him to possess every sick, twisted part of me.

"Make it hurt," I beg.

He hums, then says, "You like to bleed." Grabbing the back of my neck, he holds up a pocket knife in front of my face—a knife I didn't know he had on him. "Remember this? You made me use one on you." His touch is bruising, his words are poisonous, yet I love every second.

The knife disappears out of sight. I try to look behind me, but he keeps me locked in place with his hand on my damp neck. A sudden, sharp sting burns my hip as he chuckles cruelly. I hiss, angling my hips away out of instinct, and he presses the bloodied blade against my throat.

"Stay still," he warns, his cock digging into me from behind.

With the knife pressed to my throat, he swipes fresh blood from the slash on my hip and lubes up his dick. My mouth dries up. I feel him at my entrance—so fucking hard. "Tell me one thing, *Blaise,* when did you first screw around on me with Tiago?"

A cry rips from my lips when he rams his cock inside me and slaps his hand over my mouth to muffle my sounds while shushing me.

"Shut the fuck up, Blaise." *Thrust.* "Did you fuck him all this time?" *Thrust.* "Did he feel better than me?"

I breathe through my nostrils. My ass feels as if someone poured gasoline over it and set it on fire. Cole snaps his hips, and the blade in his hand threatens to cut me with every powerful claim.

"I doubt he fucked you as good as this, huh?" He drags his wet tongue up the side of my neck and presses his lips to my ear. "I swear to fucking god, I will leave you bleeding and covered in cum, then I'll hunt him down and kill him so fucking slowly he wishes he never put his hands on you."

I sink my teeth into the fleshy part of his hand, and he hisses as he rips it away. "I never touched him."

"No?" *Thrust.* "Have you already forgotten I broke his fucking nose in the cafeteria for kissing you?"

I groan with his next deep, savage thrust. He fucks me like he hates me and wants to brand himself on my soul. A tingle starts at my spine, and my balls draw up tight. His cock in my ass hurts so fucking good—his *anger* feels so fucking good.

"You don't like it, do you? You don't like that you're jealous," I taunt, just to get a reaction. "Tiago has the softest fucking lips—"

He rams his cock deep, and it pulses as he snarls, "Shut the fuck up!"

Chuckles vibrate my chest. I can't help but love how my dick leaks precum when he is this angry and possessive. I almost want to taunt him some more, but Cole is already at his breaking point, and he might snap if I do.

He presses the tip of the knife to my jugular, making my heart rate spike. "You're mine, Blaise."

"I'm yours," I reply. "Only yours."

My words seem to soothe the chaos brewing inside him. The knife falls to the floor, and he hauls me away from the door and slams me down on Mia's vanity desk. Makeup products clatter to the floor, and the front legs lift off the ground with every hard thrust.

"Fuck," I grunt and curl my fingers around the edge for something to hold on to. The vanity crashes against the wall, more items toppling to our feet. Blood smears the white surface.

Cole fists my hair and yanks my head up. Our eyes meet in the mirror. His are heavy with heady lust, a jaw clenched tight. A light sheen of sweat dampens his forehead.

"I'm gonna come inside you so fucking hard," he says, watching my ass swallow his cock.

Moaning, I study my face and flushed cheeks in the mirror. I never thought I'd see the day I took a cock in my ass. I always thought of myself as a topper, but I'll bend the rules for Cole. I'll let him unleash his inner demons on me, if only to see the pure erotic sadism in his eyes.

"Fuck me harder," I plead, my dick pulsing and throbbing.

He smacks me hard, and I groan at the sharp, sudden sting on my ass cheek. Fuck… Cole is ruthless.

Three more thrusts. "Fuck…fuck, fuck, fuck." He buries his cock deep and grabs my neck while his cock pulses his release. A guttural groan rumbles in his chest. The feel of his hot cum spilling inside me has me moaning his name and trembling.

Before we can catch our breath, he drops to his knees behind me and spreads my ass cheeks. "I love seeing my cum drip from this perfect ass."

"Jesus Christ," I choke out when his wicked mouth descends on my back hole. *Holy fuck.*

"Fuck yourself," he orders, lapping up his cum as it leaks out of me. "Make yourself come." His tongue circles my entrance, and he groans as he grips me tighter and forces his tongue inside me. He slurps and licks before biting my ass cheek while I jerk my length almost frantically. My panting breaths steam up the mirror in front of me. There's a photograph of me and Mia at the ski resort taped to it. She looks so fucking happy in my arms, beaming at the camera. I break out in a cold sweat—so close, so fucking close.

"Such a filthy little brother."

I can hear the smile in his voice before he sucks my balls into his mouth. "Fuck, that feels good," I grunt, and he sucks harder. A hiss escapes through my teeth. I'm right at the edge.

My arm is cramping up. I groan and bite my lip. The sound of slapping skin mixes with my heavy breaths.

I'm just about to fall over the edge, when Cole pulls me up by my arm. He guides me over to the bed and lines his chest up with my back before reaching around to circle his fingers around my dick. "Hands at your sides," he whispers against the curve of my neck where it meets my shoulders. "Now…" His damp lips find my ear. "You're gonna be a good boy for me and leave your ex a parting gift."

Shuddering, I fist my hands. His touch feels out of this world. He works my dick like a pro with firm strokes that drive me wild.

"I want you to come all over her pink sheets, fluffy cushions, and teddy bears, got it? You gonna come hard for me? Harder than you ever have?"

My head falls back against his shoulder. I can't think about anything but the sensation of his big hand on my cock.

"She could never make you feel this good, could she?"

I shake my head and wet my lips. "No…"

"That's right. No one can. You're mine. Only fucking mine. From this moment on, no one, and I mean fucking no one, touches this dick except for me."

He bites down hard on my earlobe, and I fall over the edge. My muscles tense. Ropes of cum rain over the pink sheets in quick spurts. "Cole," I moan.

"Look at all that cum," he breathes, smiling against my skin as another squirt spills onto the blanket. "What do you think she'll say when she comes back here later to see how hard I made you come?"

"I didn't know how possessive you could be," I reply and turn around on shaky legs, out of breath. We put our dicks away in silence, glancing at each other. The moment I'm done tightening my belt, he pulls me to him and drops his lips to mine. I fist his hair and force my tongue into his hot mouth. Heaving breaths and deep grunts. Cole curses before biting my lip, assaulting the tender flesh. I grab his stubbly chin and suck on his tongue. Then something changes, and our touches turn reverent, gentle.

Cole breaks away first and presses his forehead to mine, fingers hooked in my belt hoops. "I'm sorry I ghosted you... I should have talked to—"

"Shut up." I shake my head. "I'm the one who should apologize. What I did..." My throat jumps. "I drugged you and... Fuck..." I can't even finish the sentence. Guilt gnaws at my insides. I wish I could turn back time and talk some fucking sense into myself.

"Hey..." Cole catches my eye. "Look at me. Let's just..." Wetting his lips, he inches closer. "Forget about the past. Forget about all the fucking bullshit."

Instead of replying, I cup his face, and his stubble scratches my fingers. I brush my lips over his and whisper, "I love you."

His trembling breath fans my mouth. He kisses me, a soft press of lips. "I love you too—"

The door flies open. A police officer enters the room. His gun is drawn, and his beady eyes bounce between us. The world slows to a stop. Beside me, Cole's face drains of color. I shove him behind me and square my shoulders.

"It's good to see you again, son," Cole's dad says, skirting the length of the room and circling us. "You should answer your phone once in a while."

"Don't fucking talk to him," I snap, and he swings the gun in my direction. Cole tries to barge past me, but I whip my arm out to keep him back.

"Would you look at that," Cole's dad taunts, cocking his weapon. "My pathetic son is a faggot." His harsh laughter turns my stomach. My jaw tightens as he flashes his yellowed teeth that look like nubs. His pores reek of alcohol, and his greasy hair hangs limply over his forehead. How he hasn't lost his badge yet is beyond me. The man is a fucking mess—a corrupt cop, if there ever was one.

"You're drunk," I say. "Put the weapon down."

"You don't make the fucking rules here, faggot. I do." He jostles the gun. "Step out of the fucking way. Let me talk to my boy."

Cole puts his hand on my arm. "Blaise, let me talk to him—"

I cut him off with a single glare. Fuck that. I'm not letting his dad anywhere near him.

The gun is aimed at my head. It would be a quick death if he decides to pull the trigger—over in a heartbeat. One moment, I'm here, defending Cole's honor and then...nothingness. Sweet oblivion. Only death doesn't seem sweet if it means losing Cole, but if I have to die to protect him, then so be it.

"Step out of the fucking way," he spits, saliva droplets flying from his mouth.

I glare at him.

"I'll blow your fucking head off." He can barely stand up straight, swaying and hiccupping. "I've had enough of this shit. Cole is my son. His mom is my fucking wife—"

"Ex-wife," I point out, and he narrows his eyes.

"She'll always be *my* wife." He sniffs, his mustache twitching. Then he roars, *"And Cole will always be my son!"*

I swear I hear Cole choke out a sob behind me, reminding me

of a wounded animal—a terrified dog shying away from its owner.

My heart thrashes. Adrenaline rushes through my veins.

"Here's what's gonna happen," he says, sweating profusely. "I'll count to three. If you haven't moved out of my way by the count of three, I will put a bullet between your eyebrows, understood?"

When I remain silent, he counts "One," and a sly smile spreads across his lips. My heart slows to a dull thud. I zero in on the barrel. This is it. I'll die at the hands of Cole's crazy father —murdered in cold blood for loving his son.

"Two." His eyes gleam with sick excitement. He's enjoying this. He wants to pull the trigger. In his mind's eye, he visualizes blood spraying over the walls. I swallow hard, resigned to my fate—

Cole shoves me out of the way, and I crash against the vanity table. A shot goes off. Cole clutches his stomach. His eyes lift, and the confusion I see there breaks something inside me. He looks at me, his dad, and the blood pouring between his fingers.

"Look what you fucking did," Cole's dad snarls, gripping him by the arm and hauling him across the room. I dash after them, but come to a sudden halt. The gun digs into Cole's temple. His father inches backward toward the door, kicking a stray bunny slipper out of the way. "Don't follow us. I will kill him if you do."

"No, you won't."

"You want to test me on that, boy?" With the gun pressed to Cole's head, he opens the door.

My mind spins. What the fuck do I do? I need to phone the cops. Tell them that one of their colleagues shot and kidnapped his own son.

The deep red stain on Cole's T-shirt is slowly spreading. Nausea ripples through me. I tear at my hair as they exit the room. What the fuck do I do?

Spinning around, I search everywhere for my fucking phone.

I need to call for help. Where the hell did I put it earlier? I find it on the floor beside the bed and throw myself at it. It takes me three attempts to unlock the screen and dial the cops.

With my phone pressed tightly to my ear, I wait for it to connect as I run into the hallway. Mia's gone, probably to her friend's house nearby.

"Nine-one-one, what's your emergency?"

CHAPTER 34.
BLAISE

The police arrive minutes after Cole's dad kidnaps him, but it is too late. They're gone. A blonde female officer leads me out of the room to ask me countless questions while my head spins with possibilities. What if he hurts him? He already has. Cole has been shot. There was blood. Lots of blood. Where is he taking him? What is he planning?

Fuck...the unhinged look in his eyes—a man who'd lost everything and finally snapped. Cole's dad is dangerous.

A paramedic tries to check me over, but I send her away with a hard glare.

"Did you find his mom?" I ask the police officer, interrupting her mid-question.

Her brows draw close together. "They're trying to get hold of her now."

"Fuck!" I tear at my hair and pace on the spot—two seconds away from driving my fist into the cement wall. My knuckles would take one hell of a beating, but the pain would be worth it. This restless energy coursing through me demands me to do something. I can't stand around while they inspect Mia's room as though they'll find any clues in there. They won't. Only a cum-covered bed and our blood.

It's also pointless to phone Cole's mom. She won't pick up. He took her—I know it in my gut.

They finally decide they're done questioning me and arrange

for another police officer to drive me home. The streets pass by in a blur. *Everything* is a muted blur.

The moment I shut the front door, smearing the chrome handle with blood, Dad pops his head out of the kitchen. "The trip got canceled—" His eyes widen, and he enters the hallway. "What happened?"

I stand there, seeing but unseeing as the fight leaves me. I don't know when Dad crosses the hall, when he palms my cheeks to inspect my injuries, or when he pulls me into his embrace.

His arms constrict around me. It feels weird. Unlike Tiago's mom, I can't recall the last time he hugged me. Even when I was little, the extent of his affection was a pat on the shoulder or a ruffle of my hair. I was so happy on the rare occasions when he mussed up the short strands and told me that I'd been a good boy.

Dad means well, but he's cold.

"Did Cole do this?" he growls, and my thoughts crash to a halt.

His Boa-arms squeeze tighter, or maybe it's my imagination. I can't breathe. I'm slowly suffocating to death. Crushed, like a tin can.

My muscles object as I untangle myself. I was too high on adrenaline earlier to feel the extent of my injuries, but now it hurts to move. "Why are you so quick to blame Cole for everything?"

Dad opens his mouth to speak, but I cut him off, "Do you even know where your wife is? Do you care?"

He frowns as I shoulder past him.

I can't stand still. I need to move. I need to act.

Where would Cole's dad take them? Back to their old house? No, it would be the first place the authorities check. He knows that—he's unhinged, sure, but he's not stupid.

Dad pulls me to a stop just as I'm about to escape upstairs. My foot barely touches the first step when his long fingers curl around my shoulder, and I look down. I'm still wearing my shoes, but the laces are undone.

"What happened, Blaise?"

I don't get to tell him. There's a knock on the door.

Dad sighs before the weight of his hand disappears, and he crosses the hall to open the door.

The same female officer who questioned me at Mia's dorm introduces herself to my dad. They walk past me and enter the living room.

Their voices drift through the thin walls. Another officer shuts the front door, his eyes finding mine as he walks past. He offers me a small, apologetic smile before he, too, disappears into the living room.

I stay rooted to the spot with one foot on the first step. Cole's name is mentioned more than once before I finally hurry upstairs. Why are they talking and not out there looking for him?

As soon as I enter my room, I make a beeline for my laptop on the desk. The dark night outside seeps through the glass, and when I lift my gaze, I'm met by my own haunted reflection in the window. I look like shit: cheeks smeared with blood, an eye that's almost swollen shut, and a busted lip. There's more dried blood on my hands and underneath my nails. My knuckles are split, too. They sting like a motherfucker when I flex my fingers, but the pain is soothing. At least it gives me something else to focus on instead of the pit in my stomach.

I type in Cole's dad's name and scroll through the search results. There's not much, but maybe I'll find something that'll give me a clue if I keep hunting.

My phone vibrates in my pocket, and I slide it out to check the caller ID. Tiago. After silencing the call, I toss the phone onto the desk. Guilt gnaws at my gut, but my head is all over the place. It continues ringing. I wait it out, watching Tiago smile on my phone screen before it goes dark. Breathing out a sigh of relief, I lean forward to click on another article—

The door opens behind me, and I straighten up. Dad enters the room, looking significantly more tired than he did earlier. He has loosened his tie and runs a hand through his dark hair.

"Have they found them?" I ask as he slides his hands into his pockets. He shakes his head once. "No," is his response. "They haven't."

"Well?" I ask, my voice wobbling like my chin. "What did they say? Are they out there looking for them? Have they got any clues of where he took them?"

"I don't know, son."

We stare at each other.

I feel helpless. Dad always has the answers. Always knows the right thing to say or how to handle difficult situations. He never looks this...defeated.

Swallowing hard, I dip my chin to my chest. I should jump in my car and drive around town. They can't have gone far, right? Maybe I'll spot them somewhere.

Dad walks deeper into the room and, without asking questions, pulls me into his arms again. I'm stiff at first. Dad doesn't do emotions. He shouts and stomps around the house like a dictarian.

"The police will find them," he says.

"What if they don't? What if he hurts them?"

"He won't."

"What makes you so sure?"

Instead of replying, he steps back and puts his hands on my shoulders. "We have to trust the police. They have their best men on the case."

"Trust the police?" My voice is shrill. "Cole's dad is a cop. He has a restraining order against him, yet they let him keep his fucking badge. They're all corrupt."

He looks at me peculiarly, then sighs and drops his hands. "Try to get some rest, son."

"Try to get some... Try to get some rest? Your wife is missing. Don't you fucking care?"

"Don't swear at me," he replies. "Of course, I care, but there's nothing else we can do tonight."

"So we do what? Nothing?"

"We'll know more by the morning." He crosses the room to the door, and I call out, "They could be dead tomorrow."

Dad stops in his tracks, his shoulders stiff. "They won't be."

He leaves the room without another word, and I slump back against the desk. My anger rears at his blasé attitude. Why isn't he as frantic as me? His wife is missing—kidnapped by her ex-husband.

"Fuck," I groan and scrub my hands over my face. My phone vibrates on the desk, sliding sideways with each '*brrrrr.*'

I pick it up and unlock the screen before it can fall to the floor. It's Tiago again.

"Don't ignore me when I call you," he says the moment I press the phone to my ear.

"Look, tonight is not a good time—"

"I know what's going on."

I stiffen. "You do?"

"It's on the news."

Crossing the room, I switch on the TV on my dresser. Two pictures, side by side, of Cole and his mom fill the screen. My butt meets the springy mattress. I swallow hard. Tiago's voice drifts in and out of my consciousness. It didn't feel real earlier, not like this.

"What can I do to help?" he asks. "I've got Ronnie on the other line, too."

I lower the phone and stare at his smiling photograph before pressing it to my ear again. What can he do? Maybe my father is right. Is there nothing we can do? We don't know where they are or even where to start searching.

"I don't know," I reply, feeling so damn useless. Cole must be so scared. My heart aches at the thought, and the urge to smash something to bits—to break and destroy things—floods through me. I'm up on my feet in the next second, the phone forgotten on the bed.

Tearing the lamp from my nightstand, I throw it full force at the wall. Nothing survives my burning fury. I throw and punch and kick and rage. I overturn the desk chair and unleash all my pent-up anger by driving my boot into it over and over again until my T-shirt sticks to the sweat on my back and my muscles burn with exertion. I barely notice.

When I finally look up, I pause.

Dad stares at me in the doorway, shock written on his face. It's only now that the extent of my fury dawns on me. My gaze drifts over my destroyed bedroom, which looks like a tornado swept through it and uprooted everything. I'm shaking all over with adrenaline. My teeth chatter.

Dad's eyes meet mine, and then he turns around and leaves. I stare at the gaping doorway, but he doesn't return.

Exhaustion swoops in, and I plop down on the mattress, which is now void of pillows and a blanket.

Tiago's tinny voice disturbs the silence. "Blaise? Talk to me. Are you okay?"

CHAPTER 35
COLE

Burning pain seers up my ribs, warm blood seeping from my fingers as the car speeds out of the parking lot and onto the road. The trunk is large in the cop car, and I bounce around as he takes a sharp left, hitting my head on something hard.

I hiss through the pain. I don't know if the bullet went right through, or if it went haywire inside me. All I know is that I feel dizzy and I'm lying in a pool of my own blood.

I can hear my dad talking, yelling, telling whoever is on the other end of the line to set something up. He shouts my name, but all I can do is tense everywhere and try to stay conscious. I can't pass out. I can't fucking close my eyes and let myself go. I need to fight through this somehow.

Rolling onto my left, I spit a curse through my teeth as I move onto the wound.

Sweat clings to my skin, or it's blood. I don't know. It's sticky and warm, and my eyes sting as I force myself to stay awake. Feeling around the roof of the trunk, I hunt for a lever or a button, but my arm keeps getting tired, and my hand drops.

My breathing grows heavy, my eyes heavier, and when he goes over a bump, I try to snap out of the daze. I haven't adjusted to the darkness. I can't see shit, but I can hear him speeding up.

"Fuck," I mutter. Each breath feels like I'm inhaling fire into my lungs. I think every time I move, the skin splits even more, and shit, it hurts.

Blinking through my dizziness, I use my free hand to feel around again as the car slows, turning right. Dad is yelling again, telling someone to be ready because I'm injured.

Who? Who is helping him?

Where are we going?

I wince as I roll onto my side again, holding my breath and counting until the extreme pain settles, but it only gets worse when I roll again, each time he turns the car.

The smoothness of the wheels on the ground changes. Bumpy. Gravel. We're on a gravel road, or a dirt road?

He's not yelling anymore.

The car slows to a sudden stop, and I hear the car door being thrown open and slammed. "Do you have what you need?" I hear my dad ask someone. They must nod or whisper a reply. "He's in the trunk."

Their footsteps grow close. Someone is standing right there, and I think I might be sick. My eyes are so damn heavy, but I need to fight. I need to get the fuck away from him.

As soon as that trunk opens, I'll fucking dive on them, throw my fists and make sure I don't let him win this time. He can't use any weakness on me, because Blaise isn't here, and my mom is—

The trunk flies open to my mother's worried, traitorous eyes.

Every atom of my being wants to ask her what the fuck she's doing, and with my mind trying to fucking work against the darkness, my eyelids fall shut, their voices becoming an echo as I'm jostled and yanked from the car. My hand slips from the gunshot wound as I'm lifted in death's arms, and although my heart is aching at her betrayal and desperate for answers, my fight leaves me.

"Woah, dude. What the fuck happened to your eye?"

Chokehold

I shoulder past my friend and head for my locker. He tries to catch up, getting in front of me again and pressing his hand to my chest.

"Don't do that. Talk to me, Cole."

Talking doesn't help. It only makes things worse, because no one truly helps a deputy's son from abuse. Not a soul in this town is going to report him, not even my school—four teachers know about my home life. And they only know because I opened my mouth to one teacher and they decided to run theirs.

But do any of them help me? No.

My dad getting his promotion was the worst day of my life, because since then, he's been on a power trip. Only, he mainly takes it out on my mom. She accepts every shitty word. Every smack. Every time he comes home smelling like another woman. I walked in after school one day to some teenage girl who looked only a few years older than me with his shirt on, no pants, cooking breakfast while my mom was tending to my dying grandma.

She smiled at me, and my dad didn't like that.

I had to listen to them for days before it stopped.

Then he came into my room and started talking to me about sex. How to be safe, ways to make sure I don't get caught if I'm already with someone. He even went as far as telling me he'd make it easier for me by seeing if one of his girls would take my virginity.

I was thirteen.

Safe to say, I declined and told my mom. I think that was the first day he physically hurt her in a place the world could see, so she wasn't allowed to leave the house and I was to keep my mouth shut.

It became a normality. My friends definitely know. I don't even need to say anything. They take one look at my hand-me-down clothes that don't fit me, the skin and bone of my frame, and the shaggy hair in desperate need of a cut, and they know my home-life is fucked up.

"You wanna hang out at my place after school? Some of the guys are coming over too. My parents are out of town until Monday and my babysitter is hot."

I shake my head. "I need to go home."

323

Or I'll be the next missing kid on milk cartons and plastered all over the news.

I dodge any more questions and head to class. I'm just on time before the teacher walks in. I sit next to Georgina, my usual lab partner, and glance at everything she has set out. Fuck. We have a test today? I haven't missed a single class in months. When were we told?

"It was posted on the school's online board two days ago," she tells me, seeing the worry all over my face. "Here. I printed extras for you."

I'm not allowed on the internet. Social media, YouTube, gaming. All of it is cut off for me. Always has been. My parents are strict and think it will melt my brain or cause an addiction, and if I end up screwed in the head, I'll never be able to be a provider for my future family.

Because I have no choice but to carry on the family name, so my full focus needs to be on my grades, and making sure I'm settled before I'm twenty-one.

My parents set the goal, not me.

Anyway, I'm sure the main reason we don't have the internet in the house is because we're borderline broke. Sure, Dad is a cop, but he doesn't put food on the table or give my mom cash when she asks so she can buy groceries.

Honestly, I have no idea what he does with his money. Gambles, maybe. Or he pays for girls to sleep with him, which is something I've heard my mom scream at him for once.

I never want to be like my dad.

Georgina gives me a soft smile when the teacher tells us to begin. She's cute, has blue eyes that you can't help but stare at, and she's nice to me. Maybe Dad will tell me to marry her one day.

An hour later, I hand in my test results and leave the classroom, my stomach growling when I walk by the canteen filled with students eating their lunch. I go to the bathroom, huddle in the stall, and lock it while I pull out the half-eaten sandwich from yesterday. I pull a hair from it, check the rest, then finish it in two bites.

By the time school ends, I've successfully swerved any questions about the swollen, bruised eye. Georgina did ask me if I was okay before the bell rang through the halls, so I was able to hide in the swarm of students and vanish out of the building.

Dad's car is parked outside the house, and I can hear yelling. I take a deep breath, grip the frayed straps of my school bag, and stop at the front door.

"She was sixteen, Malcolm! Sixteen! You do know you're going to jail, right? There isn't a chance you can get away with this, you lying, cheating, piece of shit!"

"It's her word against mine. Who are they going to believe? Some bratty teenager, or a full grown man with a badge?"

I hear a slap, and then there's silence.

My heartbeat accelerates to an unhealthy pace as I open the door, freezing when I see my dad on top of my mom, his hands around her throat.

He's so zoned out that he doesn't hear me come in, or when I grab one of his golf clubs from his trolley. I don't wait for a second to swing the metal at his head, knocking him over.

Mom gasps for air at the same time as saying my name. Coughing, she rolls onto her side to try to fill her lungs while I grip the golf club tighter and point it at my dad. It's shaking, fucking trembling, and he has blood staining his hair.

"You," he starts, pressing his palm to his head, bringing it away to see the blood staining his hand. "You fucking little shit!"

Dropping the club, I turn to run, my heart in my throat, but he catches my hood and swings me to the side, both choking me and hitting my head against the wall. The knee connecting to my jaw knocks me back, and I don't have a chance to feel any of the pain because he's fisting my hair and dragging me across the floorboards.

I kick, trying to tear into the skin of his hand with my blunt nails, but he's too strong. I'm too weak to save my mom. She's lying on her front, tears in her eyes as she watches my dad pull me right into the kitchen.

Without letting go of my hair, he grabs a knife from the block, and it's enough to slap me into panic mode, and I fight back against him. I *twist beneath him, kicking at his shins, managing to hit him between the legs to make him release my hair.*

And I run again.

He catches up, slamming the front door when I pull the handle, and something like burning hot pain slices my hip. My dad doesn't care that he just slashed me; he's chasing me up the stairs. I jump over my mom, helpless on the floor.

Terrified. Frozen in place as her husband chases her only son. She's not even trying to stop him from hurting me.

I get to my room, slam the door, and attempt to drag my dresser in front of it. Being so thin and weak, I barely nudge it from the ground before I hear his heavy footfalls, yelling, mocking me that I'm a little pussy who needs to be taught a lesson.

I pull harder, thankful the dresser shifts with the terrified adrenaline rushing in my veins. I twist and turn once I block the door, looking for a weapon. My window doesn't open, and I'm not strong enough to smash it. I'm trapped.

I'm gonna die.

Gulping down bile when I touch my side and see blood on my palm, my bottom lip trembles. My dad bangs against the door, and my body jolts, my heart stopping, tears spilling down my cheeks.

This is it. He's going to stab me, remove me from the equation so he can have all of Mom's attention. He never loved me anyway. I was always in the way, a nuisance, the weirdo child who couldn't hold down a friendship or learn things as easily as other kids. I wasn't like his friends' kids either. He'll be glad to get me out of the way.

Maybe they'll have another child who isn't like me.

Mom's voice is in my head, begging me to go to my hiding spot. There's another bang on the door, moving my dresser forward, and it's enough to rocket me toward my bed, scurrying under it. I push myself right to the other side, planted against the wall, and try to hide myself with the bags of used toys and large clothes Mom is waiting for me to fit into.

I jolt and freeze, holding my breath as the dresser tips over, and the door swings open. *I can't see him through all the stuff hiding me, but I can hear him walking into the middle of the room.*

"Cole?" *He says my name through his teeth, footsteps going to my window.* "I'm sorry, Cole. I shouldn't have hurt you."

I grit my teeth so hard, my jaw hurts, and more tears threaten to slip free as a demonic laugh sounds around the room. "Come out so I can see where you're hurt," *he drawls, pulling open my wardrobe and slamming it harshly, showing his anger.* "Where the fuck are you?"

He hums to himself, then I flinch as something smashes on my wall. The only thing it could be is the picture of me and my mom that sat next to my bed. The version of my mother I miss. The version who vowed to protect me, love me, care for me. Not this new version who forgets to make sure there's food in the house or to unlock the door while she's gone for two days with Dad.

He steps on the glass, getting closer. Closer. Until I can see between bags that he's kneeling next to my bed, and I stop breathing, shaking, fucking trembling as he leans down.

He has blood on his cheek from the dripping wound I made on the side of his head. Good, I hope it hurts nearly a fraction of what you put me and Mom through.

"I can see you."

It's the last thing I hear before he grabs my leg and drags me out from under the bed.

"Dad, please!" *I scream as he drags me over the glass from the smashed picture, little cuts on my back making me wince. He grabs my jaw painfully, forcing me to look up at him, but before he can speak, I say,* "Please. I'm sorry. I'm sorry, Dad, please."

He mocks me with a baby voice. "Dad. Please. Sorry. Don't. Please. The same tune, different fucking day with you." *His hold grows painful, and I think my jaw might dislocate or snap when he brings the knife to my cheek.* "Why can't you be normal? Why do I need to be stuck with a defective kid?"

"I'm not," *I try to say.* "I am normal."

He laughs in my face and lets go of me, causing me to fall back on the glass, cutting my palm. It hurts, but not as much as my hip. It's bleeding through my clothes from the wound.

"I'm sorry," I cry quietly, tears soaking my cheeks in terror. "Don't hurt Mom."

Touching the cut on the side of his head, he stares at his blood, glaring at me. "When I found out we were having a boy, I was excited. I told your mom I was going to raise him to be just like me. I was going to teach him sports, take him to games, and show him how to become a man. I was going to make sure if we ever had another kid that he could hold his own and have their back against bullies. I wanted a son I could be proud of for doing well in school, getting a job, marrying someone who would pass on the family name."

He flips the knife in his hand, staring at me. "But I got you instead. Pathetic. Useless. Fucking weak."

Dad goes to drop the blade down on me, but Mom tackles him from behind, making the knife drop and them both to topple to the side.

"Run, Cole!" she screams, hurrying for the knife as she quickly crawls away from Dad. "Run!"

I don't run, though, because when I get to my feet, Dad grabs my mom by the throat and snatches the knife from her grip, and I catch his wrist before he can swipe it at her neck. Adrenaline overtakes, and the dire need to save my mom.

My knee drives into the back of his, bringing him down, and I start punching him in the face with a tight fist. I've never hit someone like this before. It hurts my wrist, but I keep going until he falls back and I'm on top of him.

"Fuck you, fuck you, fuck you!" I yell as I keep hitting him, seeing blood coming from his nose and lip. "I fucking hate you!"

The punch to my side catches me off guard, and I fall off of him, winded, coughing, my eyes bulging from the force of it. I try to get up, but Dad grabs my foot again, turns me on my back, and my eyes widen as he grabs the blade and hits the sharp edge against my shin like he's using an ax.

I scream and scream and scream, begging for him to stop when he keeps going. Slashing, axing, mutilating my right leg until Mom grabs him from behind and pulls him off.

Dizziness mixes with the agonizing pain. I'm shaking on the ground, hearing my mom crying for him to stop, a scream from him slapping her.

My head lifts, eyes dropping to my leg. Just below my knee is gushing with blood, flesh ripped apart from the assault from my father, and bile rises in my throat as he picks up the knife again, heading straight for me.

Mom screams like she's being strangled, tugging at his arm, and I push my hands into the ground and slide myself back, back, back, until I hit the wall. I cover my eyes, waiting for his next attack, but it doesn't come, because my mom has thrown herself to her knees and begs him to leave me alone, crying to him that she won't leave.

We'll stay a happy family while I sit in a puddle of my own blood.

That night, when my mom rushes me to the ER, I'm treated, labeled as self-harming, and from then on, I'm the psychologically fucked-up kid who needs constant surveillance, a psychiatrist, a "buddy" when I'm at school.

The scars are there, covered in ink. Hidden. Like all the abuse and torture I endured while living with that monster until Mom finally chose me.

Until the monster came back for me to finish the job.

CHAPTER 36
BLAISE

T wo days pass. The police are as useless as a sloppy condom in a trash can. I've lost count of how many times I have checked my phone, praying to hear from Cole while also knowing I won't. What's he going to do? Message me?

Hi Blaise, my battery died. We're at Starbucks. Come meet my dad.

Seated with my elbows on the kitchen table, I smack my head, muttering, "Fucking stupid." I hit my head again, but the dull ache doesn't help.

Detective Calleary, a middle-aged man with a beer gut and impressive sideburns, and his colleague, Jones, look at me equally pityingly. My father remains a statue beside me while the coffee machine splutters in the background, filling the air with its rich aroma.

"It's the least I can do," Dad said when the detectives entered the kitchen to inform us about their progress or lack thereof.

Dragging my hands down my face, I blow out a long, tired breath. The coffee machine falls silent, but no one moves. I've lived in the same black hoodie and jeans since the night Cole was taken. I had a quick shower to wash away the blood, then dressed like a robot. I pulled the hoodie over my head, barely aware of sliding it down over my T-shirt.

Lowering my hands, I stare at my abused cuticles. My cracked knuckles are slowly healing, and something about that—the proof that time moves on even when we don't want it to—angers me. I don't want another fucking day to pass until they catch Cole's dad and lock him up for good. I haven't slept for more than an hour or two at a time. I'm fucking tired. No, scrap that, I'm exhausted. The anger inside me boils over, and I slam my hand down on the kitchen table. No one reacts, not even when I shoot to my feet and kick over the chair.

"Blaise," Dad tries, sounding tired.

"Fuck you," I snarl, ripping the stupid fucking coffee machine from the wall and tossing it into the sink. Scalding water splashes onto my arms and hands, but I don't give a shit about the pain.

Detective Jones stands from the table and puts his meaty hand on my shoulder. I shrug him off, breathing like a bull.

He takes the hint and holds up his hands in a surrendering gesture. "Sorry…"

I look between them all, feeling like a scared animal backed into a corner.

"You're hurt," Jones says, jutting his chin to my hands.

I'm bleeding.

My skin is bright red from the hot water, and the crusts on my cracked knuckles have opened back up.

"Look," he says, speaking to me like I'm a flight risk.

Am I? The urge is definitely there to bolt.

"We will find them, Blaise."

"The fuck you will! They've been missing for two days…" I look away, my chest rising and falling rapidly. "Two fucking days."

"I've got my best men on the case," Detective Calleary says across the table. "They're out there right now, chasing clues."

"Blaise," Dad breathes, fed up with my mood swings. "Sit down, son."

"Shut up!" I roar. "Shut the fuck up, Dad." I point out the window. "They're out there somewhere. You didn't see the look in Malcolm's eyes. He has lost it. Do you hear me? Lost it! He doesn't care what he has to do to get his family back."

Dad sighs, and it pisses me off even more.

Detective Jones tries to reach for me again, but I shrug him off with a hard glare, then look at the unfeeling man who fathered me. "Don't you get it? He will kill them before turning the gun on himself. He'll try to play happy families for a while. But he will snap sooner or later. He's unstable."

"Blaise," Detective Jones says carefully. "If you don't calm down, we'll have to take you in."

"Take me in?" I frown. "Are you fucking serious?"

"It's for your own protection. They'll be able to get you something to calm you down."

"Fuck you," I sneer. "We're in this fucking situation because Malcolm was allowed to keep his fucking badge. This could have been avoided if the police department would've done their job instead of brushing it under the carpet."

"That's not true," Dad interjects, and I look at him. Betrayal gnaws at my insides when he rises to his feet. "Badge or no badge, it was a restraining order. He was free to walk the streets. No piece of paper could have stopped him from taking what he wanted."

"Clearly," I spit bitterly before pushing past Detective Jones on my way out.

They don't stop me, which is just as well. I don't know what I'll do if someone tries to keep me here. My skin crawls like there are hundreds of worms beneath it. I'm a restless, caged circus animal.

I jog down the porch steps and cross the lawn to the car. Gunmetal gray clouds roll across the sky from the south. As I climb into the car, the first raindrop slams down on the windscreen with a dramatic splash. More follow until it hammers on the roof like a stampeding herd.

I need to get out of here.

After reversing out of the drive, I slam my foot down on the accelerator. The wipers work overtime, and the road is barely visible in the heavy downpour. I take a corner too fast and nearly lose control of the vehicle. Panic seizes me as the tires skid on the wet surface.

Spooked, I pulled over by the side of the road and cut the engine. My heart slams around inside my chest. I need to calm myself the fuck down, or I'll crash into a tree or, worse, another car. My sanity is slowly slipping between my fingers.

I grip the steering wheel like my life depends on it, and blood seeps from my knuckles. The cuts split open more as I white-knuckle the leather. I hate feeling so helpless. What if Cole is dead? Two days without treatment for a gunshot wound is bad fucking news. What if he bled to death?

My head falls back against the headrest, and I close my eyes.

I will myself to think clearly, but it's a lot easier said than done. All I want is to burn the fucking world down for Cole. He's buried underneath my skin, and now it feels like I've lost the other half of my soul.

I lift my head off the headrest, then slam it back again. The ache in my chest won't subside. Guilt twists my insides. I couldn't save him from his dad. I promised him I'd keep him safe but broke my word.

I wring the steering wheel while my mind torments me. I should have saved him. I shouldn't have let his dad take him. I should have told him I loved him more often.

So many things I should have done but didn't.

As a car whizzes by outside, briefly rocking the vehicle, I drive my fist into the steering wheel, then try to rip it out but fail miserably. I hit it again and again, exerting whatever little energy I have left until I break down into sobs.

My shoulders shake from the force, but I'm done fighting the foreign emotions that have resided inside me ever since I met Cole. No walls high enough could have protected me from this.

I saw my arm across my damp eyes and fetch my phone from my pocket. There are no new messages or calls from Cole.

"Fuck," I whisper, willing it to vibrate with an incoming text. "Please, just tell me where you are."

Tossing the phone back down, I rest my elbow on the door where it meets the window, and rub my lips with my middle and forefingers. The rain bounces off the pavement as the wind whips through the branches of the trees lining the road.

It's a miserable fucking day.

I pick my phone back up to google his father while the windows slowly steam up. When that doesn't return anything I haven't already read, I look up our local police department and spend endless minutes skim-reading pointless articles. But at least I'm doing something. That's what I tell myself when a logging truck thunders past.

An incoming text from Tiago steals my attention. He has checked up on me more times than I can count in the last couple of days. I appreciate it, but I also wish he would leave me alone.

Swiping the notification off the screen, I reach for the keys and turn the ignition. The engine roars to life, and I check my mirrors before pulling away from the side of the road.

The drive across town to Cole's childhood home doesn't take long. I park outside the derelict house and peer through the passenger window. It's just as depressing as last time.

After unbuckling the seat belt, I exit the car. The rain has stopped, and I skirt around puddles in the cracked pavement.

I cast a look down the street to ensure no one is around to pay attention. I'm alone. The gate squeaks open ominously on its rusty hinges. My lungs expand on a shaky inhale, and I ask myself, not for the first time, what the fuck I'm doing. The police have already searched the property. They're not here.

But I have to check it out for myself. I can't sit around a minute longer while the police flounder like washed-up, gasping fish.

I jog up the sagging porch.

A wind chime attached to the roof plays a tinkling, haunted

tune. There's something inherently creepy about this place—an evil that lingers in the air and refuses to leave.

I almost wish I had brought sage or something to cleanse this place of ghosts and I don't even believe in that crap.

As I apply pressure to the rotten wood, the door creaks open, and dried leaves drift across the floor. I step over a console table that lies upturned on the mucky floor and breathe in the dank and stale air.

When was the last time someone opened a window?

As I make my way deeper into the house, it soon becomes obvious that it has been abandoned for some time. Damask wallpaper peels away from the corners, dark mold grows on the roof in blotchy patches, and a thin layer of dust covers every surface. I struggle to picture Cole growing up here, but this is the horrifying truth of his past. These are his roots.

I pause in the living room doorway and scan the dark room. Heavy, moth-eaten curtains frame the windows, blocking out the daylight. A small sliver breaks through the gap, and dust mites float peacefully in an eternal dance, forever adrift.

Crossing the room, I skirt the flowery couch and pull the curtains open to flood the room with light, then cough when it disturbs the dust. "Fuck…" I waft the air, looking around.

A forgotten can of beer still sits on the coffee table, like the owner of the house rose from the armchair one day, walked out, and never returned.

As I drift my fingers over the dusty couch, it dawns on me how little I know about Cole. I want to know every secret he's ever told, every nightmare that's kept him up at night, and every fantasy he's pictured while touching himself.

The less I realize I know, the more I want to dig beneath his skin until I unearth all those secrets he guards close to his heart. I don't care if I have to carve him open to get at what he's hiding at his core.

I walk the length of the room, drifting my fingers over every surface, feeling an inexplicable urge to touch his past.

Disturbing the dust on the empty bookshelf, I imagine a much younger Cole doing the same.

A freestanding lamp in the corner lacks its lampshade. The electricity has long since been cut, so nothing happens when I pull the string, but I still picture it flooding the room with an ambient golden glow.

I'm just about to turn around and leave the room, when my eyes snag on a framed medal on the wall. I walk closer, tilting my head sideways. It looks out of place in this run-down, miserable house.

It's an award. A bravery award with Cole's dad's name, to be exact.

Huh...

Cole never mentioned it. And it's also difficult to imagine the drunk, unhinged man who fired the gun on his son as the recipient of such a prestigious award.

My phone vibrates in my pocket, and I rip it out so fast, I almost drop it. Tiago again. Disappointment weighs heavily on my chest as I swipe the screen and press the phone to my ear.

"Miss me already?"

"Har. Har. Have you heard anything yet?"

"No. The cops are fucking useless," I say as I cross the room to a set of drawers. "I don't know what the fuck to do..." My voice bleeds with frustration.

Tiago is silent for a moment. I pull open a drawer and root through its contents.

"Just...don't do anything stupid, alright?"

I scoff, inspecting a sepia photograph of an elderly man in suspenders on a sun lounger with a cigar in his mouth. I drop it back down, then pull open the next drawer. "I can't make promises."

"Where are you?"

"At home, debating if I should binge-watch *Friends* or *Gossip Girl*."

"Fucking liar," he chuckles. "I went by your house, and your dad said you left."

"I couldn't sit around."

"You're up to something, aren't you?"

"Whatever gives you that idea?" I ask, pulling open the third drawer and rooting through paperwork. There's no system to any of it. Someone rammed it all in here.

I pull out the contents, phone balanced between my ear and shoulder as I flip through the unpaid bills and letters. They sail through the air and flutter to the floor.

"You have that tone in your voice."

"I don't have a tone in my voice."

"Stop lying to yourself. Just..." He hesitates. "You could hinder the investigation."

"I don't give a fuck about the investigation right now," I reply. "Cole is injured..." I drift off when I spot a yellowed cutout news clipping amongst the letters.

'Police officers win bravery award.'

I feel a frown on my forehead as I let my eyes roam over the photograph of two young, proud officers. One of them is definitely a much younger version of Cole's dad.

I scan the news article to find the date. Quick math tells me this was published years before Cole was born. His dad was in his early twenties, fresh out of the police academy—

"Blaise?" Tiago asks.

"I have to go."

"Fuck that. What did I say about doing anything stupid?"

I hang up on him, then pocket my phone while reading the article. Cole's dad and a colleague won a bravery award for neutralizing a shooter who entered a local warehouse and opened fire on the workers.

How come no one talks about this? And what the hell has happened to Malcolm? He could never replicate that moment and, according to my diligent research, he got into trouble at work for turning up drunk. It spiraled from there.

I look over at the medal on the wall, then back down at the article. A grainy photograph shows the warehouse nestled amongst fir trees.

Fishing my phone out of my pocket, I google the address. Call it a hunch or a sixth sense, but something tells me it's important.

The paper clip trembles in my hand. It's probably a long shot, but I have to check it out to see if there's even the slightest chance that he took them there, back to a place of immense pride and nostalgia, back to a time when he felt like he could go somewhere in the world—back to the beginning.

The news article flutters to the floor, and I stride back out with a renewed sense of urgency.

CHAPTER 37

COLE

"I'm going to get us out of here," a voice whispers. It's soft, calming. The person is stroking my hair, gripping my hand tight, repeatedly telling me that we'll be okay.

The voice keeps going, saying soothing words while the hand keeps stroking. I feel like I'm in an oven one second and shaking with how cold I am the next.

When the hand vanishes, I feel something tug at my side, and I flinch all over and try to sit up, but the person pushes down on my chest to keep me still.

"I need to change your bandage. Stay still, Cole." There's silence, and then she whimpers. "The infection is getting worse."

I blink my eyes open, my vision distorted. I can only see shadows, so I blink a few more times, screwing my eyes to focus.

Someone, a woman, with long hair and a warming, sad smile, stares down at me. "Don't move. The stitches aren't my best since I didn't have much to work with." She sighs, discarding the bloody bandage into the trash can beside her, then opening a saline water pack. "You need—"

Her voice is cut off by someone coughing, their footsteps coming closer. She pales, her hands shaking as she cleans around my wound and then pulls the bandage from its packaging.

It hurts, but I'm more focused on her face. It comes in and out of view and she has bruises on her cheek and jaw, her lip cut as if she was punched.

"How is he?"

My father comes into view, my vision still blurring, but I can see claw marks down his face. Mom put up a fight. Good. But he'll look better six feet under.

"He needs to go to a hospital," Mom says, her voice filled with desperation. "I can't stop the infection."

With a hum, he crouches down beside me, inspecting my side like he's praising his work. "He'll survive. Pack up. We're leaving in an hour."

Her eyes go wide, and she stands when my dad does. "Where?"

"I told you. The fucking unit is out looking for me. I know a guy who can make us disappear."

"You must be more insane than I thought if you think I'm going anywhere with you. I hate—"

She topples onto the ground with how hard my dad back-hands her, and she pants, gasping, tears springing in her eyes as she looks up at me.

I want to stand up for her like I used to. I want to get to my feet and jam my fist in his mouth and snap the motherfucker's neck, but I'm too weak to even keep my eyes open as they fall shut again.

"He's bleeding through the bandage," Dad scolds her. "Clean him up and get ready to leave."

He grabs my jaw, squeezing as he leans down to me. "I promise we'll be a family again, son. If you stop fighting me, I'll be proud of you. I'll be your father, not your enemy." He shoves my face. "Sort him out, Rachel."

Then he's walking out again, grabbing a gun from the table filled with tools and straddling the seat, studying the weapon.

My attention flicks back to my mom, who's trembling as she kneels beside me, tears soaking her cheeks, her jaw rattling so much I can hear her teeth clashing together. "I'm sorry," she whispers. "I'm sorry, Cole."

I want to tell her not to be, but I cough instead, and it causes pain to rocket through my body like I've been struck by a car at high speed.

She gives me a drink of water that sputters from my mouth when I cough again. Fuck. I feel like my body is shattering with each harsh breath.

"I did what I could with what I have," Mom says, her eyes glassy. Her lip twitches when she looks down at my wound. "Your father made me become a nurse. He wanted me to treat his abuse at home, so no one would ever be suspicious."

I stay silent, staring at her.

A tear slides down her cheek. "I failed you. I failed you so badly, Cole. I should have run with you sooner. The moment he became aggressive, I should have packed our bags and snuck out while he was at work. When he said I should go study to be a nurse, I thought he was getting better." She lets out a breathy, fed-up laugh. "I should have known he only wanted me trained so I could treat us at home."

My lips flatten. I never saw it that way.

"You deserve to be happy, Cole," she says. "You deserve a good life. If you hold on for me, I can figure a way out of this. We can get home, fix your relationship with Allie, and if you need to, we can move away. Or I can give you money for you to move away."

Dad scoffs in the distance. "You are home. And why would he want her? He doesn't even like pussy. Ain't that right, son?"

My body hurts too much to pay him any attention, but he keeps going anyway. "Did you know he was fucking your stepson?" He lets out a haunting laugh that echoes around the warehouse. "Or was *he* fucking *you*?"

"What are you talking about? Cole has a girlfriend."

"No, I don't," I grit out painfully, and the words make my body vibrate with even more pain, so I close my mouth and screw my eyes shut.

"Stop talking. You're only hurting yourself. I said we can sort this out. All of it," she says. "You can fix whatever is going on between you and Allie. She'll forgive you for whatever you've done."

Dad springs up from his seat and marches toward us, gripping a flashlight now. "He's fucking gay, Rachel. Did you not just hear what I said about your new, piece-of-shit husband's son?"

Her brows draw in. "No. Blaise and Cole can't stand one another." Glancing down, she looks at me questioningly. "What is he talking about?"

I roll my eyes, tensing as I try to shift to the side to put distance between us since she's still kneeling beside me and stroking my hair. "He's not lying."

She frowns deeper. "I'm not following."

"It doesn't matter. Cole is done with the Rowle family, and so are you." Grabbing Mom by the hair, he yanks her to her feet. The urge to stand and attack him is strong, but the pain and weakness is worse. He drags her to the table and forces her to bend over it.

I try to get up. I fucking *try*, feeling the stitches my mom did ripping as I force myself to sit upright the moment he unzips his pants.

Seeing stars and feeling blood piss out of my wound and down my leg, I put one foot in front of the other, dropping to a knee with a wince and getting back up again. Vomit rises in my throat. My fingers curl around a pipe, but the dragging of the metal makes my dad freeze his movements before he can enter her, my mom's cries hitting every wall around us, begging him to stop.

He turns to me, tucking himself away and letting out a laugh. "What are you going to do with that?"

Everything around me goes in and out of focus, my lungs seizing as sweat coats my face, unable to put my foot forward for one more step. I gulp down a lump, swaying back and forth, the pipe slipping from my fingers before I fall forward.

Dad catches me, still laughing. "I think it's time to tie you up." He steps to the side, dragging my limp body with him, even though my mind screams for me to fight.

He sets me down on the ground, holding me up against a metal beam built into the structure of the warehouse. My arms are pulled behind me, and I hear the click before the cold metal tightens around both of my wrists.

"That'll keep you out of my way until it's time to leave." He slaps my cheek. "I'm proud of you for wanting to protect your mother, though. Really fucking proud. Maybe you're not weak, after all."

Mom cries as Dad pulls her toward me. "Sit behind him," he orders.

He cuffs her to the beam too, our cuffs crossing over, and I can feel the warmth of her body, even though there's a metal beam between us. I'm mentally being comforted by my mother – my mind is tricking me into a dream where I'm safe, under the bed, hidden, and my mom is protecting me like she should have when I was a kid.

His footfalls grow silent as he goes outside. I hear him talking to someone on the phone—forty-five minutes until someone arrives. Something about a boat to somewhere, new identifications too.

"Cole didn't have his phone. I saw it lying on the ground when I took him." There's silence, and then he adds, "No, I smashed her phone up and threw it in the quarry."

My eyes focus on the sign near the entrance. Allertons Factory. I've heard of it before, but I can't remember where.

I roll my head to the side. "Mom?" I think it says it audibly—maybe I mouthed the word?

"Yeah?"

"Can you...reach my back pocket?"

Her fingers move around, and she freezes when she feels the burner phone my dad must've missed. She pulls it out, but it drops. We both stop breathing, my eyes lifting to the entrance, even though my sight is shit and I can barely see, I know he didn't hear it.

I reach for the phone, groaning as I try to turn on my side, my eyes straining to look as I type out a message to Blaise. I drop the phone twice, and the pain that rocks through me every time I move is indescribable.

"What the fuck have you got there?" Dad bellows, and my fingers go faster as I hear his heavy boots, just like it used to be when I was younger.

I have no idea if it sends before he grabs it and tramples all over it. He crushes it to pieces, launching it off the wall before marching out of the warehouse entrance and tossing it down the well.

"You think you're fucking smart?" he grits, and my hearing vanishes as he smashes his boot into the side of my face, making my mom scream at him to leave me alone.

I smirk up at him, spitting blood at his feet. "F-fuck you."

"If you do one more thing to step out of line, I'll take it out on your mother." My smile drops, and he grins, shaking his head as he walks away. "Fucking weak-ass pussy."

The next half an hour, I think I fall in and out of consciousness, and my wound is gaping, stinging, and fucking burning like I've been chucked in a fire. My entire body aches. My mouth is dry, and I have sweat layered all over.

I think I might die. I know I'm already heading in that direction and Dad isn't going to get me any medical attention. He's a delusional asshole who needs to be sectioned, or better yet, killed.

"If I..." My words stop as I grit through the pain, and I cough, making the pain even worse. "If I don't make it."

"You're going to be okay, sweetheart."

"Tell Blaise...I love him."

I love him so fucking much; he's all I can think about as I slip in and out of the darkness. Death is waiting for me with his scythe grinning, impatiently tapping his foot with his black cloak.

Blaise Rowle gave me a few months of life. I wasn't the defective, useless asshole who let a girl treat me like a doormat, or a son who couldn't follow simple rules, and I wasn't the stepson who was hated. I was Cole Carter, and someone loved me back.

Mom claims to have always loved me, but she didn't protect me like she should have. Not right away. Blaise, however, other than drugging my ass and fighting me every step of the way, loved me.

I swallow, tasting copper—that can't be good. My side is burning more, and it feels like a golf ball is lodged in there.

She's silent for a beat. Two beats. Three. "You can tell him yourself, okay? Because I won't let him take us. I'll make your dad take you to a hospital."

Bless her heart. She has no idea how ridiculous that sounds, considering Dad is packing bags into the new truck, loading guns into a satchel before hiding them under the seat. He doesn't give a fuck about my condition, or that the chances of me walking are slim to none. I can't even sit up properly without thinking I'm about to die on the spot, and I've lost all feeling in my legs.

There's no stopping him. He'll take us. And what happens next, I have no idea. Hopefully, I die before I find out.

"Change of plan. They're at a meeting point. It's a twenty-minute drive from here. Let's go," he says, marching over to us and unfastening our cuffs. "Stand up."

He grabs my mom and pulls her away from me. She doesn't fight or stop him from kicking my leg to try to wake me up. My eyes are open, are they not?

Barely.

Mom worries her lip, hugging herself. "He can't. He's really sick, Malcolm. The wound is getting even more infected, and if we don't get him treated, he will probably go septic if he isn't already."

"We'll take those chances. Grab all the medical supplies and get your ass in the car. I'll deal with him."

She stands over me to stop him from grabbing me. "A few bandages and gauze aren't going to help him. If we don't get him help, our son will die. Do you hear me? Our son is *dying*." The last word cracks in her throat, and she covers her mouth. "Please don't take my boy from me. I'll go with you. I'll do whatever you want. Just take him to the hospital."

My heavy eyes glance up at him. I want to tell my mom that there's not a chance in hell she's going with him or giving herself up for me, but I'm so weak, too fucking tired. I want to kick him in the balls and put a hammer through his skull, but I can't do a fucking thing.

He grinds his teeth, getting up close to her, and she shrieks as he snatches her throat. I try my best to sit up, to move my hand to grab his ankle, but I can't. I fucking can't.

"You took Cole from me, so fucking sue me if I want to do the same to you. If he dies, then he dies. Less dead weight."

The slap echoes around us as my mom's hand swipes at his cheek.

He growls and drags her to the car, tosses her inside, and tells her if she gets out, he'll put a bullet in my head. By the time he gets to me, I have one eye open, my pain is starting to subside, and I can barely see.

If this asshole is the last person I see before I die, I'm going to be more than pissed.

"I should leave you here. You're going to be nothing but a nuisance, but I need her to love me again, and she's never going to do that if I let you die." He grabs my arm, yanks me up, and fists my hair with his free hand. "Walk to the fucking car."

He shoves me, but I just fall on my face, my skull smacking the ground. I can hear it rattle, the way the bone connects with the hard surface, but I don't feel anything.

I'm tired. So fucking tired. I just need to sleep. When I open my eyes again, I'll be beside Blaise, and this would've all been a dream. A fucking nightmare I can't wake up from. This isn't real. None of this is happening. My dad isn't dragging me along the ground by my ankle, and my mom isn't screaming my name as if I'm already dead.

It doesn't hurt anymore.

Fading in and out of consciousness, I feel arms around me. My back is to someone's chest, and there's a hand stroking hair from my forehead. They're shushing me, even though I'm silent. Rocking me like a baby. Tears. Sobs. Pleads.

I've needed my mom my whole life. I did everything I could to make her happy. Even when we moved in with Blaise and his dad, I tried to be on my best behavior, but I failed. I couldn't even hold down a girlfriend for her, because I couldn't fall in love with Allie.

I tried.

I forced myself to stay with that girl for two years for my mom. I saw how happy she was when I brought Allie around and they'd sit and chat away for hours before telling me I better marry her one day.

And I was going to. I was going to marry Allie to please her, to keep seeing the smile my father snuffed out years ago. Fuck, I even tricked myself into thinking I could have a family with her, fall for her along the way. That my broken soul would fix itself for someone I didn't care for.

Then I fell for her stepson. I started needing him more than I needed air filling my lungs. I still do. I wish I could see him. One last time, I'd tell him how important he is to me. I'd tell the world he's mine and I'm his.

I'd do anything to go back. I'd change so much.

"Fuck!" Dad shouts as he swerves right, but it's too late.

Something rams into the side of us, and blinding hot pain rips me back to reality.

CHAPTER 38
BLAISE

I 'm losing control.

I can sense that my fragile hold over the panic festering inside me is slowly withering away. Cole has been missing and injured for two days. The more I think about it, the more irrational I become.

I'm speeding down a country lane leading to the abandoned warehouse. The odds that he took them there are slim, but a nagging sensation in the pit of my stomach and a sense of urgency have me pressing down harder on the accelerator.

I check the speedometer as I tighten my grip on the steering wheel. What if he's not there? What if I'm too late?

My phone vibrates in my lap. It's Dad.

"Sorry, can't talk right now," I mutter, declining the call. The rain has stopped, but dark, ominous clouds still paint the sky a deep shade of blue as thunder rumbles in the distance.

When Dad rings again, I curse under my breath. I don't want to talk to him right now. I don't want to fucking talk to anyone.

"What?" I bark, phone pressed to my ear.

Dad is quiet for a moment. Under normal circumstances, I would never speak to my dad like this, but I'm not myself. His unfeeling, collected, stone-faced son is nowhere to be found as the car flies down a country road in the aftermath of a summer downpour. Water sprays from the wheels as I drive through yet another large puddle. If I'm not careful, I could waterplane, but the thought of the car spinning out of control and crashing into a

348

tree seems like a welcome idea if I'm forced to exist in a world without Cole.

I've been a goner from the moment he chased me through the forest and wreaked havoc on my entire fucking world. Back then, while hiding his identity behind a mask, he shook me up from the inside like a snow globe until he stirred up all these complex, fucked-up emotions. Emotions that I don't know what the fuck to do with. And he did it with such effortless ease; I had no say in the matter. So no, Cole doesn't get to leave this fucking world without me. I refuse to let his dad take him away from me. I fucking refuse.

I will find him.

I *have* to find him...

I taste salt, and it's then I realize I'm crying again. I've never cried a fucking tear in my life until Cole.

"Fuck," I breathe in a shaky tone and wipe my cheeks with the back of my hand.

"Where are you?" Dad asks, his tone softer than I've ever heard it.

"Why did you always hate Cole?" I ask, ignoring his question. "You never gave him a chance."

Dad is silent for a moment before he blows out a soft breath, and I picture him pinching the space between his brows. "It's not that I hate—"

"Then what, Dad?" I interrupt.

"He has too much of his useless father in him," he responds as if that's a reasonable excuse. It's not. Cole is nothing like his dad, and he'd soon see it, too, if he gave him a damn chance.

"I worried he would have a negative impact on you."

If he only knew how Cole turned my world upside down. "That's bullshit, and you know it." The clouds light up as lightning streaks across the sky in the distance. "You didn't like that you couldn't control him like everything else in your life."

"Blaise—" he starts, but I cut him off.

349

"No, you listen to me for once. I'm sick of you behaving like a tyrant. When we get them back, you owe them an apology."

"Just…" Another deep exhale. He changes the subject. "Where are you?"

I'm about to reply, when a text message from Cole's burner pops up on the screen, almost causing me to drive off the road.

"Fuck!" I blurt and grip the steering wheel as I ease up on the accelerator. My heart races. I'm surprised my life didn't flash before my eyes just then. I hang up on my dad with trembling fingers before pulling up the message. I swallow, bouncing my attention between the wet road and the screen.

> Unknown: allersfac45minleavinghury

Shit…

If my heart was racing before, it's thundering now like the clouds overhead.

My body trembles all over as I drop the phone and grip the steering wheel with both hands. "Calm down, Blaise. Calm the fuck down! He's alive. He's still alive," I chant, failing to get my raging emotions under control. *If Cole can't type properly, then that means… No. Don't think like that.* Something inside me hardens, and I slam my foot down on the accelerator with renewed determination. Time is running out, but I know where he is. My gut instinct was right all along. His crazy father chose to take his family to the one place he thought no one would look, and he didn't think anyone would find the link tying him to this place.

"I'm coming, Cole. Hang in there, just a little bit longer."

The countryside blurs on each side of the road, and trees and farmhouses pass by in my periphery.

Where is his dad taking them? What if I arrive too late? What then?

"Shut up!" I white-knuckle the steering wheel as though I can get a semblance of control of my fear and crippling anxiety. It's a useless battle and one I can't win, but at least there's a shimmer of hope—Cole is alive, and I have a location.

Now I need to call the cops and let them know where they are.

Picking up the phone, I swipe the screen and start to type in the emergency number, but I'm trembling so much with adrenaline that the cell slips from my fingers and lands in the footwell.

"Fuck..." My heart sinks to my stomach. *"Don't do anything reckless,"* Tiago's voice whispers in my ear. If he were here now, he'd tell me in his calm, steady voice to pull over by the roadside, retrieve the phone, and call the police. What he wouldn't tell me is to ignore it and continue driving. But that's what I do.

I don't have precious minutes to spare. Cole is waiting for me.

My jaw tightens as I picture him sending that text. When I get there, I'll skin his dad alive for even thinking he could take him from me. No one touches what's mine—

My thoughts grind to a halt when I approach the turn-off to the warehouse—a dirt road barely visible behind a cluster of trees. A car approaches the junction before pulling out on the main road.

Cole...

Cole is in that fucking car. I can't see into the vehicle from here, but there's no doubt in my mind that it's his dad's getaway car. Who else would visit the warehouse? No one. That road isn't used, as evidenced by the tall weeds and wildflowers.

"Fuck it..." The blood in my veins boils. Cole's dad messed with the wrong person.

I don't even think as I chase their car. No matter what it takes, I won't let him get away. Not a damn chance. It will be a cold day in hell before I allow anyone to take Cole away from me.

Gaining on them, I lock eyes with Cole's dad through the driver's window. We're side by side, flying down the road at breakneck speed.

Time slows, and the sounds around me grow muted until all I'm aware of is my heart's steady beat.

Cole's dad sweats profusely, his eyes blown wide with panic. He's not thinking straight. Neither am I.

In a swift move, I spin the wheel and ram my car into the side of his. We collide in an ear-splitting crunch of metal. "Stop the car, you motherfucker," I roar as I fall back, only to do it again. Tires squeal on the road. Malcolm tries desperately to overtake me, but he loses control as we approach a sharp bend in the road, and I watch in slow motion as their vehicle hurtles toward a cluster of trees.

It all happens so fast. One moment we're side by side, then the next, their car slams into a tree and erupts in flames.

I've never been more terrified than when I hit the brakes. The car comes to a sudden stop, and I sit for a moment and stare at the inferno in front of me while their car's horn blares. My mind roars, struggling to make sense of the situation. Flames engulf the hood, and dark smoke rises into the air. A part of me expects Cole to exit the car and order me to run before he chases after me in his mask—to be his usual bossy self. But no one leaves the car.

Reaching for the handle, I push open the door and climb out with my heart in my throat. The strong scent of burning metal and plastic pricks my nose as I stare at the tall, wild flames. I can't believe what I'm seeing.

Cole...

Crossing the road, I almost slip down the embankment before stumbling toward the car. The hood is wrapped around the tree trunk, reminding me of a crushed can.

Peering inside, I see his unconscious dad trapped between the steering wheel and the seat. Blood trickles from a deep gash on his head, and the seat belt digs into his throat. Static noise fills my ears as I spot Cole in the backseat with his head in his mom's lap. He's out cold, by the looks of it, but his mom is slowly coming to. I swallow hard at how pale he is, his hair matted with blood.

"Blaise?" his mom chokes as she blinks her eyes open. They widen when she sees the wild flames.

I don't need to look to know what she sees—I can feel the heat from the fire. They need to get out of the car before the toxic fumes become suffocating, or worse, the car explodes.

"Blaise..." Her voice is small and shaky. "Help me move him. I can't... He's too heavy."

I spring into action, trying to open the passenger door, but it's stuck. I try again, yanking hard on the handle. It's fucking stuck and I can't open it on the other side either because the car is jammed against a large fir tree. Even if I manage to open the door, the gap is too small to fit through.

"Fuck..." I open the other passenger door beside the driver's seat and start to climb in, but soon retreat with a loud curse. The windshield smashed when the car crashed into the trunk of the tree, and now the air is too fucking hot. I don't dare try to haul an unconscious Cole through the middle of the front seats. I don't even think I can, not on my own, and certainly not before the car is engulfed in flames or goes off like a bomb.

Pacing on the spot, I tear at my hair. Think, Blaise. Fucking think. There has to be another way.

A loud bang comes from the hood, and I duck. Fuck me... What the hell was that? Cole's mom shouts my name from inside the car, and I whip my head around in search of...something.

A large rock amongst the dried grass catches my attention, and I pick it up before running back over to the car and ordering his mom to shield her face. The window shatters on impact as I drive the rock into it. Glass crunches underfoot as I use the rock to knock out the last remaining jagged edges. After tossing the rock aside, I lean in and lift Cole by the shoulders while his mom shifts to grab his legs. Cole is heavy when he's conscious and awake, but now? He weighs a ton.

My shoes slide through the dried grass, and I use every ounce of adrenaline to pull him out through the window.

We collapse to the ground, and I scramble upright to pull

him to me. Tears gather on my lashes while I run my fingers over the scratches and bruises on his pale face. "I'm sorry..." I brush his matted hair off his brow, then shift his arm out of the way to inspect his gun wound. Nausea rises in my throat as the hole in the blood-soaked material comes into view. I reach for the hem of his T-shirt, about to slide it up when his mom puts her hand on my shoulder. "We need to take him to a hospital, Blaise."

My first instinct is to hold on to him. I don't want to lose him again. When his mom crouches down, I tighten my arms around Cole and shake my head.

Soft fingers slide over my cheekbone. "Look at me, Blaise."

Her eyes glitter with unshed tears. A roadmap of mud streaks and bruises decorates her pale skin.

She smiles softly. "He's hurt, Blaise."

My chin trembles, and I start to shake my head again, but she puts her hand on my arm. I drop my gaze to Cole and pull his unconscious body to me, wishing I could turn back time and protect him somehow. "It's my fault."

"No..." Her voice softens even more. "None of this is your fault."

"I should have done something—"

"You couldn't have stopped him." She casts a fleeting glance at the tall flames behind me, then squeezes my arm. "Cole needs medical attention. Help me carry him to your car."

The tears in her pleading eyes slide down her mud-streaked cheeks, and I whisper, "Okay," before climbing to my feet.

We work in silence, carrying Cole to the car and placing him in the backseat. Shutting the door, I stare at him for a moment. He almost looks as if he's asleep.

In the distance, thunder rumbles.

"Come on," Cole's mom says, her hand on my shoulder. "We need to go."

"You go ahead." My voice hardens as I look over at the burning car.

She follows my line of sight. The fire has spread to the cabin. "He's dead."

"I need to see his pathetic corpse burn with my own eyes."

"Blaise…"

"Go." My hard voice doesn't broker an argument, and she stares at the fire with me for a moment before she drops her hand from my shoulder and climbs into the car.

I focus on the flames. Overhead, a raindrop falls from the sky and hits my cheek.

More follow, soaking my hair and clothing. I can sense Rachel's hesitation before she steps on the gas.

I don't let myself feel relief. Not yet. Not until I know for a fucking fact that Malcolm is dead. I won't leave here until he burns to a crisp.

The rain is coming down heavier, bouncing against the pavement, threatening to extinguish the flames.

I jog across the road, slide down the embankment, and approach the burning vehicle. The fire hisses as if it fights its inevitable demise. I hold a hand up to protect my face from the intense heat, but I can still feel it threaten to singe my exposed skin.

Bending to look into the cabin, I frown when I find the front seat empty.

"What the fuck?" I breathe out in a disbelieving voice before straightening up to look around, but it's too late. A hard blow to the back of my head knocks me to my knees, and I groan as hot pain radiates through my skull.

The world spins out of control.

Rough hands fist my T-shirt and haul me up, and then a sour breath laced with alcohol assaults my confused senses. "You really need to stop playing the fucking hero, boy." The grip on my T-shirt loosens, and I fall to the ground.

Malcom kicks me hard in the stomach, causing me to curl in on myself. Violent coughs rack my body, but he's far from satisfied. His next kick sends me flying.

I try to crawl away, clawing at the dried grass, vaguely aware of the hissing fire beside us. Malcolm stalks me. He could easily catch up with me and end this torture once and for all while he has the upper hand. Instead, he hunts me. He puts one foot in front of the other, humming under his breath. "Where are you going?"

This time when I cough, blood splutters from my mouth, and that's when I know I'm in deep trouble. I can barely breathe.

My fingers dig into the dried grass and soil. I wince as a sharp stab of pain stabs at my temple.

Another hard kick in my side forces me closer to the burning car. The heat scorches my back, threatening to melt my clothing if I get too close.

When I try to get up, he knees my chin, and I fall back.

I groan in pain, then choke as more blood floods my mouth, my ribs throbbing with an icy pain that's at odds with the unbearable heat. I'm weakening.

I spit, trying and failing to push up from the ground.

"You shouldn't have gotten in my way." His distorted voice drifts in and out of my consciousness. "I could have been with my family now if it weren't for you."

He fists my short hair, and a rippling pain spreads across my scalp.

Cold metal digs into my temple. Malcolm sneers at me. "You won't get between me and my family again."

"Fuck you," I hiss through bloodied, gritted teeth.

I'm convinced he'll pull the trigger—his finger threatens to— but he chuckles instead before the pistol whips me with such brutal force that my head snaps to the side. I laugh, delirious. If I'm going to die at the hands of a crazy fuck, I might as well show him my true colors.

He might be a drunk whose life spiraled out of control until there was nothing left but ashes, but I don't accept defeat. And I certainly don't lose.

"You're pathetic." I'm still chuckling, and his eyes darken with anger. "You want to kill me. Do it."

"With fucking pleasure," he growls, cocking his gun and lifting his arm.

I launch myself at his ankles, and we crash to the ground. Malcolm tries to kick me, but I'm soon on top of him, fighting to steal his gun. It's easier said than done. I'm bleeding profusely, my ribs throb with each inhale, and my strength is waning.

A shot goes off, sending birds erupting from nearby trees. Grabbing his wrist, I bang it against the ground. Again and again. The weapon drops from his fingers, but before I can get it, he throws me off, picks it up, and aims it at my head. I barely manage to roll out of the way before he pulls the trigger.

"Shit!" I curse, jumping to my feet and sprinting for cover behind the burning vehicle. It's too fucking hot, and I'm scared to get too close in case it explodes. Any moment now, it could go *boom*.

"Stop hiding, you faggot."

Clutching my sore arm, I wince when my hand comes away slick with blood. I was too high on adrenaline to realize or even feel the pain when he shot me. I doubt he hit an artery, but it's still bleeding heavily.

I lean back against a tree and rest my head against the trunk. I'm soaked through from the rain, my clothes sticking to my bruised body.

My odds of survival aren't great. I have a useless arm and no weapon. For the first time, fear trickles into my heart—not of death but of losing Cole. What if I never get to see him again?

More coughs rack my frame, and I grimace as sharp pain lances through my skull and assaults my ribcage.

His boots disturb the grass as he rounds the vehicle, his weathered face coming into view. A raindrop clings to his nose as he lifts his arm and aims the gun at my face.

It strikes me as humorous, and laughter bubbles up from my

chest. Here I am, staring death in the face, yet all I can focus on is that single raindrop. We're comrades, both of us clinging to life.

I wonder who will give up first? Me or the drop?

I try to sit straighter, clutching my midriff, then spit a wad of blood on the dried grass and leaves.

This is it.

The end of the road.

"Any last words?" he asks, his finger steady on the trigger.

"Eat a dick and die."

A bitter chuckle climbs up his throat for a brief second, but it dies just as quickly, and he pulls the trigger.

Click.

His eyes meet mine and widen. We look at the gun. He tries again.

Click.

Click.

Now I'm laughing for real.

I can't stop it.

My ribs throb with pain as my stomach muscles contract. Tears stream from my eyes for a different reason.

Malcolm's eyes harden as a cold rage seeps from his pores. He tosses the gun to the ground and comes for me.

I'm ready for him as I stand up.

When he's within reach, I use the last of my remaining strength to rugby tackle him. My shoulder connects with his chest, and the breath gets knocked out of him. I shove him hard.

The world slows.

Everything slows.

Malcolm extends his arms as if asking for help, and a pleading look enters his eyes before he cartwheels his arm in a last attempt at regaining balance.

It's already too late.

He topples back against the car and in through the open passenger door. His shrill, ear-splitting scream fills the air as the sizzling flames engulf his thrashing body.

The air soon fills with the stench of burning clothes and flesh, and I press the back of my bloodied hand against my nose, wafting the air.

Moments later, his screams fall silent, and I cock my head curiously. His upper body and head are burning, but his legs and feet remain outside the car, strangely untouched by the flames.

It's almost as if I expect them to twitch or something, like in the movies.

When they remain unmoving, I blow out a bored breath and stumble past the burning car toward the road.

I'm growing dizzy, blood dripping from my fingers with every step. I clutch my arm in a bid to stem the bleeding, but I'm struggling to stay upright. I feel like I might faint.

I finally step onto the road and sway on the spot. What do I do now? My phone is in the footwell of the car.

The same damn car Rachel took to the hospital.

My weak laughter rattles my diaphragm. I stumble, barely managing to right myself in time.

I tip my head back and lose myself in the rain against my lashes and cheeks. Maybe I'll die here today, but at least I can feel the rain on my face one final time.

A wave of nausea comes over me, and I topple back. In the distance, sirens draw nearer.

Maybe it's my imagination.

Maybe I'm already dead.

Cole's smiling face is the last thing I see before the world turns black.

CHAPTER 39
COLE

Beep. Beep. Beep.

Continuously, the beeping fills my ears like a haunting melody. It's constant—the reminder that I'm not dead. Unless I am, and I'm stuck listening to this fucking sound for the rest of my dead life.

Or when people said you see the bright light, they lied, and you actually hear the incessant beeping right before you take your last breath.

Unless I am dead already and this is Hell, because the high-pitched noise is getting annoying the more awake I am. The bright light nearly blinds me as I open one of my eyes. Wincing, I close them again and try to lift my hand to my face, but it's then I become aware of someone holding my hand.

"He's waking up," I hear a voice. A soft voice I know belongs to Allie.

"Go get the nurse," my mom says to my left. It's her that's holding my hand. Her thumb is stroking the top of it, squeezing every few minutes while I fight to stay awake.

Is she okay? Did Dad let her take me to a hospital? Is he standing in the corner of the room, gun drawn, waiting for me to get treated so he can take us away? Did my mom scream for help?

I flinch as I try to move. Everywhere hurts – my side and back, my head, my chest. It's like I was hit by a—

My eyes open. The last thing I remember is a car ramming into us.

The beeping intensifies, and a hand rests on my chest. "You're okay, Cole," my mom says, trying to soothe me. "Please relax. Please. You're still very fragile."

"The nurse is coming," Allie says, and I turn my head to look at her. She has no makeup on, her eyes red, and she's wearing sweats and a hoodie I'm certain belong to Jackson. She hugs herself. "Hi," she says, her voice low, like an echo. "How do you feel?"

I grit my teeth and turn to my mom. "What happened?" I ask, my voice all croaky and dry. It takes me everything to try to swallow, like I'm gulping down nails against sandpaper.

"Blaise found us," she says, and my heart thuds even harder, the machines alerting us that my heart rate is picking up. "He told me to take you to hospital."

"Dad?"

She chews on her lip. "He's dead. Blaise put up a good fight against him."

"Bl—" I stop, my eyes instantly stinging. My face snaps to Allie, then back to my mom. "What...?"

My mind is about to explode, because I'm not following. I think the drugs pumping into me are making me lightheaded, or it's my erratic breathing.

I look down at my arms, their voices falling in and out of focus, even as the nurse comes in and checks me over. She tells me I was lucky to be brought in when I was. The bullet was removed, and it's been two days since surgery. I have fluids and antibiotics pumping through my body to fight the infection, stickers on my chest from them trying to trace my heart, and my side is bandaged.

My temperature is still high, but not dangerous, and the wound still has some pus, but not as bad as it was when I was brought in.

I was lucky, she keeps saying.

Over and over and over again. Lucky. Lucky. Lucky.

Where's Blaise?

Blaise was there. He found us. So he must've received the message I sent. Did he call the cops and make sure he had help? Dad is trained in combat, and in how to use a firearm. Blaise, as much as he's a hard-ass, would be nothing on my dad.

I hold my breath when a shot of pain runs up my side. The nurse tells me my throat will still be scratchy from the breathing tube. I still needed it for a few hours after surgery because I was declining, but they put me on their strongest antibiotics.

"Calm down, Cole," Allie says, and I want to tell her to fuck off. She has no reason to be here. But then my mom leans over me and cups my cheek, her bruised face filled with worry. "Breathe, sweetheart. We're safe now. Blaise saved us."

Blaise.

Why aren't you here?

There's not a chance in hell I've lost him.

My heart drops at the thought, stopping altogether. I look around the room, and I don't see any of his things. His bag, his phone charger, his keys. Blaise wouldn't leave my side if he was here. And he wouldn't be sitting around and allowing Allie to be here. He'd tell her to get the fuck out.

My breaths are shaky as my eyes land on my mom again. "Is Blaise... Is he...?" I gulp painfully, not wanting to hear the words that will shatter my world forever.

"He was brought in shortly after you. Blaise was in a bad way. If the emergency services got there even a few minutes later..." Her words trail off. "His ribs were broken, and one of them punctured his lung. He was shot in the arm too. And he has quite a lot of internal bruising, but he's okay. They worked quickly on him."

I sit up, or try to, and wince at the pain in my side. Sweat layers my skin, and I feel sick, but I don't care. I need to find him.

"No. You need to stay in bed and heal, Cole."

"Where is he?"

"He's on this ward. Please, just rest. We'll take you to him soon."

Allie sits down beside the bed and tries to take my hand. I pull it away before she can. "Why the fuck are you here?"

"I was worried about you. It was all over the news. I came straight here and found your mom."

"I'm fine." I groan as I try to sit up once more. "You can leave now."

Tears brim her eyes. "Don't push me away."

I stare at her, blinking. "I don't want you here. You have no reason to be here."

Standing, she hesitates. "I'm sorry. About everything. Jackson will leave you both alone, I promise. Will you ever forgive me for how I was in our relationship?"

"I'll forgive you if you leave. I'm fine." I sigh at the sadness in her expression. "Thank you for checking on me."

She nods, smiling at my mom. "I'm glad you're both okay. Thanks for always being there for me."

"Of course, dear."

Allie gives me one last look before she leaves. The door shuts behind her, and my head turns to the side to look at Mom. "Why'd you let her in here?"

"She was screaming down at the reception looking for you. I thought it would be better for everyone to let her in. She was a big part of your life for years, Cole."

"*Was*," I repeat, pointing out the important word in that sentence. "And she cheated on me constantly and treated me like shit. I wasn't ever happy with her."

Her eyes round, but she softens them. "You never told me that."

"It doesn't matter."

She flattens her lips when I try to sit up again. "Where are you going?"

"Blaise is on the ward. I'm not just fucking lying here."

"You're hurt."

"And so is he!" I raise my voice, then hate myself. "Please take me to him, Mom. You heard what my dad said. You know what he means to me."

Mom freezes, her bottom lip curling as she tries to stop herself from crying, but fails as I push up fully, ignoring the burning sting on my side. I tug out the needles from my arms, and when I get to my feet, I feel like I've been hit by a fucking truck.

Mom rushes to my side, but I shrug her off and force one foot in front of the other. I need to get to him. I need to know he's okay.

Fuck. It hurts, and there's warm liquid trickling down my arms from pulling the needles out, but I keep my eyes in front of me as I step out into the corridor, my mom right behind me as she yells for a nurse.

I stop in my tracks as I see someone limping down the corridor, throwing his arm off someone trying to grab him. My vision is still blurry, but I know who it is. I limp probably worse than him from how tender my body is. As my arm presses to my side, I hold my breath and rush to him, gritting through the pain as I hear a nurse telling me to get back to my room.

Closer, Blaise comes toward me, trying to speed up. His dad is trailing behind, his eyes sunken in like he hasn't slept a wink while his son fights him off once more.

"Cole," he breathes as he reaches me, and we collapse against one another in a warm, painful embrace. His arm, the one not in a sling, wraps around me as my arms hold him to me.

I'm finally home. I know I'm not dead. And neither is Blaise, because my heart hammers against his, beating as one.

Everything aches. I'm sure I can feel my stitches pulling, but I don't care. Because I have Blaise in my arms and we're okay. His body shakes against mine, and my own does the same as he buries his face into my neck.

My hand slides up into his hair, sticky with blood and mud,

and I fist at his strands and pull him to me more. My eyes open, staring at my stepdad. He's frozen in place, unable to move or say a word.

I have his son in my arms, tears in my fucking eyes, and if he thinks for a second that he'll take him from me, he'll be the one in a hospital gown next.

Because Blaise is mine, and I'm his.

CHAPTER 40
BLAISE

"**W**hat do you think they want to talk about?" Cole asks as we pull up outside the house.

Our parents asked us for a 'meeting' this afternoon. I'm not worried, but Cole fretted all day. I can see the tension radiating off his stiff shoulders when he tightens his grip on the steering wheel as though he has to hold on to something physically to ground himself. I just wish it was me instead of an irrelevant piece of plastic.

Note to self: Have the car scrapped and invest in a horse and carriage instead. On second thought, he'd probably bond with the horse or, god forbid, the horseman, and then I'd have to find a way to hide a body.

Let's just stick with this car for now.

Yes, I am jealous of it. I'm growing more possessive of Cole by the day, especially after almost losing him, which made me realize how deep my emotions run. Cole has carved his name on my damn heart.

Ever since we returned from the hospital, the atmosphere in the house has been…tense, for lack of a better word. Dad has yet to comment on my closeness with Cole or the embrace he witnessed in the hospital. In fact, he has kept out of my way as much as possible and is spending more time at the office. Meanwhile, Cole's mom dotes on her son at every opportunity. We can't enter the house without her asking to check him over or bringing him food. I think she feels bad for forcing Allie on

366

him all these years. And I know she feels guilt over the shooting.

"What do you think they want to talk about?" Cole asks again, and I tilt my head to study him. His dark hair is longer, falling over his eyes and curling at his nape. I'm sure he'll cut it soon, but I love this look on him. It makes him look rebellious in the best way.

"Are you not listening to me?" he asks, his lips thinning in disapproval, which somehow makes him even more attractive.

"What?" he asks, uncertain, when I remain silent. "Why are you looking at me like that?"

Unclipping my seat belt, I palm the back of his head. His eyes widen and he opens his mouth to say something, but I shut him up with a hard, possessive kiss. He grunts, sending a jolt to my hardening dick, and his stunned surprise is the opening I need to invade his mouth.

"I was thinking," I whisper, sucking his bottom lip between my teeth and tugging the waistband of his shorts, "about how much I want your taste in my mouth when we face our parents."

"Are you crazy?" A full-body shudder grips hold of him. "Anyone could see us."

I free his fat cock and wet my lips in anticipation while stroking the impressive length. "You better hurry up and come down my throat, then."

"Jesus fuck," he grunts when I lean down to swallow his cock. His thighs tremble beneath me, and harsh panting breaths gust out of him. I deep throat him the way I know he likes, my own cock straining against my jeans. There's no hotter sight than Cole in the throes of pleasure, and sometimes, like now, murderous thoughts torment my mind when I remember that his ex has witnessed this look on his face. Next time I see her, I might have to snap her neck, after all. My self-control only extends so far.

He grips the lever on the roof as his gaze flicks from left to right to make sure no one is around. The moment he spots Mrs.

Lovejoy across the street, an elderly lady who takes great pride in her rose bushes, he pales and pulls on my hair to make me stop, but I trap his wrists with one of my hands and jack his dick.

"What's the matter?" I tease, smirking like the cat who caught the canary. "Worried she might see you get a blowjob from your stepbrother?"

"Fuck...she's waving at us," he says through clenched teeth, the tips of his ears burning with embarrassment. His heaving breaths gust across my face as he yanks his hand free to wave hello to her with the fakest smile I've ever seen.

Amused, I duck out of sight, and he chokes on his own breath when I pay extra attention to a thick vein on his cock. I trace it with my tongue all the way to the tip, where a nice, fat drop of precum waits for me. "What do we have here?" I lick it off, humming with approval before sucking him down again.

Cole bites his knuckles, his thighs tensing as my head bobs in his lap, but I couldn't care less if the lady across the road can see us. Cole is now too busy chasing his impending orgasm to care about potential witnesses either.

"Fuck, Blaise..." He sucks in a breath, then slams his hand down on my head and forces me to swallow more of his cock.

My gag reflex kicks in, and I choke around his throbbing length, but it only turns me on more to feel his rough fingers dig into my scalp.

"Fuck, that's it. Choke on it." His fingers twist, pulling the strands tight, and salty cum shoots down my throat. I swallow every drop, savoring his taste, then straighten up and drag my thumb over my lips to catch anything I might have missed.

Cole watches me for a moment before he looks down at his spent dick. Even soft, it's big, and I'm already hungry for another taste.

He stuffs himself away and runs a hand through his hair. His nerves are back, making me briefly contemplate fucking him in the backseat until he's too damn tired to worry about our parents and what they might have to say.

Cole stares out the window with a faraway look before glancing back at me. "What if they refuse to let us be together?" "That won't happen." My voice is deadpan.

Cole's lips twitch for the briefest of seconds, and then he blows out a shaky breath. "I don't know..."

"Well, I do. I won't let anyone get between us."

I go to kiss him again, but he moves back, fingers pressed to my lips to stop me from claiming his mouth again. "We can't keep them waiting forever."

Gripping his wrist, I slide his hand from my lips and place it over my rock-hard erection. "See what you do to me? How fucking crazy I am about you? Do you think I care about our parents? The only person I care about is you. Besides, my dick is in agreement with me for once and says we should skip this 'meeting' and drive somewhere quiet so I can stick my dick in your hot ass and fill you up with my cum."

A low chuckle leaves his lips, the sound teasing my balls, and then he escapes the car before I can grab him again.

I fall back against the seat with a tortured groan. Why does he have to care so much about others? I know he loves his mom, and it's because he loves her that I also have to respect her. They've reconnected since the kidnapping, and while that makes me happy, I don't like that I have to share him. Even if it's family.

"Fuck me," I whine, then glare down at my throbbing cock. I swear it's laughing at me for being such a whipped fucker. "What the fuck is so amusing? You're the one with blue balls."

I throw the door open and exit the car while grumbling under my breath at the unfairness of it all. The only consolation is Cole's taste on my tongue. But even that is like only eating one Pringle, when we all know that once you pop, you can't fucking stop. And that's the fucking truth. It doesn't matter how many times I fuck him and claim him as mine; I still want more.

Is it too late to tie him to my bed in a country far away, preferably on a distant planet or, better yet, a different galaxy, where no one but me can have access to him?

Okay, maybe I need help. But in my defense, I thought I'd lost him.

"Try to smile," Cole says, pulling on the corners of my lips with his forefingers. He tilts his head, his nose scrunching up. "Maybe not. You look like Joker with that psychotic smile."

I follow behind like a kicked puppy as he walks up the drive and jogs up the stairs. His shorts show the strong muscles in his thighs from training, bunching with each step. If we didn't have to play nice with our parents, those shorts would be around his ankles now.

He turns and rubs his neck while I ascend the last two steps like a lazy cat. "Just...don't run your mouth in there, okay?"

"Run my mouth?"

His Adam's apple bobs on a swallow. "If your dad is against..." He lowers his hand and gestures between us. "...this. If he's against us. I know you can be protective and—"

"Damn right." I fist his T-shirt and pull him to me with such force, he crashes against me. "If he says a single bad thing about you, I won't hesitate to acquaint him with my fist."

"Blaise," he chuckles, uncertain. "He's your dad."

"I don't fucking care. I almost lost you. You were bleeding all over me and..." I drift off, needing a moment to rein in my emotions. My heart always aches whenever I think of his pale, blood-smeared face and broken body that day. "I'll never let anyone hurt you again, and that includes words."

"I can stand up for myself—"

One moment, he's giving me his old spiel about how he doesn't need or want me to defend him, and the next, I have him trapped against the railing with my hand clamped over his mouth to shut him up. "I know you can stand up for yourself, but that's beside the point. I'm your boyfriend, Cole. Your man. Your battles are my fucking battles. Don't you dare try to fight alone! Not anymore. Not over my dead body. I love you, for fuck's sake. You don't ever have to stand up for yourself anymore, not when I'm here." I shove away, my body trembling with rage.

Rage at the world for not accepting all types of love, no matter age, race, or gender. I fucking hate that Cole has to worry about our parents' opinion of us. They wouldn't bat an eyelid about our union if I were a girl. But I have a dick, and therefore, he spent the day fearing their rejection, and that makes me want to break shit.

I don't deal well with these emotions. It fucking pains me to witness Cole's anxiety. Who the fuck cares what our parents think? Fuck them.

Cole cares. He cares a lot.

I rub my eyes vigorously before dropping my hands and meeting my stepbrother's worried gaze. "C'mon. Let's see what they have to say."

He doesn't object when I reach for his hand, and that makes me feel like I've won a trophy. For the past week, Cole has kept his distance from me around my parents, only kissing me or touching me behind closed doors.

I squeeze his damp palm as I pull open the door and enter the house. The rich smell of steak and peppercorn sauce is the first thing that greets us.

Exchanging a look with Cole, we find his mother in the kitchen. The table has been set, and a fresh vase of flowers sits in the middle.

Releasing my hand, Cole walks up to his mom and kisses her cheek. "It smells lovely."

A pink hue touches her cheeks, and she peers past him at me. "I hope you're hungry, Blaise."

Smelling a trap, I walk deeper into the room. What's with the meal? I expected a much more arctic atmosphere than this. It's almost as if…his mom is trying to distract us.

"Sit down," she offers just as my dad enters the room,

looking tired. He pulls out the chair beside mine, barely sparing me a glance, and Cole's mom plops down next to her son.

Red flags. Red fucking flags everywhere.

I pick up my fork and knife for something to occupy my hands with while Dad cuts into his steak without a preamble. Silence falls over the table, and I try to catch Cole's eyes, but he looks anywhere but at me. I kick him under the table, and he gulps his glass of water.

My teeth gnash.

There's nothing I hate more than to be ignored. Especially by Cole. It always makes me want to choke him, but since our parents are here, acting weirder than usual, I can't exactly launch myself across the table, steaks be damned, and choke the daylights out of him to drive home the point not to shut me out.

Instead, I cut a perfectly symmetrical square of steak and eat it like a normal person who isn't occupied with murderous thoughts. I can do this. I can be normal.

I'm so fucking normal.

Normal. Normal. Normal.

"Gavin and I are divorcing," Cole's mom blurts, making me choke on the steak.

Across from me, Cole pales while I hack up a lung. I reach for my glass of water, then down it in one. While I expected this to be an intense talk, I didn't expect them to announce their divorce.

When I can finally breathe again, Cole asks, "Is it because...?"

"No," she replies in a soft, reassuring voice. "Not at all. It's not about you, boys. Gavin and I... Well..."

My father blots his mouth with a napkin. "We talked and decided it's for the best."

"But why?" my boyfriend asks.

I love calling him that. My boyfriend.

Mine.

Cole's mom fidgets, mulling over her words. "Ever since your dad, I've existed in survival mode. You're grown up now, and well…" She lifts a shoulder and lets it fall. "I think I need some time alone to find myself again."

"And you're okay with this?" I ask my dad, who is unusually quiet beside me. I would even go as far as to say he looks contemplative.

Tapping his forefinger on the table, he nods. "Yes, I think it's for the best, too." He lifts his gaze and looks at Cole. "I love your mom but haven't been a good husband. I realize that now. I think that…maybe we married for the wrong reasons. And your mom is right. She deserves space away and freedom to find herself again."

I look over at Cole's mom, seeing tears cling to her lashes, but she looks…happy.

"What about money?" Cole asks.

"That's already taken care of. I wouldn't leave her penniless."

Silence falls on the table. I wait for someone to mention the elephant. No one does.

I meet Cole's eyes and address the room. "Cole is my boyfriend. I love him. I have loved him for a very long time. Probably from the first day I met him, even when he was stubborn and decided from day one that he hated me."

"I love you, too," he mouths, and we share a small, nervous smile.

"Are you gay?" Dad asks me.

"No, I'm not gay."

Cole narrows his eyes, like he always does, and a smidgeon of jealousy creeps into his gaze. It doesn't matter how many times I tell him that he doesn't need to worry about women. Or men. I only have eyes for him.

"I'm bisexual," I explain.

Dad rises from his seat, walks up to the fridge, and pulls out a bottle of vodka. Cole's mom offers me a smile while my dad pours a large glass and takes a sip, studying me from across the kitchen.

"You like both genders?"

I shrug. "I guess."

"You guess?"

"I only want Cole. I only have eyes for one person, and that's your son." The last part is directed to Cole's mom. "I promise I'll always look after him."

Dad drinks his vodka like it's soda, then blurts, "Fuck," when he spills some down his shirt.

I rise from the chair and round the table. "Talk to me, Dad."

He glances at the back of Cole's head, making me stiffen, but then he puts his empty glass down and slides his hand over his tie. I wouldn't say he looks happy about the prospect of Cole and me, but he doesn't look at my boyfriend like he wants to murder him anymore either, and that's a start.

My boyfriend.

My heart does a little jolt.

Dad puts his hand on my shoulder. It's awkward at best. He pats me once, twice. "It will…" He clears his throat. "It will take me some time to get used to."

Clenching my jaw, I look down. I guess that's all I can expect from him, but a part of me still feels disappointed. The idea that anyone could be against us or find the idea of us difficult to swallow leaves a bad taste in my mouth, but that's the reality we live in.

"I understand."

His fingers dig into my shoulder briefly, and then he pulls me to him and wraps his big arms around me. "I want to be a better dad to you, and that starts with accepting you for who you are and who you love."

I tentatively slide my arms around him and hug him back, my nose buried in his shoulder. "Thank you."

"I haven't forgotten what you asked of me."

Easing back, I look at him questioningly, but he's no longer focused on me.

His sole attention is on Cole.

Leaving my side, he puts his hand on my boyfriend's shoulder. "I want to apologize for how I've treated you all these years. It wasn't fair on you or your mom. I know it's a little too late, but I hope with time, you'll accept my apology."

"Thanks," Cole replies, his eyes sliding in my direction, brimming with emotions.

"And I will always love you, no matter what," his mom says, stroking the back of his head. "All I've ever wanted for you is to be away from your father's shadow."

"He's gone now," Cole says in a choked voice. "That monster will never hurt us again."

He looks at me then, and it takes all my willpower not to drag him upstairs like a caveman.

COLE SHUTS THE BEDROOM DOOR, his eyes taking me in with an intensity I feel to my core, but for once, I don't have sex on my brain.

Well, that's a lie.

I always want to fuck, but I actually have something else in mind.

"What are you doing?" Cole asks when I hold my hand out.

"Don't you trust me?"

He flips the lock, the sound whispering filth to my dick, and then he walks up to me where I wait by his bed with slow, purposeful steps. "That's a very loaded question."

I drop my gaze to the outline of his hard dick inside his shorts. "It's a yes or no question. Don't overthink it."

He smirks, hiking a brow. "It depends."

"On what?"

"On what you have in mind."

"Take my hand and you'll see."

Slowing to a stop in front of me, he slides his hand from his pocket and lets it hover above mine.

"What scares you, Cole?"

He finally trails his calloused finger across my palm, tracing the lines with his warm touch before entwining them with mine. "Nothing anymore."

A smile spreads across my lips, and I kiss his knuckles.

"What are you doing?" he asks when I release him and disappear beneath his bed. His socked feet shuffle closer, and then he kneels and peeks at me.

"Join me."

The corners of his lips twitch. "Why are you under my bed?"

"Stop asking questions and join me."

"Fine..." he grumbles. "Bossy."

I scoot over to make room for him when he slides underneath the slats. There's almost no space for two grown men, but I doubt Cole cares. I know I don't.

"This is the first place you let me in."

Cole stares up at the slats before he turns his head and searches my face. "What are you scared of, Blaise?"

I ease up his T-shirt and trace his scarring with a featherlight touch. "I'm scared to wake up and learn that our happy ending was only a dream." My fingers brush through his happy trail, and I smile when he shivers.

A sharp V points the way to Cole's cock, like a dangling carrot. While I'm not a reindeer, I still deserve a fucking medal for resisting the strong urge to pull out his cock and suck the soul from his body.

"Do you think Jackson will leave us alone now?" I ask.

Cole's brow furrows. "You don't have to worry about him. That shit is over."

"And Allie?"

"Are you jealous?" he asks teasingly, looking pleased and a little smug. It takes a Herculean effort not to take the bait. Instead, I shift over onto my side, cursing the small space. My shoulder squishes against the slats, which is fucking uncomfortable, but it's worth it to be here in Cole's safe space.

I stroke his cheek. "I'll always be possessive of you."

"You're very territorial."

"And you're not?"

Cole scoffs, a smile teasing his lips. "I'm above petty jealousy."

"Is that so?" I hum, tracing his dark brow. "It didn't seem like it when Tiago stood too close the other day and you threatened his existence."

"Threatened his existence?" Cole has the audacity to sound offended. "I would never—"

"You said, and I quote, *stand that close to him again, and I'll string you up by your balls.*"

A blush colors his cheeks before he can stop it. "I didn't say it *quite* like that."

"I'm pretty sure those were your exact words. Want me to phone Tiago and Ronnie to confirm?" My hand falls away from his cheek when he shifts onto his side.

We stare at each other in the semi-darkness, and then he drops his eyes to my mouth and licks his lips. My heart beats harder in response. Cole always has that effect on me.

"I've seen him kiss you, Blaise. Short of bleaching my eyes, I can't eradicate that image from my mind."

"Trust me..." I kiss his lips. "You have nothing to worry about. You're the only one I see. Besides, Tiago is as straight as they come."

When I lie back down, Cole does the same. He takes my hand as I cushion my head with my arm. The feeling of his fingers entwined with mine is all I can focus on. That, and the soothing sensation of his thumb stroking the back of my hand.

Exhaling a content breath, I close my eyes.

For once in my life, I'm where I need to be.

I'm home.

EPILOGUE
PART ONE.

Cole, 5 years later

Samson's head rests on my shoulder as he snores. He's been like this the entire bus journey home from our game two states over. We're all exhausted. After nearly ten failed away games, it was about time we got a win.

Ever since I got scouted at my last ever college football game, my world has kind of been insane. Between my mom going to work in London after her second divorce to Gavin, I barely see her unless she FaceTimes, and even then, she's in a different time zone and we usually miss each other.

I know she's there for me, just like she knows I'm there for her. She's happy, and that's what matters. Her divorce from Gavin was pretty quick. Within weeks, she was free, and he remarried months later.

When I graduated and landed a spot on the team, I was worried about how me and Blaise would figure out our relationship. He was still in college, I was out in the wild, and we were trying the whole "living apart" for the worst two years of my life. Seeing Blaise only on the weekends and holidays was horrible. We were both needy and miserable, but we made it work.

I stare down at the ring on my left hand. It's a plain white-gold band. Blaise has the same one, both with our initials engraved inside. He'd dropped to one knee when he showed up at my apartment in Cal a week after his graduation, and everything has been full steam ahead since.

The bus slows to a stop in the small neighborhood near

Blaise's company building – a businessman who lands deal after deal, completely dominating my income. I nudge Samson off me, and he groans.

"You sure you don't want to stay at our place until tomorrow?"

He shakes his head and rubs his eyes. "I'll wait at the airport."

"Right." I tell my team I'll see them at practice in two weeks, since we now have time off, and I grab my bags and climb off the coach.

It drives away, leaving me with my suitcase rolling behind me, a yawn on my lips as I pull my luggage up to our gate. Entering the code, I check to see if any of the lights are on, but none are.

My phone ran out of battery this morning, and I haven't had time to charge it, so I haven't spoken to Blaise. He'll be worried. He hates it when I travel, always checking in to make sure I'm okay. So my husband is probably losing his fucking mind right now.

Even though my dad is dead, thanks to him, he still panics.

The memories are there. The worry. The voices in our heads that haunt us. We both have nightmares that have us waking up in cold sweat, but we're always there to comfort the other. My anxiety attacks have since vanished from the moment we bought this place.

I open the front door, and both Wesley and Boomer run to me —our golden retrievers who have only just left the puppy stage and stopped chewing up everything and shitting all over the house like they're competing for the World's Worst Puppy award.

Tossing my keys in the entryway bowl and dropping my bags, I crouch to fuss with their ears and get kisses, and then I glance around the dark house.

"Blaise?" I call out, listening for a TV or shower or even the fucking snores, but silence…

I stand. "Blaise? Are you home?"

Sighing, I pull the charger from my bag and plug my phone in, leaving it sitting there as I push my hands into the pockets of my sweats and hunt the house. The kitchen is dark, but a glass of wine sits on the counter, the bottle still full. The sitting room is empty, and when I check upstairs, I see the bedroom, bathroom, and spare bedrooms are all dark too.

He must be out with Tiago and Mia—they've been insufferable about spending time together ever since they decided to go official from their friend-with-benefits status.

I was always against it, seeing as Mia was Blaise's ex and all, and the fact we both fucked her, but it's not like that. She's happy for us, and she's happy too, so we all win.

Fuck knows what Allie is doing. Probably on her second husband by now. Jackson got bored of her real quick and they've been radio silent on social media since.

I sit down on the bed and lie back on the mattress, yawning again, but something out the corner of my eyes has me glancing out of the balcony doors. A flicker of orange.

Getting to my feet, I open the door to the balcony and tilt my head, leaning my elbows on the stone wall. Blaise is standing in front of a small fire, staring intently into the flames like he's in a trance.

Even from here, I can see how handsome he is. The sharp contours of his face illuminate from the flicker of embers around him, and I watch as he blows out a breath and runs his hand through his hair.

It takes me less than a minute to get to the back door, and I head into the yard. The moon lights up the expanse of it. We wanted to buy somewhere with a large area around the building, a few acres of woodlands too.

I gulp as I reach him, standing in front of the flames opposite him. And when he doesn't look up or speak, I grow nervous. "Hey."

Nothing. His jaw ticks, and he blinks twice.

"Is something wrong?"

His eyes snap up to mine. "You tell me."

I huff and put my hands in my pockets again. "You're the one sulking in the yard at three in the morning."

"Samson had his arm around you in that picture that was posted a few hours ago. And you didn't reply to my messages."

A smirk pulls at my lips, and I stifle a laugh. "Is my husband jealous?"

He glares at me. "I'm not jealous."

"No?" I say, walking around the flames until I'm in front of him. I look him up and down, loving the way he doesn't even have on a shirt. My name is inked over his heart. "Then what are you, if not jealous?"

"I'm pissed," he retorts. "Your phone was *off.*"

"It died." I grab his jaw, tugging him to me. "Are you going to stand here and sulk, or are you going to kiss me and come to bed?"

"Neither," he replies, shoving me in the chest so hard, I take a few steps back and frown at him. He opens a bag I never noticed at his feet and tosses me something.

I catch it, staring down at the blank, black face mask in my hands. I look at him in confusion, my head tilted.

My heart instantly accelerates as he grabs another mask. His eyes light up at my expression, at the way my cock hardens between my legs and rises in my sweats as he slides the mask onto his face.

A white one with a crack down the side. The same one I wore all those years ago.

EPILOGUE
PART TWO

Blaise

L et me ask you one thing before I chase the love of my life and fuck him into the dirt: can you think of that *one* small moment in your life that changed the trajectory of your future. Think hard. Let's call it your *before* and *after*. Something happened that changed everything. Maybe it even seemed insignificant in the moment, but without that one event, however big or small, you wouldn't be here today. It's also known as the one moment that defined your *now*. We all have one. It's almost as if we're dancing to an imaginary tune. Maybe that moment and every moment since seem like a random sequence of events, but looking back in the rearview mirror, you realize all those moments where you felt lost, held your hand all along.

The flickering flames dance across Cole's sharp facial features. Time has been kind to him. If anything, he's more handsome now than five years ago when he chased me down in the woods.

You guessed it.

That was *our* moment.

He stares down at the black mask in his hands, his eyes brimming with emotion.

Life has a way of coming full circle.

"Put it on."

Cole's blue eyes flick up, and his Adam's apple bobs on a swallow.

"I won't tell you again."

A small smile plays at the corners of his mouth, easing his sharp features. It doesn't matter how many years pass, Cole still brings me to my damn knees. Sometimes, like when his fucking phone dies, I can't stop the fear creeping into my heart at the prospect of losing him. I almost did once. Never again.

I tilt my chin in his direction. "Mask on now."

The fire shoots sparks into the night sky.

"Bossy," Cole teases, but follows my order.

My heart hammers harder in response. Back then when he first claimed me, it was me running through the dark woods with Cole hot on my heels. I didn't know who it was, but one thing was clear as day: I wanted it to be him. I wanted it so fucking badly.

When the mask is on, Cole drops his arms by his sides and blinks at me through the holes while awaiting further instructions.

Nothing excites my dick more than his submissive side. Especially after he has spent days away, letting his aggression out on the football field. Not that I allow my thoughts to drift in that direction. Last time I watched him play, I almost stormed the pitch and choked the fucker who shoulder sacked him and then had the fucking audacity to lie on top of him.

My eye twitches just thinking about it.

Fuck that... I need to bleach my brain or act on my murderous instincts. Either will do. But since Cole is less appreciative of the little psycho devil on my shoulder, I have to let my jealous side out to play in the bedroom instead. Besides, Cole secretly loves it, which is why he teased me earlier. He should know better than to poke the bear.

I tilt my head to the side, a smile spreading across my lips beneath the mask. "Five years ago, you chased me down and made me choke on your dick." Cole watches me closely as I bend over to pick up the hockey stick in the grass. I straighten back up, resting it on my shoulder, and Cole's eyes widen. "I'm curious what went through your head when you realized it was me. I mean..." Chuckles rumble in my chest. "It's quite obvious what went through your head, if you get my drift. You were hard as a rock."

Cole steps back, but his eyes never leave the hockey stick. Noticing, I twirl it. "Nice touch, don't you think? Maybe I should whack you in the head with it, like you did to me at the swimming pool, remember? I always liked your brand of foreplay."

More sparks erupt from the fire, the flames crackling in the night. "Here's what will happen." I press the hockey stick against his chest. "I'll count to ten real nice and slow while you run like your life depends on it. The faster you run, the harder I'll fuck you. Hear me? I want to fight for it. If you make it too easy for me, I'll fuck you soft and gentle, like I imagine your team's physiotherapist, who keeps giving you the fucking eyes would do." I shove him with the hockey stick to drive home the point of how much I want to murder that man. "You should let me dispose of him, by the way." I shrug, like we're discussing what color of tie to wear for his next media event. "I don't see the problem."

Cole looks toward the trees, already trying to figure out what direction to run, so I place the stick beneath his chin and guide his eyes back to mine where they belong. "My point is, he would make sweet, tender love to you. But that's not what you're into, is it? You like it rough and hard. You crave the fight as much as I do."

Cole slowly walks backwards, and I follow him step by step. The anticipation darkens his usually pale blue eyes to a deep shade of cobalt, which excites me almost as much as his next swallow. I love how all of these little nervous tells seduces the darkness in me.

"Next time he inspects a strain injury of yours, I want you to remember this." I pretend to inspect the hockey stick. "He wouldn't dream of whacking you in the head with it. But I would." Our eyes meet, and my dick demands we cut this little chit chat short. "I would bruise you, mark you, and then make you come harder than you ever have."

Another delicious step back.

"What's the matter, Cole? You look nervous? Maybe even a little scared." I wet my lips beneath the mask, basking in the hunt. "That's good. You should be scared." Resting the stick on my shoulder, I pause with my feet planted wide and my head tilted to the side. "Now, be a good little husband and run."

Cole hesitates, his chest rising and falling in rapid succession.

"One…" My voice lowers. "Two."

He dashes toward the trees, and I crack my neck in anticipation while continuing to count. The night is alive with sounds. Crickets chirp in the grass, the damp logs crackle in the firepit, and an owl hoots in the distance. We're still hours away from the sunrise.

"Eight," I shout, flexing my fingers. "Nine."

A mild breeze teases the hairs at the nape of my neck.

It's almost time.

My dick strains against my zipper. Is he still running, or is he hiding behind a tree or boulder somewhere to catch his breath?

"Ten!" I spin the hockey stick. "You better be running." With a final chuckle and a bounce on my heels, I sprint toward the trees, batting fir branches out of the way.

It's like entering another realm. Sounds grow muted, the air feels moist, and the temperature drops. I slow my strides, listening for sounds. Cole knows how much I enjoy the hunt, and how I like to drag it out.

Sticks break underfoot as I tighten my grip on the stick. He's nearby. It's almost like my body is fine-tuned to his.

I follow the invisible string that connects us, my boots pounding the damp moss. Sweat soon dampens my forehead and the space between my shoulder blades, but I push on. "Run, little rabbit. Fucking run! I'm coming for you."

A darting shadow shifts somewhere to my left, and I skid to a halt. In the distance, a swooshing sound and a surprised cry cuts through the silence.

Walking forward, I smile wide at Cole thrashing in the swaying net suspended from a branch. "Well, well, what do we have here?"

"What the fuck?" he chokes out. "What the actual hell, Blaise? The fuck is this?"

"It's called a trap, and you ran straight into mine." My head tilts, and I chuckle as I poke him with the hockey stick, making the net swing past me. "Looks like I caught an angry rabbit."

"Fuck you!" he snarls, wriggling enough to make the branch creak from his weight. I wonder briefly if it'll break and send him crashing to the ground.

"You do some twisted shit," he spits, "but this beats it all. You're insane, Blaise. Fucking insane."

"Such sweet talk. Nothing says I love you more than being called insane by my lover."

"Let me down."

"But you look so cute trapped in a net."

"Cute?" He's so angry and pent up on adrenaline that he doesn't care that his mask sits at an angle or that his T-shirt is twisted and halfway up his stomach. "I'm not fucking cute, asshole."

"Agree to disagree."

"Let me the fuck down."

I look at my big bulge. "What do you say, Blaise junior, shall we free him?"

"Are you talking to your dick now? Are you fucking serious?"

"What?" I ask, looking up. "His opinion matters, too. You deprived him for the full weekend."

Cole lets out a frustrated, angry groan, and I can't stop my lips from twitching at seeing him so enraged.

After tossing the stick to the ground, I fish out a butterfly knife from my pocket and take my sweet-ass time approaching him. "A *pretty please* would go a long way now."

He stops thrashing and tosses me a loathing glare, which makes me snigger as I circle the dangling net with my catch inside. "For my first attempt, I think I did a good job."

"What's next? A fucking bear trap?"

"Now there's a thought. Keep the ideas coming. Maybe I'll dig one of them big holes in the ground and then cover it up." I place my hand on Cole to stop the net from swinging, and when I rest the blade against the rope, he pales—well, half the side of his face visible beneath his mask.

"What are you doing?"

"You asked me to let you down." I can't quite keep the laughter out of my voice.

Cole shakes his head almost frantically. "Blaise, no."

"No? Make up your mind."

"I'm in the fucking air. I'll get hurt."

"Well...what a pickle."

Cole curses, sweat beading on his brow—again, the one visible.

I really should tell him to right his mask or remove it completely.

"I love you," he says, playing on my heartstrings. "Remember when I hurt myself while cutting onions the other week? You nearly tore the kitchen apart."

"You're very accident prone," I mutter.

"Yes... You hate it when I get hurt."

"That's different."

"How is it different."

"It's outside of sex," I reply, sawing the rope.

Cole looks like a ghost, his eyes wide and terrified. "What the fuck are you doing?" he repeats with more panic.

"What does it look like? I'm letting you down. Besides, I know how much fear gets you off."

The rope begins to split, thread by thread.

We exchange a glance, and then Cole rips off his mask, his glassy eyes pleading for mercy. Before he can open his mouth to speak, the rope snaps and he crashes to the ground with a loud thud.

Groaning pitifully, he writhes, and I study him closely while circling like a hungry predator.

"Jesus fuck…" He grimaces in pain, forehead pressed to the sticks and wet leaves on the ground.

"What's wrong?" I taunt, using my foot to shove him over onto his back. "Can't handle it?"

"I can handle it," he grits out as he watches me unbuckle my belt.

"Are you sure about that? I can always turn to someone else if it's too much—"

Cole flies up to his feet and shoves me back, his body vibrating with possessiveness. "Don't you fucking dare finish that sentence."

This is a game we play. Who can make the other the most jealous.

But that's all it is. There's no other man for me but Cole, and he knows it. I would rather claw out my eyes and feed them to our dogs than let another man touch me.

Deep down, no matter how insecure I feel at times when he travels away, I know I'm *it* for him too.

I press the knife to his throat, his eyes holding mine as I guide him back against the nearest tree. A drop of red trails from the shallow cut, and I lower the blade a fraction before leaning in close to drag my tongue through it.

Cole groans and grabs my upper arms to push me away, but it's half-hearted. While the intent is there, his body speaks a different language. He wants me to hurt him and fuck him and make him bleed all over his designer clothes.

I smile against his throat, and then whisper near his ear, "Did you miss me?"

"So fucking much," he grunts, his hips chasing my touch as I palm his hard dick through his shorts.

"Is that why your phone was turned off?"

"I told you…" His heavy eyes take in my mask, and he wets his lips. "The battery died."

Shoving his shorts halfway down his thighs, I grab his hard length. Cole shudders, his lips parting.

I stroke his dick like I own it—stroke it until his soul trembles and his knees quake. My touch drips with possessive intent. I press the tip of the knife to the pulse point in his neck and nick the skin on purpose. A bead of blood rushes to the surface, and Cole sucks in a breath, his dick twitching in my hand.

I observe the hitch in his breathing and swipe my thumb through the precum formed at the tip. Lifting my mask, I lick it off while tipping his chin up with the flat end of the hilt. His cobalt eyes appear almost black, the blue swallowed whole by his blown pupils.

"Kneel." Swiping more precum from the crown, I smear his lips, resisting the urge to sink my teeth into the soft flesh. My dick has its own heartbeat as I watch him slowly lower himself to the damp ground.

I reach out a hand and grab him by the throat. His pulse thunders beneath my punishing grip as he stares up at me. A small part of me wishes he would put up a fight, but he looks damn delicious at my mercy beneath a canopy of leaves and gnarly branches, which crawl across the sky overhead like a roadmap of veins. Moonlight barely manages to stream through, its silvery hue appearing ghostly.

"Next time your phone dies, I'll have no choice but to punish you."

Cole's throat jumps on a swallow, and I tighten my hold and then unzip my jeans with the hand holding the knife. My fingers drop by my side, and I jerk my chin. "Get my cock out."

Cole wastes no time pulling my jeans down to reveal my aching dick. The moment it bobs free, he wets his lips and stares at the angry veins and weeping head with so much longing, it's by some fucking miracle I manage to resist the urge to ram it down his throat.

My husband has always had a natural submissive streak in him, even before he admitted to his feelings for me, and it gets me so hard every damn time. He flicks his eyes up and watches me drag my tongue through the blood on the knife's flat end. I make sure to leave some on my chin, knowing how carnal it makes Cole when I look monstrous.

Closing my hand over the blade, I drag it across my palm and form a tight fist. Blood soon drips to the ground.

Tap. Tap. Tap.

Cole shivers visibly when I fist my dick.

Stroking in long pulls from root to tip, I use the knife to shift some of his dark hair away from his brow. "Show me how much you want your husband's dick. What a needy slut you are." I release my cock and tilt my head to the side. Patience has never been my strongest virtue.

He grabs me by the hips and sucks on the head—a move that drives me insane because it's not enough. I'm not happy unless my crown is smashing against his damn tonsils. He knows it, which is why he's being a brat now.

I entertain his games for all of two seconds, then say, "Unless you want it to hurt when I take your ass, I suggest you lick it clean of blood. Get it nice and wet."

Quiet chuckles rumble through his chest at the sound of the barely veiled frustration in my voice, and he takes me deeper, staring up at me as he slowly sinks lower on my cock.

"Shit," I grunt, fisting his matted hair with my bloodied hand. "You're so fucking hot on your knees with my dick in your mouth."

His tongue swirls, and his cheeks hollow. This is what it feels like to have one's soul sucked from the body. Shivers rush through me, and I grit my teeth against the blinding pleasure that threatens to confiscate my control.

"Fuck," I groan, my head falling back, my hips stuttering.

Cole swallows around my dick and slides his hand from my hip. My breath hitches when he pushes a single finger against my back hole, breaching the tight entrance.

It's all it takes. After all these years, my husband knows how to play me like an instrument.

I pull out and yank his head back to bare his neck. He hisses at the sharp hold I keep on his hair, but I don't ease up. If he can be a fucking brat, he can sure as hell take a little pain while I jerk my dick in front of his face.

With his hands fisted at his sides, he stares up at me. Cole has expressive eyes.

Eyes that goad me to give him my worst.

Fuck...

Cum erupts from my dick, and I clamp my teeth together, quivering from the strength of the orgasm. It goes on forever. At least that's what it feels like. I struggle to stay upright.

Strings of cum rain over Cole's face while I hold him prisoner with my death grip on his hair. There's something inherently carnal about seeing him covered in my release.

Shoving him away, panting hard, I run a hand through my sweaty hair, almost forgetting the mask I'm still wearing. I circle a finger through the air. "Turn around."

Cole obediently shuffles until he's facing away from me, and I fist his dark hair. He barely manages to suppress a sharp hiss when I pull on the strands. I'm not gentle. Hurting him turns us both on.

My spent dick is already thinking about another round, so I give it a helping hand, stroking the thickening length while pulling and tugging on Cole's hair. He tries hard to keep his pathetic little whimpers under control, but fails miserably. Pain has always been his Achilles heel—the one thing that will make him putty in my hands.

Releasing him, I toss the knife on the forest floor, then pull the belt from the loops, ensuring he can hear the seductive slide and clank of the belt, and then I secure it around his neck before slowly lowering myself to my knees behind him.

"Do you want my cock?"

"Y-yes."

"Is that so?" I taunt near his ear before removing my mask and sucking and nibbling on the lobe. I bite down hard, and Cole nearly comes on the spot. "Hands behind your back."

When he doesn't immediately cooperate, I reach into my back pocket, pull out the cheap handcuffs I got from a sketchy website, then secure his wrists one handed. Cole struggles for the first time tonight, but it only excites me more.

The latch finally clicks into place with such finality, I'm surprised the sleeping birds don't wake up and erupt from the branches overhead.

Cole tries to look at me over his shoulder as he wrings his wrists to escape the cuffs. It's fruitless. While they're cheap, I've already double and triple checked their durability. No scared, aroused husbands can escape these bad boys.

I lean in close to his ear again and whisper, "Now, be a good boy and open your mouth."

This time, he obeys, and I waste no time placing the small key on his tongue. "I'm gonna fuck you so damn hard, you won't be able to walk tomorrow. Try not to swallow the key, alright? If you do, you have to explain to the paramedics how you ended up swallowing the key to the handcuffs." My voice drops. "...with my cum dried on your face, and leaking out of your ass."

I can feel him stiffen, and it makes me chuckle.

Reaching between our bodies, I tease his butt crack with my dick. "Such a good fucking boy, Cole, playing my twisted games. Don't do anything stupid. If you spit the key out, I won't let you come. Not today, not tomorrow, not the day after. Remember the last time I denied you an orgasm?"

He stays silent, unable to talk with the key to his freedom resting on his tongue. I bet his mouth is filling with saliva.

I release my dick and reach into my other back pocket to retrieve the sachet of lube. I tear it with my teeth, spit the torn corner on the ground, and squeeze a healthy dose onto my fingers. The cool liquid threatens to slide to the forest floor. I lube up his back hole, smiling to myself as he trembles from the contact.

"I didn't let you come for two weeks. This time, I'll leave it a month."

Cole whimpers pitifully and shakes his head. If he didn't have the key on his tongue, he would beg and plead for me to fuck him. If that didn't work, he'd try to push my jealous buttons. That's a neat little trick in his back pocket that always gets his way when we play our cat-and-mouse sexual games.

"For once," I whisper against his pulse point, feeling it thrash beneath my lips, "I'm ahead of you." In one quick move, I bite down hard and simultaneously ram my dick inside him.

Cole grunts at the sudden intrusion, his neck breaking out in a cold sweat, his body stiff.

"Fuck," I breathe through clenched teeth, my forehead pressed to the sensitive area where his neck meets his shoulder. "Fucking fuck! You feel so good."

He shudders, and I reach around to stroke his massive cock. I brush my lips up against his ear again and whisper, "Did you swallow the key?"

Shaking his head, he moves his hips, chasing an orgasm I won't let him reach just yet. Not until I've fucked him so damn good, he feels me every time he sits down for the next week.

I want his ass sore next time he attends a team meeting.

"Mine," I growl, sliding out to the tip and thrusting back in with such force, he would topple over if it weren't for the belt around his neck—a belt I have rolled around my palm.

I pull him back, so his spine is glued to my chest, and then I pound his tight hole. My thighs quiver and burn, but even that feels good. Everything feels like heaven when Cole groans like my big dick in his ass is the best thing to happen to him.

His own length throbs in my hand, angry and impossibly swollen. I stroke him slowly, teasing him until he's right on the edge. The moment I feel him tremble, I release his cock and force my thick fingers into his mouth. Saliva trickles from his lips, and I press down on the key on his tongue while ramming into his ass so hard, I'm surprised we're still upright.

Cole gags, and more saliva pools in his mouth. I bite down hard on his earlobe, then soothe the sting with my tongue. "I have the best fucking husband in the world. You take my dick so well, don't you, Cole? I'm so fucking lucky. Feel that? Feel my cock taking what belongs to it? What has always belonged to it even when you were a stubborn brat who used to push me away? I'm the only one who has fucked this ass and the only one who will ever stick my dick in you."

Raging possessiveness courses through me the more I talk. I apply more pressure to his throbbing cock, then smirk when he groans and chokes around my fingers.

He's close.

One more filthy, degrading word, and he'll ejaculate all over the tree in front of us.

Now I'm jealous of nature.

I slide my fingers from his mouth and slam my hand over his mouth and nose. Cole's eyes blow wide open.

He stands no chance with his oxygen gone, my cock tearing through his ass—pounding and fucking pounding—and his dick pulsing in my hand. Two more strokes, three, and cum squirts from his cock. A guttural groan vibrates his chest. I let go of all control, becoming more animal than man as I fuck him into next Sunday.

The moment the orgasm hits, we collapse forward and pant like we've raced a marathon. Cole trembles beneath me as my heart hammers against his back, and I burrow my nose in his neck to breathe in his masculine, citrusy scent.

"I missed you." My voice cracks at the end. The things I feel for Cole—the sheer magnitude of my feelings—scare me at times like these. My dick is still buried inside him, but I don't want to roll off him yet. I want to stay here, breathing him in, whispering how much I love him until the morning sun streams through the canopy of leaves overhead.

The key appears from his lips, and he spits it out amongst the leaves. "I missed you too."

"Don't leave me again."

"We can't be attached to the hip twenty-four-seven."

"Says who? I'll kill them for putting such nonsense ideas in your head."

Chuckling, he shifts onto his back, and I reluctantly let him. My cock misses his heat already.

Squirming, he tries to free his cuffed hands trapped behind his back. "Space is good sometimes. Would you have fucked me this fiercely if I hadn't been gone?"

I scoff. "What kind of a question is that? Of course I would have."

Instead of replying, he blinds me with his smile. It's effortless for Cole. His smiles were always rare until recently, but they never lost their potency. "I love you so fucking much." He lifts his head off the ground and kisses my nose. "Guess what?"

I peck his lips, whispering, "Tell me?"

More squirming. Cole nips my bottom lip. "We got our happy ending."

My heart clenches with a surge of happiness, which used to be a foreign emotion but now makes an appearance every time Cole whispers sweet nothings that don't include *you're insane.* Those kind of phrases are reserved for the bedroom with all his other colorful word choices.

"You say that like our story is over."

"You defeated the villain."

"There are plenty more villains hiding in the shadows. My job as your husband is never done."

"What other villains?" His voice drips with contagious humor.

"Your team's physiotherapist, for one. He's on my kill list."

"Isn't our dentist on that list?"

"Of course. He's had his fingers in your mouth more times than I can count."

"Uh-huh... What about our doctor?"

"Mr. Greenwell? Have you not noticed? He magically disappeared after he suggested future prostate exams."

Cole's eyes glitter. Overhead, the sky is slowly lightening.

"Mr. Greenwell was in the produce section last week, remember?"

"Weird. He must have a twin brother."

Cole laughs, the sound doing wicked, dangerous things to my heart. It's like being blinded by a thousand suns.

"Are you gonna remove these cuffs now?"

"Ask nicely, and I'll think about it."

Cole sinks his teeth into his lip to stop from laughing. "Please, my beautiful, amazing, considerate husband, will you free me from these handcuffs so I can show you properly how much I missed you while I was away."

"Amazing, huh? Beautiful." I wink, reaching for the key, my fingers sliding through leaves and pines.

I pause and frown. Noticing, Cole asks, "What's wrong?"

"The key..."

"The key? What about it?" He shifts to the side, and I move out of the way. We stare at the ground, exchanging a brief glance, and then I spring forward, tearing at the leaves and wet moss.

"Where did it go?"

"Fuck if I know. It's got to be here somewhere."

"This was all your idea."

"Don't pretend you weren't into it. Fuck..." I grumble, rolling over and brushing pine off my wet dick.

Cole kicks a pinecone in my direction, making us both laugh. "They're cheap, right? We can break them."

I pull a face, remembering how I tested them out beforehand. "Are you sure you didn't swallow the key?"

"You saw me spit it out," he replies, laughing disbelievingly.

Climbing to my feet, I pull him up by the arm. We slide our pants up—well, I have to help him since his hands are secured behind his back.

Cole scans the ground, but the key is nowhere to be found. Note to self: next time, get a spare key cut.

"Where are you going?" Cole asks when I walk back toward the house.

"Maybe we have an axe or something. It worked for Jack and Rose, remember?"

Cole catches up, playfully shoving my shoulder with his. "If you chop my wrist off and I die from blood loss, I will haunt you for all of eternity."

"That's fine," I grumble, running a hand down my face. "Just stay away from other ghosts' dicks."

The End.

ABOUT THE AUTHORS

Leigh Rivers and Harleigh Beck are two authors from the UK who write dark and gritty romances. Connect with them below:

Connect with Leigh Rivers @authorleighrivers
Connect with Harleigh Beck @author_harleighbeck

Made in United States
North Haven, CT
15 July 2024

54835110R00225